ICK.

TURN TO ME

Also by Tiffany Snow
No Turning Back, The Kathleen Turner Series
Turning Point, The Kathleen Turner Series
Blank Slate

TURN TO ME

Book Two in The Kathleen Turner Series

Tiffany Snow

Montlake
Romance

Text copyright ©2012 Tiffany Snow
All rights reserved.

Published by Montlake Romance, Seattle

www.apub.com

ISBN-13: 978-1-611-09962-1
ISBN-10: 1-6110-9962-5

Printed in the United States of America.

This book is dedicated to my mother, from whom I inherited my love of reading. Rarely do I recall seeing you without a book in your hand.

Thanks, Mom. This one's for you.

PROLOGUE

K ade Dennon rose silently from the bed, the brunette next to him still sleeping. The moonlight that filtered through the blinds on the window provided enough illumination for him to find his clothes.

After he'd dressed, he retrieved his holster and gun, attaching them firmly to his hip. He ran his fingers through his thick, dark hair, the locks tousled at the hands of the brunette. Pausing for a moment, he frowned in concentration, trying to remember her name. When it didn't immediately come to mind, he shrugged, grabbed his leather jacket, and quietly let himself out of the woman's apartment.

Outside was bitter cold, December having hit Buffalo hard. The streets were empty. The snow and freezing temperatures had driven even the panhandlers and criminals inside.

For a brief moment, Kade longed for a cigarette. Despite having kicked the habit years ago, the cravings lingered. He slipped into his car, the engine of the Mercedes coming to life easily despite the weather.

Kade's watch signaled the hour was getting late, but he pointed the car in the direction of downtown. He had an appointment to keep.

A short while later, he parked his car on the street outside a tiny bar, the neon sign blinking tiredly in the night. Pushing open the door, Kade stepped inside. The smell of beer and stale cigarette smoke permeated the air. His gaze swept the room.

The place held only a few patrons. Two men sat at the bar, nursing beers and avidly watching the television hung on one wall, bleating out some kind of sports program. Another man sat alone at the far end.

The bartender, his sluggish movements betraying too many years doing the same work, looked up, saw Kade, and quickly looked away.

A shadowy figure sat at a table in the far corner. Kade rested his hand on his gun as he made his way through the bar past empty tables. He slid into a chair across from the man waiting for him. Neither of them was seated with his back to the door. When Kade saw who awaited him, he relaxed.

"Donovan," Kade greeted him. "Didn't know they were sending you."

"Dennon," the FBI agent replied. "Glad you could come."

"I can always make time for the federal government," Kade said dryly.

"How's freelancing going?" Donovan asked.

Kade hesitated. The agent was well aware that Kade hired his services out to a select few—those for whom justice had been an illusion, victims of various crimes whose perpetrators had been able to evade the best efforts of police and litigators.

"It's a living," Kade replied vaguely.

"Saw what you left for us in Pittsburgh," Donovan continued. "Glad you got the bastard."

Kade knew what he was referring to. A man named Travis Haney had murdered his mother and his grandparents, then kidnapped his eight-year-old daughter and been chased by the FBI across four states. Kade had found him holed up in a motel in the middle of Bumblefuck, Utah.

The girl had been scared to death, her father ranting and raving, and she hadn't been fed for two days. Kade had watched through the scope on his M40 rifle, trained on the window, tensing each time the man waved the gun in the girl's direction. Finally, the man had stayed still long enough for Kade to shoot him.

Kade had called Donovan, then dropped the girl off at the nearest hospital. She'd clung to him, crying. Kade still remembered her little hands clutching his jacket.

"No problem," Kade said uncomfortably.

"You saved that girl's life," Donovan pressed.

Kade shrugged, smiling tightly. "I wouldn't want to pay for the years of therapy she'll no doubt need."

Donovan sighed, conceding Kade's point. "Are you sure you won't come back?" he asked. "I could get you a sweet position in DC. You wouldn't be stuck in some remote field office."

Kade shook his head. "I like my freedom. So, what do you have for me?"

Donovan reached into his jacket and produced a brown envelope. He placed it on the table.

"This was handed to us from Homeland Security. Coded transmissions coming out of Iran," he said. "They're having issues breaking the code."

Kade took the envelope, sliding it into his jacket. "What's it worth?"

"Break the code and it's two hundred grand in your bank account," Donovan said.

"I thought the FBI was under a budget crunch," Kade replied.

"There's always money for certain things." Donovan glanced at his watch and stood. "Gotta get going. You know how to reach me."

Kade nodded, watching the FBI agent as he left. He stood and went to the bar, sliding onto one of the stools. The bartender warily approached.

"Vodka. Neat," Kade ordered.

The bartender set the glass down in front of Kade, who threw the shot back quickly and signaled for another. The second he nursed more slowly.

The latest job from Donovan was going to require him to go to either his office or his home for the equipment he needed. The former was in Boston, the latter in Indianapolis.

He didn't want to go to Indy. Everything inside him rebelled at the mere thought. The woman he both wanted to see and needed to avoid at all cost was there.

Kade stared at the mirror behind the bar but didn't see his reflection. Instead he pulled out a memory, one he refused to contemplate very often—that of a woman with long, strawberry blonde hair and eyes as blue as the summer sky. He recalled the softness of her skin when he'd held her, the curves of her body beneath his hands. For a moment, he allowed himself to remember the look in her eyes when he'd last seen her. She'd trusted him. Trusted him to keep her safe, take care of her.

His phone rang, vibrating in his pocket. A glance at the caller ID had Kade cursing, as though the mere thought of her had conjured the phone call.

"Yeah," he answered curtly.

"Kade, it's me," Blane said.

"What's up, brother?" Kade asked, forcing his mind from the image of Blane's girlfriend, guilt assailing him.

"Can you come back to Indy? It's important." A pause. "Kathleen is in danger."

Kade frowned, his grip tightening on the cold glass in his hand. "What's going on?"

"I'll tell you when you get here," Blane replied.

"Are you sure you're not overreacting?" Kade asked, stalling for time, trying to think of a way he could refuse.

"I need you."

Blane's bald confession made Kade pause. He took a swallow of his drink.

Kade's silence prompted Blane to speak again. "You know I wouldn't ask otherwise."

"I know, man, it's just—"

"I don't ask much from you, you know that," Blane interrupted.

Kade cursed. "Fine. I'm on my way." He disconnected the call and finished his drink in one swallow.

It looked like he was going back to Indianapolis whether he liked it or not. Meeting his own eyes in the mirror behind the bar, he muttered softly, "This isn't going to end well."

CHAPTER ONE

Hey, pretty girl, give me your cash and I won't mess up your fancy dress."

I started, my pulse picking up as my brain processed the words. I was cold. Freezing, actually, and my feet were killing me. December in Indianapolis was bad enough—add to it walking the streets alone at night wearing nothing but an evening gown and four-inch heels, and you had the ingredients for a truly wretched experience. Well, at least I'd thought that was the worst it could get. Apparently, I'd been wrong.

Turning, I watched as a man stepped out of the shadows. He was a hulking brute, big enough to easily outweigh me by a hundred pounds or more. The scattered light from a nearby streetlamp glinted off the knife he was holding and I swallowed heavily. I hated knives. Knives meant pain, whereas guns meant death. Maybe I was in the minority, but death was the preferred of the two to my way of thinking. I wasn't a big fan of pain.

"I don't have any money," I said, trying to stay calm. I glanced around, keeping an eye on him as he advanced toward me. Unfortunately, no one was around. I backed away as he got closer but knew I didn't stand a chance if I tried to run, not with these shoes.

"Then I'll take the pretty necklace," he sneered, leaping forward and grabbing my arm. I shrieked in surprise but was silenced when he pressed the cold steel of the blade to my neck.

"Shut up, bitch," he snarled.

I was breathing hard, fear and adrenaline pumping through my veins. He towered over me, pushing against me until my back was against the cold brick wall. The rough stones abraded the exposed skin of my back.

"Give me the necklace or you'll regret it." His breath was hot and fetid against my face.

"No," I said, helpless anger rising in me. I'd been given the necklace mere hours ago, Blane fastening it around my neck as I'd gotten dressed for this evening.

It suddenly seemed terribly ironic that a night that had started with such promise was ending in terror.

~

The day had begun well enough. I'd had the day shift at The Drop, a local place where I tended bar. I know the current in-vogue term was *mixologist*, but neither I nor the patrons had any illusions about what I did—which was pour drinks. On Saturdays I usually worked the night shift, but today I'd traded with Lucy so I could have tonight off to be with Blane.

Blane Kirk was my boyfriend, although the term was at once both too adolescent and too committed to actually describe him and our relationship. Blane was a high-profile lawyer in Indianapolis, with aspirations for public office.

A former Navy SEAL, he was over six feet of male perfection, complete with dirty blond hair, a square jaw, and eyes a tantalizing mix of gray and green, the color drifting more one way or the other depending on what he was wearing. Women had been an interchangeable accessory to Blane, and I wasn't sure that wouldn't be the case with me. Blane and I had started dating about six weeks ago, right after Halloween. I know that doesn't sound like very long, but considering how often Blane usually changed girlfriends, I was cautiously optimistic. Optimistic about what? Well I wasn't sure of that either.

Considering the differences between us, it was difficult most days to believe that Blane would choose to be with me. As the daughter of a housewife and a police officer from Rushville, Indiana, Kathleen Turner—yeah, that's me—wasn't a name people knew. I take that back. People knew the name, but I wasn't *that* Kathleen Turner. Turner was the family name, and choosing a celebrity to be named after was the tradition. Just ask my dad, Ted Turner, or my grandma, Tina Turner. Except neither one was with me any longer, so I alone was left to carry on the Turner tradition or curse, depending on your point of view.

I'd moved to Indianapolis eight months ago and had taken a job working as a runner for Blane's law firm. It took both gigs to make ends meet and I hadn't given up the day job, even though I was sleeping with the boss. Incredibly tacky of me, but I needed the job. We kept it discreet because while Blane didn't care at all what people said, I did.

Blane had asked me to go with him to a victory dinner/fund-raiser tonight for someone he knew that had been reelected to Congress in the last election. I'd seen in the paper that plates were seven thousand dollars each. I'd swallowed hard and hoped the food would be really good for that kind of price tag.

After my Saturday shift, I had dashed home, hopping into the shower to quickly wash my hair and shave my legs. I had time to blow my long, strawberry blonde hair dry, pin it up, and throw on some makeup before I heard his knock on my door.

I'd learned a hard lesson a few weeks ago about checking the peephole in my door, and I remembered that tonight. I checked first before opening the door, and my breath caught, as it nearly always did, when I saw Blane.

My doorway was filled with wide shoulders encased in a charcoal-gray suit jacket that tapered to lean hips. A white shirt peeked from beneath his jacket and tie. Currently, a hand was braced high against the jamb of my door, opening his jacket enough for me to see the gun tucked into the holster against his side. Indiana was a conceal state, and Blane had a permit to carry, which he always did. That habit had saved my life once.

"You're early," I said, smiling and opening the door wider to let him in. He unfolded his tall frame from where he'd been leaning and came inside, closing the door behind him and stepping into my personal space. The whole apartment seemed smaller with him in it, not that it was very big to begin with. He took in my appearance—I was still wrapped in a towel from my shower—and the gleam that came into his eyes made my heart beat faster.

"How early?" he asked, his voice a low rasp as he moved even closer, his hand coming up to trace the top edge of my towel. Words failed me when his lips and tongue touched the bare skin of my shoulder. I tipped my head to the side, my eyes fluttering shut. He sucked lightly at the juncture of my neck and shoulder and I inhaled deeply, the scent of his cologne enveloping and enticing me. When I felt him loosen the towel and it dropped to the floor, I found my voice.

"You'll mess up my hair," I managed breathlessly as his hand slipped between my thighs. I clutched at his shoulders for support, his fingers moving with practiced ease and causing my legs to tremble.

"There are ways to avoid that," he whispered in my ear, sending a delicious shiver through me. And indeed, there were, as he proceeded to show me.

Half an hour later, I was slipping on my dress and repairing the damage done to my lip gloss. True to his word, not a hair of mine was out of place, though my skin now had a telltale flush.

My dress was a deep midnight blue, and I thought it brought out my eyes, since they were nearly the same shade. It was a long, satin sheath with a sweetheart neckline, the straps reaching over the outer curve of my shoulders. The cut emphasized my cleavage, something I'd been blessed with plenty of. A long slit ran up the side, shifting and revealing my legs as I walked. I stepped into a pair of silver heels that helped make up for my sad lack of stature and surveyed myself with a critical eye in the mirror. The dress demanded a necklace, but jewelry—even the costume sort—was an unnecessary expense when I worked two jobs just to pay the bills. I'd found a pair of rhinestone earrings that now dangled from my ears and sparkled when I turned my head.

"You forgot something," Blane said, surprising me as he stepped into the mirror's reflection. I looked at the couple we made and was gratified by the sight. We looked good together, I thought.

My eyes widened as I watched his hands come up to place a necklace on me. As he did the catch, my jaw dropped at the sight of the large, oval sapphire pendant now nestled between my breasts. Surrounded in diamonds, it glittered brightly as it hung from a long double chain.

"I'll let you put on these," he said, his arm reaching around in front of me.

I glanced down to see he was holding a velvet jewelry box, opened to display a set of matching diamond-and-sapphire earrings. I reached out cautiously to touch them, the movement causing them to sparkle in the light.

"Blane," I began, "I . . . I don't know what to say. It's too much." I was stunned. I had never been given something like this. Tears pricked my eyes and the earrings swam in my vision. I blinked them back. It would totally ruin the moment if my mascara ran.

"Say you'll wear them," he cajoled, his lips at my ear as his other arm slid around my waist to pull me back against his chest. "The stone reminded me of the color of your eyes. I want you to have them."

I put on the earrings as he watched me and left the rhinestones on my bureau. A thought occurred to me and my eyes flew to his in the mirror. Was this my "going away" present? Blane always gave a gift to his girlfriends when he broke up with them, though usually they were chosen by his secretary, Clarice.

"You're beautiful," he complimented me, the warmth in his eyes easing my worry. The heat from his hands seeped through the thin satin, and I berated myself for thinking he had other motives for the gift.

He glanced at his watch. "We'd better go."

I grabbed the silver clutch bag I'd gotten to go with the dress and headed for my apartment door.

"Wait," Blane said. "Where's your coat?"

I grimaced. I hated wearing coats and usually only did so when Mother Nature forced the issue by spreading snow on the ground.

"You have to wear a coat," Blane insisted, going to my tiny coat closet and pulling out the long black trench coat he'd given me a few weeks ago. "It's freezing outside."

I reluctantly let him put it on me, though I didn't think it went with my dress at all, and locked my apartment door on the way out. I lived on the top floor of a two-story building in an area of downtown Indy where you made sure to lock your car at night.

Blane took my hand as we went down the stairs, and I was grateful for his solid presence next to me, unpracticed as I was in walking in heels this high. It's not like I went many places where I had cause to dress up—except church occasionally, but somehow I didn't think silver strappy sandals with a four-inch heel were Sunday morning Baptist attire.

He helped me into his black Jaguar, which, let me say, was difficult to get into in the getup I was wearing. As he watched me carefully swing my legs into the car, Blane let out a chuckle.

"What?" I said, my voice testy.

"I was just wondering if you were going to emulate Britney again," he said, propping his arms against the door as he leaned toward me. My cheeks grew warm as I realized he was referring to my beloved pop princess, Britney Spears. I was a huge fan and could do a dead-on impression of her singing, which I'd had cause to do this past Halloween when all the girls at The Drop dressed up as pop divas for the holiday bash. In this instance, I didn't think Blane was referring to Britney's singing so much as her inadvertent flashing of some very private areas when climbing into and out of cars.

"You're assuming I'm not wearing anything under my dress," I said breezily, deciding to give as good as I got.

"Are you?" I noticed the gleam was back in his eyes as they dropped to where the cut of my dress had opened to expose the length of my thigh.

"If you're lucky, you might find out later," I teased. His lips curved in a wicked grin and he stepped back, shutting the car door.

A few minutes later, we arrived at the hotel. The fundraiser was taking place in one of the large ballrooms of the nicest and most expensive hotel in Indy. A valet took the keys and Blane helped me out of the low-slung car. I emerged as gracefully as I could without exposing anything I shouldn't. Offering me his arm, we went inside, where Blane checked our coats, pocketing the small ticket for retrieving them.

I was really nervous. This was the first public function I'd been to with Blane. He'd taken me to dinner and on other casual dates, but this was the first time I was his "plus one" at something relating to his job. I knew Blane was ambitious; his career was on the fast track to public office, though he hadn't said which one. He came from a family of lawyers and politicians, with a grandfather who had been a senator and a great-grandfather who had been on the Massachusetts Supreme Court. Blane was only fourteen when he had a falling out with his father, then cemented the divide when he joined the Navy, but politics was still in his blood.

There would be a lot of people here tonight he'd want to connect with to increase his network of contacts, people who could help or hinder his future plans, whatever those might be. I didn't want to embarrass him in any way, though I felt far out of my element as I observed the ballroom and foyer full of people. They milled around chatting in groups, most with a cocktail or glass of wine in their hands. I swallowed hard, my palms clammy from nerves.

"Don't worry," Blane whispered, settling his hand on the small of my back. "You'll be fine. I promise, I'm the only one who'll bite you."

I smiled, my eyes catching his, and breathed easier. His attempt to tease me, make me smile, had bolstered my courage. I nodded, took a deep breath, and didn't resist when he led us to a group of people nearby.

"Kirk! There you are! We wondered when you'd be arriving." The greeting came from a man who looked to be about Blane's age and height but was much slighter of build. He had dark hair and eyes, and was holding a highball glass with a clear liquid inside. A woman stood next to him, as tall as he, wearing a black-velvet gown that wrapped around her torso and legs before flaring at mid-calf. I wondered how she was able to walk in it. Her dark hair was piled in loose curls on top of her head, a few escaped coils trailing down her ears and neck. The darkness of her dress and hair accentuated the fairness of her skin. She held a glass of champagne in one manicured hand.

"George, good to see you," Blane replied, shaking the man's hand. "And I see your wife, Sarah, is looking as lovely as ever." Sarah smiled back at him, giving him a quick once-over. Blane had his politician's smile firmly in place. I called it that because it was wide and friendly but never really reached his eyes. "Congratulations on your win," Blane continued, returning his attention to George. "But that was never in doubt, was it?"

George laughed, clapping Blane on the shoulder. "I never lose, my friend. Something you should keep in mind when you decide to stop keeping secrets and tell me what office you want." George's gaze flicked to me and I pasted on a bright smile.

"I'd like to introduce Kathleen Turner," Blane said, his hand moving again to my back. "Kathleen, this is George Bradshaw. He is the campaign manager for the senator. This is his wife, Sarah."

"Pleased to meet you," I said, politely grasping hands with first George, then Sarah. Sarah's fingers barely brushed mine before she dismissed me, turning back to Blane.

"Likewise," George said. I noticed he took in my appearance with a calculated gaze, his eyes lingering on the pendant Blane had given me. At least, I hoped it was the pendant though it could have just been my cleavage. "And what do you do, Kathleen?"

My smile grew forced. I hadn't thought about this part. I should have known someone was bound to ask that question. I flushed as I realized I had only two answers to give, neither of which I wanted to say.

"She works at the firm," Blane smoothly interjected.

"A fellow lawyer," George said, assuming what my job was. "Always knew Blane would find a like-minded woman." He lifted his glass as if to toast me.

16

"Not . . . exactly," I stammered, not wanting to lie. Lies always came back to bite you in the ass.

We were interrupted by another man stepping into our small circle. He was an older man with silver hair who carried his age well though he had to be in his sixties. About Blane's height, he stood straight and tall in a dark suit and tie. He vaguely reminded me of Blane, exuding a palpable presence and energy that made him the center of attention. George and Sarah stepped back in deference as the man clapped Blane on the shoulder and grasped his hand firmly.

"Knew you wouldn't let me down, Blane," he said, smiling warmly. I watched as Blane responded in a much more natural way, grinning broadly and giving the man's hand a firm shake.

"I know better than to do that, sir," Blane replied with a twinkle in his eye. "Let me introduce you." And just like that, my nerves were back. I could tell this was someone Blane genuinely liked. I just hoped he wouldn't ask me what I did for a living.

"This is Kathleen Turner," Blane said. "Kathleen, this is Senator Robert Keaston."

My eyes widened in surprise. I had known this evening was for a senator, but I hadn't realized it was this particular one. Even I, who followed politics not at all, knew the name, as often as it was in the news. Robert Keaston was a powerful senator who had been elected and reelected so many times, I wondered why he was still subjected to the formality.

"Pleased to meet you," I managed to squeak out through lips frozen into a smile.

"Likewise, my dear," the senator said, giving me a quick look-over.

"Where's Vivian?" Blane asked, diverting the senator's attention from me before he could ask any questions.

"Oh, she's over there with some other hens wanting to talk her ear off about some charity or another," answered Keaston with a wave of his hand. "You're sitting with me tonight, aren't you, Blane?"

"I don't think so, sir," Blane said regretfully. "I'm sure they have me seated elsewhere."

"Well, we'll fix that," Keaston replied, gesturing to a woman hovering nearby. She quickly came forward and he said something to her too low for me to overhear. With a nod, she left to do his bidding.

"That's not necessary, sir," Blane protested, but Keaston waved his hand dismissively.

"You may not be of the right party," Keaston said with a mock glare of disapproval, then he smiled, "but you're family."

Shock went through me and I couldn't stop a quick look at Blane. He glanced uncomfortably at me before returning his attention to Keaston.

Family? Blane was related to one of the most powerful men in the US Senate? That would have been helpful to know. If I'd felt out of place before, now I felt like a downright intruder.

"I have to do the rounds, Blane," the senator said, "I'm sure you understand."

Blane nodded. "Of course."

"But I'll see you at dinner." Keaston looked my way and gave a short nod of dismissal. "My dear."

I automatically smiled and watched as Keaston ambled toward another knot of people, all of whom turned his way with fawning smiles. George and Sarah had drifted off as well, leaving Blane and me with a blessed moment alone in the midst of the crowd. I looked up at Blane.

"Family?" I asked, hoping that perhaps the senator hadn't meant it in the blood-relation sense.

"Great-uncle," he answered shortly, dashing that hope.

"Why didn't you tell me?" I asked, trying to keep the dismay from my voice.

"I didn't think it mattered," he replied quietly, taking my hand. "Does it?"

I didn't know what to say. I felt like the proverbial fish out of water and my mouth moved soundlessly, as if I were gasping for air. How was I to explain to Blane, who no doubt had never felt out of place in his life, how this news had impacted me? I was saved from replying as yet another couple came by to greet Blane.

I had underestimated the number of people who knew Blane and wanted to ingratiate themselves with him. I lost track of the names almost immediately after I was introduced, but I marveled at how Blane was never at a loss for a name or a smile. I watched with admiration as he wove his magic around those with whom he spoke, seeing in their eyes how he captivated them as he made each person feel special, sending them on their way with the certainty that they were important to him. It was amazing and I was proud of his skills, which seemed to come very naturally indeed. My smile grew less forced as it became clear that no one had any interest in me. They barely paid me any attention at all. I was glad to melt into the background at Blane's side.

Blane and I made our way around the room, and I was feeling more relaxed since it seemed nothing was really expected of me except to smile and nod. Blane's hand was reassuring on the small of my back as we turned toward another couple. I stiffened immediately.

It was Kandi-with-an-*i*, the woman Blane had dated just before me. She'd been none too happy about losing Blane and had expressed her contempt for me on Halloween, showing up at The Drop dressed in a fairy costume that I'm sure cost more than I had made that night. She was beautiful and had made no bones about the fact that she felt Blane was slumming it by being with me. Tall with long, straight blonde hair, tonight she wore a red dress that hugged her body. She was absolutely stunning and I hated her.

"Nice to see you again, Blane," she greeted him, ignoring me completely.

"Kandi," Blane replied evenly, "I didn't realize you'd be here this evening."

"I'm here with my father," she said with a smug smile, tipping her head toward a knot of people standing a short ways away. "You know what good friends he and the senator are."

Blane gave a curt nod. "Of course," he said. "How are you?"

She moved closer to him, insinuating herself between us so Blane's hand was forced to release mine.

"I'm very good, as I'm sure you remember," I heard her say huskily. Her breasts brushed suggestively against his arm as she leaned into him.

My eyes narrowed. The tramp. I may not have grown up with her wealth and privilege, but at least I had manners, though I was having a hard time remembering them at the moment. I very much wanted to grab a hunk of her pretty blonde hair and yank. Hard.

"Call me," I heard her whisper in his ear before she walked away, her hand trailing lightly across his chest.

"Sorry about that," Blane said quietly, a grimace passing quickly over his face when he looked at me. I made my lips stretch into a tight smile.

"She's very pretty," I said diplomatically. I struggled not to sound jealous or bitchy. I didn't think I'd succeeded.

"Most people would say so," he replied. He slid his arm around my back and tugged my stiff body closer to him, overcoming my resistance with ease. "But she's not my type. Not anymore."

"Oh, really?" I said sarcastically, trying to ignore the effect of the heat from his body as it warmed me through the thin material of my dress. "What's your type?"

Blane bent and leaned close to me. "I prefer a woman with long hair the color of the sunset and eyes as clear blue as a twilight sky. She's got an Irish temper and likes her bourbon. Her guilty pleasure is a certain well-known pop princess and she has a passion for rocky road ice cream. Her skin is the color of peaches bathed in cream and is as smooth as silk."

His lips brushed against my ear as he spoke, sending a thrill of heat through me. I looked up at him and couldn't hold on to my irritation at Kandi. I melted into him, as he had no doubt known I would. The corners of his lips were tipped up ever so slightly, as if he were thinking about smiling. I was mesmerized by the stormy gray of his eyes, flecks of green sparkling from their depths.

"And if I were to tell her about the perfection of her breasts," he continued, the huskiness of his voice making me shiver, "that her body was made to fit mine—or how the noises she makes when I make love to her drive me crazy—she'd blush nearly to her toes."

My mouth dropped open at his audacity and I blushed, as he'd predicted. Regardless, I couldn't help smiling and as he let out a small huff of laughter, the tension Kandi had created began to dissipate.

"Let's find our seats," he said, his eyes twinkling. "I'm starving."

Blane took my hand and led me to a table near the front. It seemed Senator Keaston was as good as his word, because our seats were with him and a woman I assumed was his wife. She looked to be only in her fifties, though I thought looks might be deceiving. To my dismay, I saw that Kandi and a man who was obviously her father were also seated at the table. George and Sarah Bradshaw were there, too. One other couple we'd met that evening rounded out the seats, the man a member of the senator's staff, though I couldn't remember either of their names.

"Blane!" the older woman happily exclaimed. She went to rise from her chair but Blane quickly stepped to her side, forestalling her and pressing a chaste kiss to her cheek.

"Good evening, Vivian," Blane said warmly. "Don't get up."

"Robert said you were here tonight," she said as Blane held out my chair for me to sit down. "Thank you for coming to support him."

"I wouldn't have missed it," Blane replied, sliding into the seat on my left. He'd seated me beside Vivian. I wanted to grumble about Kandi's place at his left side, but that would have been catty.

Blane introduced me to the very kind and gracious Vivian. I liked her immediately. I could tell that Blane was very fond of her as well. Tall but slight, she had a powerful presence about her.

Dinner was served and I kept quiet as I ate, listening to the small talk at the table and trying to make sure I didn't drip anything on my dress. Kandi chatted easily with the senator and Vivian as well as the others. I tried not to feel like a kid at the grown-ups' table.

I observed with growing dismay as Kandi drew Blane into conversation with George and Sarah, frequently laying her hand possessively on his arm. Blane couldn't very well be rude to her in front of everyone, but I was disgruntled to see how friendly he was with her as they joined in the laughter around the table.

I ate a tiny bite of some kind of fish they'd served, my appetite now gone, and pushed my food around on my plate in glum silence.

I think Vivian must have felt sorry for me being left out of the conversation, because she turned to me and asked, "Kathleen, isn't it?"

I swallowed the lump of fish, quickly passing my napkin over my mouth as I nodded. "Yes, ma'am."

"Please, call me Vivian," she said with a smile. "And what do you do for a living, Kathleen?"

I shifted uneasily, but knew I couldn't lie to her. Fortunately, everyone else was still involved in their own conversations, so no one was really paying attention to us. "I work for Blane as a runner," I said, "and I tend bar at night."

Vivian's eyes widened a fraction in surprise before she masked it. "I see," she said kindly. "And are you from Indianapolis?" Beyond her, I saw the senator's eyes flick in our direction, and I knew that while he was talking to his staff person next to him, he was also listening to us.

"No, ma'am," I answered, unable to shake my mother's lessons in manners enough to call Vivian by her given name—respect for my elders had been drilled into me. "I'm from Rushville, Indiana. My parents grew up there."

"And what do they do?"

"My dad was a policeman," I said. "My mother stayed home. They both passed some years ago."

"I'm so sorry," Vivian said sympathetically, and to my surprise, her hand reached out to grasp mine. "Do you have other family? A brother or sister, perhaps?"

I shook my head. "I have an uncle and cousin, but we don't keep in touch." Truthfully, I couldn't even say where my dad's brother and son lived anymore. It had been years since I'd heard from them, since Mom's funeral, actually.

Vivian's grip on my hand tightened, her face creasing in a frown. "You're awfully young to be on your own," she remarked thoughtfully.

My smile was tense. I was unsure how to respond. I didn't want her pity, but neither did I want to appear rude. "I do all right," I said, slipping my hand from hers.

"So, Blane," the senator said, bringing everyone's attention to him, "are you going to tell us how the Waters trial is going? A lot of important people in Washington are watching to see how this turns out. You win this case, it'll be the biggest moment of your career. So far."

Everyone's eyes turned to Blane. All were waiting for his answer, their interest in this topic obvious.

I looked at Blane in confusion. What Waters trial? Biggest moment of his career? What was Keaston talking about? Blane didn't usually say much about his work. I didn't know why—if he just didn't want to talk work after hours, or if he didn't think I was interested. While you might think I'd know everything going on at the firm since I worked there, regardless of what Blane did or didn't tell me, I was frequently out of the office making runs. Even when I wasn't in the office, I was still separated from Blane by four floors.

"It's going well," Blane replied, his face a mask of polite indifference.

Senator Keaston chuckled. "From what I hear, it's going better than that, son," he said. "You win this case, your name will be on everyone's short list."

Short list? Short list for what? My confusion increased. I tried to catch Blane's eye but he just shook his head, not looking at me.

"I don't know about that," he said. "The prosecution is pretty tough. We'll just have to see how it turns out. It'll be in the jury's hands."

"You'll beat James," Kandi said confidently. "He's no match for you in front of a jury and everyone knows it."

"James?" I interrupted incredulously. "James Gage?" This time Blane did turn to look at me, his expression unreadable.

"Yes, dear." Kandi was the one to answer my question. Her voice dripped condescension. "You do know the name of the district attorney, don't you?"

25

My face heated at her disdain but I refused to look at her, my gaze still locked with Blane's. I couldn't believe he hadn't told me.

James Gage was the son of the former senior partner at Blane's firm of Gage, Kirk, and Trent, now just Kirk and Trent. His father, William Gage, had been indicted for fraud and accessory to murder. William had been behind the recent scandal that involved a local computer company, TecSol, rigging online election voting. He'd also been responsible for the death of my friend Sheila and her boyfriend, Mark, who had worked for TecSol. James had been involved as well but had gotten off scot-free, even winning the election for Indianapolis District Attorney.

James and I had gone on one date—a date he felt gave him license to be jealous of Blane's attention to me. Remember I said I'd learned the hard way about checking the peephole in my door before opening it? That was because of James, who had hit me and tried to choke me when he found out Blane and I were together. Only the quick actions of CJ, my neighbor at the time and someone I'd thought of as a friend, had saved me from even graver injury.

James had always been jealous of Blane, waging a competition to which Blane had been oblivious. I was alarmed that they were going up against each other in what was apparently a very important trial, and hurt that Blane had said nothing about this to me. James was dangerous and volatile, not to be trusted. Would he do something stupid if he lost a big case to Blane?

My dismay must have shown on my face, because Blane's jaw clenched tightly before he looked away. I realized everyone was watching us now, and I focused on my plate to keep from meeting all those eyes. I was embarrassed—everyone had known about something quite vital in Blane's life except me, his girlfriend.

"We missed you and Kade at Thanksgiving," Vivian said to Blane, changing the topic of conversation and taking the attention away from me. It was the kind of comment my mother would have made. It demanded an explanation, even if she hadn't asked for one.

"We celebrated here," Blane replied.

I was surprised Vivian knew about Kade. Kade was Blane's illegitimate half brother. Their father had been unfaithful to Blane's mother, though he'd refused to claim Kade as his when Kade's mother died.

Kade went by Kade Dennon and, as far as I knew, very few people knew of the relation. Kade was a former FBI agent, specializing in cyber crimes. I hadn't known any of that when I'd first met him, though, and had known only that he was an assassin for hire. Kade had quit the FBI a few years ago and gone freelance, something Blane abided but didn't necessarily condone. Kade was as dark as Blane was light, with black hair and piercing blue eyes, though he had the same charisma and aura of danger as his older brother.

Blane wasn't quite being truthful with Vivian—we had celebrated here in Indy, but Kade had not joined us for the festivities. He'd disappeared several weeks ago, right after the election. Blane said Kade stayed in touch with him, but I hadn't asked where he was and Blane hadn't offered the information.

Kade was an enigma to me—we'd begun by hating each other, but he'd saved my life when I'd been moments away from being raped and killed. I'd never breathed a word about it to Blane and to my knowledge, Kade hadn't either. The shame and humiliation of the incident still sometimes haunted my nightmares, and the last thing I wanted was to see pity in Blane's eyes when he looked at me.

Kade had also been paid twenty thousand dollars to kill me, then had turned around and given that money to me. It seemed Kade and I had called an uneasy truce, though I'd wondered if my being around was what had kept him from Blane at Thanksgiving. Kade was utterly loyal and devoted to Blane, and I felt a pang of remorse that his dislike of me might have been the reason he'd stayed away from his brother for the holiday.

Blane deftly turned the conversation to other topics and I kept my mouth shut, regretting my earlier outburst that displayed my woeful lack of knowledge about his life. Thankfully, dinner was over soon and people began drifting to the dance floor, the strains of a slow jazz number coming from the five-person band. The smoky sound of the saxophone drifted through the room as I contemplated what Senator Keaston had said.

"Dance with me," Blane said quietly, resting his arm on the back of my chair and leaning over me. He caught a loose tendril of my hair and gently wrapped it around his finger. Our eyes met. I nodded and he rose, helping me from my chair and taking my elbow to lead me to the dance floor. I could sense Kandi's glare burning a hole in my back as we walked away.

Blane took me in his arms and I felt my body stiffen, holding myself slightly apart from him; I was angry after all. I stared eye level at his shirt, crisp and white as it peeked out from beneath his jacket, and said nothing, still reeling from the realization of what he'd kept from me.

After a few minutes of dancing in tense silence, I finally spoke. "Why didn't you tell me?" I asked, unable to hold the question in any longer.

He sighed. "I know how you feel about James," he answered, "and this doesn't involve you. He's my problem now."

My temper flared and I glared up at him. "So my role in this relationship is to look pretty, keep quiet, and warm your bed, but not really be a part of your life?"

His hands dug into my hips. "I never said that," he replied, his eyes narrowing. That usually signified a warning that his anger was close to the surface, but I ignored it.

"It's what you don't say that speaks volumes, Blane," I bit out, my heart hurting at the truth of it. "What did Keaston mean by 'short list'? What short list will you be on if you win this case?"

I didn't think he was going to answer me, his jaw locked tight, but finally he spoke.

"Governor. He was talking about the short list for governor."

My jaw dropped open in shock and my feet stumbled. Only Blane's tight grip kept me from falling.

"Of Indiana?" I squeaked, then wanted to kick myself for the stupid question. Blane gave a curt nod, watching me.

"Excuse me," I said, stepping out of his grip. I had to get away for a few minutes, regain my control and equilibrium. I didn't want to break down into tears in the middle of the dance floor. He let me go, watching as I walked away.

I found a ladies' room and hid in a stall, taking deep breaths.

I had hoped Blane felt more for me. I wanted to be more than another transient woman in his life and his bed. I'd known Blane was a player, had seen him discard women without a backward glance. Why I thought I'd be different, I had no idea. My naiveté was my own undoing. I wanted to be a real part of his life, but the fact that he hadn't told me about the case, that he had thoughts of running for governor, made my wants seem laughable. Sometimes my outlook on life was too hopeful for my own good.

I realized I couldn't hide in the bathroom all night and surveyed myself in the mirror, tucking a few strands of hair that had gotten loose back up into some pins. The light caught on my necklace and I touched it, remembering the look in Blane's eyes when he'd given it to me mere hours ago. A hint of doubt crept into my mind. Maybe I was wrong; maybe Blane had a good reason for not telling me about all this. It wasn't like I'd given him a chance to talk before rushing off.

I resolved to give him a chance to explain, to tell me why he'd kept this news from me, and that resolve lasted until I walked into the ballroom and saw him dancing with Kandi in his arms.

Well.

Turning on my heel, I walked out and didn't stop walking until I hit the street. It was cold and I shivered, belatedly realizing I'd left my coat inside. I couldn't have retrieved it anyway; Blane still had the ticket.

It was late and the streets were nearly empty, the sidewalk even more so. I had my purse with me but only had a few dollars, not enough for a cab. There was a bus stop a few blocks away, so I trudged onward. I'd catch the bus toward my apartment and walk the last few blocks from where it dropped me off. It was nearly ten and I knew it picked up every hour.

I walked morosely, watching the sidewalk so I didn't trip. I was regretting the shoes now, but it wasn't as if I'd known I'd be hiking in them by the end of the evening. I sniffed, telling myself it was the cold making my nose run. My toes were numb and I was freezing. I wrapped my arms around myself to try to stay warm. The wind went right through the satin fabric of my dress and before long I was shivering. I cursed the cold, my choice of attire tonight, the fact that I'd agreed to come with Blane in the first place, and Kandi-with-an-*i* on general principle. It was quite clear she had more of a history with Blane than I'd realized or that he'd bothered to tell me.

I turned down a side street and saw the bus stop a block away. Finally. I picked up the pace a little but was brought to a jarring halt by the voice echoing out of the darkness.

"Hey, pretty girl, give me your cash and I won't mess up your fancy dress."

∽

"Give me the necklace or you'll regret it," the mugger said, jerking me back to the imminently dangerous here and now.

"My husband is on his way," I lied, grasping for straws.

He laughed cruelly. "You're a shitty liar," he scoffed. His hand closed around the pendant and yanked, the chain of the necklace biting painfully into my skin before it broke. He stepped back, admiring his prize.

"No!" I leapt forward and grabbed his fist, clenched tightly around the pendant. I had to get it back. Surprised, he turned sharply to avoid my lunge, the movement causing the knife to bite into the skin of my arm. I ignored the sharp burn. "Give that back!"

"Get off me," he growled, shoving me away. Furious, I came back at him again, grabbing the hand holding my necklace and sinking my teeth into it. He yelled in pain. Unable to get any leverage between us, his arm came down hard and he slammed a fist into my back. I was forced to release him, the painful blow knocking the wind from my lungs and leaving me unprepared for his punch to my stomach. I doubled over, the pain excruciating.

His hand closed around my neck and he pulled me upright before carelessly tossing me away. I hit the concrete hard, my hands taking the brunt of it, but still smacked the side of my face on the ground. I couldn't move. My face ached and my thigh burned from where it had scraped the asphalt, and I struggled to breathe through the pain in my back and stomach.

"Fucking bitch," he muttered angrily. His shoe scraped behind me and I made myself turn over, not wanting to have my back to him. I saw the kick coming too late to protect myself, and I cried out when it connected. I curled into myself, trying to become as small a target as possible. He hauled back to kick me again.

A shape came hurtling out of the darkness, tackling the mugger to the ground. I watched them grapple. The knife glinted briefly in the light before it was kicked out of the thug's hand. The sound of grunts and flesh hitting bone filled the alley.

I struggled to sit up, gasping at the aches and pains, and saw my rescuer had gotten the upper hand as he straddled the attacker. His fists continued to pummel the man, though I thought for sure the mugger was unconscious by now, as still as he was.

I stumbled to my feet, tottering forward carefully on my ill-used heels. He still wasn't stopping, his blows landing punishingly hard as I winced, afraid he was going to kill him. I moved as close as I dared.

"Stop," I implored, grabbing onto one of the man's arms with both of my hands. "You're going to kill him!"

The man easily jerked his arm out of my grip, turning his head sharply to face me—and I froze in shock.

It was Blane. I didn't know where he'd come from or how he'd found me, but he had. His face was a mask of rage as he took in my appearance and I took a shaky step back, afraid of what he might do. I watched as the anger drained away from his face. He spared one last glance for the unconscious mugger and I heard him snarl, "Fucking piece of shit," then he stood and was at my side in an instant.

"Are you all right?" he asked, turning me toward the light. He sucked in a breath and I knew I must look awful, blood trailing in a thin stream down my arm from the shallow cut the knife had made. I could feel my cheek swelling from where I'd hit the concrete. Blane's finger gently brushed my cheekbone, coming away with blood. Quickly removing his jacket, he placed it around my shoulders, pulling it tightly closed. Shock started to set in and I began to shake.

"Shh, Kat," he whispered, pulling me into his arms. "You're safe now. I've got you."

Tears spilled over my eyes as I leaned into him and basked in the comfort he offered, deeply breathing in cologne mixed with the musky scent of his sweat.

"Thank you," I mumbled against his shirt. In response, he pressed his lips lightly to my forehead.

"Let's get you someplace warm," he said, turning us toward the mouth of the alley.

"Wait!" I scrambled out of Blane's arms and ran back to the mugger. Prying open his fist, I grabbed my necklace. The man groaned but didn't open his eyes. I was glad Blane hadn't killed him, though I wondered briefly what would have happened if I hadn't stopped him.

As I returned back to Blane, he looked questioningly at me. I shrugged. "He took the necklace you gave me."

Blane didn't move. "You fought him over the necklace?" he asked, his tone chilling.

Grimacing, I muttered, "You gave it to me. I didn't want him to have it."

"Christ, Kat!" Blane exploded. "I would have bought you another one! It wasn't worth your life! He could have killed you!"

I bit my lip, knowing he was right but not wanting to admit it. I had acted irrationally, but hadn't been able to stop myself. I'd just been overcome with anger that he would dare to take something precious to me. It wasn't even that it was an expensive necklace—it was just that Blane had given it to me. I said none of this, just looked up at Blane and hoped he would drop it. Huffing with exasperation, he pulled me to him, wrapping me tightly in his arms and resting his chin on top of my head.

"Never a dull moment, Kat," he said with a sigh.

We emerged from the mouth of the alley to find two police cars pulling up, sirens blaring. A blinding light flashed at me and I realized there were a few photographers there, too. A quick glance at Blane made it obvious that he'd been in a fight. His hair was tousled and a bit of blood marred the corner of his mouth. His once-white shirt was stained and torn, the cuffs open from where the buttons had come off. I saw his knuckles were raw, scraped and bloody from the fight. The veneer of gentility he'd worn earlier was gone. He looked altogether masculine and dangerous.

A cop stepped up to us, blocking the photographers. "Mr. Kirk, is that you?" he asked. At Blane's nod, he turned his attention to me. "You must be the victim. Someone heard you scream and called 911. You all right, miss?"

"I'm fine," I said, my voice too weak for my liking. The cop nodded and stepped past us toward the prone and now groaning mugger lying on the ground.

"Hey! That's Blane Kirk!" The words came from one of the photographers and seemed to ignite a frenzy of flash-bulbs.

Turning me gently toward his chest, Blane hid my face from the cameras as we moved forward through the photographers and a small crowd of onlookers that had gathered. Flashes continued to go off, and I didn't know how Blane wasn't blinded by them. When we reached the street, he let out a piercing whistle and a passing taxi pulled to a stop.

Blane opened the door, eased me inside, and carefully shut it. Leaning into the open driver's window, he spoke to the cabbie. "Take her home and help her inside."

I saw him give the driver several bills before he turned to speak to me. "I'll handle the cops and press," he said. "I'll come by when I'm through."

I nodded silently, grateful to be going home. The adrenaline was wearing off and my body was forcefully reminding me of the abuse I'd just endured.

With one last searching gaze, Blane backed away. The driver pulled into the street and I turned in my seat to look out the back window. Blane stood watching until I was out of sight. Flashbulbs brightly illuminated his torn white shirt and body every few seconds, the silence of the scene from the confines of the cab making it appear eerie as the flashes bathed Blane with their cold glare.

CHAPTER TWO

The adrenaline was gone now, leaving only the pain of my injuries in its place. I sniffed, scrubbing a hand across the tears on my cheek.

"Are you o-k-kay?"

I looked up, focusing on the driver who was taking quick glances in his rearview mirror at me while watching the road.

Clearing my throat, I said hoarsely, "Yeah, I'm fine."

"I c-c-c-can t-take you to a-a hos-hospital," he insisted, a very pronounced stutter making it difficult to understand him.

"No, really, I'll be fine," I replied. "I just want to go home." My dress was stained and torn, my entire body ached, I had a massive headache throbbing in my temple from where I'd hit the sidewalk, and on top of all that, my feet hurt.

He still seemed uncertain, his expression anxious as he watched me, but didn't press the issue.

I was touched that he was concerned; it seemed genuinely nice people grew harder and harder to find with each passing day. "What's your name?" I asked.

"F-Frankie," he answered.

I forced a smile, though my face ached with the effort. "Nice to meet you, Frankie. I'm Kathleen."

"Nice t-t-to m-meet you, t-t-too," he stuttered back.

With a tired sigh, I laid my head back on the seat, and the few miles to my apartment passed in silence.

When he'd parked, Frankie jumped out of the car and opened my door. I eased out of the taxi gingerly, wincing at the pain in my abdomen, and unfolded myself from its confines. I clutched Blane's jacket to me, shivering as the icy wind blew my hair into my face. The pretty updo I'd done earlier was nowhere to be seen, the thick strands having fallen free from their pins. I sighed, feeling a little like Cinderella after the ball, except Cinderella never got beat up.

I headed for the stairs and had taken two steps up them before I realized Frankie was following me. I stopped and turned. "You don't have to come with me," I said.

He shook his head adamantly. "The man s-s-said t-to help."

I was too tired to argue, much less in the freezing cold. Grimacing, I clutched the railing and climbed the flight of stairs to the top floor. I fumbled in my purse for my keys, opened the door, and collapsed gracelessly on the couch. I didn't think I'd ever been so grateful to be home.

Tigger, my marmalade-colored cat who thought himself more human than feline, jumped on my lap. Absentmindedly, I stroked his soft fur, his purring making his body vibrate under my fingers.

Frankie fumbled for a minute before locating the light switch and flipping it on. I squinted in the sudden brightness. It was my first good look at Frankie and I was surprised at how young he appeared to be. He was tall but lanky, his hair and eyes were both a nondescript brown, his features plain but not unattractive. Frankie shifted uneasily at my scrutiny.

"You n-need s-s-some ice," he said, gesturing jerkily to my face.

I lifted my hand to my cheek, realizing it was slightly swollen and bleeding from scraping the asphalt. Before I could say anything, Frankie had hurried into the kitchen. It took him a while and I wondered if I'd have to help, but finally he was back and handed me a small bundle of ice wrapped in paper towels.

"Thanks," I said, pressing it to the side of my face. It eased the pain.

Frankie shifted from foot to foot as he watched me, shoving his hands in the pockets of his faded jeans. He wore a T-shirt and thin jacket, his shoes well-worn sneakers. He reminded me of a lost puppy and I wondered about his family.

"How old are you, Frankie?" I asked.

"Twenty," he answered obediently.

"Do you live with your family?"

He shook his head. "Not anymore," he said flatly.

His answer didn't invite more questions, so I was at a loss as to what to say when he suddenly blurted, "You l-look l-l-like my little s-sis-sister."

My eyebrows shot up in surprise. "I do?"

"C-Chrissy," he said. "I t-t-take c-care of her."

"By yourself?" I couldn't imagine him taking care of anyone—he barely seemed capable of taking care of himself. I tried not to think unkindly, but Frankie didn't seem to be very bright. Eager and kind, but not too smart.

He nodded. "She's f-f-fifteen."

Good lord, he was a child taking care of another child and apparently made a dubious living as a taxi driver in Indy. My chest tightened in sympathy as I imagined them trying to get by on that salary. Painfully rising from the couch, I went into the kitchen and dug inside the cookie jar. When I returned, I handed Frankie a small wad of money.

"Thank you for your help tonight," I said.

Frankie took the money, glancing uncertainly back up at me. "B-but that man p-p-paid," he protested.

"Well, I'm paying, too," I said firmly. "Take care of your sister, okay, Frankie?"

He nodded but made no move to leave. He opened his mouth to try and speak, but his stuttering had grown worse and he couldn't manage to get out a sentence. It seemed to really distress him, and I chewed my lip in sympathy, waiting. Finally, he was able to be coherent enough for me to understand.

"Th-th-that man," he stuttered anxiously, "d-d-did he d-do that t-t-to you?" He pointed to my face.

That man? It took me a second to figure out that he meant Blane. "No," I denied, shaking my head for emphasis. "I was being mugged. That man rescued me. He'd never hurt me." Again, I was touched at his concern. It seemed, like Blane, Frankie's protective instincts ran strong.

Frankie nodded in acknowledgment, breathing hard from the exertion of getting that last sentence out, and he didn't bother trying to speak again. Impulsively, I gave him a hug.

"Thanks again," I said warmly. He awkwardly patted my back before leaving. I shut and locked the door behind him and wearily headed to the bathroom for a shower, dropping my ruined dress carelessly on the bathroom floor. Usually I was pretty tidy, but I was too tired to care.

I slipped on an old T-shirt and curled up on the couch with a blanket and Tigger, grabbing the remote and flipping on the news. Both the couch and television reminded me of Blane, since he had purchased them. When my apartment and belongings had been trashed several weeks ago, Blane had taken it upon himself to be my benefactor. He'd completely refurnished my apartment, right down to the underwear in my bureau drawers.

I watched the news with half my attention, the other half listening for a knock on the door that would signal Blane's arrival. I hoped he hadn't had a bad time with the cops, or the press. I had never seen photographers descend on Blane like that before, though I knew he was often in the papers. It had been rather disconcerting, though Blane had handled the attention like he was used to it, which I supposed he was.

My attention was suddenly caught by the news anchor, and I realized he'd said Blane's name.

". . . Blane Kirk, a local lawyer now turned local hero, saved a young woman from being mugged this evening in downtown Indianapolis," he intoned seriously. "Authorities have not revealed the identity of the woman, only that she was not seriously injured, thanks to the timely rescue by Mr. Kirk."

I watched avidly as footage played of Blane and me walking out of the alley. My face couldn't be seen clearly, since he'd had the foresight to turn me toward him. I watched as the cameras filmed him putting me in the taxi, before abruptly cutting away.

"What made you decide to attempt something as dangerous as stopping a mugging?" a reporter asked, shoving a microphone into Blane's face.

"People should be safe on the streets of our city," Blane replied.

"Did you know the woman you rescued?" someone else asked.

"A fellow attendee this evening," Blane answered, which was true, though I noticed he wasn't really answering the question.

"Blane Kirk is the defense attorney defending Kyle Waters, a Navy SEAL currently embroiled in a wrongful death suit here in Indianapolis. Of course, Mr. Kirk is a fellow ex-Navy SEAL himself, tonight putting his life on the line to rescue a woman he didn't even know. That's a hometown hero for you. And now for the weather."

I flipped the TV off, the last image of Blane—standing, calm and collected despite his torn shirt and bloodied lip—as he answered the reporters' question, burned into my retina. Now that the reporter gave more information about the Waters trial, I realized I had peripherally heard about this on the news the past few weeks. I hadn't paid much attention. Terms like "Rules of Engagement" and "enemy combatants" sounded as foreign as the cities they spoke of in Iraq, but now I realized this was a big deal. Huge. And Blane hadn't breathed a word. Had he expected me to know? No doubt everyone else at the firm probably knew about this case. Did he think I was an idiot blonde by not realizing the significance?

I watched the clock, my heart sinking a little more with each passing hour. What was taking him so long? A tiny part of me wondered if he was with Kandi. She'd certainly seemed eager to resume their relationship.

Finally, a little after one, I gave up on Blane and climbed off the couch. My side ached where the mugger had kicked me, so I grabbed an ice pack out of the freezer, tossing the melted mess Frankie had sweetly made for me into the trash. I wondered if I should use a heating pad instead—I could never remember when I was supposed to use heat and when to use cold.

I curled up in bed, pulling the covers up to my chin, and wondered how a day that had started so promisingly had turned to crap so quickly. My mind was filled with things I didn't know about Blane, things he hadn't told me—the important case he was working on, his plans to run for governor, his relation to Senator Keaston, and his history with Kandi.

I fell asleep with all these things spinning through my mind.

I woke suddenly, not knowing why. It was the dead of night and I lay still in my bed, listening. I went to sit up then fell back down, moaning as the aches and bruises in my stomach and back made themselves forcefully known.

"Don't get up. I didn't mean to wake you."

I jerked upright, ignoring the sharp stab of pain, before realizing it was Blane sitting down next to me on the bed. The familiar feel of him, smell of him, surrounded me. I breathed easier, just now realizing how on edge I'd been, even asleep, without him here. But I made myself be still and not throw myself into his arms, not knowing how he was feeling.

"What time is it?" I whispered, unwilling to disturb the quiet in the warm silence of the night.

"A little after three," he said, his voice low as well. "I'm sorry it took so long. I didn't mean to wake you."

"It's been a hell of a night," I said dryly. "You could've gone home. I wouldn't have minded." He'd beat the snot out of a mugger and had taken a few hits himself. He had to be tired.

Blane didn't reply immediately. The light from the streetlamp outside filtered through the window, casting his face into light and shadow as he studied me. His fingers lightly traced my scraped cheek. I shivered, unable to look away from his gaze, which seemed to see through me.

"I had to see you. Touch you. Know you were all right," he finally rasped.

I swallowed. "I am. Thanks to you."

His brow creased slightly, almost as if what I'd said pained him, then he kissed me. It was the lightest of touches, tender and sweet. His hand threaded through my hair to cradle the back of my head. I tentatively brought my hands to his shoulders and leaned into him.

When he broke off the kiss, I expected him to pull away. Instead, he drew me close and wrapped his arms around me. I rested my head against his chest with a sigh.

"Saw you on the news," I mumbled.

"Did you?" he asked, but he didn't sound surprised.

"Yeah." I didn't stop to think before I blurted, "You didn't tell them I was your girlfriend."

"Of course I didn't," he said. "I don't want reporters camped outside your door."

"Oh." I hadn't thought of that. "How'd they find you anyway?" I asked. "And the cops?"

"Someone heard you scream," he explained. "They called the cops. The photographers were just ones that heard about it on the scanner. Reporters are notoriously nosy, you know."

I nodded like I knew all about reporters.

"No more questions?" he asked more gently.

"Well, it just took you a long time to get here," I finally said, wincing at the pout in my voice. "I thought maybe you were . . . catching up . . . with friends . . . or something." Again, the words bypassed my brain on the way out of my mouth.

Blane went still for a moment, thinking, before he saw through me. "You mean Kandi," he said flatly.

I was glad he couldn't see my face, since I could feel my skin heat in embarrassment. A part of me could not believe I was acting out the cliché role of jealous girlfriend, especially after the events of tonight, but I couldn't make the little voice inside my head shut up, so I went into denial mode.

"No, of course not," I stammered in protest, pulling away from him. "I meant . . . you know . . . the senator . . . and his wife," I finished. His eyes glittered in the shadows as he watched me squirm.

"Is that why you left?" he asked. "Because I was dancing with her?" His voice had taken on that flat edge that made me nervous. When I didn't answer, his fingers lightly grasped my chin and lifted it so our eyes met. I cringed at the anger I saw there.

"It was unavoidable," he explained tightly, "and meant nothing. I would have told you that if you'd asked, rather than leaving and nearly getting yourself killed."

"Sometimes I can be a little . . . spontaneous," I weakly defended myself, relieved to hear that their dance hadn't been something more. I told the little voice in my head to shut the hell up. I held my breath as I waited to see what he'd do, then relaxed when his lips finally twitched in an almost smile.

"Impetuous, you mean," he said dryly.

"Perhaps," I agreed without malice. "Am I forgiven?" I cuddled back into the warmth of his arms, which came up automatically to wrap around my waist and pull me onto his lap. Pressing my nose into the crook of his neck, I inhaled, the remnants of his cologne still lingered on his skin. His hand rose to cup my breast, his thumb brushing against the nipple through the thin cotton of my T-shirt. My body tightened in response, already conditioned to his touch.

"You owe me," he said, his voice rougher now. "And don't think I won't collect once you're feeling better."

I shivered at the promise and threat in his voice. "You know, for a knight in shining armor, you're not very gallant," I teased.

"Knights are overrated," he replied, picking me off his lap and putting me back down on the pillows. He straightened and I sat up again as well, reaching for his hand. His warm, callused fingers engulfed mine.

"Stay tonight?" I asked. We didn't make a habit of staying over at each other's places. I guess I was still a bit old-fashioned in some ways, but I felt he should have his home and I should have mine. However, tonight I wanted him here.

"Of course," he said, kissing the top of my head before gently pushing me back down on the mattress. I watched as he stood and stripped off his stained shirt and slacks before sliding into bed with me. He pulled me back toward him spoon-fashion, draping an arm over my waist. I threaded my fingers through his and sighed contentedly.

"Are you feeling all right?" he asked, his warm breath brushing my ear. "He didn't hurt you badly, did he?"

I shook my head. "I'm fine. A little sore, that's all."

His grip tightened on my hand, but he didn't say anything else. My mind drifted and I sleepily wondered if this was what it would be like to be married. I immediately scolded myself for even thinking such a thing—we'd only been dating for a short while. The fact was, though, that I really liked having someone to be with, someone to talk to about my day with, someone to hold me at night . . . I don't think I'd realized how lonely I'd been before Blane.

It had really meant something to me to have people to spend Thanksgiving with this year. Usually, I just heated up a TV dinner and watched the Macy's parade. But this year, Blane's housekeeper, Mona, who had also been his nanny when he was growing up, had made a fancy turkey with all the trimmings. Although it had just been Mona, her husband, Gerard, Blane, and me, it had been homey and nice. Remembering it put a smile on my face.

When I awoke, Blane was no longer in bed with me. I stretched, hearing the sounds of the shower running. I winced at a few aches and pains, but overall I felt better than I had last night. Rolling out of bed, I shivered in the cold air and quickly pulled on a pair of sweats, shoving my feet into hot-pink fuzzy slippers. Stopping to glance in the mirror, I grimaced at the livid purple and blue bruise on my cheek. The scrape on my cheekbone had scabbed over as well. Lovely.

Mercifully, Blane had already made coffee. I poured a cup and carried it to the living room. Looking out the window, I was delighted to see that it was snowing. I disliked the cold but loved the snow. Go figure. Too bad you couldn't have one without the other.

I sipped my coffee for a few minutes, watching the thick flakes settle on the ground outside, already blanketed with what looked like two or three inches. The trees had turned into works of art, their dark branches now starkly outlined in white. Even the grunginess of the neighborhood in which I lived seemed briefly washed away by the curtain of falling snow.

I heard Blane come out of the bathroom and felt him behind me. His arms slid around my waist in a light hug and I leaned back against him. We watched the snow falling outside my window.

"Good morning," he said, squeezing me lightly.

"Good morning to you," I replied with a contented sigh. "Thanks for making the coffee." Blane knew that my morning priority was always getting my hands on that first cup. Seriously. Don't even speak to me until I've had my coffee.

It was a nice moment and I was loath to ruin it, but I had questions, things Blane and I needed to discuss. I steeled my resolve and shook off the compulsion to just ignore what had happened last night and pretend everything was okay.

"When were you going to tell me about the trial? James? Running for governor? The senator?" I asked, my gaze still fixed outside. "Were you going to tell me at all?"

Blane stiffened. I tensed as well, unsure how this was going to play out. He could very well call it quits at this point, after all, that was his MO—women were a diversion and none of them were allowed to get close. I knew what I was asking, but after last night, I realized I wanted to be a part of his life. I wanted to know what worried him, what he cared most about, what kept him awake at night. I wanted more than great sex and a dinner companion. I just wasn't sure if he was willing to offer it.

After a few tense moments, he answered me. "It's not like I've been hiding the trial from you, Kathleen," he said reproachfully. I winced. He was using my whole name, not Kat, which wasn't a good sign. "It's been in the news. I just haven't spoken about it much."

So he had expected me to know about it, probably thinking I was a featherbrained idiot for not knowing. My face heated, but I came back at him. "And James? You didn't think it significant to tell me you were up against him? You know how crazy he is and he's obsessed with beating you."

"I didn't want you to worry," he said calmly. "I can handle James."

"I care about you," I said stiffly. "Of course I'm going to worry."

He turned me around, his jaw locking tight when he saw my bruised face. The backs of his fingers gently brushed against my skin and his eyes glittered with an unnamed emotion.

"Likewise," he said softly.

I softened at this. Blane didn't often put his feelings into words—he was more a man of action—so I treasured it when he did.

"You know what your apartment needs?" he asked briskly, changing the subject, and I shook my head. He'd filled it with everything I could need and then some, so I had no idea what he was thinking. "A Christmas tree," he said, as if it were obvious.

I broke into a wide smile. "Really?" I asked. "You'd help me get a tree in here? A real one?" I hadn't been able to get a real tree by myself and usually put up the little fake four-foot tree I'd had growing up.

"Absolutely," he said, his eyes, made even greener because of the hunter-green sweater he wore, twinkled at me. "We'll pick it out and cut it down ourselves."

"That sounds perfect," I enthused. I loved holidays and Christmas was no exception, though the past few had been more sad and poignant than I wanted to think about. But this year would be different—I'd have someone to share it with. Since Christmas was less than two weeks away, today would be perfect to get a tree and decorate it.

"But where in Indy are there places to cut down trees?" I asked. It's not like there was a tree farm in the middle of the city.

"There are a few places south of here," Blane said. "We used to go to Tower's in Columbus when I was a kid. You'll like it."

I hurried to get ready, throwing on jeans, a long-sleeved shirt, and a sweater over that. Tying my hair back in a French braid, I added a little mascara and lip gloss. Surveying the bruise on my face in the mirror, I grimaced. I concealed it the best I could with foundation and powder. I threw on some socks and boots, and I was ready to go. Blane had already eaten, so I grabbed a bagel, fed Tigger, and we headed out.

Before we left, I knocked on my neighbor Alisha's door. She was twenty-five, only a year older than me, and lived by herself. She worked in the library at Purdue. It was good to know your neighbors, especially if you both were young, female, and lived alone. Alisha had been living here for only a few weeks, but we'd hit it off from the first.

She answered the door wrapped in a blanket and holding her dog, a little dachshund named Bacon Bits. I had known I'd like Alisha the moment I'd learned her dog's name—bacon should have its own food group, along with rocky road ice cream.

"Hey!" I said by way of greeting. "We're going out to get a Christmas tree. Do you need anything from the store or something?"

Alisha pushed her glasses up her nose before answering. "I'm good, but thanks." She glanced at Blane. "Did you measure?" she asked him. "Because you don't want to be like Chevy Chase in *National Lampoon's Christmas Vacation* and have it be too big. And make sure there aren't any critters hiding in it. You'll have sap everywhere, you know, and needles. Make sure you cut off the lower branches before you bring it inside or you'll really have a mess. And don't forget to drill a hole in the trunk so it can draw more water."

I grinned. Alisha acted older than her years and was the queen of telling people what they ought to do as well as the myriad consequences if they did not. She had what some might call eccentric advice on everything from what kind of fabric softener I should use to how to properly make coffee ("never use the tap in the bathroom—that's toilet water"). If she wasn't so genuinely good-hearted and sweet, it might be annoying. As it was, I found it humorous, especially since many times her advice turned out to be correct, except the toilet water thing—I didn't buy that. She was a little odd, a lot obsessive-compulsive, and very genuine, and I had liked her immediately.

Blane just sort of stood there in stunned silence at this rapid-fire litany of advice. I bit back an even bigger smile and decided to save him.

"You bet," I said seriously, tugging at Blane's hand, "we absolutely will do that. Catch you later."

"Drive safe," she called out to us, "and try to get behind a plow truck if you can."

"Okay," I hollered back, giggling a little as I made my way through the snow on the stairs.

"Is she always like that?" Blane asked.

I laughed again. "Yeah. She means well, she's just very opinionated, that's all. I don't mind."

It looked like Blane had exchanged his Jaguar for a Range Rover last night, as he led me to the large black SUV in the lot.

"How'd you know to get this?" I asked as he helped me step up and into the vehicle. The interior was freezing and dark, all the windows covered with snow.

"I watch the weather," Blane said, a smirk on his face. I rolled my eyes. Smartass. He knew I hated watching the weather—I preferred to be surprised.

He shut the door and rounded to his side, starting the engine and getting the defroster going before scraping the windows clear. I huddled inside, flicked on the heater for the leather seats, and watched him, something I never tired of doing. The windows were tinted, so I could see him but he couldn't see me.

We stopped by his house so he could grab a stand for the tree, then we headed south on I-65. The snow had stopped falling and the highways were clear, though not very busy.

"I liked Senator Keaston and his wife," I said after a while.

"I'm glad," Blane said.

"Vivian was very nice." I paused for a moment before adding, "I didn't realize you're related."

"Robert is my grandfather's brother," he said. "He was around a lot when I was growing up."

"I was surprised they knew about Kade," I said, not really wanting to bring him up but curious just the same as to what he'd say.

"Robert and my father were very close," Blane explained. "Robert helped him out of some of the messes he got himself into. I'm sure he knew about Kade long before I did."

I thought for a moment, wondering if I should say what I was thinking. "Kade told me about how your dad wouldn't take him in," I said hesitantly. "How you wanted him to and that you went to find him after your dad died."

Blane's eyes swiveled to mine, his gaze shrewd. "Did he, now?" he said.

I swallowed nervously. Kade had told me a lot of things about their family, and I wasn't sure how much Blane would have wanted me to know. "Is that a problem?" I asked.

"Of course not," Blane replied, looking back at the road. "I'm just surprised. Kade doesn't usually tell his life story to people."

"He didn't tell me his life story," I quickly contradicted. "I just wanted to know how you found each other, that's all."

"Kade was in state custody when I found him," Blane said. "He'd run away from foster home after foster home, living on the streets and stealing to get by."

"Why did he run away?"

Blane shook his head. "He never would tell me. Maybe not all the people they put him with were bad, but enough of them were. When I brought him to stay with me he had nightmares—talked in his sleep. He was only six when his mother died."

"Did things go okay once he came to live with you?"

Blane let out a little huff of laughter. "Hardly. I was only eighteen and they wouldn't grant me guardianship, even though I was his brother. Robert had to step in and pull some strings. Kade was scared, defiant. He ran away a few times. But I tracked him down and brought him home. I think it finally got through to him that I wasn't going to leave him. But it took time and patience. He'd learned not to trust."

The story fascinated me even as it tugged at my heart. I felt sorry for Kade, enduring such a childhood, and I was amazed at the strength of character and loyalty Blane had displayed even as a teenager. He had managed to track down and take in his brother, working with him to gain his trust and affection.

"Who took care of him while you were in the Navy and at school?" I asked.

"Mona and Gerard," he answered. "They never were able to have children. They took him in like he was their own and raised him. Mona was upset that he didn't come home for Thanksgiving. He usually doesn't miss a major holiday with them."

I hadn't realized Mona had been upset on Thanksgiving; she'd hid it well. I asked the question that I'd been wondering about for the past couple of weeks. "Why didn't he come?"

"He didn't really give much of a reason," Blane said thoughtfully. "Just that he was working and couldn't make it. I didn't press him for details."

The thought again came to me that perhaps he'd stayed away because of me, but then I chastised myself for thinking such a thing. Kade was tough as nails and twice as hard.

A memory replayed itself in my head of Kade standing in my bedroom, his hands resting on my hips as he towered over me:

"You didn't tell him about us," Kade had said, referring to Blane.

"There is no 'us.'"

"You sure about that, princess?"

The idea that he might feel something for me and want to stay away because I was with Blane was ridiculous and narcissistic.

Blane interrupted my thoughts. "Do you want to tell me what really happened to Stephen Avery?"

I turned to him, my eyes wide in surprise. "What . . . what do you mean?" I stammered, panic flashing through me. Stephen Avery had been the man who'd intended to rape and kill me. Only Kade's timely intervention had prevented him from doing exactly that.

He looked at me, exasperation evident on his face. "Kathleen, I'm not stupid. Stephen Avery was a VP at TecSol. You and Kade went with him to Chicago that night. Then he ends up with a broken neck in his hotel room, supposedly an accident from slipping in water on the floor? Please."

I turned away to gaze out the window. The palms of my hands were clammy with sweat as I remembered that night, remembered Avery attacking me, hitting me. I'd been more terrified than I'd ever been in my life.

"Did Kade kill him?"

I didn't look at him as I gave a short nod, staring sightlessly out the window.

Blane cursed and I jumped at the harsh sound.

"Why the fuck would he do something so stupid?" Blane asked angrily. "He could have just knocked him out, tied him up rather than kill him. And he had to involve you in it as well! I swear, the next time I see him, I'm going to hit him just for being stupid."

I was alarmed now at Blane's anger toward Kade. Kade didn't deserve that. He'd had a reason for killing Avery, and it wasn't one I could disagree with. When it's either you or them in a matter of life and death, you tend to pick yourself.

"Blane, it wasn't like that!" I protested, wondering how I could get Kade off the hook without revealing too much. "He had no choice."

Blane's astute gaze met mine and I realized even that little information had tipped him off that there was more to the story.

"Tell me," he ordered.

I shook my head in wordless denial, turning to look out the window again. Unwittingly, the memory came back with a vengeance: Avery's hand wrapped around my throat as he held me pinned against the door, squeezing until I nearly blacked out. His hands were on me, shoving my face into the mattress as I fought to breathe, knowing my last moments were going to be horrible—dying of suffocation while he raped me. It was the utter helplessness I'd felt that still woke me up some nights.

Staring out the window, I saw none of the scenery going by. That night with Avery replayed in my mind, of Kade rescuing me, holding me while I wept. Avery had been dead on the floor, his sightless eyes staring up at me.

I was abruptly shaken from my distraction by Blane, and I realized he'd stopped the car on the shoulder of the road.

"Why are you stopping?" I asked, confused. I jerked in surprise when Blane grasped my chin, turning my face toward his.

"Kat, I've been talking to you and stopped when you wouldn't answer me."

"I . . . I'm fine," I stammered, alarmed and embarrassed that I'd apparently been so out of it I hadn't even heard him talking to me. "I'm sorry . . . I guess I just didn't hear you." My excuse was lame, and when my gaze met his, I knew I wasn't fooling him for an instant.

He studied me intently before finally saying, "Just tell me one thing. Would I have killed Avery, too?"

It was a loaded question. I remembered the man who'd tried to mug me and how Blane had beat him unconscious. There was little doubt in my mind that Blane's response would have echoed Kade's actions if it had been him there that night.

"Yes," I said simply.

Blane studied me for a moment, then pulled me into his arms, resting his chin on top of my head. "I'm sorry I upset you," he apologized. "We won't discuss it again, okay?"

I nodded. Blane's understanding eased my anxiety, and I was grateful at the concession he'd just given to me.

After a moment, I pulled out of his arms and self-consciously smoothed my hair. Clearing my throat nervously, I watched in my peripheral vision as Blane silently studied me before sliding behind the wheel and pulling back onto the highway.

"Do you have decorations somewhere for a tree?" Blane asked. It was obvious he was changing the subject and I gratefully latched on to it.

"I have some things of my parents' in storage from when I was a kid," I said. "Christmas was a huge deal in our house." I smiled, remembering. "My dad would fight the lights every year when he decorated the outside. He cussed a lot."

"Did you have white lights or colored?" Blane asked.

"They started out white," I said, "but my mom told me that when I was five, I insisted he put up multicolored lights because I thought they were prettier. Apparently, I was quite persuasive."

"I can see that," Blane teased. The tension from earlier was gone, thank God, and I appreciated his effort to turn the mood around.

"What about you?" I asked. "Did your dad hang lights?"

Blane shook his head. "Not himself, no. We had professional decorators that did the outside lights and the inside. There was a Christmas tree in nearly every room—each with a different theme."

"Wow!" I said, impressed. "That must have been really pretty." Professional decorators. Huh. Somehow I doubted his decorators would have approved of my homemade construction paper chains that had wrapped around our tree.

"It was," Blane agreed. "The house was beautiful and perfect." His voice was slightly bitter.

"I thought you said you came to this place we're going when you were a kid?" I asked, confused.

"Mona and Gerard brought me with them to get their tree," Blane explained. "That was the Christmas tree I remember decorating—theirs, not ours."

I wasn't sure what to say to that; it sounded so sad. Blane was matter-of-fact about it, the bitterness no longer present in his voice.

"One year we went the day after Thanksgiving to get our tree," I finally said, "and it was perfect. The absolutely perfect shape for a Christmas tree. We brought it home and decorated it, which always took forever because my parents had been collecting ornaments for each other and our family since before they got married. We finally finished and were so excited to have the perfect tree. Unfortunately, it was dead less than a week later."

"Dead?" Blane asked incredulously. "That quick?"

I giggled. "Yep. The whole thing had turned brown and needles were falling by the bucketful. I was crying because our Christmas tree looked horrible and Dad was cussing a blue streak about getting ripped off at the tree place. We had to take the whole thing down and get rid of it. I think Mom and Dad would have been fine without a tree, but I certainly wasn't. It was still four weeks until Christmas! So that was the year we bought an artificial tree."

Blane laughed with me, reaching across the console and threading his fingers through mine. We spent the rest of the drive recounting favorite stories from our childhood Christmases. Well, it was mostly me telling the stories. It seemed to me that Blane didn't have a lot of favorite memories from his childhood. I told him about the time I'd gotten my Barbie Dreamhouse, the best Christmas present ever, and how my mom and I used to sing Christmas carols by the fire. Sometimes my dad had joined in, but more often than not he had just watched us, a smile on his face.

We arrived at the tree farm about an hour later as it began to snow again. The place looked like a winter wonderland with Christmas lights peeking out from under their gloss of snow. Christmas carols drifted through the air, playing over the sound system inside the large barn where Blane led me. It was warm and cozy inside, the air thickly coated with the scent of pine and balsam.

"May I help you?" a kindly man asked, appearing to be in his early sixties.

"We're looking for a tree," Blane said with a genial smile.

"Well, you came to the right place! I'm George and I can help you get started."

He gave Blane a saw to use and pointed us in the direction of the trees. "Just find one you like, make sure it's not too tall—they all look smaller in the outdoors than they will in your living room—and cut it down. Bring it back here and we'll finish it up."

We thanked him and started walking in the direction he'd pointed. Not many people were at the farm, and I figured it was probably the weather keeping them away. Not that I was complaining. The farther we walked, the more magical it seemed with just Blane and me in the silence of the snow-covered woods.

He held my hand, helping me through the drifts, some of which were up to my knees. We talked quietly, pointing out different trees to each other and inspecting them for flaws. I laughed at how particular he was—I didn't mind a tree with a bare spot or two.

At last, we found one we both could agree on, which was a good thing since it was starting to get dark. I got down on my knees, helping Blane scoop the snow away from the trunk. When it was finally clear enough, I watched as he sawed through the trunk and cheered when it fell over.

"Ooh, Blane," I cooed, batting my eyelashes at him. "You're so str-o-o-ong." I giggled at the expression on his face, then squealed in surprise when he started to chase me.

I laughed as I ran, scooping up a handful of snow, which I quickly packed into a ball and hurled at him. He ducked and it sailed over his head.

"Ha! Missed me!" he gloated just as I lobbed another that hit him square in the face.

I erupted in gales of laughter now, but had to take off again as a barrage of snowballs came flying at me. I ran behind a stand of trees, huffing from the exertion. Scooping up some snow, I waited, packing it into a tight ball. When I didn't hear anything, I cautiously peeked from behind the trees.

I screamed, startled as Blane stepped directly in front of me, then started laughing at how he'd gotten the drop on me. He was grinning, watching me as my giggles gradually subsided. I noticed his long eyelashes were wet from the snow.

"You're terrible at this game," I said loftily, nose in the air. "I think I won."

"I don't know about that," Blane said, his voice a husky rasp that made my laughter die in my throat. Putting his hands on my hips, he tugged me closer to him. The look in his eyes was one I knew well, and my heart started beating faster. "I'm pretty sure I won this game."

My breath caught in my throat as his gaze lowered to my mouth. Bending down, his lips settled on mine. My eyes drifted closed.

A sudden loud noise startled me and I jumped just as the bark on the tree next to us exploded. The sound came again and I gasped in shock as Blane shoved me to the ground.

"What are you doing?" I gasped. "What's that noise?"

"Gunshots," Blane replied grimly. "Someone's shooting at us."

CHAPTER THREE

Another crack of a gunshot sliced through the air nearby as Blane grabbed hold of the collar of my coat, picked me up bodily, and yanked me behind the trees. I was too stunned to do much more than stumble to where he led me.

The sound of a gunshot was much closer this time, and I nearly jumped out of my skin, then I saw it had come from the gun in Blane's hand.

"You brought your gun Christmas tree shopping?" I hissed. "Seriously?"

He just gave me a look. I rolled my eyes, then yelped and covered my head with my arms as a bullet smacked through the branches above us.

"I'll provide cover," Blane said. "You run as fast as you can back to the barn."

"What? No way," I said, shaking my head firmly. "I'm not leaving you."

"We're an easy target out here in the snow," Blane said, before squeezing off another round and ducking back behind the tree. "If I can keep him occupied, you can get back and send help."

I chewed my lip in indecision. I really didn't want to leave Blane by himself, but there was little I could do to help him. After all, he was the one with a gun.

Blane cursed as another shot hit the tree we were standing behind. "On three," he commanded, and I reluctantly nodded. "One . . . two . . . go!"

I took off running the best I could, back in the direction we'd come from, hearing Blane's gun spit bullets as he provided cover. The snow impeded my progress, but I reached more trees and darted in among them. I was breathing hard now and my legs burned from the exertion of running.

I could still hear sporadic gunshots, so I kept moving as fast as I could. I had to find help for Blane. What if he didn't duck behind a tree fast enough? What if he ran out of bullets? The what-ifs terrified me and I prayed he would be okay.

After what felt like forever, it started to snow yet again, the fat flakes resting gently on my nose and eyelashes. I realized I should have been back to the barn by now. Blane and I had walked a ways, but I'd been running back. Stopping, I looked around in confusion. Dusk was fading, the falling snow becoming a thick curtain that was difficult to see through. Everything looked the same around me—endless rows of Christmas trees. As I turned around, I realized I couldn't tell which direction I'd just come from, my footprints already disappearing under a new layer of snow.

I fought down panic. I couldn't be lost—we hadn't gone that far. The barn should be right up ahead, past this grove of trees. I hurried forward, certain I was right. Stepping out from the trees into a large clearing, I was dismayed to see how wrong I'd been.

There were no man-made structures in sight, just woods. Not even the neat little rows of planted Christmas trees now, just naturally growing ones. Uncertain what to do, I walked farther into the clearing, wondering if I should stop walking and stay put. Wasn't that what my dad had always told me to do if I got lost? Except I didn't know if anyone would be coming to find me.

I wondered if Blane was okay and frustrated tears stung my eyes. If my failure to get help had resulted in his getting injured, or worse . . . but I couldn't finish that thought.

A movement caught my eye, and I was relieved to see a man standing about fifty yards away at the edge of the clearing near the trees. I couldn't see him very clearly because of the snow, but I could tell he'd spotted me.

"Hey!" I shouted. "Can you help me? I'm lost." I started shuffling quickly through the snow toward him, grateful that I'd found someone who would hopefully know where I was. The man moved and I froze.

He was pointing a gun at me.

My breath seized in my chest as I realized this had to have been the man shooting at Blane and me. If he was here, did that mean he'd shot Blane? Oh God, no.

That thought was abruptly cut off at the sound of a loud crack and I flinched. I'd thought the sound came from his gun, but to my horror, the ground suddenly shifted and gave way underneath my feet and I was plunged through ice into freezing cold water.

I realized what was happening just in time to keep my head above water. I grabbed on to the surrounding ice, which broke under my scrabbling fingers. The shock of the cold water was incredible—I'd never felt anything like it—and I started gasping, my breath coming in short, quick pants.

I knew I'd hyperventilate if I kept breathing that way, so I struggled to stay calm and take slower, deeper breaths, and most important, stay afloat. Looking back at the far bank of what I now guessed to be a small pond or large creek, I saw the man was still standing there. As I watched, he turned and disappeared into the trees, leaving me to my dubious fate. Bastard.

After a few moments, I was able to breathe better and take stock of my situation. I'd had a fear of drowning since as a child I'd accidentally gotten stuck underneath a raft in the neighborhood pool. I could still feel the panic of my lungs burning with the need for air as I tried fruitlessly to surface. But dying hadn't been on the agenda today and I wasn't about to pencil it in.

Bracing myself, I tried to haul my body out of the water and onto the ice I'd been walking on before—that had held me well enough. But I couldn't seem to get more than my upper body out of the water; the leverage I mustered just wasn't enough to get my balance of weight onto the ice. My sodden coat, clothes, and boots were like dead weight, tugging me downward.

My body was going numb now, the cold not so bad, but I could feel my energy ebbing. I tried twice more to heave myself out but couldn't do it. It was getting harder not to panic and I wondered if I would die here, my body locked underneath a layer of ice.

Fear threatened to overtake me, sapping my strength. There was no way out. No one was coming to help me.

I was going to die alone.

That thought gave me a burst of adrenaline, and in a fit of desperation, I kicked my feet like I was trying to swim as I hauled upward. To my surprise, that was enough to propel me out and onto the ice.

Gasping from the exertion and cold, I just lay there for a moment, relieved to be out of the water. I knew I wasn't out of the woods yet, literally, and I still had to make it off the ice. Common sense said I probably shouldn't stand up on the ice, but maybe if I crawled . . .

Getting gingerly onto all fours, I began to slowly crawl away from the hole toward the trees. When I was near enough that I judged it to be safe, I got to my feet. To my relief, the ground beneath me held. I'd never been so grateful to hug a tree as I was when I finally reached one.

My brain was foggy, but I tried hard to think. Judging by how dark it was, I had to have been gone for nearly an hour. Looking around, I realized that the full dark actually was better than dusk had been. The snow was reflective and now I could see what I couldn't before—lights off to my left, their brightness amplified by the snow falling from the sky above them.

Wearily, I headed that way, careful to keep in the trees. Each step was an effort that got more and more difficult. I was shivering violently from the cold, which seemed to reach down into my bones with icy fingers. I was so tired. It was tempting to sit down and rest for a few minutes, but I was afraid if I did that, I would never get up. So I kept moving, putting one foot in front of the other.

Finally, when I was wondering if I could take it anymore, I broke out of the trees and saw the barn about a hundred yards away. If I'd had the energy, I would have cried in relief.

I went to step forward again and realized with dismay that my body wouldn't obey. My knees buckled and I landed hard in the snow. Through bleary eyes, I saw people moving by the barn, and with the last of my energy, I called out for help. No one seemed to hear. I tried again, even as darkness crowded my vision.

~

I slowly became aware of several things—I was lying on something soft, was wrapped in something deliciously warm against my naked skin, and Blane was speaking quietly to me.

Blane.

My eyes flew open. Blane was sitting in a chair beside me, watching me avidly, lines of worry on his face.

"Blane," I choked out, trying to maneuver an arm out from the piles of blankets in which I was swaddled, "thank God you're okay." I finally managed to get my arm out and I reached for him. His hand tightly grasped mine.

"*I'm* okay?" he repeated incredulously. "Christ, Kat . . ." He shoved a hand through his hair and took a deep, ragged breath.

"What? What's wrong?" I was taken aback by his demeanor. His usual iron control seemed frazzled.

"What happened?" he asked urgently, ignoring my question. "Why didn't you come back here?"

"I got lost," I admitted. "Then I fell through some ice. I'm so sorry, Blane."

In an instant, he'd joined me on the bed and gathered me into his arms, blankets and all. "I'm the one who should be apologizing," he said gruffly. "I should have stayed with you, not sent you off on your own like that."

"You were trying to protect me," I defended him. "It was my own crappy sense of direction that got me lost."

Blane pulled back so he could look into my eyes. His smile was warm and tender as he brushed my hair back from my face. "Your sense of direction isn't to be trusted. Good to know."

"I'm just glad you're okay," I said quietly. "I kept worrying that you were hurt and I hadn't sent anyone back to help you."

He shook his head. "I'm fine, as you can see. The guy ran off a few minutes after you left. I tried to follow your trail, but the snow had started coming down again and I lost it."

"He found me," I said, grimly reminded of my encounter at the creek. "He had a gun pointed at me, then the ice broke and I fell in."

"He found you?" Blane asked. "Had a gun on you then watched you fall in the water?" His voice was flat and hard.

I nodded. "He left and I was able to get out."

Blane closed his eyes at this and he rubbed his forehead wearily. I realized we'd had a lot of drama this weekend, more than I really wanted or needed, and wondered uneasily if Blane was thinking the same thing.

Looking at Blane with these thoughts rattling around in my head made me anxious, so I glanced away. Checking out the little bedroom I was in, I saw the walls were painted a cheery buttercup yellow, the sparse furniture white. What looked like a handmade quilt covered the bed and another was wrapped around me. A small lamp burned on the bedside table, giving a warm and cozy feel to the room.

"Where are we?" I asked.

Blane raised his head with a sigh. "The upstairs of the barn," he said. "George and his wife, Martha—"

"Really?" I interrupted. "George and Martha?" I grinned. "Please don't tell me their last name is Washington."

Blane's lips twitched in a small smile. "I don't think so, no. But they were helping me organize the search for you when you came out of the woods. They offered me this room so you could get warm."

"Well, that was thoughtful of them," I said. I thought for a moment. "Do you think they'll give us a discount on the tree?"

Blane was silent as he stared at me.

"What?" I asked. "I think we should get a discount, don't you?"

"Absolutely," he said, deadpan. I cracked a grin.

A knock at the door interrupted us and it opened to reveal a small older woman wearing faded jeans and a thick green sweatshirt with *Ho! Ho! Ho!* emblazoned in shiny red letters across the chest. Sparkly silver bell earrings dangled from her ears, making her jingle as she walked.

"Oh good, you're awake!" the woman said, setting a small tray on the bedside table. She took in the sight of Blane cradling me in his arms with an indulgent smile. "See, young man, I told you she'd be just fine. Nothing that blankets, some hot tea, and a little TLC won't fix."

"You were right, Martha," Blane agreed, his arms tightening around me.

"Of course I was. Drink the tea, that'll warm you right up. Your clothes should be dry soon. Now, if you two need anything else, just let me know," she instructed.

"Thank you so much," I said. "I'm sorry for the trouble."

"No trouble at all, dear," Martha replied, shutting the door behind her.

"Here, drink this," Blane said, picking a steaming mug off the tray.

I reached for it, keeping the blanket pulled up to cover myself. The warm tea was heavenly and I finished the whole cup. Blane took it from me.

"Hungry?" he asked, tucking a lock of hair behind my ear. I rested back against him.

"Not right now." I sighed contentedly, curling into him. "What time is it? How long was I out?"

"About thirty minutes," he answered.

"Oh, so not very long," I said, relieved. "That's good. I thought it had been longer."

"It seemed long," Blane murmured, almost to himself.

I tipped my head back so I could see him. He looked down at me, his fingers lightly combing through my hair. His face was serious, the lighthearted banter of a few moments ago forgotten.

"What's the matter?" I asked quietly, almost afraid of the answer.

He shook his head a fraction, his eyes not meeting mine but following the motion of his hand instead. When he didn't answer, I decided to try a different tactic.

"So why would someone be shooting at us in the middle of nowhere?"

"I honestly have no idea," he said. He finally met my gaze and my stomach clenched at the look in his eyes, grave and intense. It seemed like he wanted to say something, and I waited, but his jaw tightened and his lips became a thin line instead.

"Maybe I just attract trouble?" I mused, only half kidding. I was hoping to lighten his mood, unsure what had caused the sudden thick tension between us. He didn't reply as he gathered me closer and kissed me. The kiss wasn't tender and gentle, but hard and demanding, his tongue sliding against mine as he cupped my jaw in his hand.

I no longer felt cold as Blane's hands moved under the quilt, heating my skin as he unwrapped me from my cocoon. His lips moved to my bare neck and shoulder. He grasped my leg and turned me so I straddled his thighs. I was breathing hard now, my pulse racing, and I bit back a moan when his hands moved to my breasts.

The quilt fell from my shoulders to puddle on the bed behind me. With a groan, Blane pressed me to his chest, his mouth claiming mine again. He kissed me with an urgency that both thrilled and frightened me. I gasped when his hand curved behind my thigh to slip between my legs. Fire licked my veins at his touch and I whimpered against his lips when he slid a long finger inside me.

"Undo my pants," he said, breaking off the kiss. I drew back, trying to keep a coherent thought in my head. "N-no, we can't," I said breathlessly. His hand moved a certain way and I lost my train of thought. I struggled to remember why we should stop. "It would be rude . . ." I managed to say, "and . . . tacky."

"Ask me if I care," he growled. "Undo them."

When he put it that way, who was I to argue? I prayed Martha wouldn't walk back in as my hands fumbled at his belt and zipper, which seemed much more complicated devices than I remembered them being, but I finally succeeded in my task. He was thick and heavy in my hands, and I'd barely gotten my fingers wrapped around him before I was lying on my back and he'd pushed inside of me in one hard thrust.

His mouth swallowed my cries and Martha was utterly forgotten as he moved inside me. He was everywhere, surrounding and overwhelming me with the force of his passion, and I drank in every moment, wanting to commit it to memory.

It was hard and fast and I couldn't hold on, my body splintering apart into a million pieces under his. A moment later, his body jerked forcefully into mine and he bit out my name from between clenched teeth.

I struggled to regain control of my breathing and my thighs ached as he lay between them. I didn't mind, though, my hand combing aimlessly through his hair as he rose up on his elbows to look at me.

"Sorry that wasn't exactly gentle," he apologized, his fingers brushing the side of my cheek.

"It's all right," I said with a soft smile. If he felt that passionate about me, then I certainly wasn't going to complain. "I'm tougher than I look."

I knew instantly I'd said something wrong, because that pained expression came across his face again before he masked it.

"Yes, you are," he agreed more seriously than I felt my comment warranted.

A knock sounded at the door and I froze, my mouth agape in horror. It would be so incredibly awful if Martha walked in, I didn't think I could withstand the sheer embarrassment. Before I could voice my fear, Blane had pulled me upright and wrapped the quilt around me. I saw him quickly zip his pants back up and fasten his belt before he called out, "Come in."

Martha reappeared in the doorway, holding a stack of clothes. "Your clothes are dry, dear," she said, setting them on a nearby wooden chair.

"Thank you," I said, blushing to the roots of my hair. If she hadn't known what we'd just been doing, no doubt my bright red face clued her in.

With a knowing smile, she turned and left again. When the door shut, I hid my face against Blane's chest, groaning in embarrassment. He chuckled softly.

"I can't believe we just did that," I said with dismay. "We're never going to be able to come back here again!"

"Speaking of which," Blane said briskly, "you get dressed and I'll see about getting that tree."

"You're not going back to get the one you cut down, are you?" I asked in surprise, abruptly sitting up so I could see him.

"No," he said with regret, "though it was the perfect tree. They have some precut ones."

"It's really not a big deal," I protested, knowing he'd had a long day as well, "we don't have to get a tree."

"I promised you a damn Christmas tree and I'm not leaving here without one," he said stubbornly. He rose from the bed.

"All right," I capitulated with a sigh, "but don't say *damn* and *Christmas* in the same sentence." He looked at me. "It's sacrilegious," I explained, as if it were obvious. His lips twitched in a small smile before he pressed a quick kiss to my mouth, then he was gone.

I made use of the tiny half bath attached to the bedroom, dressing in the warm and dry clothes and finger-combing my hair. My French braid was long gone and my hair now hung in waves down my back. Examining myself in the mirror, I saw I was a little paler than normal, but I have fair skin, anyway, so that wasn't saying much.

My boots were nowhere to be found, and I grimaced when I realized there was no way they were going to be dry yet even if I did find them. Looking at the rumpled bed, I made a quick decision, folding up the quilt I'd been wrapped in—and on which Blane had made love to me. Carrying it in my arms, I headed downstairs.

The tiny wooden staircase led into a brightly lit kitchen, and I saw Martha bustling around the stove. I cleared my throat and she turned around, a bright smile on her face. She reminded me of my grandma, and I returned her smile.

"Thank you so much for the hospitality," I said.

"You're welcome," Martha said, "I'm just glad you're all right. That man of yours was fit to be tied when he came back and you weren't here."

I grimaced. I bet he had been. After all, who gets lost on a Christmas tree farm, for crying out loud?

"George told him we'd put together a search party to find you—he knows this land like the back of his hand—but he wouldn't wait," she continued. "Was determined to go back into the woods by himself to search. And when you came staggering out, collapsing like that in the snow . . ." She shook her head as I waited, engrossed in her story. "Well, I've never seen anyone move so fast. He had you in his arms, carrying you inside here before we hardly knew what had happened. Like something out of one of those romance movies."

"Really?" I asked, wondering if she was stretching the truth a little.

"Oh my, yes," she said with a chuckle, turning back to stir a pot of something steaming on the stove. "I'm sure he wouldn't like me telling you this. He seems as though he likes to play his cards close to his chest, and believe me, I know the type. But he was worried something fierce, sweetie. Terrified, I think, that you weren't going to wake up. He refused to leave your side. Of course, I knew you would. We raised five boys here with the Indiana winters and I knew you'd be just fine once you warmed up."

"Huh" was all I could think to say, my mind still trying to wrap itself around Blane's reaction to my accidental dousing.

"He certainly loves you a great deal," she said with a twinkle in her eye, turning back to me. I stood, stunned, as she moved closer and gestured to the quilt in my arms. "Here, let me take that for you."

I finally managed to speak. "No—I mean, I really love the quilt and was hoping I could buy it from you?" My mind scrambled for equilibrium after hearing her assertion that Blane loved me.

"You like it that much," she said, "you can have it. It's the least we can do after all you've endured today."

"Thanks," I said gratefully. "Um, do you know where my boots are?"

"They're still wet," she said, "but I have some old ones you can wear to get home. Let me get them for you." She disappeared and returned moments later with a well-used pair of boots. I pulled them on, glad they fit good enough for the trip home.

"I'm going to take this outside to the car," I said, heading to the door with the quilt in my arms. "I'll be right back."

It was dark and cold outside, the snow had stopped, and I could see the stars twinkling above me in the clear moonless sky. Without the city lights, I could see so many more than usual. It was beautiful. I walked to the car, my steps crunching on the thick snow, and put the quilt in the back. I could hear Blane talking with George, and I saw them carrying a tree toward me. I smiled, wrapping my arms around myself to stay warm. As I turned back to go inside, something tucked under the wiper blade caught my eye. I reached for it, realizing it was a piece of paper.

Curious, I turned it toward the light spilling from the barn, realizing there was some writing scribbled on it. As I read, my mouth ran dry.

"What's that?" Blane asked, coming up behind me. George was tying the tree to the top of the SUV. Blane glanced over my shoulder when I didn't respond, still staring at the paper. Gently, he took it from me, turning it so he could read the words as well: *Watch your back.*

Blane didn't move for a moment, seeming as stunned as I was, then quickly pocketed the note. "Let's get out of here," he said crisply. I nodded in agreement, following him as he walked quickly to the kitchen door.

"We'll be going now," he said with a wide smile for Martha after we'd entered the kitchen. Again I admired how effortlessly he could turn on the charm, no matter what the situation. "Thank you so much for your assistance today."

"I'm glad we could help," Martha said, handing him a large paper sack. "I put some dinner in there for you, just some bread and soup I made."

"Thank you," I managed, the shock of the note wearing off. "Have a merry Christmas."

"You, too," Martha said, giving me a hug while George and Blane shook hands. "Don't forget to invite us to the wedding, won't you?"

"Wha—?" My confused question was abruptly cut off as Blane pushed me unceremoniously out the door. He wrapped his arm around me, holding me close against his side as we walked quickly to the car. I couldn't shake the feeling that he was using his body as a shield for mine. It was only after we'd gotten in the SUV and started down the road toward the highway that I spoke.

"Wedding?" I really didn't think I had to add anything else.

Blane glanced at me uncomfortably. "I had to tell them we were engaged," he explained. "Otherwise, she wasn't going to let me stay with you while you were naked." He hesitated before adding gruffly, "She said it wasn't proper."

I couldn't help grinning. The idea of a little old lady like Martha telling Blane he couldn't do something struck me as funny indeed. I wished I'd been conscious to see it. The thought of being engaged to Blane made butterflies dance in my stomach, but I ignored them. Best to let the conversation drop there. I was well aware of how men viewed women who talked about marriage mere weeks after dating, and it wasn't good.

I cleared my throat before changing the subject. "The note . . ." I began, then was at a loss for anything else to say.

"I know" was all Blane said, his voice flat.

The rest of the trip was quiet, each of us lost in thought. It wasn't until we'd reached my apartment and were hauling stuff inside that Blane spoke again.

"You have the quilt?" he asked, pulling it from the back-seat.

I shrugged. "I asked and she let me have it."

He nodded before wordlessly carrying it upstairs for me. After another twenty minutes, we were looking at a naked Christmas tree standing in a corner of my living room.

"Where are your decorations?" Blane asked.

"Downstairs in storage," I answered, "but let's eat first. I'm starving."

Martha's soup was incredibly good, a thick and hearty vegetable beef that made me sorry I hadn't asked for the recipe. The bread was homemade—crunchy on the outside and chewy on the inside. The meal was fantastic and my mood was considerably better when I was finished. After all, I'd gotten to spend the day with Blane, we'd found a great tree, made love, and had a homemade dinner. Yeah, I'd fall-en through ice and nearly froze to death, and yes, someone had shot at us, but I chose to look at the positive.

Blane carried up my boxes of ornaments and decora-tions from the apartment building's storage room while I threw the quilt in the washing machine. Though it was get-ting late, we strung lights on the tree and hung the orna-ments. Many of them had a story and I told Blane about them, showing him the ornament my parents had gotten while on their honeymoon in Niagara Falls, the first ornaments they'd given each other while still dating, the one commemorating my first Christmas, and the one they'd purchased when they'd moved into their first house.

"This must be you," Blane said with a smile, holding up a handmade ornament with a tiny school picture of myself glued on.

I laughed at the sight. "Yes, I think I was eleven when that was taken," I said.

Blane studied it. "You were cute." He glanced back at me, mischief in his eyes. "I would have pulled your ponytail, put frogs in your desk, done anything to get a scrap of attention from you."

I rolled my eyes but couldn't resist the rush of pleasure his words gave me. "I think you and I would have been in completely different crowds," I said. I imagined him being with the popular kids, the football player all the girls drooled over but only the head cheerleader had a shot with. I, on the other hand, had been a quiet loner for the most part. Books had been my friends. Shy and reserved, I'd rarely sought attention, avoiding it if at all possible.

We finished the tree, standing back to admire our work once the lights had been lit. Blane wrapped his arms around me, pulling me back against his chest.

"It's beautiful," I said softly. "This is the first time in a long time I've had a tree large enough to put all my parents' ornaments on." I looked up at Blane. "Thank you."

His arms tightened around me. "You're welcome, Kat," he said, his voice gentle in my ear. We stood in the dark, the only light coming from the strands wrapped around the tree. I leaned my head back against him, my hands resting on his arms across my abdomen. It was a moment I knew I wouldn't soon forget.

The shrill ring of his cell phone shattered the silence and the mood. With a sigh, Blane released me, reaching into his jeans pocket for the phone.

"Kirk," he answered. I tried to step away but he reached out, grasping my hand in his and tugging me back.

I couldn't hear the other side of the conversation, so I just stood in front of him, watching his face. I grew concerned as his expression turned hard, his jaw clenching tight.

"No," he said angrily, "that isn't what we agreed on." Dropping my hand, Blane turned away and took a few steps toward the window, quiet again as he listened.

"That's none of your fucking business," he growled, fury now etched in every line of his body, starkly outlined against the glowing whiteness of the snow outside.

I grew tense as I watched him on the phone, his emotions emanating from him. Blane's charisma and presence ensured that he set the tone and atmosphere of any room, and it was no different when I was the only audience.

"You do that and I'll have Judge Reynolds chewing your ass in his chambers tomorrow at dawn, you fucking prick," Blane threatened. A pause and then, "Watch me." Blane flipped the phone closed with enough force to make me jump.

"Who was that?" I asked, my eyes wide.

Blane hesitated before answering. "James," he finally said. "He likes to create problems, try and keep me off balance."

"So what was none of his business?" I asked.

Blane's face turned into that expressionless mask I knew very well when he replied, "He wanted to know if I was with you tonight."

I was so surprised, I didn't know what to say. James had been complicit in nearly having me murdered by Jimmy Quicksilver, a hit man his father had used to kill my friend Sheila and her boyfriend, Mark. Not to mention that James had punched me in the face and would have strangled me if not for CJ, my neighbor at the time, who had intervened—with a gun.

"Why would he want to know that?" I asked weakly.

Blane shook his head. "Don't worry about it," he said. "James isn't foolish enough to try anything with you. He's just trying to goad me into doing something stupid."

I wanted to ask more questions, but Blane interrupted me.

"I have to go," he said. "I need to check on Kyle. Here, take this." He reached under his sweater and lifted his gun from its holster before handing it to me.

"Why are you giving me your gun?" I asked, alarmed. I stepped back, but Blane caught my hand, pulling me back and placing the gun in my grip.

"Because this case is a high-profile one and volatile," he explained quietly. "We've already had someone shooting at us today. If it happens again and I'm not around, I want you to be able to shoot back."

I swallowed hard, the gun feeling cold and heavy in my hand. I was familiar with guns—my dad had taught me to shoot when I was a teenager—but I didn't know if I could actually shoot someone, should the need arise. Not deliberately anyway.

"What about you?" I asked, my voice sounding small and worried in the quiet of the apartment.

"I have another at my place," he said reassuringly.

"You know I don't have a license to carry this," I reminded him. It was all well and good to carry a gun for protection, but if the police found out I was doing so without a permit, I'd be paying a hefty fine—or worse.

Blane's mouth tipped up at the corners. "Don't worry. I know a good lawyer."

He kissed me once before grabbing his coat and heading out the door. I watched from the open doorway as he went down the snow-covered stairs, got into his SUV, and drove away. Only then did I shut and lock the door.

CHAPTER FOUR

The next morning dawned clear and bright. It was still well below freezing, but the sun shone in a cloudless sky. The snow-covered trees and ground sparkled as if they were covered in diamonds. My breath clouded in the frigid air as I cleared the snow off my car.

The streets were dry as I drove to work, the gun Blane had given me shoved inside my purse on the seat next to me, though I could feel its presence like it was a living thing. I worried about how long Blane expected me to keep his gun. I tried not to dwell on the incident yesterday, but I had a sinking feeling that we hadn't seen the last of whoever had been shooting at us. I knew the firm sometimes defended people who weren't always safe, or innocent, and I wondered if the gunman might be someone tied to an old case of Blane's, though his current case seemed to be a likely culprit as well.

Thirty minutes later, I arrived at the firm, situated north of downtown Indianapolis in the nicer suburbs. I parked and hurried inside, taking a quick glance at the parking lot and noticing that Blane's car wasn't there in his usual spot. He probably was already in court this morning.

I put my coat, purse, and travel coffee mug in my tiny cubicle on the first floor. Although I was out of the office a lot, making runs, I had a little spot of my own with a computer. So much paperwork flowed through the firm, they were forever trying to keep up, and if I was through with my runs, I often helped out.

After dropping off my things, I faced the most dreaded part of my day—checking in with the firm's office manager, Diane Greene. A heavyset, no-nonsense woman, she'd taken a dislike to me almost from the moment I'd started almost a year ago. When James had found out about Blane and me, he'd had Diane fire me, which she'd seemed to relish doing. Blane had hired me back, but Diane had become even more antagonistic toward me and I despised having to work for her. Not that I'd ever said a word about it to Blane. It smacked too much of wanting special treatment because of our relationship. Besides, anything he might do to try to alleviate the situation, short of firing Diane, would no doubt just make things worse, and I wasn't about to ask that he fire her.

"Good morning, Diane," I said politely, a fake smile plastered on my face as I stepped into her office.

She looked up from her computer, her eyes narrowing as her gaze fell on me. I kept still as she scrutinized me, despite the instinctive need to squirm under her inspection. It was rare that Diane didn't have something critical or disparaging to say about either my work, my appearance, or both.

"Don't think that the weather is going to give you an excuse to not make your runs today," she said brusquely. "I have a large stack for you and they all need to be delivered this morning."

My smile became strained as I replied. "The streets are fine," I said calmly. "I shouldn't have any problems."

"Then don't let me keep you," she said, gesturing to a stack of files on a nearby table. "And make sure you check in with me when you get back. There's plenty of work to be done, so you won't have time to waste socializing." She made "socializing" sound like it was pornographic.

I gritted my teeth, biting back the angry retort on the tip of my tongue. She was implying my visiting Blane, of course. It didn't matter that I rarely went up to his floor, except to see if Clarice had any files for me to run. I grabbed the stack and took it back to my desk.

"How was the dragon this morning?" Lori asked, stepping into my cube. She was a paralegal whose cube was adjacent to mine. No one held any particular affection for Diane, and her treatment of me had not gone unnoticed.

"The usual," I said with a shrug, not wanting to complain. Most everyone still treated me the same, even though it was common knowledge that Blane and I were dating.

"I can't believe she's stupid enough to treat you the way she does," Lori said, sipping from the cup of coffee she was holding. "I mean, come on, you're the boss's girlfriend, for crying out loud."

"She probably figures it's just temporary," I remarked, knowing Diane was probably right on that score.

"Still," Lori protested, and I noticed she didn't contradict me, "you'd think she'd try to be a little nicer."

"I'd better get going," I said ruefully, "before she checks to make sure I'm not socializing too much."

Lori rolled her eyes at this and I silently agreed.

I headed to the elevator, punching the button for the seventh floor. Blane had moved his office to the top floor when James Gage Sr. had been indicted. Derrick Trent, the remaining partner, had expanded his office on the fifth floor.

"Hey, Clarice," I said, sliding into an empty chair across from her large mahogany desk.

"Morning!" Clarice said with a smile.

I eyed her speculatively. "You seem to be in an awfully good mood this morning," I said, teasing her. "Would Jack have anything to do with that?" Clarice was divorced, with two kids, and dating a high school science teacher named Jack. They'd been seeing each other for several months now.

Clarice's smile grew even wider. "Maybe," she said mischievously. "It was a good weekend."

"Good for you," I said with a grin. "You deserve it." Clarice was being cautious about being involved with someone after her first marriage had ended, but she and Jack had gotten progressively more serious. I was glad things were going well for them. I'd met him a few times and he seemed like a really nice guy. Clarice had finally introduced him to her kids a couple of months ago.

"What about you?" she said. "How was your weekend?"

I hesitated, unsure if I should tell her all that had happened. I decided that being vague was easier. "Good. It was good. Blane and I got a Christmas tree."

"That sounds promising," she said. Clarice had been thrilled to find out Blane and I were dating. She had a soft spot for Blane and had worked for him long enough to see him go through woman after woman. I think she was hoping it would be different with me. "I saw Blane on the news

Saturday," she continued. "What was that all about? Was that you he rescued from that mugger? She sure looked like you."

I nodded. Clarice's eyes widened.

"Are you okay?" she asked worriedly.

"I'm fine," I replied, shrugging off her concern. "Blane got there pretty quick. I had a few bruises, that's all." She looked like she was going to ask more questions, but I hurriedly changed the subject.

"Clarice, I was wondering," I began, "are there any outstanding cases or clients that are particularly hostile toward Blane?" I figured that was the best place to start looking for a connection between the shooter and Blane.

"How much time do you have?" she asked. "He's always had the odd nut job or two, but the case he's on now seems to have brought them out of the woodwork. Take a look at this."

She pushed a file folder toward me, full of papers. Bemused, I opened it. I read the first few and my hands turned to ice.

The papers were all death threats, some more hideous and grotesque than others. The vividness of the more elaborate ones had bile rising in my throat. I paged through them slowly, aware that Blane had mentioned none of this to me.

"How long have they been like this?" I asked quietly, swallowing the nausea.

"A couple weeks," she answered with a sigh. "I took them to the police, but they didn't do anything. They think it's just a few crazies, nothing serious."

"I don't know about that," I muttered. "What is it about the case he's on now, the Waters trial, that has people so upset?" I asked, handing back the folder.

"Blane's defending a friend of his, a man named Kyle Waters. Kyle is a SEAL sniper," Clarice explained. "He fought in Afghanistan and Iraq. On one particular mission, they were supposed to capture or kill some sheikh who was an al-Qaeda leader. Well, on their way, a shepherd stumbled across them. There were only four of them, they couldn't capture him. They determined he was an immediate threat, that he would warn others that they were there, so they killed him."

I processed this. "So now he's on trial for wrongful death?" I asked.

Clarice nodded. "Turns out that supposed shepherd was really an American citizen."

My jaw dropped. "Oh my God," I breathed.

"Not so fast," Clarice said. "He was an American citizen who renounced his citizenship, converted to Islam, changed his name to Ahmed el Mustaqueem, and moved there to fight for the other side."

"Oh." Well, that certainly put things in a different light.

"Exactly," Clarice said knowingly. "But you still have the people that are all pissed off that they killed him, not that I particularly see it that way," she added.

"How do *you* see it?"

She looked me in the eye. "I think it's a hell of a lot easier to play armchair quarterback from behind a desk than it is on the other side of the planet, surrounded by people who want to kill you. If that guy wanted to go fight for the other side, then he knew the risks. I think Kyle's a hero and what's going on is disgraceful. The man has been through three deployments and has a list of commendations and medals as long as my arm."

Her vehemence surprised me.

"Does Blane feel the same way?" I asked.

"I haven't asked him," she replied. "I assume so. He served in Afghanistan, so I would think he has an opinion on the matter."

I was confused. "If it's a wrongful death suit, why is James prosecuting? Wouldn't it be a private suit, not a county one?"

"Usually," she replied. "But in this instance, the man was from Indianapolis originally and the family got the county to bring the suit. If James wins, it sets a precedent that's never been done before—a state government prosecuting a soldier. It's disgusting what James is doing."

I thought for a moment before asking, "Do you think I could look at the Waters file?" I wanted to read through it, see if there was anything I could find that might shed some light on who had tried to kill us yesterday.

"Sure, but don't tell anyone. Technically, you work for the firm, so you could be legitimately helping with the case, but I don't want to get into trouble."

"No problem," I assured her. "I won't breathe a word."

"Come by later," she said. "The files are in the conference room and you can start there."

I agreed, thanking her before heading back downstairs to grab my stack and head back out into the cold for my deliveries.

I finished my runs and was on my way to the courthouse for my last delivery, which had to be there by noon. Suddenly, I noticed my steering wheel was pulling to the right and an odd sound was coming from my car. I slowed down as it got progressively worse, finally forced to pull off to the side of the road. Grabbing my gloves, I pulled them on as I got out of the car. As I walked to the front, I saw what the problem was and groaned. My right front tire was flat as a pancake.

I stood staring dumbly at it, wondering what the heck I was going to do now. I knew how to change a tire but shied away from doing it in the freezing cold, with all the slush and snow lining the road. I was sure to get filthy trying to change the tire by myself, and while I wasn't opposed to having to do that, I really didn't want to.

Cars flew past as I contemplated my predicament. Not only did it look like I was going to have to lay out cash for a tow truck and new tire, there was no way I was going to be able to get my delivery to the courthouse in time. Diane was going to be pissed.

As I wavered in indecision, a taxi pulled up and off to the side of the road in front of me. Surprised, I turned to see a familiar figure get out and walk toward me.

"Frankie?" I asked as he got closer.

"Hey, K-K-Kathleen," he stammered, shoving his glove-less hands into the pockets of his jeans. "What hap-hap-pened?"

"I got a flat." I gestured helplessly to the deflated tire.

"D-d-d-do you n-need a ride?"

I brightened. "That would be great!" If I could get to the courthouse, I could get the documents delivered on time and then I'd just call a tow truck from there.

I went to grab my purse from the car and hesitated—I still had Blane's gun. There was no way they'd let me in the courthouse with it, that was for sure. Making a quick decision, I opened the glove box and pushed the gun inside, then grabbed my purse and the files from my car before locking it and following Frankie to the taxi. It was blessedly warm inside his car.

"Where t-t-to?" he asked once he was behind the wheel.

"The courthouse, if you don't mind," I answered, meeting his eyes in the rearview mirror.

He nodded once and we set off. I was glad for the stroke of luck that had him nearby. After a few minutes, I ventured a question. "How have you been, Frankie? And your sister?"

"G-g-good. C-Chrissy loves the s-s-s-snow."

I smiled. "Me, too. Especially here at Christmas."

"Your f-f-face is b-better," he offered.

I assumed he meant the bruises from the encounter with the mugger the other night. I lightly touched the still tender skin of my cheek. "Yeah, thanks," I said, surprised he could see them, considering how much makeup I had pancaked on this morning.

We made it to the courthouse with about fifteen minutes to spare, and I hurriedly dug inside my purse for money, glancing at the meter to see how much the ride had cost. I had just enough cash on me to cover it.

"Here you go," I said, holding out the money.

Frankie tried to not take it, shaking his head. "You d-d-don't have t-to p-p-pay," he protested.

"I absolutely do," I insisted. "I don't work for free and you don't either. Come on and take it—I've gotta go."

He reluctantly took the money, then handed me a scrap of paper.

"M-my cell. In c-c-case you n-need a c-c-cab," he stuttered.

I smiled my thanks, grabbed my things, and hopped out, slamming the car door shut behind me. "Thanks again, Frankie," I tossed over my shoulder. "You were a real life-saver today."

He waved at me and I spared a hand to wave back as I jogged up the courthouse steps, being careful of icy spots that looked slick.

"Well, if you aren't a sight for sore eyes!" Hank exclaimed, a twinkle in his eyes. Hank was the head security guard, a large, imposing black man. While he may have looked threatening, Hank was about as likely to take somebody down as he would be to drop-kick puppies. I liked him immensely, and he seemed to have a soft spot for me, too.

"Hi, Hank," I said with a grin, handing him my purse for his cursory inspection as I walked through the metal detector. "Finished Christmas shopping for those kids of yours yet?" Hank and his wife, Theresa, had five kids, all under the age of ten.

"Aw, Kathleen," he said, a pained expression on his face as he gave my purse back to me, "you know I hate the mall this time of year."

"You hate the mall any time of year," I retorted with a laugh.

He grinned broadly and laughed as well. "You got that right," he said.

I made my delivery, then called a local towing company to tow my car to the tire shop to get the flat fixed. After that, I milled the hallways in indecision, wondering if I should call Clarice for a ride back to the firm. I thought about how Diane was going to react to finding out the runner had no transportation, and no good scenario came to mind.

As I was putting off going back to the firm, and Diane, a thought occurred to me and I walked back to Hank. I waited until there was a break in the flow of people coming inside before interrupting him. "Hey, Hank, could I ask a favor?"

"Anything for you," he said with a wink.

"I was wondering if there's any room left in the gallery for the Waters trial?" I really wanted to see Blane, especially after reading those letters this morning. I was sure he was fine, but I couldn't shake the lingering unease.

"That one's pretty crowded," Hank said, "and been a bitch to keep secure with all the people wanting a piece of the action."

I sighed, disappointed.

"But I think I can get you in," he continued, glancing at his watch. "If you come with me, they just took a short recess and have about another hour to go before lunch."

I brightened immediately. "That's great! Thanks so much, Hank."

I followed him through the halls to the largest courtroom in the building. There was a crowd of people in the hallway outside the door, the buzz of conversation reverberating loudly off the walls. Another security guard stood by the entrance to the courtroom, checking people's badges before allowing them through. I kept up with Hank, as his large size caused people to move to the side to allow him to pass.

"This one's with me," Hank told the guard, who nodded as we moved beyond him through the doorway.

"Find a spot and settle in," Hank directed, gesturing to the rows of benches, all of them filled nearly to capacity.

"Thanks, Hank," I said gratefully, and he gave me a smile in return before leaving. I looked around, finally spotting a narrow strip of empty space on the bench directly behind the prosecution's table. I was reluctant to take it, not wanting to be in such close proximity to James, but had no choice. Hurrying down the aisle, I muttered an apology to the bench's occupants as I squeezed into the nearly too small space. The man sitting next to me gave me a dirty look. I ignored him.

A few minutes later, the prosecution attorneys filed in and took their seats. My heart seemed to skip a beat when I saw James. He was standing, talking with another lawyer. James was dressed in a dark suit, with a white shirt and navy tie. He looked professional and honest. You'd never know what he was capable of just by looking at him. It made a chill go through me to watch him, remembering how his father had so easily condemned me to die and how James had done nothing to stop it. I wondered if the apple didn't fall far from the tree. Would James stoop to murder to achieve his ends? Could it have been him out in the woods yesterday?

I froze when James glanced around the courtroom as he talked quietly, taking in the number of people filling the gallery. His gaze brushed past me and I let out a sigh of relief. Then I saw him stop speaking and his gaze flew back and met mine.

I didn't breathe and my palms grew sweaty under his scrutiny. I swallowed hard but refused to be the first to break the stare, not wanting him to know how much he unnerved me.

His eyes were cold and his mouth curved in a smirk as he watched me. I finally let out the breath I'd been holding when he casually turned away, dismissing me.

My attention was diverted by Blane's arrival. Conversation in the courtroom buzzed more loudly as he and his client took their positions at the defense table.

I was able to get a good look at Kyle Waters now, and he didn't seem like the devil incarnate the press made him out to be. At least a head shorter than Blane, he nonetheless carried himself with dignity even amid the stares and whispers currently flying around the room. Appearing to be in his late twenties to early thirties, he wore his Navy uniform; his dark hair was neatly trimmed and his face clean shaven. Blane spoke quietly in his ear and I saw him nod in response.

"All rise," intoned the bailiff. Everyone got to their feet, with much shuffling and noise as the judge walked in. I realized that must be the Judge Reynolds that Blane had spoken of to James last night. As everyone resumed their seats, I looked curiously at him.

I'd expected him to be old, at least in his fifties or sixties, but he couldn't have been much older than Blane. He had dark hair and wore a mustache, and I could see faint scars on his face, pockmarks, like the kind you get if you scratch too much with chicken pox or from particularly bad acne. The scars didn't make him unappealing, though, rather they lent him an air of no-nonsense gravity.

The judge struck his gavel twice and the courtroom fell silent, anticipation heavy in the air. I watched as a man took the witness chair. He was wearing a Navy uniform as well.

Tall with dark hair and eyes, he was broad shouldered and lean.

"Remember, you are still under oath, Lieutenant Sheffield," Judge Reynolds said. His voice was deep and had a gravelly sound to it.

"Yes, sir," the lieutenant responded calmly, his voice resonating.

I watched as James got up from his seat, buttoning his suit jacket shut as he walked toward the witness stand.

"Lieutenant," James began, "you work for the Judge Advocate General's Corps, correct?"

"Yes, sir."

"And you were informed of the murder of an unarmed American citizen?"

"Objection, Your Honor," Blane interjected as he stood. "Presumes facts not in evidence."

"Sustained."

"Who informed you about the shooting?" James rephrased.

"Staff Sergeant Troy Martin," the lieutenant answered.

"What did Staff Sergeant Martin tell you?"

"That the team had been forced to kill an unarmed male combatant." Sheffield's tone was matter-of-fact.

"Did he say the man threatened them?"

"No."

"Did the man try to run away?"

"No."

"Did Martin think he had a weapon at the time?"

"No."

"No further questions, Your Honor."

James sat down and Blane stood, approaching the stand.

"Lieutenant, what were the Rules of Engagement for this mission?"

"The team was authorized to remove any threat they deemed necessary to their survival and the success of the mission."

"Do you think their actions fall under those rules?"

"Objection, Your Honor," James said. "The question calls for the witness's opinion."

"Considering the witness is employed by the US Navy to render judgment and opinion on matters of military law, I'd ask you for leniency, Your Honor," Blane responded.

"I'll allow it," the judge said, nodding toward Blane.

"Lieutenant?" prompted Blane.

"It is quite common in Iraq for even unarmed combatants to alert others as to the presence of military forces," Sheffield said. "It's happened before, and good men lost their lives showing leniency. I considered it covered under the ROE and closed the case."

"Thank you. No further questions."

Blane sat back down while the judge dismissed Sheffield. James was poker-faced, but I could tell by the rigidity of his posture and the clenching of his jaw that he wasn't happy. I was enormously satisfied at how he'd been outmaneuvered by Blane.

A messenger came in and handed an envelope to Blane. I watched as he opened it, then went very still. His client looked curiously at him and Blane wordlessly handed him the packet. Kyle looked through it as well, his face expressionless, before giving it back to Blane, who stuffed whatever it was back in the envelope as James called another witness.

About an hour later, they broke for lunch. I hoped I could say a few words to Blane, then hop a bus to take me to my car. The tire should be fixed by now. I glanced at the defense table. Blane looked really preoccupied, his expression grim, and I hesitated to approach him. I doubted he'd really want his girlfriend bothering him right now, so I quelled my urge to talk to him and left the courtroom with the tide of people.

I walked to the back of the building, looking for the bus schedule that I knew was taped to one of the walls by a rarely used side exit. Few people were around and I started when someone suddenly grabbed my upper arm from behind me.

"Excuse me, but are you Kathleen Turner?"

I turned to see a man about my height standing there. He looked like a lawyer, his suit neatly pressed, and my instinctive panic receded.

"I am," I answered. "Who's asking?"

"Would you please come with me?" he asked, ignoring my question. His grip tightened as he tugged me forward.

"Where are we going?" I asked, reluctantly forced to walk with him.

"Someone needs to see you," he said cryptically.

I was confused for a moment, then thought it might be Blane. He must've seen me in the courtroom and sent this guy to get me. I followed the man as he led me down a dim corridor into an office. I walked inside and turned to see him leaving, closing the door behind him.

"So glad you could join me."

I spun back around, my mouth falling open in surprise to see James step out of a darkened corner. He'd shed his coat and stood with his arms folded across his chest, a sneer on his face as he surveyed me. I closed my mouth with a snap, trying to ignore the fear that had spiked in me at his unexpected appearance.

"What do you want?" I demanded with more bravado than I felt.

"I'm hurt, Kathleen," he said snidely. "I would've thought you'd be glad to see me."

"The last time I saw you I was nearly killed," I retorted. "And you didn't lift a finger to help me." I paused, feigning confusion. "You know, some might call that being an accessory, right?"

His smile faded. "Don't play with things you don't understand, Kathleen," he said angrily.

"Then what do you want, James?" I asked. "Your flunky brought me here for a reason, I'm assuming?" I crossed my arms defensively over my chest.

He moved until he was right in front of my face, grabbing my upper arm and yanking me toward him. I yelped in surprise and pain as his fingers dug in, bruising my skin.

"Listen up, Kathleen," he hissed. "You tell that son of a bitch you're fucking that he's going down and he doesn't even see it coming. This isn't some case that no one gives a shit about." He shook me roughly. "Important people, very powerful people, are watching. This case is going to make my career and no one is going to stand in my way. Especially not Blane Kirk."

His threat sent chills down my spine even as it pissed me off. "Let go of me," I ordered through gritted teeth, trying to pull my arm out of his grasp. He abruptly released me and I stumbled back, glaring at him.

"Don't you dare threaten Blane," I spat at him. "He buried you in there and I'm positive he'll do it again. You're no match for Blane. You never have been and you never will be."

"We'll see just who is buried when this thing is done," he said icily. "This isn't a military trial. Logic can only get you so far in a case like this. Wait till I put the orphaned son on the stand, or the grieving mother. Emotions carry further than logic when it's a jury of your peers."

His eyes were dark with anger and I stepped back, remembering how easily he'd lashed out at me before. I jumped when my cell phone rang, the shrill sound shattering the tense silence. I scrambled blindly in my purse for it, keeping my eyes on James as I backed toward the door. My hand closed on the knob just as James spoke again.

"You be careful, Kathleen," he said, menace lacing his voice. "It would be a shame if something happened to you."

I turned the knob and fell out into the hallway. I didn't bother taking time to shut the door, just turned on my heel and hurried away. I didn't want to run and show how much he'd unnerved me, but neither could I make myself walk. My groping hand finally found my still ringing phone and flipped it open.

"Hello?" I answered breathlessly.

"Where are you?" Blane asked, his voice tight.

"I'm in the courthouse," I said, wondering why he sounded angry. "Why? What's wrong?"

He blew out a breath and I could almost see him in my mind's eye, shoving a hand through his hair. "Meet me in room 115, by courtroom two."

"Okay," I agreed. "I'm right around the corner."

I flipped the phone closed and quickly found room 115. I knocked only once before it was jerked open. Blane stood there, his face an emotionless mask as he looked me up and down.

"What is it?" I asked, confused.

Reaching out, he took my hand and pulled me inside the small conference room. Behind him, I could see Kyle seated at a conference table, Blane's briefcase and papers laid out on its surface.

"Kyle, meet Kathleen," Blane said. "Kathleen, Kyle."

"Nice to meet you," I quickly interjected, and Kyle gave me a short nod.

"We have a problem," Blane said cryptically. I watched as he picked up an envelope, recognizing it as the one that had been delivered to him in the courtroom. He dumped the contents into his hand before handing it to me.

Looking down, I saw he'd given me photographs. Examining them more closely, I realized with a start that they were pictures of me—pictures taken today as I stood outside my car, gazing down at a flat tire. That would've been creepy in and of itself without the big red *X* drawn over my face.

I silently flipped through the small stack, coming to one that had words scrawled across it. *Easy target,* I read silently. I swallowed, hard.

"It's a bit . . . dramatic, don't you think?" I asked tentatively. "Like somebody's watched too many movies or something."

"I don't give a fuck if they've seen too many movies," Blane said, frustration evident in his voice. "Somebody got close enough to take pictures of you. Where is this? What were you doing?"

I shrugged helplessly. "My car. I got a flat today while I was making deliveries."

"Where's the gun I gave you?" he demanded.

I hesitated. I really didn't want to answer that, especially with Blane being in the mood he was in. As it turned out, I didn't have to say anything because Blane read the answer on my face.

"Christ," he huffed in exasperation, pushing a hand through his hair as he paced a few steps away from me, stopping to stare out the window, his hands on his hips.

"I knew they wouldn't let me in the building with it," I explained to his back. He could be mad all he wanted. I knew not even Hank would have let me inside with a weapon.

"I'm really sorry about this, Kirk," Kyle said, speaking for the first time.

Blane sighed. "It's not your fault." Turning back to Kyle, he crossed his arms over his chest. "Any ideas?"

"No clue, man," Kyle said regretfully. "Could just be a whackjob."

"Maybe."

Kyle hesitated, then added, "If they're going after her because of you, maybe you should cut ties."

My stomach flipped inside out. "Cut ties" sounded very ominous. I waited to hear what Blane would say. I didn't have to wait long.

"Agreed."

"Wait, what does that mean?" I asked. Neither man answered, so I continued, "Does this have anything to do with those horrible death threats you've been getting?"

Blane's eyes narrowed as he focused on me and I felt a twinge of unease. Probably shouldn't have mentioned that I'd seen the letters. But it seemed to me that if I was getting dragged into this, it would be beneficial to know all the facts.

"Those letters aren't anything to worry about," Blane said roughly. "The usual fanatics sending their hate mail. But this," he gestured to the pictures I was still holding, "this is something else entirely."

"Oh, so it's not a big deal if you're the one threatened," I said sarcastically, "but if it's me, then it's another story."

"Exactly."

I glared mutinously at him, but he didn't waver, his gaze level and undeterred by my anger.

"I think I'll wait outside," Kyle said uneasily, rising from his seat. He went out the door, letting it swing shut behind him.

"Kyle's right," Blane said. "The only reason they're screwing with you is because of me. We need to stay away from each other for a while. Until the case is over."

That was not something I wanted to hear at all. I thought about what James had said to me, the message he'd wanted me to deliver, and abruptly decided against telling Blane about it. In the mood he was in, I wouldn't put it past him to track James down just to beat the pulp out of him. Not that I objected to that plan in theory, but it would be a pain in the ass if Blane got arrested.

"Why did you take this case?" I asked, changing the subject.

"Because he's a SEAL, and my friend," Blane said flatly. "This case is one of the reasons I went into law and why

I'm going into politics. The troops need more advocates in government. This case is a prime example of why. Too many people second-guessing after the fact, putting unrealistic constraints on the men over there."

"But he killed someone," I said quietly. "An American."

Blane looked at me. "Yes, he did," he said. "Someone who hates America and everything it stands for to the point of going to fight for the other side. It's very likely he would have alerted other men with weapons who would have killed Kyle and his team."

"You don't know that he would have done that," I protested.

"And you don't know that he wouldn't have," Blane retorted. "War really is hell, Kat, and it's not always just soldiers who die. Better the enemy than four SEALs."

That made me pause. What if it had been Blane on that mission? A chill went through me at the thought. Somehow, I thought my armchair quarterback judgments wouldn't matter a hill of beans to me if Blane had been the one in danger.

Blane watched me and I moved closer to him, tipping my head back. "I understand what you're saying," I told him. "I really do. If it had been you, I'd want you to do whatever you had to do, so long as you came back alive."

The tightness around Blane's eyes and mouth eased, and I realized he'd been waiting to hear what I would say, to know if I supported him in this case or not. I was surprised and humbled that he cared what I thought.

"I'll have Clarice come get you and take you to your car," Blane said, pulling out his cell phone. "Keep the gun I gave you on you at all times. And I don't want you making any more deliveries. Stay at the office tomorrow."

"Great. Diane will love that," I muttered, grimacing when I thought of her reaction to what she'd see as special treatment from Blane.

"What did you say?" Blane asked, the cell phone at his ear.

"Nothing."

Clarice must have answered then, because Blane began talking to her. I listened with half an ear as he asked her to come get me, flipping through the pictures as I did so. There were only about a half dozen of them, but it was still unnerving to know someone had been watching me, *photographing* me, without my knowledge. I knew that what Blane was saying made sense. The fact that the photographs had been sent to him made it obvious that the person behind them intended to hurt him through me.

Blane had ended his call and now stood next to me. He took the photos out of my hands and set them aside. I didn't look at him. I wasn't afraid exactly; I was more upset about the staying away from each other part. He lifted my chin until I was forced to look at him.

"It's just temporary," he said gently. "I need you to be safe."

I nodded, clearing my throat before I said, "You were great in there today."

"You were in the gallery?" he asked, surprised.

"For a little while," I said. "I think you're going to win. The jurors—they like you, they listen to you."

"I hope you're right," he said with a sigh. "This case can't be over soon enough for me."

"Anything I can do to help?" I asked.

He shook his head. "Just help me keep you safe. Don't do anything . . . spontaneous," he said dryly.

I remembered our conversation from Saturday night and smiled. "I don't know what you're talking about," I said innocently. "I always think things through first."

He snorted in derision. "Right," he said, and I could tell he wasn't buying it. His eyes twinkled at me. I needed to touch him, so I straightened his already straight tie and smoothed down the collar of his shirt and the lapels of his jacket. The wool was soft against my fingers. A knot was forming in my stomach, which I tried to ignore. If I thought about it too much, it felt like we were breaking up, so naturally I chose to not think about it.

"Kat," Blane said softly, and I raised my gaze to his.

The air grew charged between us as he gazed into my eyes. The dark suit made his eyes appear more gray than green, their depths stormy in my imagination. His hand lifted to my hair, catching a lock and slowly wrapping its curl around his finger. He tugged gently and I obediently moved closer, sliding my hands around his waist under his jacket.

Both of his hands threaded through my hair now, tipping my head farther back as his palms cradled my head. My breath caught in my chest when he leaned down, his mouth meeting mine. His kiss began tender and sweet, like I was a precious thing, and I took advantage of the moment to open my lips beneath his—I needed to feel a deeper connection.

He took my invitation, his tongue sliding against mine, and I whimpered deep in my throat as I molded myself against his body. One of his hands stayed in my hair while the other arm wrapped around me, holding me tightly.

The kiss turned into hunger and need, my hands sliding up his back to hold him close, and I tuned everything out but him—the hardness of his body, the smell of his skin, the slight abrasion of his five o'clock shadow, the demands of his mouth and tongue.

"Oh my! Excuse me!"

The startled voice and slam of the door caused me to abruptly return to reality and I tore my lips from Blane's. I would have stepped back, but his arm tightened, holding me in place.

"Who was that?" I gasped, trying to get my breath back as my heart pounded in my chest.

"Clarice," Blane replied evenly, his fingers brushing my cheek.

I was annoyed but not surprised to see him unruffled by our interlude or its interruption, though his eyes blazed as he watched me. He released me and I moved a safe distance away, self-consciously combing my fingers through my hair, hastily repairing the disarray Blane had inflicted.

He went to the door and opened it. "Come in, Clarice," he called. She stepped inside the room, a huge grin lighting up her face when she saw me. I recognized that smile and inwardly groaned. I knew I was going to have to listen to her enthusiastic optimism about Blane and me all the way to picking up my car.

Blane stepped into my personal space again, and I swallowed as I looked up at him.

"Stay safe," he said quietly, his thumb brushing my jaw.

"No worries," I said, forcing a smile. I hated that some-one was using me to get to him; he had enough on his plate without worrying about me.

Blane turned to Clarice. "Make sure Hank or another security guard walks you to your car."

"Yes, sir," she agreed.

I grabbed my purse, threw one last look at Blane, and followed Clarice down the hallway.

Hank readily agreed to see us safely to her car, and be-fore long she was dropping me off at the tire repair shop. I was surprised—Clarice had actually been good and not gushed about Blane and me, though that satisfied grin of hers remained as we chatted.

"Can I still see those files?" I asked.

"Absolutely," she said. "They're all in the conference room for you. His older case files are in storage in the base-ment. The keys are in my desk, if you need them."

"Thanks, Clarice," I said as I got out of the car. "And thanks for the ride, too."

"No problem!" she said cheerily. I waved to her as she drove out of the lot.

Unfortunately, the tire had to be replaced, and I wasn't surprised to hear that the tire had a gash in it. The mechan-ic told me it looked like it had been slashed. No accident then. I decided to keep that information to myself. It took a while before they were finished and I impatiently whiled away what was left of the afternoon waiting.

As I wrote the check to cover the bill, my mind drifted longingly to the twenty thousand dollars Kade had given me. I'd thought long and hard about what to do with it. Ultimately, I'd decided to report the money, which had meant I'd had to pay taxes on it. After the government took its rather large chunk, I'd decided to send the rest to pay against my mother's medical bills. Her fight with cancer hadn't been very long, but it had been expensive, and it was a relief to know I'd be able to keep the creditors off my back for a while with the large lump sum payment. But sometimes, like now, I really wished I'd kept some of it to pad my checking account.

The only thing I hadn't been able to resist doing was buying a pair of shoes, as Kade had told me to. Though no doubt he would roll his eyes in derision at my choice—a pair of sky-high peacock-blue heels I'd been coveting for months at Nordstrom. They'd cost more than my entire paycheck, but I hadn't been able to resist splurging. I also hadn't worn them, leaving them in their box in the back of my closet.

I'd never told Blane about the money Kade had left. I didn't know how he'd react if he knew about it, and I didn't want to find out. He'd want to know why Kade would do that, and I had no answer to give him. The gesture had bewildered me, Kade's motives a mystery. It wasn't as though it was going to be repeated and the money was spent, so what was there really to tell?

It was after three by now and I was hungry. I'd given all my cash to Frankie to cover the cab ride, so I'd skipped lunch. I swung by the grocery store, grabbing one of those shrink-wrapped premade deli sandwiches and a Pepsi, before heading to the firm. If I wanted my life to get back to normal, I needed to see if there was anything I could dig up on this case of Blane's or any of his old cases.

After checking in with Diane, who had no further deliveries for me, I headed up to the seventh floor. True to her word, Clarice had left the files in Blane's conference room. Several boxes sat on the table, all filled to the brim with papers. I grabbed the nearest one and started digging.

I ate as I read, some of the files and motions unrelated to anything I was looking for, though I wasn't positive what that even was. Hours passed. I found confirmation of what Clarice had told me. Kyle Waters was a highly decorated professional warrior who had enlisted and then reenlisted with the Navy, serving three tours in Afghanistan and Iraq. Married once with no children; his ex-wife had divorced him after he'd reenlisted.

There was a file for each of the people on the prosecution and defense witness lists. I read through them carefully. Three other SEALs had been on the same mission with Kyle: Ron Freeman, Brian Bowers, and Staff Sergeant Troy Martin, the CO.

Kyle had been court-martialed after the incident but had been found innocent of any wrongdoing. Looking through the witness list, I saw Brian Bowers was scheduled to take the stand in a few days. I jotted down where he was currently staying for the duration of the trial. Maybe he would have some insight into who might be trying to kill Blane. Thinking along the same lines, I added Ron Freeman's name and current residence as well.

In reading Staff Sergeant Troy Martin's file, I saw he had a girlfriend named Stacey Willows who happened to live north of Indianapolis in Carmel. Although Martin had already shipped back to Iraq, Stacey was on the list as a character witness. She might be worth talking to as well. I wrote her address down, too.

Now I had three people I could talk to who might have some insight into who would be targeting Blane, and consequently, me. It was better than nothing.

The comment James had made about Blane "going down" still bothered me. That could definitely be taken as a threat. Maybe I should be looking further into what he might have meant by that. I turned the idea over in my head, wondering if I should pursue it. I decided to put that on hold for tonight. James was a dangerous guy with even more to lose now.

I wanted to go downstairs and review some of Blane's older cases, but I was tired, the words on the page blurring as I read. With a sigh, I returned all the files to their proper boxes, tucking my list of names and addresses in my purse. I flicked off the lights, making sure the conference room door was locked as I pulled it shut.

It was still and silent outside, no one around at this late hour, and I could see my breath in the cold. I hurried to my car, a faithful blue Honda that had over a hundred thousand miles on it but thankfully ran like a top.

As I unlocked the door, a weird sensation came over me and I paused, glancing around uneasily. The parking lot was empty of vehicles, yet I searched the darkened corners. The trees and bushes surrounding the building loomed as silent, dark sentinels, their depths impenetrable in the night. I couldn't shake the feeling that I was being watched. It was creepy and unnerving.

I scrutinized the trees until a sudden movement made me jump, startling a brief scream from me. Then I blew out the breath I'd been holding as a deer came bounding out of the trees, leaping gracefully over a hedge and disappearing into the darkness.

Good lord, I was going to give myself a heart attack. My heart was pounding and adrenaline was making me shake. Obviously, the photographs and incident over the weekend were having a larger impact on my peace of mind than I'd thought. With a snort at my own paranoia, I climbed into my car and headed home.

It was late and the apartment building was dark. I had a pang of guilt when I thought of Tigger being home by himself all day. He wasn't going to be happy. I climbed the stairs, my eyes on the ground to make sure I didn't misstep. I walked wearily to my door, flipping through my keys for the right one.

"Hey, Kathleen."

My head jerked up in surprise. A small dark figure stood outside my door.

"I thought you weren't ever going to get home."

I narrowed my eyes as I peered into the darkness. The voice was familiar, as was the scent of cigar.

"Who's there?" I asked.

The figure stepped into the dim light. My keys fell from my fingers in shock.

CJ, the girl who had both saved and betrayed me, stood staring at me.

CHAPTER FIVE

CJ was obviously freezing, despite her casual words, so after she'd stubbed out her half-smoked cigar, I brought
her inside. Perhaps not the wisest thing to do, given what
she'd done, but she looked very young and very frightened.
Of what, I had no idea.

I gave her a blanket and she huddled on the couch with
it wrapped around her while I made some coffee. It was a
little late for caffeine, but I had a feeling I was going to need
it. I handed her a cup and she thanked me while I sat down
next to her and waited for her to speak.

"I know you're probably wondering why I'm here," she
said, fixating on the mug she held with both hands instead
of looking at me. "I'm surprised you let me in, actually. Well,
maybe not," she amended. "You've always been too nice to
people."

"Too nice to people who don't deserve it?" I asked, my
voice bitter.

She winced. "Yeah, maybe." She took another sip of coffee. "I'm sorry about before, Kathleen. I didn't want to do
what I did."

Her voice was thick and I was shocked to realize she had
started to cry. The CJ I knew—cigar-smoking, gun-toting,

friend-betraying CJ—had never struck me as someone who cried. Ever. Even now—with her straight black hair, dyed red streak still intact, numerous piercings and all black clothes—I couldn't believe she was crying.

"Hey," I said anxiously, taking the cup from her hands before she spilled the coffee. "It's okay. Everything turned out fine. I wasn't arrested or anything." I patted her shoulder awkwardly.

She nodded and roughly wiped her cheeks, taking a deep, shuddering breath.

"So why did you do it?" I asked once she'd regained control. "Why did you change the code so the election results would get routed to China, of all places?" It was a question that had been bothering me for weeks.

"I can't talk about it," she snuffled, wiping her nose on her sleeve.

"What do you mean you 'can't talk about it'? Then why are you here?" I asked, my voice harder than I had intended. I didn't want to make her cry again, but I thought I deserved an explanation.

"Because I didn't have anywhere else to go," she said baldly. "Some people, bad people, are after me. I can't go home. I'm afraid they're going to kill me." Tears started leaking from her eyes again, but I don't think she even noticed.

I knew I should stay angry with her, but my heart wasn't in it. I didn't know what she'd gotten herself into, but I believed that she was afraid.

I grabbed a box of tissues from the bathroom and gave them to her, waiting while she blew her nose and wiped her eyes. She'd never told me her age, but she couldn't have been more than nineteen, twenty tops. Black streaks from her makeup now marked her skin, which made her look even younger. Despite what she'd done to me, I felt bad for her.

"Who's after you?" I asked much more gently. "What did you do?"

She shook her head. "Anything I tell you would put you in danger, Kathleen," she said resolutely. "I spent hours just making sure I wasn't followed here."

That made me pause. I already had someone stalking me. I didn't need someone else with an ax to grind knowing where I lived.

"I'll understand if you kick me out," CJ said, interrupting my thoughts. "I just really needed a place to stay. Just for tonight," she added hurriedly. "I won't be in the way or anything, I swear."

"Don't you think I deserve more of an explanation," I said, "especially if you've brought trouble to my doorstep?"

She hesitated before finally saying, "It's illegal, what I did, really bad. But I did it for my family, and I'd do it again. I never meant for you to get hurt, Kathleen. You were the only friend I'd had in a really long time and I'm sorry."

I thought about it, but I knew in the end that I didn't have it in me to turn down her plea. I wanted to ask more questions but thought I should wait until morning. She seemed exhausted and agitated.

"Okay," I said with a sigh, "you can stay." There was no way I was going to kick her out to make her own way on the streets, and I believed her story. CJ had always seemed very capable, despite her age, but her guard was down now, leaving her vulnerable.

"Thanks, Kathleen," CJ said gratefully, and she visibly relaxed. "I really appreciate it."

CJ took a shower while I made up the couch with linens and a pillow. She ate a sandwich I made for her, barely able to keep her eyes open and yawning constantly. Soon she was tucked under the covers, sound asleep. I watched her for a moment, thinking it felt somewhat like having a little sister, which was kind of nice. Considering what she'd done, I probably shouldn't have been feeling so protective of her. But after the events of the last few days, it felt good to help someone else for a change rather than just worrying about my own neck. And she had saved me twice—once from James and once from Blane and Kade.

I knew CJ said she was only going to stay the night, but I hoped I'd be able to convince her to stay longer in the morning once she'd had a good night's sleep. Maybe there was some way I could help her, or maybe Blane could—Lord knew he had friends in high places. The comment she'd made about her family concerned me. I couldn't imagine what they could possibly have to do with her hacking attempt.

My sleep was uneasy, nightmares of being chased through the darkness as I tried to find Blane haunting me. I could hear his voice but couldn't find him, a faceless figure behind me getting closer and closer. I jerked awake, my heart pounding. Then I realized the pounding was coming from the front door.

Hurriedly slipping on some knit shorts to go with the old T-shirt I slept in, I headed for the door. I jerked to an abrupt halt when I saw that CJ was no longer on my couch. The sheets and blanket had been neatly folded and I saw a note sitting on top of them: *Thanks.—CJ.*

The pounding came again and I crumpled the note in my fist, worry gnawing at me that CJ had gone before I'd had a chance to talk more with her. I looked through the peephole and saw Alisha standing there, holding her dog.

"Thank God you're awake," she said with relief, pushing past me into the living room.

"How could I not be with the racket you were making?" I snorted, rubbing my tired eyes and closing the door on the frigid air from outside.

"I need a favor," Alisha said, not sounding the least bit sorry as she set Bacon Bits on the floor. He started to sniff the carpet. I watched the dog warily. He seemed very interested in my furniture now. I prayed he wouldn't pee on anything. My furniture was leather.

"What kind of favor?"

"I need you to watch Bits for a few days."

"What?" I jerked my attention from the sniffing dog back to Alisha. "I have a cat, Alisha," I said. "Dogs and cats do not get along."

As if to prove my point, Bits suddenly spotted Tigger lying on the back of the couch, eyeing the newcomer through half-closed eyelids. The dog began to bark excitedly. Tigger didn't bat an eye but started licking his paw, dismissing the noisemaker entirely.

"See what I mean?" I said loudly in exasperation, motioning to the scene.

"They're just meeting for the first time," Alisha protested. "They'll be fine. Listen, I have to go back home. My grandma is sick and needs someone to stay with her for a few days. My mom can't, she has to work, but I can take some time off to take care of her."

"Why can't you take the dog with you?" I knew where this was going and was scrambling to find a way out.

"Because she has a dog, too, and they really don't get along," she said. "I'm afraid he'll hurt Bits. Please, Kathleen," she entreated, "I don't want anything to happen to him and I trust you. You'll take care of him for me. Please?"

"What about a kennel?" Last-ditch effort.

"Those cost a fortune," Alisha said. "I can't afford that."

She looked at me, her eyes hopeful. The dog was still barking. Damn it.

"Fine," I relented, throwing up my hands. "I'll do it."

Alisha beamed at me, but I pointed my finger at her. "You owe me," I said with as much force as I could muster before my first cup of coffee.

She nodded quickly, smile still intact.

"Here's his schedule," she said, pulling a folded paper from her pocket. "His food, leash, and pillow are right here." She opened the door and dragged in a stack of items.

"Schedule?" I asked, bewildered. I skimmed the paper, wondering what I'd gotten myself into. The paper was legal size and filled with writing.

"He likes to stay on a schedule," she insisted, putting a huge hot-pink dog pillow in the corner. "Don't forget to add a little chicken broth to his food. He likes it moist, not dry, but don't put in too much liquid, like with cereal—it should be more like chunky soup. Serve it promptly at 7:00 a.m. and 7:00 p.m. in the glass bowl I brought. He doesn't like metal or paper containers. He needs to go outside three times every day, at 7:30 a.m., 6:30 p.m., and 10:00 p.m., and you have to say, 'Go toodles, Bits. Go toodles for Momma!' in a high-pitched voice or he won't know what to do. If there is snow, you have to dig out a little area where he can see the grass. That is very important—the grass and toodles part— because if he doesn't toodle on the grass, then he will toodle on your bed. At night he needs two dog treats and a drink of water, then point to his pillow and say, 'Go nee-nee, Bits. Go nee-nee.' Otherwise he will stay up all night and pace and whine. If he barks three times in a row, that means he wants to look out the window—you'll need to pull back the shades so he can see. On Tuesday nights he likes to watch *Hollywood Dawgs*. I think he has a crush on Sandy, the surfing Siberian husky. Any questions?" She took a deep breath, the first in several minutes, I think, and raised her eyebrows in inquiry.

Five minutes later, she was out the door and I was left with Bacon Bits's schedule and his pink pillow, special food and chicken broth, leash, and assorted doggie toys.

To my surprise, somehow Bits managed to jump up on the couch with his short little legs, scrambling up the back to try to reach Tigger. With a yowl, Tigger sprang to his feet, his back arching as he hissed at the still-barking Bits.

I sprang forward, scooping Bits up in my arms. He struggled and for a second I thought I might drop him, his fur was slippery, but I maintained my hold.

"Enough!" I yelled, desperate for the barking to stop. Bits abruptly shut up, his tongue lolling out of his mouth as he looked up at me curiously. I decided separation would be the order of the day, so I put Bits in my bedroom before hauling all his things inside there as well. He curled up on his huge, gaudy pillow, watching me, his big brown eyes forlorn at being deprived of his entertainment. With a sigh, I headed for the shower, closing the bedroom door behind me.

A hot shower and two cups of coffee later, I was feeling better. CJ's arrival and abrupt departure still bothered me. I worried about the things she had said, but I had to get to work. I took Bits outside to "toodle" before returning him to my bedroom, filling up his food and water dishes and shutting him inside.

It had snowed again overnight, leaving a fresh dusting of snow on everything. I didn't mind. This close to Christmas, I wanted as much snow as possible. I hummed a carol as I walked to my car, wondering what I was going to get Blane for Christmas. What do you get the man who has everything? I'd been racking my brain lately but still had no ideas. Maybe inspiration would strike. Until then, I was at a complete loss.

I'd had to park farther away from the building last night because the haphazard snowdrifts left by the plows in the parking lot made it difficult to sort out parking spaces. I picked my way carefully over to my car, not wanting to wipe out on a patch of snow or ice. It wasn't until I was a few feet away that I noticed.

The whiteness of the snow covering my hood had been marred with red streaks. Squinting in confusion, I slowed as I got closer, studying the marks. My eyes widened in shock when I realized the streaks were actually writing: *Kirk's whore.*

I stood frozen in place as I stared. I looked down at the ground by my door and saw something furry lying in a crumpled heap. It wasn't very big. As I edged closer, I nudged the thing with the toe of my boot, then jumped back as it fell sideways to reveal a dead possum, its throat cut.

Nausea bubbled in my throat, but I swallowed it down. Fear and anger filled me. I didn't want to think about being scared, so I embraced the anger.

Pulling open my door, I yanked out my scraper, quickly pushing the bloody snow on the hood off onto the ground. I couldn't bring myself to touch the dead and mutilated possum, so I just sort of scooted it with my foot to the edge of the lot before climbing into my car. With a shaky breath, I started the car and headed for the firm.

I dropped my things off in my cube and headed to Diane's office. Not even the unpleasantness I was sure to be greeted with could make an impact on the numbness I'd felt since seeing my car this morning.

"You have a different assignment today," Diane said curtly, breaking into my reverie.

"What's that?" I asked.

"Clarice is sick," she informed me, "and Mr. Kirk has requested you fill in for her until she's feeling better." Diane's mouth puckered in distaste at this, making her look like she was sucking on a lemon.

I wondered if Clarice was really sick or if Blane had told her to take a few days off so I'd have to fill in, and he'd be sure I didn't leave the building.

"Okay," I said indifferently, though inside I was excited by the thought of working more closely with Blane, even if it was only temporary.

"Make sure you attempt to keep up at least the appearance of professionalism," Diane sniffed. "This firm has a reputation to uphold and I don't want any sordid stories getting out of what goes on behind closed doors here."

My cheeks flamed at this, my blood pressure skyrocketing, and it was all I could do to keep my mouth firmly shut and not slam the door behind me when I turned on my heel and walked away. As if that ship hadn't already sailed, I thought sourly, what with Mr. Gage being in the news for his indictment as an accessory to murder.

Her insinuations rang in my ears as I grabbed my things and headed for the top floor. I took deep breaths, trying to cool off, and shoved Diane to the back of my mind. I had more urgent things to worry about. I debated whether I should tell Blane about the message on my car, then decided I'd wait to see what mood he was in before I said anything.

I tossed my things onto Clarice's desk, glancing at Blane's closed door. I could hear voices inside but couldn't tell what they were saying. I settled into the chair and reached for the stack of files waiting to be organized and rewritten, recognizing Blane's handwriting on them as he'd revised them for Clarice.

Picking up the phone, I dialed Clarice's home number from memory. She picked up on the third ring.

"Hello?"

I could tell immediately that she was really sick and I regretted having to call her. "Hey, Clarice," I said, "I'm so sorry to bother you. I'm filling in for you today and I need the password to your computer. How are you feeling?"

"Awful," she moaned. "Stomach flu. I'm trying to stay away from the kids so they don't get it. Thank God they're not out for Christmas break yet."

"Do you need anything?" I asked.

"No," she replied, "Jack brought some things by this morning and he's going to check on me at lunch."

I was glad she had someone to help her, and if I was being honest, I was a little jealous. That's when you knew someone really loved you—when they held your hair while you threw up. Now that was devotion.

She told me her password, and before we hung up, I reassured her that I would take care of things, that she should concentrate on resting and getting better.

I'd logged onto the computer and was pulling up one of the files when I noticed how quiet it had gotten in Blane's office. I listened with half my attention as I typed, wondering who he was meeting with this morning. A few minutes later, my question was answered when the door opened and Kandi stepped out.

I froze mid-keystroke, my eyebrows flying upward in surprise. With dismay, I took in her appearance. She was dressed in a form-fitting ivory cashmere dress that clung to her curves. A heavy gold bracelet adorned her wrist and she wore four-inch gold heels. Her hair had been twisted up onto her head and she looked both businesslike and sexy, a look I couldn't pull off in a million years. Her gaze met mine, and she took in my long black skirt and white sweater with haughty disdain, her mouth curving in a faint mocking smile that only another woman would catch.

As she brushed by my desk, she sneered quietly, "The secretary? Really? How cliché."

"You seem cranky," I said snottily. "Better pick up some more batteries on the way home."

Her eyes narrowed and shot daggers at me. I returned the look, with interest, my hands clenching into fists as she turned away, her heels muffled by the thick carpet as she walked to the elevators. A cloud of expensive perfume drifted in her wake. I made myself start typing again only after I'd heard the elevator doors slide shut, resolutely refusing to look into Blane's open doorway to see what he was doing. I was not going to ask him what she'd been doing here. Uh-uh, no way.

I caught sight of Blane out of the corner of my eye, leaning against the doorway to his office, his arms crossed over his chest. He watched me in silence as I worked, which I pretended to ignore, though every sense was focused on him.

"You're probably wondering why Kandi was here," he said.

"Did the slutty princess try to screw you in your office?" Well, that's what immediately sprang to mind. "It's not my business" was what I actually said, still not looking at him. Maybe his "we have to stay away from each other" thing was also a way for him to let me down easy, killing two birds with one stone. Was he already moving on to someone else? I didn't want to believe that, though that cold, hard knot was back in the pit of my stomach.

Blane moved to stand behind me. I typed even faster, trying to ignore him. I jumped about a foot when his hands came down on my shoulders.

"What are you typing?" he asked in bewilderment. I looked at the computer monitor to see what he was talking about. To my utter humiliation, the document I'd been working on was now filled with gibberish.

"You *can* type, can't you?" he asked.

I spun around in my chair, making him drop his hold on me. "Of course I can," I snapped. "I just don't like being watched, that's all." I waved my hand vaguely toward him.

He smiled and butterflies did a little dance in my stomach. Damn it.

"That's right," he said slowly, "you were typing gibberish that night you were here late—the night I first took you to dinner."

"Technically, it wasn't dinner," I corrected him. "I just had soup. That doesn't count as dinner."

His smile widened, temporarily mesmerizing me. He was leaning against the desk now, towering over me, his dark suit jacket falling casually open. To my surprise, he suddenly leaned down, his lips brushing mine in a soft kiss.

"You have nothing to worry about," he said softly. "Kandi was here to invite me to their annual Christmas party Friday night. That's all. Her father insists I come. Robert and Vivian are going to be there as well."

His words might have carried a little more weight if I hadn't caught another whiff of Kandi's perfume lingering on his jacket.

"Are you going?" I asked, trying and failing to keep the jealousy from my voice.

"Yes, we are," he replied.

I looked up hopefully at him. His fingers brushed my jaw.

"If you'll go with me, that is," he amended.

I nodded, then said, "But I thought we were supposed to stay away from each other."

"We can drive separately," he said. "There won't be any reporters there; it's a private party."

"Okay then." I smiled, my heart much lighter now than when I'd seen Kandi come out of his office.

"I have to get to court," he said, stepping away. "Remember, stay at the office today, all right?"

"No problem," I said.

A few minutes later, he had grabbed his overcoat and briefcase and was gone, leaving me alone in the vast silence of the seventh floor.

After I'd finished the typing Clarice had stacked in her to-do pile, I grabbed another box from the conference room and began reading more on the Waters case. Deciding that the Internet was the best place to look for those most passionate about the case, I started searching. Discussion boards and chat rooms led me to people who were seriously worked up over the dead man, saying vile things about Kyle Waters, the US military, and America. It was all sobering to read.

I thought about what James had said yesterday. Powerful, important people were watching this case? Who, in James's view, were powerful, important people? The only thought that immediately occurred to me was politicians. Ick. The only job with a lower public perception than a lawyer was a politician. Or maybe a reporter.

Except for the ticking of the grandfather clock Blane had brought up from the fifth floor when he'd moved, the space was eerily quiet. The phone rang several times during the morning and I wrote the messages down for Blane.

I took a break for lunch, eating the sandwich I'd packed and running downstairs to the first floor to grab a Pepsi from the vending machine. The candy in the machine next to the soda looked tempting and I bought a Snickers.

Other than trying to talk to Ron Freeman and Stacey Willows, I was at a loss as to how else I could help find out who was behind the shooting, photos, and bloody message on my car. Looking through the file, I wrote down the address of the JAG officer who had testified yesterday, Lieutenant Sheffield. It might be worth talking to him, too.

I felt better knowing I was doing something to take control of the situation, and not just sitting back and letting whoever it was terrorize Blane and me even more. But I also wasn't stupid enough to think I should tell any of this to Blane. As protective as he was being, there was no way he'd let me go do any investigating of my own.

I glanced at my watch. I'd spent much of the day hunched over the keyboard and stretched to ease the tightness in my shoulders. It was getting late and my stomach rumbled hungrily. The Snickers snack had been a while ago. I wondered when Blane was going to be back.

As if my thoughts had conjured him, I heard the ding of the elevator and turned to see Blane stepping off and then heading in my direction. He discarded his coat and briefcase before coming around my desk to lean back against it once again.

"Good evening, dear," I said with a grin. "How was your day?"

He chuckled, pushing a hand tiredly through his hair. "Better, now that I see you're safe and sound," he replied. "No incidents today?"

The bloody words on the pristine snow flashed through my mind, but I smiled and said, "Nope. All quiet."

Blane blew out a sigh, the tension in his body easing. I felt guilty that he'd been worrying about me again.

"How's the trial going?" I asked.

Blane shook his head. "Not good. James is getting nasty, bringing in doctors who examined the photos and are trying to say the guy was shot twice, not once. Unfortunately, it's just my expert's word against his."

Blane seemed lost in thought and I remained quiet, watching him. He was very close and I enjoyed the view, now that I could look with impunity. He'd rolled his cuffs back, which I loved, and his tie was loosened. His ankles were crossed as he rested against my desk, and his proximity and position gave me an idea. It would do him good to relax a little. I could certainly help with that.

"Shall I buy you dinner?" he asked, shaking himself from his reverie and focusing back on me. "And not just soup?" I could tell he was oblivious as to the direction my thoughts were taking.

"Maybe later," I said coyly, rolling my chair closer to him. I placed my hands on his thighs and slid them upward toward his crotch, which was really at the perfect height for what I was planning.

My hands reached the bulge in his pants and I heard Blane take a sharp breath. I chanced a quick look up at him to find him watching me intently, his eyes darkening. Then my attention was drawn back to his crotch as I felt his cock stiffen under my questing fingers.

I found the zipper and tugged, the expensive fabric easily parting. Blane was a boxers kind of guy and I was easily able to free what I wanted. My mouth went dry at the sight of him.

I moaned as I leaned forward and took him in my mouth. I heard Blane's breath hiss between his teeth, but I was too distracted to pay much attention. I breathed deeply through my nose, the scent and taste of him causing my hormones to spike and sending a warm wetness between my thighs.

I'd gotten much better at this and had found, to my surprise, I enjoyed it a lot. Though it seemed submissive, it wasn't. I liked the sense of power it gave me, however briefly and illusory, over Blane.

He buried his hands in my hair as I slid up and down his length, relaxing my throat to take as much of him as possible. It was always gratifying if I could make him forget himself enough to thrust into my mouth. He was afraid he'd hurt me by doing that and held tightly to his control so he wouldn't. I noticed with satisfaction that his hips jerked upward when I did a certain thing with my tongue, so I did it again.

Blane ground out a curse and lifted me off him. I whimpered in disappointment before his mouth claimed mine, our tongues sliding against each other in an attempt to become as close as possible.

He quickly rearranged his clothes then lifted me against him, his hands supporting me as I wrapped my legs around his waist. He took me into his office, setting me on my feet before closing and locking the door. I grabbed the hem of my sweater, yanking it over my head and letting it fall to the floor. Then Blane was back, our mouths colliding again. His hands found the zipper of my skirt behind me and I felt the whisper of the fabric as it slid down my legs to puddle on the floor. I toed off my shoes and now stood dressed only in a white lace bra and matching panties. They were the expensive kind that I never would have bought for myself, the ones that Blane had purchased when he'd paid for replacing my entire wardrobe.

"Virgin white today, Kat?"

The roughness of his voice sent a shiver through me, but I couldn't answer or take my eyes off his. I wanted him so badly, I didn't care that we were about to have sex in his office like the tramp Kandi and Diane thought I was.

With a swipe of his arm, just like in the movies, he cleared a place on his desk and lifted me onto it. He tugged the scrap of satin and lace down and off my legs, and I leaned back to brace myself on the palms of my hands. I saw him shove the fabric into his pocket but had no time to wonder about it. Blane bent my knees so my feet were planted on the desk as well, only too far apart for any modesty.

His eyes on me made my cheeks burn, but before I could get uncomfortable, his mouth was on me, his tongue inside me, and my eyes slammed shut.

Under his skilled lips and tongue, my body was soon convulsing, cries falling from my lips. In the corner of my mind that still retained a semblance of dignity, I noticed I sounded like a bad porn movie. I couldn't help it, I started to giggle.

"What's so funny?" Blane asked, his mouth pressing against the skin of my abdomen as he moved upward. His fingers found the clasp on my bra and I arched my back so he could remove it.

"Me," I said, still laughing. "I make ridiculous noises."

"You sound fucking amazing," he growled, abruptly cutting off my giggles as he thrust inside me.

I moaned, raising my hips to meet his. I couldn't touch him without losing my position, so my hands remained on the desk behind me.

Blane's mouth found my breast and his hands dug into my hips as he lifted me to a better angle, which I strongly agreed with, judging by the moans and whimpers I couldn't suppress.

I didn't care how I sounded, I just wanted it harder and faster and right there, and told him so. I teetered on the edge for a blissful moment, then felt Blane's teeth close over my nipple. My scream was muffled by his hand over my mouth and I held on as his body pounded into mine, my thighs trembling with the aftershocks. He stiffened against me, his teeth marking me as he made his own happy noises, which I must say, sounded much better than mine.

We lay there for a moment, catching our breath, before I started to notice how hard the desk was and how chilly the air had become. I shivered and Blane pulled back, rearranging his clothes before lifting me down to stand on trembling legs.

I retrieved my bra and sweater and put them on while Blane found a tissue. He wiped gently at the wetness between my thighs while he kissed me, long and deep. I noticed with satisfaction that the aroma of sex hung in the room, obliterating any last traces of Kandi's perfume from this morning.

He released me with a touch to my cheek, our eyes meeting in a moment of perfectly attuned intimacy. I imagined I could see the same emotion in his eyes that was currently bubbling inside my chest, though neither of us said anything. I was afraid to put a name to it, though I knew what I felt.

I broke eye contact and looked around for my skirt. I tugged it on over my bare skin, deciding against the idea of saying anything about what Blane had tucked into the pocket of his slacks. He unlocked the door while I dressed and tossed the tissue into the trash. I adjusted my clothes and pushed my feet back into my black flats, combing my fingers through my hair.

"No!"

The shout from Blane startled me and I jumped. My head jerked up in time to see him hurtling toward me. I stood in shock as he tackled me, his shoulder hitting my chest and knocking the air from my lungs. I hit the floor, him on top of me, and my head cracked painfully against a bookcase. I heard the shattering of glass, a loud bang, then everything went dark.

∼

I awoke slowly, my head pounding. I could hear a voice, Blane's voice, talking quietly. I listened as I took stock of my body. Everything ached and it took me a moment to remember why: Blane crashing into me and me crashing into the floor.

"I need you," I heard Blane say quietly. Then there was silence. "You know I wouldn't ask otherwise." I focused more intently on listening as his voice lowered even further. "I don't ask much from you, you know that."

The sound of sirens made my eyes jerk open and I saw Blane sliding his cell phone back into his pocket. I painfully raised myself up to see I was lying on the couch outside Blane's office that was tucked into a windowless corner. I groaned, clutching my head, and Blane was by my side in an instant.

"I'm so sorry, Kat," he said, sinking into a crouch in front of me. "I didn't mean to hurt you."

"What happened?" I asked. Speaking made me wish I'd kept my mouth shut, as another wave of pain crashed through my head.

"You were targeted," Blane said. I looked at him blankly. "Sighted, with a laser through the window," he explained, "right here." His finger pressed gently to my chest, directly over my heart. "You were just lucky I saw it in time. A few seconds later . . ." The words trailed off as he looked at me. My hands went cold as I realized what he was saying.

"Someone watched us have sex?" I asked in disbelief, my voice a high screech that I immediately regretted as my head throbbed. I felt violated and humiliated. What sick pervert would do that?

"I don't think you're focusing on the important part," Blane said, his voice flat. "Someone tried to kill you."

His face was hard and devoid of expression, which I knew meant he was carefully controlling his anger. I swallowed.

"Thanks for saving me," I said reflexively. I thought I might be in shock, my mind not yet fully processing what had happened. At the moment, I was more pissed off that someone had been watching Blane and me together than the fact that they'd taken a shot at me.

"It's because of me that you needed saving in the first place," Blane bit out angrily.

I couldn't answer because just then the stairwell doors crashed open to reveal a cadre of police, firemen, and EMTs.

Blane rose quickly to his feet, speaking with the police and pointing me out to the EMTs.

I had to suffer through their exam, despite my protests that I was fine. Blane hovered nearby once he was through talking with the cops. They were in his office now, examining the floor for bullets.

"You have a mild concussion," one of the EMT guys said. "You should be admitted for observation overnight."

"No way," I said, shaking my head. "I'll be fine." I despised hospitals. I'd watched both my parents die in one. The antiseptic smell of a hospital, the constant noise, the endless hallways filled with doorways through which lay people who may or may not recover from whatever ailed them—all of it terrified me. I refused to go to a hospital.

"If he says you need to go, you should probably go," Blane interjected, seating himself next to me on the couch and taking my hand in his.

"I'm fine," I said adamantly. "I will not go to a hospital."

The EMT's gaze met Blane's, and with a shrug, he packed up his equipment. When he had walked away, Blane spoke.

"Why won't you go to the hospital?" he asked quietly. "I'll take care of the cost, if that's what you're worried about."
"I just . . ." I faltered for a moment. "I just hate hospitals, okay? They're horrible. People go in and . . . they don't come out."

He didn't say anything and I looked away uncomfortably. He rose from the couch when a cop called his name. I got to my feet and followed, wanting to hear what they had to say.

"We found these bullets in your office," the cop said, handing a plastic baggie to Blane. "Looks like a .308 Win. Based on the trajectory, I'd say the shooter was on the roof of the building next door."

Blane inspected the bullets closely. "Those aren't Winchesters," he said. "They're 7.62 NATOs."

"What's significant about that?" I asked.

Blane looked at me. "This type of bullet is typically used in MK11s."

I still looked blankly at him.

"MK11s are sniper rifles and only issued to the military."

My eyes widened as I finally caught on. "So it was someone in the military shooting at me?"

Blane nodded. "Maybe even the Navy." He turned to the officer. "Did you find anything over there?" he asked, handing the baggie back to him.

"Not a thing," the cop said. "Whoever it was, he was careful to not leave evidence behind."

A few minutes later, everyone had cleared out except Blane and me. I dug in my purse until I found a bottle of painkillers, then swallowed three.

"What happened to your arm?" Blane asked out of the blue.

"What?"

"Earlier," he clarified, "I noticed your arm had bruises." He motioned to my upper arm where James had grabbed me yesterday. "What happened?"

It was so not the time for this, but I didn't see any way I could avoid telling him.

"I had a run-in with James at the courthouse yesterday," I confessed. "He was . . . agitated. Told me you were 'going down,' that this case was going to make his career."

Blane had gone very still the moment I said James's name. I could feel the anger practically vibrating through him.

"Did he hit you again?" Blane's voice was flat and cold.

"No. No, he didn't," I said quickly. "He just grabbed me, shook me a little." A dangerous light came into Blane's eyes. "You can't do anything to James, Blane," I said earnestly, tipping my head back so I could look him in the eye. "That's what he wants. If he can get you removed from this case, he'll win. No one else stands a chance against him."

Blane seemed unmoved by my argument.

"Blane," I pleaded. "Promise me you won't go after him. Not until after this case is through. It would only cause more trouble and Kyle needs you."

Finally, to my relief, he reluctantly nodded. "But I am going to find out if he's behind this," Blane amended.

"Fine," I agreed, "just don't put him in the hospital, okay?" Blane's lips twitched and I quickly added, "Or the morgue."

Blane followed me home from the firm in his car.

"I thought we were going to stay away from each other?" I'd reminded him when he told me of his intentions.

"Fuck that," he'd replied, scanning the parking lot as he walked me to my car. "I'm not leaving you alone."

That made me feel warm and fuzzy inside, though I disliked the need for his protectiveness. I also realized as we entered my apartment that I'd forgotten to warn him about Bacon Bits and the little dog flew at him, barking madly.

"How did you get out?" I asked the excited dog, hurrying to my bedroom door. I'd been so sure I'd shut it securely this morning, but there it was, standing innocently open.

"Why do you have Alisha's dog?" Blane asked, following me.

"She had to leave town for a few days," I explained with a sigh, squatting down to pet Bits. He quieted immediately.

Tigger suddenly appeared, rubbing against me, and I braced myself for the two animals to start fighting, but they seemed to have ironed out their differences. To my surprise, Tigger gave Bits a little nudge, then jogged away. Bits obediently trotted after him. Huh.

"I'll go get some dinner," Blane said as I stood back up. The room tilted for a moment and I grabbed the counter to stay on my feet.

"What's wrong?" Blane asked urgently. He lifted my chin so he could look into my eyes. "Are you all right?"

"I'm fine," I said, brushing aside his concern. "Just stood up too fast, that's all."

"You need to lie down," Blane said, hooking an arm around my waist and guiding me to the bed.

"I need to take the dog outside," I protested.

"I'll do it. Just rest, okay?"

I was suddenly too tired to argue. My head still hurt and last night's tossing and turning was catching up to me. With Blane nearby, I felt the anxiety inside me ease. I felt safe.

I let Blane push me gently down onto the bed. I kicked off my shoes and lay back while he pulled the quilt over me.

"I'll be right back," he said softly, pressing a kiss to my forehead.

I smiled tiredly. "You have to tell him 'Go toodles, Bits. Go toodles for Momma,'" I said, pitching my voice high in imitation. "Or else he won't go."

Blane looked at me. "I'm not doing that," he said flatly.

"But then he'll go on the bed," I protested.

"How about I just point my gun at him," he deadpanned.

I laughed, squirming farther underneath the quilt as I watched Blane leave the room, Bits prancing after him, tongue lolling happily out the side of his mouth.

When I awoke, it was nearly nine o'clock. My headache was gone, thank goodness, and I was starving.

I went to the bathroom and changed out of my clothes into flannel pajama pants and a long-sleeved T-shirt, not bothering with a bra. I brushed the tangles from my hair, washed the makeup off my face, and brushed my teeth. I felt much better after that and went in search of Blane.

I found him on the couch. He'd changed into jeans and a T-shirt, some clothes he'd left here before, and papers were scattered all over the couch and coffee table as he wrote on a legal pad. Tigger was curled behind him on the top of the couch while Bits lay at his feet. The scene made me smile.

He must have sensed my presence, because he looked up, a quick glance taking in my appearance.

"You look like you feel better," he said.

"I do, thanks," I replied. "Just hungry."

"There's some Chinese in the fridge. Kung pao. Your favorite."

My mouth watered just thinking about it. I grabbed the container and dumped some on a plate to heat in the microwave. When I got back to the living room, Blane had cleared a space next to him on the couch. I tucked my feet underneath me as I sat cross-legged beside him.

"Thanks for dinner," I said after I'd swallowed a mouthful of fiery chicken.

"No problem," he said, his mouth tipping up at the corners.

The television wasn't turned on, but Blane had lit the lights on the Christmas tree. After I ate, I sat in comfortable silence with Blane as he worked. Tigger moved to my lap and I stroked his fur absently. So long as we didn't talk about someone shooting at me yet again, and I didn't mention the dead possum and blood on my car, it was a real sweet scene.

I loved Christmas. It was my favorite time of the year. I could see the snow outside, the wan moonlight causing the ground to glisten. The smell of cedar and balsam permeated the apartment and the tree glowed brightly with all the lights and ornaments we'd hung on it. I found my spirits lifting in spite of the mess I was currently in.

"What are you doing?"

"What?" My attention jerked to Blane, who was studying me, his pen poised over his legal pad.

"You were humming something," he said.

"Oh," I said, taken aback. "I'm sorry." I hadn't realized I'd been doing that and certainly hadn't intended to disturb him.

"What was it?"

I thought. "I don't know. A Christmas carol, probably." I shrugged.

"Will you sing it for me?" he asked.

I ducked my head in embarrassment. "Of course not," I said, "don't be silly. Finish your work so we can go to bed. I'm tired."

Blane deliberately set aside his pad and pen and stacked his papers neatly next to his briefcase. Turning, he pulled me between his spread legs and I settled back against his chest with a sigh. With his arms around me, the night enveloping us, it didn't seem like anything bad could happen.

"Please."

Well, crap. I couldn't resist him when he said that—not that I was great at resisting him period. I wasn't that great of a singer, apart from my ability to channel Britney Spears, but I gave it my best. Looking at the tree, I softly sang the first and second verses to "Silent Night." It made me miss my mom, that song had been one of her favorites. She'd always said it set the right mood of reverence for Christmas and I agreed.

"That was beautiful, Kat," Blane said when the last note had trailed off into the darkness. His voice was rough.

We sat in silence for a while, lost in our own thoughts. I kept thinking about Kyle and the case Blane was working.

"Tell me," I said into the quiet, "about when you were in the service. Did you have to shoot anyone?"

Blane's whole body stiffened and I could practically feel him pulling away from me.

"Why do you want to know?" he asked.

"I'm not judging you," I said, twisting around so I could see his face. "I want to know what it was like for you, what you went through."

He studied me for a moment, as if deciding whether or not he was going to speak. I stayed silent, hoping he trusted me enough to open up to me.

"It's hard to explain," he began. "Life is different, more basic, in war. Your point of view is focused only on yourself and the men you're with, helping to keep each other alive. You see things, do things, that people who aren't there can't even imagine."

His eyes had taken on a faraway look and I wondered if he was seeing me or something else.

"One time we were working with some Marines," Blane said after a pause. "They needed help clearing houses and Marines aren't trained for that sort of thing. I went in first, clearing the bottom floor and they came in behind me. One of them, it was his first time out—he was young, maybe nineteen, twenty. Name was Dillon. He got too complacent once the bottom floor was cleared. He didn't realize that sometimes they would hide upstairs, waiting for us. He went up alone, careless, and the bastard hiding set off a grenade. Killed himself and blew a hole in my guy's chest. By the time I got to him, he was nearly gone. He just kept asking me to call his mom. He wanted to say good-bye. He died in my arms."

My eyes were wide as I listened. Blane was right. I couldn't even imagine what that must have been like.

"It's funny," he said thoughtfully. "You don't always remember the ones you saved. But you never forget the ones you couldn't."

There were no words I could say that would even begin to mean anything in light of what he'd just told me, so I didn't try. Reaching up, I took his face in my hands until his eyes were once again focused on me.

"You're a good man, Blane Kirk," I said. I pressed my lips firmly to his once, twice. His arms embraced me tightly as I laid my head on his shoulder.

"Did you have any problems when you came back?" I asked. I'd heard about soldiers with PTSD and wondered if Blane had ever suffered from that.

"It took a while to readjust," he said. "It was months before I could pass trash on the road without thinking it was an IED about to blow. Being on constant alert over there, it's hard to accept that you're safe, that you don't have to come awake at the slightest noise, reaching for your gun." He paused. "Kade helped me through it."

That surprised me. "Really?"

Blane nodded. "He moved in for a while. Made me go out, do things. Normal things. Go to a baseball game, see a movie, have dinner. He didn't pity me and he didn't baby me. It was just matter-of-fact, as though he knew I needed to acclimate again. I think it helped our relationship that for once I needed him, rather than the other way around."

I pondered this, unsurprised at Kade's devotion to Blane. I also had to admit that I was jealous. Some times were harder than others to be an only child. "It must be really nice to have a sibling," I murmured thoughtfully.

"It is," Blane replied.

We went to bed shortly after that, the day wearing on me even with my power nap, and I was glad to get some sleep, snuggled spoon-style with Blane. I slept soundly until a slight whimper made my eyes open a crack.

Bits was on the floor, staring up at me. He wagged his tail when he saw my eyes were open, then stood and turned around in a circle. I blearily looked at the clock. 5:30 a.m. Sheesh. Two hours earlier than the schedule. The dog obviously couldn't tell time.

Easing from the bed so I wouldn't wake Blane, I slipped on some shoes and grabbed the leash. I hooked it to Bits and he danced excitedly by the door as I slipped on my coat.

The early morning air was frigid and woke me up in a hurry. I could see my breath as I walked the dog, hoping he'd do his business quickly. I took him around to the side of the apartment building, where there was more snow-covered ground than concrete. I brushed aside an area of snow down to the grass and whispered his code words. For a dog that woke me up because he had to pee, he sure was taking his sweet time, I thought sourly.

The scuff of a shoe made my head jerk up. No one should be out at this hour, and indeed the streets were still and silent. What had seemed peaceful before, however, now took on an eerie feeling instead. The moon had long since disappeared and there were only dark shadows filling the streets.

The noise came again from behind me and I spun around, my heart racing as I searched the darkness. The hair on the back of my neck stood up and I wished I'd thought to bring Blane's gun along with me.

Tugging on the dog, I turned back to my apartment building, wanting to go inside. Bits would just have to wait until it was light out. I'd taken two steps when I saw a shadow separate itself from the darkness around it. I froze. A spike of adrenaline rushed through my veins, its chill making my hands shake. I clenched them into fists as I thought furiously.

Making a quick decision, I grabbed up the dog, turned, and ran. I didn't know where I was running to, I just knew what I was running from. A glance behind showed me I'd been correct—there was someone following me, and gaining, from the looks of it. He didn't bother to pretend anymore and I saw that he wore a dark hood as he passed under a streetlight.

Though I knew it was futile, that he would eventually catch me, I ran anyway. The only sound was that of my ragged breath and the crunch of my feet in the snow. I kept glancing behind me, but he wasn't getting closer. Yet.

Turning a corner, I ran blindly down a dark alley between two buildings. I was getting farther from my apartment building but didn't know how to double back. I burst out of the alley, turning to look behind me once again, and ran full bore into a body.

I screamed, terror peaking in me. A hand quickly covered my mouth, stifling my scream, and I struggled. Bits jumped out of my arms onto the ground and I dropped his leash, using both hands now to try and break free.

I was suddenly brought up short against the man, unable to continue to struggle as his arm tightened around me. Jerking my head up, I saw eyes bluer than I remembered, framed by dark lashes and wickedly arched brows.

"Nice to see you, too, princess," Kade said.

CHAPTER SIX

My knees buckled in relief and Kade's hold on me was the only thing that kept me from crumpling to the ground.

"Someone's chasing me," I gasped, struggling to regain control of my breathing.

Kade's expression changed, his smirk fading as he looked at me, as though he was measuring my words. Whatever he saw must have convinced him, because the next thing I knew, his gun was in his hand and he was pushing me behind him. I scooped up Bits, who'd sat nearby, tail wagging as he watched us.

"Stay close," Kade said curtly.

"No problem." He had a gun and I didn't. That pretty much meant I was sticking to him like glue.

We backtracked the way I'd come, me close behind him. I clutched a handful of his leather jacket. I probably should have let go, but I couldn't make myself. I knew I was far from Kade's favorite person, but I also believed he would keep me safe.

There was no one around. The silence of the night was profound and complete. My heart rate slowly returned to normal as we came in sight of my apartment building. I wondered what the heck Kade was doing here anyway.

"There's no one around," Kade said, holstering his gun.

"I saw someone earlier," I said, pointing. "Right over there."

We walked over to the small knot of trees and bushes. Kade stopped, crouching down to look at something on the ground.

"What is it?" I asked, my voice hushed.

"Cigarette butts," he said, holding one up, then stood. "Let's get you inside," he ordered.

He herded me up the steps, keeping close behind. With Bits in my arms, I couldn't see very well in the near total darkness and missed a step. I braced myself for the fall, but Kade's arm flashed out, hooking me around the waist.

I paused, realizing I was still shaken from what had happened. Kade no doubt thought I was a klutz since that was twice in the past ten minutes that he'd had to catch me before I ended up on the ground.

"Thanks," I said to Kade. His arm was still locked around my waist, so I tugged on it, letting him know I was fine. He released me and I bent to let Bits jump out of my arms. He trotted obediently to my door. Kade followed me inside, shutting and locking the door behind him.

Bits had curled up on his pink pillow in the corner, and to my surprise, Tigger was curled up with him. I shed my coat and shoes, pushing my fingers through my tangled hair. Kade stood in my living room, surveying his surroundings.

It made me nervous to have him here. His presence was just as palpable and overwhelming as Blane's, but I knew Blane didn't hate me. As it was, I had no idea why Kade was here, why he'd turned up at such an opportune moment, or what I was supposed to do with him.

"Would you like some coffee?" I asked politely, keeping my distance from him as I stood in the kitchen. He was looking at the tree but flicked his gaze to meet mine.

A flash of memories assailed me in that moment— Kade's loathing of me, especially when he found out I was with Blane, yet rescuing me from Avery when I would have been raped and killed. Kade carrying me across a gravel parking lot when my feet were too torn up to make it on my own, yet also threatening to kill me if I didn't cooperate and give him what he wanted.

Kade kissing me at The Drop before I had known he was Blane's brother.

I wondered if Kade was thinking something similar, but it was impossible to tell. He could have been musing on the weather, for all that showed on his face. I fidgeted under his steady gaze, nervously crossing my arms over my chest, and looked away from him to stare at the floor.

"Sure. Coffee," he finally said.

I gave a jerky nod and started a pot of coffee. Escaping from Kade's presence, I went into the bathroom. I splashed some water on my face and brushed my teeth and hair. When I was done, I just stood there, staring at my reflection in the mirror.

My face was paler than usual, the shadows under my eyes standing out prominently. For a few minutes, I just breathed.

It felt as though my nerves were a hair's breadth from snapping. Whoever was doing this to me seemed unrelenting. Each day had brought a new terror, and it was getting harder and harder to brush off the events. I didn't want to go into hysterics and cause Blane to worry any more than he already was, but after being chased in the dark by the unknown man this morning, regaining my equilibrium was very difficult. And to take matters to another level of stress and anxiety, Kade Dennon was in my living room.

I knew I couldn't hide forever, which was really too bad when I thought about it. When I finally came back out of the bathroom, the coffee was finished brewing and I poured two mugs full as calmly as my shaking hands would allow.

"How do you take it?" I asked, thinking I probably already knew the answer.

"Black," he answered, confirming what I'd thought.

I dumped half and half and some sweetener in mine before taking the mugs into the living room. He'd sat on the couch while I'd been gone and had discarded his jacket. I noticed now that he had on jeans and a black henley shirt layered over another T-shirt. His gun was firmly in the holster attached to his jeans.

I gave him the coffee, then sat at the far end of the couch, tucking my bare feet up underneath me.

"Why are you here?" I asked after a few minutes, breaking the stiff silence.

"Wondered when you'd get around to that," he said, his voice rife with the condescension I despised. "What's the matter? I can't drop by for a friendly visit?"

I snorted in derision at this. "The last time you were here, you were going to kill me, so no, a friendly visit never crossed my mind."

"That's not precisely true," Kade said, and the way he said it made my eyes dart to his.

He was talking about leaving the money, of course. I opened my mouth to say something, I wasn't sure what, when he cut me off.

"Trust me, I wouldn't be here if I didn't have to be," he said grudgingly, looking away from me and taking another swallow of the bitter coffee.

"Then why?"

He didn't answer, just shot me a look that spoke volumes about what he thought of my intelligence. Then it hit me.

"Blane asked you to come, didn't he?" I asked, knowing I was right, though Blane had said nothing to me about calling Kade.

"Ding-ding-ding," Kade mocked.

I ignored him even as my face heated. I considered this, abruptly remembering the overheard phone conversation Blane had made last night when I'd woken up. He must have been talking to Kade, which meant Kade had literally dropped whatever he was doing to get here at five thirty in the morning from wherever he had been.

"Why?" I asked the question even though I was afraid I knew the answer already.

Kade didn't bother looking at me. "I'll let Blane tell you that," he replied dryly. "Where is he, by the way?"

"Asleep."

Kade didn't reply, his eyes on the glowing Christmas tree. After a few minutes of silence, he spoke again. "It appears there's no end to the trouble you cause my brother," he mused sardonically.

I stiffened at the implication, which was grossly unfair, in my opinion.

"He put his life on the line for you once before," Kade continued, anger edging his voice. "Are you going to require he do it again?"

I felt like I'd been kicked in the gut. He turned to look at me, but I was too stunned at his verbal attack to say anything.

"Find another rich guy to screw."

I went from shocked to completely pissed off in two seconds flat. Any thoughts I'd had about thanking Kade for the money he'd left me or for being there tis morning when I'd been so scared flew out the window. I had thought Kade and I had reached a truce in Chicago. It seemed that truce was over now.

"What's between Blane and me is none of your business," I spat angrily at him, hating the fact that my eyes had blurred with tears at his hurtful words. It was all I could do not to hurl my coffee mug at his head. "I don't care about his money, not that you'd believe me or that I even care what you think! I don't even know why you're here. Why don't you just get out? Go on! Get out!"

His eyes narrowed dangerously and he abruptly moved close, so that his body loomed over mine. A shot of fear went through me and before I could quell the impulse, I shrank away from him. His face was inches away, his blue eyes boring into mine, and when he spoke, his voice was deceptively calm.

"Don't . . . push . . . me," he said slowly, enunciating each word.

The tension grew thick as we stared angrily at each other, neither one backing down.

The door to my bedroom suddenly flew open, startling me. Blane stood there wearing only his jeans, both his feet and chest were bare. I would have gone to greet him, but his gun was in his hand and his expression was cold and hard. When he saw me and Kade, his body relaxed slightly and he tucked the gun into his jeans at the small of his back.

I jumped up and hurried over to him, feeling immeasurably better now that he was there to be the buffer between Kade and me.

"Please don't do that again," he said seriously, wrapping a hand around my arm and tugging me toward him.

"Do what?"

"Leave without telling me," he clarified.

"It was Bits," I explained. "He needed to go outside."

"You went outside?" Blane asked incredulously. "Alone?"

I chewed my lip, looking at him uncertainly. I had a sinking feeling this was going to be one of those she's-too-dumb-to-walk-upright moments.

Blane took my silence as confirmation. His lips pressed into a thin line. "And I doubt you took the gun with you."

"I thought about it," I said quickly, then had to add, "after I left."

"She was running," Kade interrupted, speaking about me as if I weren't standing right there. He had stepped into the kitchen and leaned back against the counter, arms and ankles crossed in a pose very much like the one Blane frequently adopted. "Said someone was chasing her."

"Did you find anyone?" Blane asked, his attention now on Kade. His arm curved absently over my shoulders and I moved closer, sliding my arms around his waist so I could rest against him. His skin was warm despite the slight chill of the apartment. I was still furious with Kade, but Blane's touch took the edge off.

"No," Kade replied, his eyes flicking briefly to my arms as they hugged Blane. "Just some cigarette butts. Looks like whoever it was had been there a while, with a good view of the apartment."

"Why is Kade here?" I asked Blane pointedly, looking up at him. "He said you asked him to come."

"I'll step outside for this," Kade said, the corner of his mouth twisting upward in his telltale smirk. "Take a better look around now that it's getting light."

Blane and I watched him go and when the door shut, I returned my attention to Blane.

"Well?" I asked. "Why did you ask him to come?"

Blane looked down at me, and the look in his eyes made me think I wasn't going to like what he was about to say.

"I can't be around you," he said. "You're a target because of me. I asked Kade to come and help keep you safe."

I was right. I didn't like that at all, not one little bit. "You asked Kade to come babysit me?" I said angrily, stepping out of his reach.

"No one said babysit," he said. "I need you safe and can't be the one to do it. Kade's the only one I trust."

"Well, I don't!" The words fell out of my mouth before I could think better of it.

Blane's eyes narrowed. "You don't trust my brother?"

I quickly backpedaled. "It's not that I think he's not capable," I said, scrambling to put my feelings into words. "We just don't really . . . get along," I finished lamely.

"You don't have to get along," Blane said flatly. "He's here to keep you alive."

"Maybe you're overreacting," I said in a last-ditch effort. "You're the one who needs protection, not me."

"Overreacting?" Blane said, his voice a low growl. He stepped into my personal space and I retreated until I was backed up against the wall. "Need I remind you that you would be dead right now if I hadn't spotted the rifle sight on you last night?"

Okay, so maybe he wasn't overreacting, and no, I really didn't need reminding, but that didn't mean I wanted Kade hovering over me. I couldn't even sit in the same room with him and drink a cup of coffee, much less have him dogging my every move, especially when I knew he wouldn't be all that torn up if something did happen to take me out of the picture.

"He hates me," I finally said, praying Blane would understand.

His eyes softened, but his voice was still implacable. "I doubt that, but it doesn't matter anyway. I trust him."

It didn't appear I had much of a choice in the matter. I chafed under that, despite the logic behind Blane's argument. I hated the thought that I wasn't safe by myself, that I needed someone to protect me. Then another, even more unpleasant, thought occurred to me.

"Where is Kade going to stay?" I asked, afraid that I already knew the answer.

Blane didn't reply, his eyes just glanced at my couch.

"Oh no," I protested. "He is not staying here. Absolutely not." It was such a bad idea, I had trouble comprehending why Blane would even consider it.

"How else is he going to protect you?"

"I don't want him here," I said, adamantly shaking my head to emphasize my point. "We'll kill each other. He thinks I'm nothing but a trailer-trash, money-grubbing slut—"

"Don't say that." Blane's words interrupted me, harshly spoken and angry, and I instinctively recoiled. His voice gentled immediately. "You are many things," he said, his fingers combing through the hair by my face, "but not that. Never that."

Our eyes locked, and the coiled anger and fear inside me relaxed, his words warming me. I could stand Kade thinking the worst of me so long as I knew Blane didn't believe it as well.

The door opened and Kade stepped back inside, and just like that, my wariness returned with a vengeance and my defenses sprang back into place. Blane went to talk to him. I didn't want to be in the same room with Kade at the moment and disappeared into the bathroom.

I felt better after a shower, emerging from the bathroom wrapped in my fuzzy pink robe. Blane had dressed and was preparing to leave.

"I have to head home," he told me as he shrugged into his coat. "I'll see you later after court. Don't go anywhere without Kade, okay?"

I nodded unhappily. "Is he coming to the bar tonight, too?" I'd had a couple of days off but had to work tonight at The Drop.

"I'd really like it if you quit that job," Blane said, "especially now."

It was a recurring argument between us. He wanted me to quit bartending, but I wouldn't. I needed the money and refused to take it from him.

"I don't want to argue about it," I said quietly, though I knew Kade could probably hear us—my apartment wasn't that big. "You know I need my job. Both of them."

"I told you I'd take care of you."

"It would be foolish of me to quit my job," I said vaguely, not wanting to respond directly to what he'd said. How do you say, "Yeah, but what do I do when we break up?" without it sounding fatalistic?

"You'd better go," I said quickly, trying to forestall any more arguments from Blane. "You're going to be late for court." He still had to get across town to his place and get dressed.

I could tell by the clenching of his jaw that he knew exactly what I was doing, but he didn't argue further. Instead, he pulled me into his arms and kissed me.

Keenly aware of Kade nearby and possibly watching, I tried to pull away quickly, embarrassed, but Blane just tightened his hold and deepened the kiss. After a moment, I forgot about Kade watching.

When Blane drew back, I saw that Kade was ignoring us as he looked out the window. I had a moment of sheer panic as I watched Blane walk out the door and had to press my lips together to keep from calling him back. I was afraid. Afraid that Blane was going to get hurt—and afraid of being alone with Kade.

It's not that I thought Kade would physically harm me—it's what he would say to me that had my teeth clenched and a gnawing dread in the pit of my stomach. I honestly didn't think I had it in me to take more of what he'd already heaped on me this morning. Maybe another day, another week, but certainly not this one. So my first priority was to find a way to get him to leave, or if not leave entirely, then to at least get him away from me.

"You should be protecting Blane," I said to Kade, breaking the stiff silence between us as I put dirty dishes in the dishwasher. "This case he's on has got people all riled up."

"Blane can take care of himself," Kade replied evenly. Tigger had jumped up on the counter and was purring contentedly as Kade rubbed his ears.

Okay, so that tack wasn't going to work. With an inward sigh, I poured another cup of coffee and headed for my bedroom. Kade could just watch TV, pet the cat, or jump out the window for all I cared. I took my time doing the hair and makeup thing, wanting to feel fully armored before again facing Kade and his contempt.

When it was time to head to work, I emerged from my bedroom and grabbed my coat and purse. Bypassing breakfast seemed like a good idea since my stomach was in too much of a knot to eat. Kade and I didn't speak as we went out the door, and I made sure I carefully locked it behind me.

Kade followed me in his car, a black Mercedes that made my blue Honda look decidedly decrepit. To my relief, no poor dead woodland creatures awaited me this morning.

I had wanted to go see the people on my list today but had no idea how I'd accomplish that with Kade watching my every move. I was sure he wouldn't approve. I didn't speak to him as he followed me inside the firm, the silence brittle as we rode the elevator to the top floor.

Clarice had left a message on my cell, saying that she was still sick and asking if I could cover for her again today. I settled in at her desk, covertly watching Kade as he roamed the area before settling on the couch Blane had placed me on last night.

He laid his head back tiredly against the cushion and I realized he was probably exhausted from being up all night. Could it really be that easy?

"You'll be here all day?" Kade asked without opening his eyes.

"Yep," I lied, hope rising inside me.

"Okay, then I'm going to get some shut-eye. Wake me if you want to leave."

"All right," I said, careful to keep the excitement from my voice. I watched him as he turned and lay down, an arm bent behind him to cushion his head.

For the next forty-five minutes, I typed and answered the phone, keeping an eye on Kade. He'd fallen asleep pretty quickly and had stayed asleep. Careful to keep quiet, I forwarded the phones to voice mail and locked the computer. Quietly retrieving my coat and purse, I tiptoed past Kade to the stairwell, holding the door while it shut so it wouldn't slam and wake him. I didn't breathe normally until I was sliding into the front seat of my car.

Taking a slip of paper out of my purse, I saw that Stacey Willows and Ryan Sheffield lived in the northern and western side of Indy, respectively—one in Carmel and the other by Plainfield. Brian Bowers was slated for court today, so I'd have to wait to go see him. I decided to head north to Carmel and Stacey Willows.

It took a little while to find the right house, an older ranch on the outskirts of town. I made my way to the front door and rang the doorbell. After a few moments, I heard footsteps and the door swung open. A woman stood there, appearing to be in her early thirties, dressed in jeans and a thick, red cable-knit sweater.

"Yes? Can I help you?"

I smiled brightly. "Hi, my name is Kathleen Turner and I'm looking into the Waters case for the Kirk and Trent law firm. Are you Stacey Willows?"

"I am," she answered carefully.

"Would you have a few minutes to talk with me?"

"Um, I guess, okay," she said.

I smiled wider. "Great! May I come in?"

Stacey took me into the living room, the furniture clean but worn.

"Can I get you something to drink?" she asked politely.

"No, but thanks," I said with a wave of my hand. "I'm fine." I settled onto the couch and she sat on a nearby armchair.

Grabbing a pen from my purse, I put a legal pad on my lap and tried to look official. "I know you're involved with Staff Sergeant Martin, correct?"

"Yes," Stacey said. "We've been together for a couple of years."

"But not married?" I asked. That was just a curiosity question.

"I told him I wouldn't marry him until he left the Navy," she said frankly. "I don't want to be a widow."

I couldn't blame her for that. "Did he talk to you about the case against him?"

She nodded. "Thank God they didn't convict him. It would have destroyed him."

"What do you mean?" I asked.

"He's out there putting his life on the line fighting for his country," she said. Her eyes were wet but she didn't cry. "If they'd turned their back on him, convicted him for doing his job, I don't know if he could have recovered. He would have seen it as a betrayal."

"Does he plan on staying in the Navy?"

She shook her head. "No. Once this enlistment is up, he's not re-upping." She smiled. "We've set a wedding date for July."

I smiled back. "Congratulations."

"Thanks."

I decided to get down to business. "Listen, Stacey," I said, "there have been some threats and . . . incidents . . . with the defense in this case. Do you know anyone or can you think of someone who might be involved enough with the case to do something like that?"

"What kind of incidents?" she asked, frowning.

"A couple shootings," I said bluntly. "The shots were fired from a military-issued weapon. No one was hurt, but they could have been." Only by luck had Blane escaped unscathed once, and me, twice.

"I'm so sorry," she said. "That's horrible. But I honestly have no idea who could have done something like that. The SEALs are closer than brothers. So many people have stood behind us, given us their support."

I sighed inwardly. It had been a long shot, but I'd hoped she might have some useful information that would have helped. "Well, thank you for talking with me," I said, rising to my feet. "Congratulations again." I hoped her fiancé returned healthy and well from his current deployment. She seemed to read my mind.

"I just pray he comes back to me," she said quietly. "It's really hard, not knowing day to day if he's still alive or if he's hurt somewhere, or . . ." She didn't finish the sentence, not that she had to—I knew what she was thinking.

On impulse, I said, "Here's my number." I scrawled my phone number on a piece of paper and handed it to her. "Just . . . in case. Maybe you recall something or . . . just need to talk."

Stacey took it, then gave me a smile.

"Thanks," she said. "I'll keep that in mind."

I thanked her for her time and left. The overcast sky threatened more snow and I shivered as I got into my cold car. Days like today made me long for my mom's homemade chili and apple pie. Store-bought just wasn't the same.

Plainfield was about an hour away and took even longer when it started sleeting. I, of course, hadn't listened to the weather forecast, so I flipped on the radio. I listened as the weatherman called for freezing rain and sleet turning to snow later. Great. Snow, I liked. Ice, not so much.

The next person on my list was the lieutenant who had testified yesterday, Ryan Sheffield. He lived outside of the town proper and I hesitated before driving down the gravel dirt road that led to his house. It had been plowed of the recent snowfall but still had a thin layer of packed snow. I resolved that I would make this visit quick and get back to the firm. No doubt Kade was awake by now. I cringed, thinking about how angry he was going to be.

Ryan answered the door and I was momentarily taken aback. He had been very impressive yesterday in his uniform. Today, dressed in jeans and a T-shirt, he was very attractive in a manly, outdoorsy kind of way. His biceps were massive, straining the thin cotton as he held the door open and ushered me inside.

"You work for the law firm, huh?" he asked, settling down heavily in a well-used recliner.

"Yes," I said. "Just looking into some recent threats the firm has received."

"What kind of threats?" he asked, his eyes narrowing.

"It seems someone thinks we shouldn't be defending Kyle Waters," I answered. "There have been threats of violence to Mr. Kirk as well as others who work at the firm, possibly from someone in the Navy." I was vague on the last part, no need to tell him "others" meant just me. "Would you know of anyone who might want to do that?"

Ryan thought for a minute before replying. "There's always the antimilitary crowd that hate us, hate what we do. It may not be anyone at all involved in the case, just someone who's taking justice into their own hands, someone who thinks no one should defend Kyle for what happened. I can't imagine a Navy guy doing this."

My heart sank. In the back of my mind, I'd been thinking the same thing. But if that were true, trying to find that person would be like looking for the proverbial needle in a haystack. "You're probably right," I said, "I was just hoping it might be someone related to the case who had a grudge or ax to grind, something more concrete that would lead us to him."

"I'm sorry," Ryan said sincerely.

I offered him a weak smile. "I guess we'll just have to leave it to the police and hope they find him."

"If there's anything I can do, please let me know," he said. "I've been stationed here for the rest of my enlistment."

"Is this home?" I asked, glancing around.

"It is," he confirmed. "After being deployed, it's great to be back in the US of A. I'm a country boy at heart, and it's nice to be back home."

I thought of Rushville with a pang, quickly followed by thoughts of my parents. Tears clouded my eyes and I blinked them away, embarrassed.

"Hey, you okay?" Ryan asked concernedly, leaning forward in his chair to grasp my hand. "I didn't mean to upset you."

"No, it's fine," I protested quickly. His grip was large and warm. "I'm fine."

"So how's the farm business these days?" I asked, wanting to change the subject.

"It's been better," Ryan said. "This farm has been in my family for six generations. Some years are better than others."

I nodded, understanding what he meant, having grown up in the country. I could never handle being a farmer's wife. Too stressful, wondering if each year would bring prosperity or poverty.

We chatted for a few more minutes and then I gathered my things to go. I was a bit reluctant to leave, but I knew the weather wasn't going to be getting any better. I liked Ryan. He had that whole honest, homegrown, country-bred quality about him, as had so many of the boys I'd grown up with. It made me comfortable and homesick at the same time.

Ryan walked me to the porch, where I saw that it had begun to snow again. Well, at least it was better than sleet. It was a really pretty landscape. Ryan's property included a picturesque barn and acres of fields.

"Be careful driving," Ryan warned me. "The gravel road can be hard to see in this weather."

I said I would and thanked him for his time, reaching to shake his hand one last time.

"I know this may sound presumptuous," he said suddenly, holding on to my hand in his large one, "but can I take you to dinner sometime?"

I was so surprised, it took me a moment to respond. "Thanks so much for the invitation," I finally said with a smile, "but I'm involved with someone."

"Of course," he said, a small grin making his chocolate eyes soften at the corners, "a woman as beautiful as you is bound to have been snatched up already."

I blushed bright red from his compliment, too tongue-tied to say anything. With a flick of my hand, I waved as I stepped off the porch. The snow crunched under my feet and I could see my breath in the frigid air as I got into my car.

Getting back to the firm was treacherous and nerve wracking, and the drive took me nearly two hours. Traffic was backed up because of numerous accidents. My stomach growled, so I carefully pulled through a drive-thru to grab a really late lunch or early dinner, depending on your point of view. Glancing at my watch, I saw I had just enough time to get back to the firm before Blane showed up and I had to leave for my shift at The Drop.

I wondered how Clarice was doing, if she was feeling any better. Dipping into my purse with one hand, I pulled out my cell phone.

As I flipped it open, I saw I had several missed calls from an unknown number. Then I realized I'd forgotten to take my ringer off silent. Crap.

I called Clarice, who was feeling better and said she'd be back at work tomorrow. I was disappointed that I would have to go back to seeing Diane on a regular basis rather than Blane, but hid it under a cheerful tone and said I'd missed chatting with her.

It was after five when I finally got back to the firm's parking lot, my hands hurting from gripping the steering wheel so tightly in the bad weather. I was disheartened that I hadn't come up with anything today by visiting Stacey and Ryan.

Mulling this over, I got out of the car, carefully watching where I stepped as I clutched the door for support. I really didn't want to end up on my ass in the snow. Turning, I locked the door and pushed it closed. Abruptly I found myself spun around, my back hitting the car hard and my upper arms gripped forcefully by strong hands.

"Where the fuck have you been?" Kade's furious words brought me up short and I stared into his livid face, only inches from mine.

"I'm . . . I'm sorry," I stammered, "I had some errands to run. And you were sleeping. I didn't want to wake you."

"Errands that took all fucking day?" he bit out.

"It's the weather," I protested. "Traffic is horrible. I didn't mean to be gone so long." Which was actually true.

"I had to lie," Kade growled, "and normally, I wouldn't care. But I had to lie to Blane when he called to check on you."

His eyes sparked with blue fire as he leaned closer. "I detest lying to my brother," he hissed angrily.

"Then don't," I retorted, sick of him yelling at me. I pushed away from him, but he grabbed my arm, jerking me to a halt.

"If you pull something like that again," he softly threatened, "I'll save someone the trouble and kill you myself."

I wisely kept my mouth shut. As angry as he was, I believed every word he said.

"Let's go," he said, abruptly stepping away but maintaining his tight grip on my arm, pulling me along with him.

"Wait!" I said, slipping in the snow as I tried to keep up with him. "Where are we going? I wanted to see Blane."

"Blane can't come," Kade said curtly, not slowing down. "He said he'd call later."

I followed him to his car, surprised when he unlocked it and pushed me none too gently into the passenger seat.

"What are you doing?" I asked when he climbed behind the wheel. "I can take my car and you can follow me."

"Forget it, princess," he said, "I don't trust you."

"You can't just leave my car here!" I exclaimed, appalled that his intentions appeared to be just that.

"No one will steal it, if that's what you're worried about," he replied derisively.

I fumed in silence, unable to do anything about him leaving my car. Now I was without my own means of transportation. I didn't know how I was going to check on the other two people on my list—Bowers and Freeman.

I refused to speak the entire way to my apartment, jumping out of the car the moment Kade stopped. I was halfway up the stairs when I was picked up bodily and thrown over Kade's shoulder, knocking the wind out of me.

"What the hell?" I yelled, grabbing on to his leather jacket as the ground swung wildly under me.

"If you're not going to wait for me to play bodyguard," Kade said calmly as he climbed the stairs, "then I'll have to keep doing things my way."

"I. Don't. Want. A bodyguard," I gritted out.

Kade swung me back onto my feet outside my door. "Then we're in agreement," he sneered, "because I don't want to be one. Now give me your keys."

I glared at him, groped for my keys, and handed them over with ill grace. One corner of his mouth curved up in a smirk, which I longed to wipe off his face. Pushing me into the corner of the building, which was sheltered from anyone who might be watching, Kade unlocked my door, pulling his gun before he went inside.

I waited, the toe of my boot shoving at the snow as I wondered how long I'd have to endure this arrangement. I had to figure out who was doing this, not only for my continued existence but also for my mental health.

As I fidgeted, I saw that the mailman had left a small package for me. Scooping it up from the ground, I brushed the snow off it. I hoped whatever was inside wasn't ruined now from sitting outdoors.

Kade came back, motioning me inside with a jerk of his head. I brushed past, trying not to touch him. I hurried into my bedroom, closing the door gratefully behind me. I leaned against it with a sigh. I had to talk to Blane tonight, get him to make Kade leave.

I tossed my things on the bed and pulled off my boots and slacks, which were now wet at the hems. I heard the shower turn on in the bathroom. Kade must've decided to make himself at home, I thought with annoyance. The package caught my eye and I climbed onto my bed to open it. I rarely received packages in the mail and I wondered who had sent it.

I examined the outside carefully, but there was no return address. With a shrug, I tore open the tape and opened it. Inside was another little white box with a lid. Bemused, I tipped the packaging and the lid fell off, the contents tumbling out onto my palm.

It was a bloody, human eye. For a moment, I just stared at it in stunned horror, the gelatinous mass staring back at me. Then I started screaming, dropping the eye and scrambling off the bed. Blood was on my hand and I frantically swiped at my shirt. I couldn't stop screaming.

Seconds later, my bedroom door crashed open and Kade came tearing through, his gun in his hand. His eyes fixed on my shirt and a second later he stood in front of me.

"Kathleen, what happened?" he asked urgently. "Where are you hurt?" His eyes examined me, searching.

I couldn't process his words, my mind in turmoil. I'd stopped screaming and now stood numbly, tears wet on my cheeks. Wondering why Kade thought I was hurt, I glanced down, seeing the blood smears on my shirt.

"Get it off! Get it off me!" I sobbed, yanking my shirt over my head and throwing it away. My knees gave out and I slid down the wall to the floor.

"Kathleen, talk to me!" Kade demanded, crouching down next to me. "Are you hurt?"

I shook my head. "The blood's not mine," I said hoarsely. "It's from the eyeball."

"From the what?" He looked confused. I wordlessly pointed to where I'd flung the jellylike blob.

Kade got up and I watched him retrieve the box and the eye. He examined both, returning the eyeball to the box, then reached into the packaging and pulled out a folded piece of paper. Opening it, he read it, then folded it back up and returned to where I still sat huddled on the floor, knees pulled tightly to my chest.

"What did it say?" I asked. Of course there was a note. When had this freak not left a little love note?

Kade wordlessly handed it to me. With shaking hands, I unfolded the paper: *Kirk—your girl's baby blues are next. I'm always watching.*

Nausea bubbled inside of me and it took a great deal of effort to swallow it down. Tears blurred my vision again but I blinked them back. How dare this bastard threaten me? I should feel angry, furious at what he was doing. And I would be, just as soon as I got my terror under control. After all, it wasn't every day a girl got an eye in the mail.

Kade took the paper from my numb fingers as he sat down next to me, his back against the wall. Setting his gun on the floor, he pulled my unresisting body into his arms. Distantly, I noticed his skin was wet, his jeans pulled on hurriedly and not even fastened. He must have been in the shower already when I'd started screaming.

"You all right?" he asked after a few minutes of us just sitting there. His hand slid comfortingly up and down my back.

I nodded. "I'm fine," I said. I wanted to throw up whenever I saw that eyeball in my mind, which was every time I closed my eyes, and my entire body was still shaking, but other than that, I was perfectly fine, thank you very much. "Sorry for the screaming." From the little I knew about Kade, he wasn't one with a lot of patience for hysterical women.

"You're entitled," he replied evenly.

I thought I should probably move but couldn't make myself. Pathetic that all it took was a strong, capable man holding me to make me feel safe, but there you have it. I didn't want to give that up. My courage had taken a beating the past few days.

I tipped my head back so I could look up at Kade, who obligingly looked down at me as I lay pressed against his side.

"Thanks for being here," I said. I meant it. It would have been much worse if I'd been alone when I opened the box.

His mouth tipped up at one corner. "No problem," he said.

I smiled a little. Another truce would be good. I couldn't handle the terror of wondering what this deranged lunatic would do next while also fighting with Kade.

Kade brushed my hair back from my face and our gazes collided. The deep blue of his eyes momentarily robbed me of breath and I couldn't look away. I became uncomfortably aware that I was only wearing my bra and underwear. His hand still slid up and down my back, but the touch wasn't so much comforting now as it was a caress. His chest was lean, hard sinew under my hands and my gaze caught on a droplet of water that slowly trailed down his neck to his chest, following the ridges of his abdomen. I jerked my eyes back up to his, their blue depths seeming to burn now as he looked at me. His gaze dropped to my mouth.

"You know, if I didn't know what a shitload of trouble you are," he drawled lazily, "I might be persuaded to get the wrong idea." His hand dropped down my back as he spoke, sliding over the thin satin fabric of the panties I wore.

I jumped up as if I'd been burned, my cheeks flaming in both embarrassment and anger. Kade's gaze leisurely wandered over my body and I practically ran to my closet, throwing a robe on to cover my nakedness.

"You're vile and repulsive," I spat at him as I belted the robe. I was furious at his insinuations.

"I'm not the one throwing themselves at me," he protested mildly, another smirk on his face.

"Throwing themselves?" I spluttered, rage making me nearly incoherent. "You bastard! And to think I thanked you for being here!"

The smirk remained on his face as he got to his feet. I wanted more than anything to see that smug grin disappear. Looking around, I grabbed the first thing I found, a scented candle, and launched it at his head.

He dodged it easily and my groping hand found something else, I didn't even look to see what it was before I threw that, too. My anger burned white hot, and with each projectile I threw at him, I felt better. Kade suddenly came at me through the barrage and I found myself pressed against the wall, my arm pinned above my head. His grip was like iron around my wrist as he loomed over me.

By the look on his face, it probably would have been smart for me to be afraid. But I wasn't. Fury still burned inside, its flames banked but not doused.

"Enough," he ordered.

"Fuck you," I snarled.

His lips twitched at my defiance. He moved his face even nearer to mine, our lips inches apart.

"You feel that?" he nearly whispered, his voice low and intent. "You feel that rage inside? Burning hot in the pit of your stomach?"

Confused, I hesitantly nodded. What was he doing?

"That's what's going to keep you alive," he said. "Hold on to it. Fear will only sign your death warrant. Stay mad, princess."

His lips brushed my forehead before he abruptly released me. I watched in stunned silence as he grabbed the offending box and note, and then left the room, closing the door behind him.

CHAPTER SEVEN

I stood there and stared at the closed door for a full minute before I could wrap my head around what had just happened.

Kade infuriated me even as he bewildered and perplexed me. I didn't understand. One minute, he acted as though he hated the very sight of me. The next, he was comforting me and kissing me on the forehead. Which was real?

My fingers absently touched the place where his lips had brushed my skin. Memories I had deliberately pushed to the back of my mind sprang forward.

Kade gently washing my cut and bruised feet in Chicago. Kade's arms around me as he rested his head in my lap. No.

I shook my head, trying to dislodge the images. I didn't want to think about that night. It had meant nothing. I shouldn't try to pretend that Kade didn't actively dislike me and want me out of Blane's, and consequently his, life. No matter how much it depressed me to know my boyfriend's little brother hated me, there was nothing I could do about it. There wasn't time to think about it anyway. I had to get dressed or I was going to be late for work.

Fifteen minutes later, I'd changed into my uniform. Winter wear was black pants and a long-sleeved shirt. Tonight I wore black on black, which suited my mood. Romeo Licavoli, owner of The Drop, made up for the lack of skin showing on his employees in the colder months by giving us low-cut V-neck shirts to wear. Joy.

I scowled at my reflection. Too much cleavage on display and all of it white. If I could afford it, I'd tan in the winter. The paleness of my skin contrasted markedly with the black fabric. Nothing I could do about that either. I hurriedly yanked my hair up into a ponytail and shoved my feet into my shoes. Usually during the holidays I would wear something Christmassy, like my Rudolph pin with the light-up nose or my Christmas tree earrings. Tonight I couldn't bring myself to fake Christmas cheer.

When I came out of my bedroom, Kade was just hanging up his cell phone. He'd gotten dressed and I noticed a suitcase sitting next to the couch. His gaze swung to meet mine. Even from the distance across my kitchen, his gaze was penetrating and I quickly looked away.

Kade's shifting demeanor toward me made me feel nervous and wary. I had no idea what he might do or say from one moment to the next. I didn't know if I could relax or if I should keep up my guard.

"I called a buddy of mine who works for the FBI," Kade said. "He's going to get the eye and note examined, see if there's anything we can find out about where it came from." I nodded as if this was a perfectly logical thing to do with a gouged eyeball one received in the mail, which I supposed it was. I swallowed heavily before asking, "The person . . . the eye . . . They're dead, aren't they." It wasn't really a question.

Kade got up and walked toward me, stopping when he was a few feet away. He reminded me of a cat, the way his body moved—fluid and silent. In contrast my body felt like a violin string pulled too tight.

"I'd say so, yeah," Kade answered.

I nodded wordlessly, my fists clenched as I struggled not to imagine the specifics of what had been done to the poor person whose body had been violated.

"I talked with Blane," Kade said, abruptly changing the subject. "He's had a bad day."

"That makes two of us," I said.

"He said he'd come by the bar tonight and that I'm to tell you to 'play along.'"

"Play along?" I repeated, confused. "What does that mean?"

Kade shrugged. "I have an idea but I'm sure we'll find out soon enough."

I didn't reply, wishing I'd had the chance to talk to Blane myself. I wondered if I'd get the chance to talk to him tonight when he came by The Drop.

"Is there anything else that's happened?" Kade asked, drawing my attention back to him. "Anything that you haven't told Blane?"

I hesitated, thinking about the possum. My answer must have shown on my face because Kade was suddenly much closer than I was comfortable with.

"Tell me," he demanded in a tone that I couldn't disobey.

"It was yesterday," I admitted grudgingly, "in the morning. I went out to my car to go to work."

"And?" Kade prompted when I didn't continue.

"And there was a dead possum," I said flatly. "Someone had slit its little throat and they'd used its blood to write in the snow on my car."

"And it said?" Kade's demeanor had changed, his face taking on that shuttered, expressionless look that was becoming too familiar.

"It said *Kirk's whore*," I blurted. I raised an eyebrow, adding sarcastically, "Maybe a friend of yours?"

Kade's eyes narrowed but I ignored him, ducking past to put some space between us. I didn't get very far. His hand snagged my arm tightly as he jerked me back toward him.

"You didn't think that was something you should've told Blane?" Kade snapped at me, his face inches away. His blue eyes blazed the way they had in my bedroom, only this time in anger.

"Since you haven't been around to notice," I sneered back, "Blane's been a little busy. The last thing he needs is for me to be laying more crap at his doorstep."

"Usually, I would agree," Kade replied, his voice cold. "But he's been shot at twice now, and I'm not willing to let him get hurt if you're the target."

"Gee, thanks for the support," I retorted, heavy on the sarcasm. "With a bodyguard like you, I might as well just slit my wrists."

I yanked my arm out of his grip, immediately fearing I'd left some skin behind, and pulled on my coat before snatching up my purse. I didn't wait to see if he followed me, I just headed for the door. Kade was there before I'd finished opening it, shielding me as we stepped outside.

To my surprise, Kade wrapped an arm around my waist, pulling me close to his side. I noticed his gun was in his other hand. I stiffened automatically, alarms going off inside my head at the press of my body against his.

"Is this really necessary?" I hissed, trying to push away from him. My efforts were futile, he was too strong and held me in place easily.

"Shut up and walk" was Kade's only response.

We made it to the car in this fashion and I climbed into the passenger seat. I didn't speak as he got in and drove to the bar, the silence thick between us.

Kade hustled me inside The Drop in much the same fashion. I was relieved to get away from him once the door had swung closed behind us.

"I have to leave for a while," Kade said. "Meet my friend and give him the package. What time do you get off?"

"I work until close tonight."

"I'll be back before then."

"That's just great," I said with a saccharine smile. "I'll be counting the minutes."

The look in his eyes said he didn't appreciate my sarcasm.

"Try to lose the bitchy before I get back," he said, and before I had a chance to retort, he was gone.

I was relieving the day bartender, Chad. He was new and had only been working at The Drop for a couple of weeks. About my age, he was married with a toddler daughter. I'd gotten the impression he and his wife had married right out of high school. He took classes at night at the local community college, studying for some kind of business degree, but I couldn't remember what he'd told me.

"Hey, Chad," I greeted him as I stowed my purse under the bar. My blood pressure was still up from my anger with Kade, but I strove to be pleasant. Being in a foul mood wouldn't help my tips tonight.

"Hey, Kathleen," he said with a smile. "How are you?"

"I'm good," I lied. "You?"

"Great," he said. "Business was good today. Holiday shoppers and all. Hopefully, tonight will be, too."

"Yeah, that would be nice." I sighed. Business had been slow the past couple of weeks and my bank account was dipping dangerously low. "You and Holly have plans tonight?" Holly was his wife.

"Nah," he said, "just studying for a final tomorrow. But we're planning on taking Amber to see Santa Claus Friday night at the mall."

Amber was their little girl, and from the pictures he'd shown me, she was as cute as could be, with little brown curls and soft brown eyes.

"That sounds like fun," I said with a smile.

Chad filled me in on the few customers who were currently in the bar. Tish and Jill were waitressing tonight and I saw them come in to relieve their daytime counterparts.

After Chad left, it was slow for a while, then people started trickling in with more frequency. A group of five guys came in and sat at a table near the bar. They ordered a few rounds of beer and were soon laughing loudly, and sounded like they were having a good time.

We were busier than Romeo had planned for and soon I was coming out from behind the bar to help Tish and Jill deliver drinks to tables. A lot of people were ordering food as well, so Jeff, the cook, was moving fast as he tried to keep up. I was glad I didn't have time to think, and my pocket was getting heavy with tips, which was a relief.

I was delivering another round of beers to the group of five guys when they decided to pay more attention to me than usual.

"Hey, sweetie," said a big guy, catching hold of my arm, "don't run off. We could use a little company."

I smiled tightly. This wasn't an uncommon occurrence for a woman bartender. I'd had my share of overzealous drunks coming on to me over the years.

"Sorry," I said, "gotta work, guys." I pulled my arm out of his grasp and turned away, only to have him wrap his arm around my waist and yank me toward him. The move nearly upset the table, which would've spilled all those beers and really pissed me off.

"Let me go," I said, still trying to be nice but firm.

"C'mon," he slurred, his breath rank with beer, "we'd have a real good time. You've got a helluva rack, babe."

The other guys hooted and laughed, encouraging the idiot drunk who had a hold of me. Over his shoulder, I caught Jill's eye and she nodded, hurrying away. When crap like this happened and it was only women on the floor, we'd go grab Jeff. Jeff used to be in the Army and was a big guy. He had tattoos up and down his arms and shaved his head. A cigarette often hung out of his mouth while he cooked, but Romeo was too scared of Jeff to tell him he wasn't supposed to smoke in the kitchen.

The guy who had a hold of me reached over and, to my shock, pulled the neckline of my shirt so he could leer down at my breasts. Enough is enough, I thought, grabbing one of the ice-cold beers I'd just delivered to the table. With a quick flick of my wrist, I threw the liquid into his face.

He howled in outrage, abruptly releasing me. The other guys at the table seemed stunned speechless before they started guffawing at their beer-soaked friend.

I turned to beat a hasty retreat but was abruptly caught up short when the guy grabbed my ponytail. I gritted my teeth in pain as he turned me back around, his hand moving to the back of my neck and squeezing.

"You fucking bitch," he snarled, his face contorted with rage.

"Hey, Bob, let her go, man," one of his buddies said uneasily. None of them were laughing now as they watched. I also noticed none of them tried to intervene. Cowards. Looked like chivalry really was dead. Bob's hand tightened on the back of my neck and I tried not to grimace, but it hurt. I pulled at his arm but couldn't budge him. Sometimes it really sucked to be a woman, I thought grimly. What I wouldn't give to be a guy, six two and built, right about now.

"You're hurting me, Bob," I managed, hoping one of his friends might show some sense before this got even uglier. And where the hell was Jeff?

"C'mon, Bob," another guy said, "let's go somewhere else, man."

"If I already got a beer dumped on me, I should at least get to cop a feel, right, sugar?" Bob sneered.

"Let her go and I might consider not breaking your arm."

I knew that voice. My stomach knitted itself into knots even as relief flowed through me. Bob raised his gaze to peer behind me.

"Fuck off," he said dismissively.

Things happened too fast then for me to follow. All I knew was that in the next few seconds, I was free of Bob's hold and Kade had him facedown on the table, his arm bent at an unnatural angle behind his back. Blood flowed freely from Bob's nose and glass lay shattered amid the beer spilled all over the floor. Damn it. Now I'd have to mop up the whole freaking mess.

Bob's friends scrambled away, their jaws agape, and I noticed several tables nearby had gone quiet as people turned to see the commotion. Bob's face was contorted with pain. Kade bent down to whisper something in Bob's ear.

"I . . . I'm sorry," Bob babbled to me in his prone position as blood dripped from his nose to the table. "I'm a . . ." He paused as Kade whispered again in his ear. "I'm a fucking asshole and—" Kade whispered again. "—and I won't bother you anymore. I swear." He howled as Kade pulled his arm up a bit farther while hissing something in his ear.

Kade stepped back and Bob's friends quickly gathered him up and hustled out the door.

The people who had stopped to stare started talking among themselves again, and I was grateful to not be the center of attention any longer. Just then, Jill and Jeff hurried up to me.

"What happened?" Jill asked anxiously, looking at the mess on the floor and the empty table. "Are they gone?"

"Yeah," I said, shakily pushing my hair back from my face. "They're gone. Thanks anyway, though." My ponytail had come loose, so I nervously redid it, wrapping the band tightly around my hair.

Jeff gave a grunt and returned to the kitchen while Jill went to fetch a mop. Grabbing my tray from where it had fallen, I crouched and started picking up glass, my movements quick and jerky. On top of making a mess for me to clean up, they'd also stiffed me for their tab. Assholes.

"You all right?"

I looked up. Kade had crouched down next to me. He looked remarkably calm for someone who had just broken a man's arm quicker than I could tie my shoelaces.

"I'm fine," I said, forcing my lips into a smile that felt like it might crack my face.

Kade's brow lifted in a silent question that I ignored, returning my attention to the mess. After a moment or two, Kade began helping me pick up the glass. Jill came back with a mop, and before long it looked like nothing had happened.

I returned to my position at the bar, having fallen behind now, and was glad to have plenty to do. It wasn't until after ten that things began to slow down as people drifted out the door.

Since it was quieter, I could hear the Christmas music playing over the speakers, and I quietly sang along to one of my favorites, "I Want a Hippopotamus for Christmas," while I washed glasses. Kade sat at the end of the bar, nursing a cup of coffee. We hadn't said anything else to each other and I avoided going toward him.

The door to the bar opened again and I glanced up to see if someone was going out or coming in. The glass I'd been drying slipped out of my fingers and back into the water, but I didn't notice. My gaze was fixed on Blane, who had just entered, and the tiny blonde attached to his arm.

I couldn't believe it. He was bringing another woman here? Right under my nose? I blinked, pressing my eyes tightly shut before reopening them. I had to be seeing things. But no, they were sliding into a booth together.

"Excuse me, bartender, can I get a refill?"

I automatically turned to see who needed me and realized it was Kade who had spoken. Grabbing up the coffeepot, I walked down to where he sat.

"Play along, remember?" he said in an undertone as I poured more coffee into his mug. My gaze snapped up to his. His head tipped ever so slightly toward where Blane and the girl sat. With a start, I realized what Blane and he had meant. This was a setup. So whoever was stalking me would think Blane and I had broken up.

The relief I felt was so strong. I should have been embarrassed. Instead, I was just absurdly glad. I gave Kade a quick nod to let him know I understood.

"Oh my God!"

I turned around to see Tish standing by the bar, her eyes locked on Blane.

"Isn't that your boyfriend?" she asked me.

"Yeah," I confirmed grimly.

"Who's the chick?"

"No idea."

"If I were you, I'd be getting my ass over there and finding out," she advised.

We both watched as Blane took the woman's hand in his and she laughed at something he said. Jealousy spiked hard inside me, even though I knew this was a setup.

"Stay here," Tish said suddenly. "I'll get the lay of the land. Be right back."

She snagged two glasses of ice water and I watched as she delivered them to Blane's table. She chatted with them for a minute, but I couldn't hear what they were saying. A few moments later, she was back.

"Well?" I asked, anxious to hear what she had found out.

"What an asshole," she snorted. "The girl said it's their first date. He's a jerk. Cheating on you and bringing her here, of all places. You guys have a fight or something? Is he trying to get back at you?"

"No," I said. "No fight. Maybe he just doesn't like doing the breakup scene. Figured I'd get the idea if he brought someone here." I infused my voice with bitter anger, which wasn't that hard.

"Whatever," Tish said, disgust evident in her voice. "He's a dick, my friend. Better off without him."

"Should I go over there?" I asked her.

"Depends," she shrugged. "You want revenge or dignity?"

Our eyes met in mutual agreement.

"Revenge," I replied evenly.

"Dish it up, girlfriend," she encouraged.

I took a deep breath and walked over to the booth. Close up, I got a better look at the girl. She was young and petite, with long blonde hair and blue eyes. She looked up at me expectantly, a smile on her face. I ignored her and turned to Blane.

"Hi, Blane," I said pleasantly, though I could feel my palms sweating. This felt much too real and I tried to keep in mind what Kade had said. "Who's your friend?"

"Kathleen," Blane said, looking uncomfortable, "I didn't realize you were working tonight."

I smiled tightly. "Well, I am. So tell me, who's your friend?"

"My name is Apryl," the girl interjected, holding out her hand to be shaken. "But it's not spelled like the month—it's a *y* instead of an *i*." Her voice was high and delicate, like the rest of her, and I automatically gave her hand a perfunctory shake.

Yet another girl who misspelled her name. My eyes slid to Blane's. Seriously? Where did he find them? Blane's lips twitched as he read my face and he quickly looked away.

"Are you a friend of Blane's?" Apryl asked curiously.

"Well," I said, drawing out the syllable, "up until about five minutes ago, I thought I was his girlfriend. But I'm guessing that's no longer the case, right, Blane?"

"Girlfriend?" Apryl looked at Blane, alarmed. "You never said you had a girlfriend!"

"*Ex*-girlfriend," Blane corrected, his poker face back in place. "We broke up."

"You got that right," I said, injecting anger in my voice. "We are *so* over."

I grabbed a glass of ice water and dumped it in Blane's lap. That made it twice in one night that I'd thrown a drink on someone, a personal record.

Apryl gasped, and I noted with satisfaction that so did Blane. I turned on my heel and hurried away before I started laughing at the look on Blane's face. Returning to the bar, Tish held up her palm and I high-fived her. I shot a quick glance at Kade. One corner of his mouth was twisted upward in a smirk and he raised his coffee cup to me, as if in a toast, before taking a drink.

Blane and Apryl left quickly after that. Blane's slacks were soaked, which I'm sure didn't feel that great once he was outside in the freezing cold.

Glancing at the clock, I saw there were only a couple of hours until close. The bar emptied as I did my prep work for the day shift tomorrow until only Kade, the waitresses, and I remained. We stopped serving food at eleven, so Jeff was gone, too.

"You saw the schedule for the weekend, right?" Tish asked me as she leaned against the bar.

"No," I answered. "Why?"

"Romeo added you to the schedule Friday," she said.

"What?" I exclaimed. "Damn it! I had plans!" Friday was Kandi's Christmas party.

Tish shrugged. "I know—me, too. He said there's supposed to be some big storm Saturday, so he thinks Friday will be busy."

Crap. I wondered if that meant Blane would skip the party or go alone, then decided I probably didn't want to know the answer to that question.

I headed back to the storeroom to get a few bottles to replenish the bar stock. It was quiet as I searched the shelves for what I needed.

"Kat."

I spun around, my heart in my throat at hearing a voice in the dark. I watched as Blane stepped out of the shadows and breathed a sigh of relief.

"Blane," I said, my heart still pounding, "you scared me to death."

"Sorry about that," he said, moving closer. The light was behind him, so I couldn't make him out clearly.

"What are you doing here?" I asked, confused.

"I just wanted to make sure you knew tonight wasn't real, that it was a setup," he replied, stepping into my personal space.

"Kade told me," I said evenly. In the back of my mind, I wondered if Blane had kissed Apryl good night, but there was no way I was going to ask. "She is very pretty."

"Not as pretty as you," he said quietly. His hand reached out, the backs of his knuckles trailing a gentle path down my cheek.

I had to hand it to him, he could sure deliver a line. "What a smooth operator you are," I said, only half in jest.

"Is that what you think I am?" he asked seriously.

"Aren't you?"

He didn't answer, lowering his head to kiss me. At the last second, an image of Apryl and Blane kissing flashed through my mind and I turned my head slightly. Blane's lips grazed my cheek.

As if he could read my mind, Blane whispered, "I didn't kiss her." His mouth moved to cover mine and this time I didn't turn away.

It was several minutes before we came up for air, and when we did, I was tingling from my head to my toes. If the speed of Blane's heartbeat beneath my fingers was any indication, he felt the same.

"I'd better go," Blane whispered against my skin, his mouth marking a trail down the side of my neck.

"I see the cold water didn't do any lasting damage," I teased him, the hard length of him pressing against me.

"Remind me not to piss you off," he said softly into my ear. His warm breath on my skin gave me goose bumps.

Blane tightened his arms around me, pulling me up to my toes as he pressed one more hard kiss to my lips.

"Stay safe," he whispered, then he was gone.

It took several minutes, and even more deep breaths, before I felt normal enough to return to the bar. Halfway there, I realized I'd forgotten the bottles I'd originally gone into the storeroom for and that I had to go back. When I returned and started stocking the shelves, Kade took a long look at me.

"Christ," he huffed in exasperation, rolling his eyes. "Blane couldn't stay away, could he." It wasn't a question.

I looked away, embarrassed that he could read the signs so easily on me.

"Blane doesn't usually do something so stupid," Kade snorted derisively.

My anger flared and I sprang to Blane's defense. "He made sure he wasn't seen," I protested.

"You don't know that," Kade said evenly. "And neither does he. It was a dumb move."

I looked away, grabbing a cloth to wipe down the bar.

"We're going to have to fix it," Kade said.

"How?"

Kade didn't answer and my insides twisted uncomfortably. Somehow I knew I wasn't going to like his method of "fixing" it.

"Ever pick up a customer, princess?"

I spun away, hoping he was joking, though the knot in my stomach said he wasn't. Sure enough, when it came time to close he held my coat for me, one eyebrow twitching upward and daring me to protest. I pressed my lips together and pushed my arms into the sleeves. Leaving him where he stood, I went to grab my purse from under the bar.

"Hey, girl," Tish said, sidling up to me and eyeing Kade as she shrugged on her own coat. "You, uh, taking a friend home tonight?"

"Um, yeah, I guess so," I said uneasily, then tried to cover it up with a fake smile.

"He's hot," she said appreciatively, looking at Kade standing some distance away, waiting for me. "I saw him staring at you the whole night. Not really your type, though." Tish knew I never picked up guys at the bar.

"Well, my type went home with another woman tonight," I said evenly.

"Can't argue with that," she said, then grinned. "Well, have fun. Be safe. And I want to hear all about it tomorrow night." She winked and left, the front door swinging shut behind her. I locked it and headed to the back, Kade at my heels. Before I could open the door, Kade stopped me with a hand on my arm.

"Try to make it look good," he said, "or at least, believable."

I didn't really know what he was talking about, so I just nodded and followed him out the open door. I locked it, then was utterly taken aback when Kade spun me around and pressed me against the wall, his arms on either side of my head, caging me.

"What are you doing?" I squeaked, alarmed. He was so near, I could smell the sweet leather of his jacket.

"Making it look good," he said evenly. "Pretend you like me and I'll do the same."

He bent down, nuzzling the side of my neck. The stubble on his jaw scraped my skin and I shivered. This was so not a good idea.

"Put your arms around my neck," he ordered softly.

Hesitantly, I obeyed, my hands clutching the supple leather covering his shoulders.

"Blane's not going to like you doing this," I hissed in his ear.

"Blane told me to keep you alive," he replied curtly, even as his hands dropped to slip inside my coat. I stiffened when they closed around my waist. "This nut job needs to think you and Blane are through, that you have no influence over him. So I'll do what I have to do."

I jumped when I felt him press open-mouthed kisses to the skin of my neck.

"Close your eyes," he whispered, his breath warm against my ear.

I squeezed my eyes tightly shut, praying this would be over soon. I couldn't say I appreciated Kade's attitude about doing what he had to do. My feminine pride stung. Was it that much of a chore to pretend to like me, I wondered grudgingly, then I wanted to kick myself for the ludicrous thought.

Kade's arms slid around my back and he pressed closer, insinuating a leg between mine. My pulse skittered at the warmth of his body, lean and hard and wrapped around me. His tongue touched the bare skin of my collarbone and I sucked in my breath.

Warm wetness marked my skin as his lips and tongue traced the edge of my shirt over the curve of my breasts. My heart hammered in my chest and I struggled to remember this was just an act, this was Blane's brother trying to keep me alive.

My fingers had a mind of their own, threading through his hair as his head bent over my breasts. The locks were as long and silky as I remembered them being. Kade's leg pressed against a very sensitive area between my thighs and I gasped. His hands moved to cup my ass and hold me against him and I was stunned to feel his erection pressing against my hip.

"You taste like cotton candy and smell like spring after a storm," Kade said so softly, his lips against my skin, that I nearly didn't hear him. Something inside of me, something that I'd denied existed after his cruel words to me last night, soaked up his words like a parched desert. An agonizing ache bloomed in my chest and I wanted to cry with relief to see just a small part of that Kade from Chicago, the one who had lain exhausted with his head on my lap. The one who had trusted me.

"Do you always melt for a man who'll fuck you up against a wall?" Kade whispered in my ear.

My eyes flew open. His words were a cold bucket of ice water that sent a stab of pain inside me. What a fool I was.

My fingers were still in his hair and I angrily fisted a hunk of it, tugging until he lifted his head and looked at me. His eyes burned into mine.

"I just closed my eyes and pretended you were Blane," I said, my voice like sugarcoated ice. I didn't examine why I wanted to hurt him back, I just knew I did.

Kade's jaw tightened, his eyes narrowing in anger. Inside I quaked, feeling much too vulnerable pressed this close to him, his hands still on me, the echo of what he'd told me still whispering through my head.

"And who do you pretend it is when it's Blane?" he sneered. My face drained of color as I stood there, unable to reply to his insult.

Kade's eyes bored into mine until I heard him curse under his breath, then say curtly, "Let's go." He abruptly stepped back and grabbed my hand, tugging me to his car. In moments, we were speeding down the road back to my apartment.

The silence in the car was stifling and I regretted immensely not talking to Blane about Kade while I'd had the chance. I could still feel the imprint of his lips on my skin, their ghostly afterimage mocking me.

"Where were you really today?" Kade broke the silence.

"What are you talking about?" I asked stiffly, playing dumb.

"Don't give me that crap about errands again," Kade said derisively. "I'm not an idiot, princess, and I want to know where you were."

I pressed my lips tightly together and turned to look out the window, refusing to answer. My eyes stung, and to my shock, I realized I was close to tears. I couldn't keep it up, this adversarial game with Kade, not when one minute his hands and mouth were on me and the next he was making me feel like a scheming idiot.

It wasn't until we had pulled into my apartment's lot and Kade was parking the car that I found the courage to say the words hammering inside my head.

"You can't stay," I blurted, still staring out the window. "Not with me."

"You don't get a say in this, princess," Kade dismissed.

He got out of the car, slamming the door behind him.

That set me off. I jumped out of the car, rounding it quickly to confront him.

"I absolutely have a say," I spat furiously, poking my finger into his chest for emphasis. "And I don't want you here. Tell Blane whatever you have to, I don't care, but you have to leave. I know that you couldn't give a shit what happens to me, and I know you don't want to be here. So just go already!"

His brow furrowed and his lips pressed together in a grim line, his eyes searching mine.

I turned and stalked to my apartment, looking back only once to see Kade staring after me. My apartment was a welcome respite and I closed and locked the door before sinking onto the couch.

I knew I had to call Blane, tell him that I'd thrown Kade out, and I wasn't looking forward to it. Instead, I took a shower.

The water masked my tears as I had a good cry. I felt I deserved it. I'd done the stiff-upper-lip thing for a few days now, had even resisted the temptation to drown my sorrows in booze tonight. The fact that I'd been in Blane's arms and then Kade's in the same night had nothing to do with my dejection, or at least that's what I kept telling myself. Even if it had been a ploy with Kade, I still felt guilty.

Throwing on a coat and boots over my pajamas, I took Bits outside. He was mercifully quick this time and we were back in my apartment without incident. I had noticed Kade's car was no longer in the parking lot. I wondered where he went, if he'd gone to Blane's.

I took a deep breath and picked up the phone, dialing Blane's cell. It rang four times, then went to voice mail. That was a little strange. He usually kept his cell by his bed, in case he got calls in the middle of the night. Being a lawyer, he sometimes got calls at all hours. Brushing it aside, I took a deep breath and waited for the beep.

"Hey, it's me," I said with forced cheer. "Listen, I know you wanted Kade to stick around, but that's just not going to work out, okay? Don't worry, though. I'm fine. I'm sure our little scene tonight threw whoever's watching offtrack. Hope you're okay. I'm going to bed. See you at the firm tomorrow." I hung up. I'd spoken too fast, betraying my nervousness, but there wasn't anything I could do about it now.

I fell into bed, tossing and turning before finally getting to sleep in the wee hours of the morning. I must have been tired, because I slept like the dead. When I woke up, I stretched and turned over. Blearily, I opened my eyes and looked at the clock.

"Holy crap!"

I sat straight up in bed and threw off the covers. I was already a half hour late for work. Diane was so going to kill me.

Jumping out of bed, I hightailed it into the bathroom and took a three-minute shower. Wrapping a towel around me, I hurried to the kitchen. Maybe if I started the coffeepot now, by the time I got dressed, it would be done brewing. I had to have my coffee.

I stopped short at the sight of Kade sitting at my kitchen table, sipping from a coffee mug and reading the paper.

He glanced up at me, his eyes taking a slow journey downward and back up, and I wished I wasn't standing there dripping wet with only a towel wrapped around me.

"What are you doing here?" I asked through gritted teeth, gripping my towel to my chest like it was a lifeline. I was quite sure I'd thrown Kade out last night and locked my door very securely. I had hoped he'd be two states away by now, or at the very least across town.

His trademark smirk lifted the corner of his mouth.

"You didn't think you could get rid of me that easily, did you?"

CHAPTER EIGHT

Actually, I thought I had," I retorted, ignoring my own self-consciousness at my lack of appropriate armor in front of Kade.

"Doesn't work that way, princess," Kade said, taking another sip of his coffee, "especially since you have my clothes." He waggled his eyebrows suggestively, then tipped his head to acknowledge the suitcase still sitting by my couch. I noticed he'd changed into a dark gray pullover that looked warm. His hair was also slightly damp and he'd shaved. I wondered if he'd made himself at home in my shower while I was sleeping.

"I'm late for work," I said stiffly, not moving from where I stood.

"Don't worry about that," Kade said with a dismissive wave of his hand. "I called in sick for you."

"You called in for me?" I said in disbelief. "You . . . you can't do that!" Not to mention that if Diane caught wind of the fact that I wasn't really sick, she'd fire me on the spot.

"Already done. Blane thought it was a good idea," he added, "if that helps at all. Though if prior experience has taught me anything, it's that you have a mind of your own."

Water still streamed from my hair and a heavy drop trailed down my neck and disappeared between my breasts. Kade's eyes followed the path.

He suddenly cleared his throat, snapping the paper and returning his attention to it.

"Get dressed," he said flatly. "Then we'll talk."

I didn't argue but skittered back to my bedroom, where I pulled on a pair of dark jeans and a navy-blue turtleneck. I blew my hair dry, then twisted it up into a knot and pinned it. I surveyed myself critically in the mirror. My hand reached for my mascara, then stopped. If I had a day off, I usually didn't wear makeup. No need to wear it today just because Kade was here.

"Right," I muttered.

Going back into the kitchen, I avoided looking at Kade as I poured myself a cup of coffee, dumping in my usual amount of half and half and sweetener. Turning, I sat down at the table, still not looking at Kade. Instead, I saw a piece of paper lying in front of him. Reading it upside down, I realized it was the paper I'd had in my purse with the names of the witnesses I was investigating and their addresses.

"How did you get that?" I asked indignantly, reaching for the paper only to have Kade snatch it up.

"Since you weren't being very . . . cooperative," he replied dryly, "I thought I'd see for myself where you'd been yesterday."

He held up the paper so I could see my writing on it.

"Who are these people?" he asked.

I considered not answering but thought twice. Kade hadn't stopped me from going to Chicago when I had been trying to foil TecSol. He was only here because of Blane—he really didn't care what happened to me. It was doubtful he'd be overly concerned with what I had been doing.

"They're people I thought might know something about who is behind these threats to Blane," I said with a shrug.

"And how would you know that?"

"I read through the case," I answered. "Ryan Sheffield is the JAG officer who testified the other day for the prosecution. Stacey Willows is the fiancée of the man who commanded the mission. Ron Freeman and Brian Bowers are SEALs on that same mission with Kyle."

Kade silently raised an eyebrow.

"I figured whoever was doing this might be someone they knew," I explained. "Someone who disagreed with what they'd done and had the know-how and skills to fire that sniper shot at me."

"How unexpectedly intelligent of you," Kade said. "Color me shocked."

My face flushed but didn't want to get into it with him, so I didn't bother replying to his wisecrack.

"You went to see these people yesterday?" Kade asked when I was silent.

"Two of them," I answered. "Stacey Willows and Ryan Sheffield. I was planning on going to see Ron Freeman and Brian Bowers today."

"Well, you can mark Bowers off that list."

"Why?"

"Blane told me he's disappeared," Kade said grimly. "No one can find him. That makes him look guilty, makes Kyle look guilty, and makes things a hell of a lot harder for Blane. But that just leaves us Freeman to visit."

He pushed himself away from the table and stood, folding and pocketing the piece of paper. I remained sitting, stunned.

"Really?" I asked. Was he offering to help me?

"Really," Kade said evenly, bending over me and bracing his hands on the arms of my chair. "See how easy that was? If you'd just told me this yesterday, you wouldn't have pissed me off, resulting in that rather unpleasant scene when you got back."

His face was close to mine, his eyes startlingly blue and framed by dark lashes that a woman would kill for. My mind unwittingly flashed back to last night in the alley as I looked at him. His smirk faltered for a fleeting moment, then it was back.

"I'm hungry. Let's eat first."

Kade abruptly moved away and I released my breath in a rush. He opened my refrigerator and peered inside.

"Don't you eat?" he asked, his head still inside the refrigerator.

"Of course I eat," I replied, flustered. "I just haven't been to the store lately, that's all." That, and food was the easiest expense to cut when funds were tight.

"Come on," he said, shutting the fridge and shrugging into his leather coat. "I know a great breakfast place."

I was putting my coat on when my phone rang. I picked it up.

"Hello?"

"Hi, Kathleen," a woman's voice said. She sounded vaguely familiar. "It's Gracie."

Gracie! I hadn't spoken to her for weeks. She had been friends with Sheila, working in the same business as a high-priced call girl. Gracie and I had also become friends of sorts, and she'd helped me find the people responsible for killing Sheila by helping me gain entry to a private party hosted by the escort service.

"It's good to hear from you," I said as those thoughts flashed through my head. "How are you doing?" I sank down onto the couch, noticing as Kade rolled his eyes at the delay. He began examining the ornaments on my Christmas tree.

"I'm good," Gracie said, then added, "I just wish I could've called you under better circumstances."

"What do you mean?" I asked anxiously. "Are you okay?"

"I'm fine, don't worry," she said hurriedly. "It's actually you that I'm worried about."

"Why?" Surely, Gracie didn't know about what had been going on?

"I was given a message to deliver to you," Gracie said hesitantly, "and I'm really sorry."

"What is it?" I asked, a sense of foreboding creeping over me. "What's the message?"

"It's from Simone," Gracie said, naming the madam of the escort service. "She says you owe her five thousand dollars in expenses for participating in that party."

"Five thousand dollars?" I said in disbelief, suddenly glad I was sitting down. "For what?"

"Clothes, accessories, the hair and makeup, plus the fee for attending," Gracie replied. "She said she wants to be paid in full by Saturday, or else she's going to send someone to collect it."

I couldn't speak. I didn't know what to say. There was no way I could come up with that kind of money, period, and certainly not with only two days' notice.

"I know it sounds awful," Gracie said anxiously when I didn't respond.

"Why so much? Why now? It's been weeks." Once I found my voice, the questions came flooding out.

"I don't know," Gracie replied. "I wish I had a better answer for you, but she did offer an alternative."

"What's that?" I asked carefully, afraid that I knew what the answer was going to be.

"She said you could work it off," Gracie said.

"What?"

Kade winced at my high-pitched shriek.

"It's a good offer. She even said that it would be just one job and she'd call it even."

"That's a 'good offer'?" My voice was thin and strained. Out of the corner of my eye, I noticed Kade had stopped examining the tree and was now watching me.

"Yeah," Gracie replied, "it really is. You should take it. You really don't want her to send someone after you for the money, trust me. It won't end well."

I swallowed hard. No, I was sure it wouldn't end well if Simone sent her personal collection agents for me.

"Listen," Gracie said, "just go to the Crowne Plaza Hotel Saturday night at eight o'clock. At the desk, ask for Bernard and tell him you're Lorelei. He'll give you a room key."

"Um, okay," I said numbly, my mind reeling in shock at this turn of events. Perhaps some of my dismay must have come through the phone line, because when Gracie spoke again, she was soothing.

"It'll be all right, Kathleen," she said kindly. "A few hours' work and this'll all be behind you."

"Yeah, sure," I said, knowing there was no way I was going to do it but anxious to get off the phone. "Thanks for letting me know, Gracie. I'll talk to you later."

"Okay," Gracie said unhappily. "Sorry, Kathleen."

I hung up the phone, staring off into space as I contemplated my new predicament. Well, I supposed I might be dead by Saturday, so the appointment could be moot anyway.

"Who was that?" Kade asked.

I turned to look at him and saw he was holding one of the ornaments, a large golden locket.

"Gracie," I replied. At his questioning look, I explained the conversation. Kade listened, opening the locket and examining the picture inside as I talked.

"I fail to see the problem," he said curtly when I'd finished.

My anger rose quickly to the surface. "Of course you wouldn't," I snapped. "Just another day in the life, right? You think I sleep around already, so why not get paid for it?"

He turned to meet my angry gaze.

"I meant that I'm sure Blane will pay whatever the cost to make sure you don't have to fuck somebody on Simone's orders," he said evenly.

I flushed in embarrassment at his crudeness, though I supposed there was no sense in sugarcoating it. I shook my head.

"I'm not asking Blane for that kind of money," I said flatly.

"Don't be ridiculous," Kade snorted. "It's not like he doesn't have it."

I just shook my head again. It was pointless to try to explain to Kade why I couldn't ask Blane for the money. It would be humiliating, demoralizing. There was no way I was going to do it. I'd just have to figure out a way to get the money on my own, or find some other way out of it. For a moment, I half expected Kade to ask me why I didn't just pay Simone using the money he'd left for me. I didn't want to tell him how I had sent nearly every dime to the bill collectors. No doubt he'd roll his eyes and tell me what an idiot I was.

"I thought you were hungry," I said, changing the subject and shoving my newest problem to the back of my mind. Getting to my feet, I grabbed my purse. "Let's go."

Kade didn't follow and I realized he was still studying the ornament in his hand.

"Your parents?" he asked, looking inside the locket.

I stepped up to him and peered down at it. The picture had been taken before I was born, my parents posing together in front of a fireplace. They looked happy. It had always been my favorite ornament. Seeing it now was both nostalgic and poignant.

"Yes," I answered, taking it from him and carefully replacing it on the tree.

"Where are they?" Kade asked. "Where are you from, anyway?"

I realized with some surprise that Kade actually knew very little about me. It's not like we'd ever had the getting-to-know-you conversation. Our relationship, if you could call it that, had always been one of circumstances, not to mention hostile. "I'm from Rushville, Indiana," I answered. "And they're no longer with me."

I looked up at Kade, whose expression had turned very serious as he studied me. I gave him a tight smile.

"Ready?"

Kade drove us to a café I'd never been to, outside of downtown but only a block off Meridian. It was crowded and we took two of the remaining seats at the bar, the tables in the small restaurant all being occupied. There were several complex-looking coffee machines behind the counter and the smell of coffee hung heavy in the air. The friendly waitress gave us menus. Someone had hung Christmas lights from the walls and their multicolored gaiety made me smile.

I perused the menu and was taken aback. Breakfast was supposed to be cheap, but obviously this place wasn't aware of that concept. A cup of coffee alone was three dollars, a waffle nearly ten.

"What can I get for you?" the waitress behind the counter asked.

"Um," I stammered, reading the à la carte servings, "give me a sec."

"What about you?" she turned her attention to Kade.

"I'll have the house omelet with coffee," Kade said, handing the menu back to the waitress. She wrote that down and returned her attention to me.

"I'll have coffee and a plain bagel, toasted," I said.

Kade made a disgusted noise, grabbing my menu from me. "You can't live on that," he said briskly. "She'll have . . . the croissant French toast. That looks good." He handed the menu back to the waitress. "And you know what? Skip the coffee for both of us. We'll have two Bloody Marys instead."

The waitress wrote that down and hurried away.

"Why did you do that?" I asked, exasperated. The drinks alone were going to be nearly twenty dollars.

"Relax," Kade said. "You don't come to a place like this and just order a bagel. And I think if we're going to be spending the day together, some booze would help."
I couldn't say I disagreed with that last statement. His proximity alone had my nerves jangling. Something had shifted again between us, though I was at a loss to explain how or why. He was just . . . kinder. Sarcasm was his stock-in-trade, but the hard edge to his words was absent today. Still, I was careful not to let my guard down, certain as I was that if I did, he'd say or do something to hurt me again.

The waitress set our drinks in front of us, a long stalk of celery garnishing each glass. I took a careful sip of mine, delighted to discover that it had been made well. Being a bartender also meant that I was a bit of a snob when it came to my drinks.

We sat in a silence that wasn't uncomfortable. I realized the vodka did help and I breathed more easily. After a while, our food arrived and the smell of the French toast made my stomach growl. I couldn't remember when I'd eaten last.

The first bite was heavenly, nearly melting in my mouth. The maple syrup was warm and rich. My eyes slid shut in appreciation. Yum.

"Good choice?" Kade asked, eyeing me as I ate. I nodded, my mouth too full to speak. For a fraction of a moment, his mouth curved in what looked like a genuine smile.

"Want to try?" I asked, scooping a bite onto my fork and holding it toward him. I assumed he would take the fork from me, but instead he opened his mouth expectantly. Surprised, I fed the bite to him, watching with too much interest as his lips closed around the morsel and took it from the silver tines.

"Too much syrup," he said with a grimace.

"There's no such thing," I contradicted with a laugh, taking another bite of my apparently too syrupy French toast.

We ate for a while in silence, and after my plate was clean, I leaned back with a sigh of contentment. I loved breakfast—it was my favorite meal of the day—but I didn't often get to eat it out. This had been a rare treat.

Kade had finished before me and now toyed with the celery in his glass as he leaned on the counter. The waitress took away our empty plates and I sipped my Bloody Mary.

"Why didn't you come home for Thanksgiving?" I asked quietly.

In my peripheral vision, I saw Kade turn to look at me, then look away.

"I was working," he said noncommittally.

I wasn't surprised at the nonanswer. "Well, you're going to stick around for Christmas, aren't you?"

Kade shrugged.

I turned my stool toward him. "You have to," I said earnestly. "I know Mona and Gerard want you there and I'm sure Blane does, too."

He gave a short huff of laughter and watched me for a moment. "And what about you?" he asked softly. His eyes dropped to my lips and my breath caught.

"You have some syrup—" Kade said, gesturing with his hand to my mouth.

My face heated in embarrassment. I had thought for certain he'd been thinking of something other than my table manners.

Before I could grab my napkin, Kade had reached out, his thumb swiping the skin near the side of my mouth before grazing across my bottom lip.

My eyes widened, then flew to his. My lip seemed to burn from where he'd touched me. Unnerved, I looked away, grabbing my drink and taking a long swallow.

"It doesn't matter what I want," I finally replied, answering his question. "I'm not family. You are."

The waitress came by with the bill and Kade paid before I could grab my purse and offer him some money.

"Thanks for breakfast," I said as we walked out.

"Thank Blane," he said with a smirk. "I'm sending him the bill."

A storefront across the street caught my eye and I stopped in my tracks. Kade looked questioningly at me.

"Can you give me a minute?" I asked.

"What for?"

"I just need to go in there"—I pointed—"do some Christmas shopping. Please?"

"All right, but ten minutes tops," he agreed grudgingly.

He walked me across the street and I went into the small art studio. Kade browsed around the front while I went to talk to the man behind the counter in back. He was very helpful and within my allotted ten minutes, my mission was successfully completed.

"Ready," I pronounced to Kade who was staring at a print on the wall. He didn't immediately respond, so I turned to see what he was studying so intently. It was a Picasso print of a woman holding a child. I read the small description on the wall and saw it was entitled *Maternity*. I suddenly remembered how Kade's mother had passed away when he was only six. With a pang, I wondered if Kade was thinking of her.

"It's lovely, isn't it?" I said quietly as I stood beside him. I wasn't usually a Picasso fan, but this was indeed beautifully done, capturing the quiet emotion with bold strokes of the brush.

My words seemed to break through Kade's reverie and he turned toward me. To my disappointment, his face was a blank mask.

"Are you done?" he asked, and I realized he really hadn't heard me when I'd said I was ready to go. I nodded and he held the door for me as we walked back out into the cold winter morning.

The sun was shining today, casting a blinding glare off the snow. Kade pulled out a pair of sunglasses and put them on, making me wish I'd thought to bring mine. I observed him out of the corner of my eye, grudgingly admitting how good he looked. His black hair, black coat, and sunglasses made him striking. I saw more than one woman turn for a second look as we walked past.

I cleared my throat, searching for something to say. "So, can you tell me what it is exactly that you do?" I asked as we reached the car.

"I could tell you," Kade replied, "but then I'd have to kill you."

I made a face at him and rolled my eyes. "Isn't that line a little overused?" I said. "Even for you?"

"Ouch," he said. "I must be losing my touch if you think that was a line." He unlocked and opened the passenger door for me.

"You don't scare me, Kade," I retorted, turning toward him and crossing my arms defensively.

I nearly jumped out of my skin when he was suddenly right in front of me, arms imprisoning me as they braced against the car. He bent down so our faces were separated by mere inches.

"You sure about that, princess?"

His words weren't tinged with the usual sarcasm—instead they were low and threatening, and in that moment, I could see in him a man who could kill in cold blood. I swallowed hard, searching in vain for his blue eyes behind the opaque lenses. All I could see was my own pale reflection. My pulse raced, and I didn't know if it was because of his proximity or if, indeed, I feared him—maybe both.

"Do you want me to be?" The question fell out without my even considering the words.

We stood in that unmoving tableau in the frosty morning air. I don't know what possessed me, but I found myself reaching tentatively to remove his sunglasses. I expected him to stop me at any moment, but he let me take them off and I could see his eyes again.

I was astonished at the vulnerability in his gaze, as though he were grappling with something that deeply affected him. I wanted to reach out, to comfort him, in spite of the incongruity of the thought. I wondered if what Kade chose to do for a living hurt him more than he wanted to admit.

The moment was gone as abruptly as it had come. In the flicker of an eye, Kade had snatched his glasses out of my hand and walked away.

"Get in," he ordered, not looking to make sure I obeyed as he rounded the car to the driver's side. Nonplussed, I hurried to do his bidding.

As I quickly buckled my seat belt and Kade started the car, I wondered who was the real Kade. He seemed an enigma that I couldn't figure out. I couldn't predict his mood or his words. He could be as mean as a viper to me, his words cutting and cruel, then turn around and protect me like he'd done last night with the guys in the bar.

Kade headed out of town toward Ron Freeman's address. He lived a bit farther out than the other two I'd gone to see yesterday. My hands twisted nervously in my lap, the ease I'd found earlier in Kade's presence having evaporated.

"Stop it," Kade said flatly.

I jerked in surprise. "Stop what?"

"You're acting like I'm going to hurt you," he said, shooting a quick glance at me.

A slightly hysterical laugh bubbled from my throat. "And that would be a surprise how?"

He shot another look my way, his jaw tightening before he said, "I've never laid a hand on you and you know it."

"You don't have to," I said in a low, tight voice.

Our eyes met for a moment before he turned away. I broke the silence a few minutes later. "Why do you do . . . what you do?" I asked.

"You mean kill people for a living?" he shot back.

I gulped. "Is that what you do?"

He glanced at me, then back at the road. "I do what needs to be done. Last week I stopped a man from raping and murdering a fifteen-year-old girl. He'd done it before and gotten away with it. I just made sure he wouldn't be doing it again."

I shuddered, dismay filling me at the thought of that girl enduring something so horrifying. And yet, "But you can't be judge and jury," I said quietly.

"Why not?" he retorted. "Who else was going to save that girl? Or the one after that?"

"I don't have an answer," I said, turning in my seat so I could see him. "I just know that it can't be good . . . for you . . . for your soul . . . to do that."

We had pulled into a small subdivision now and Kade ignored me for a moment as he navigated the turns. The car stopped in the driveway of a small ranch-style house and he turned off the engine. Kade shifted to face me.

"Don't try to rescue me, Kathleen," he said flatly, a bitter smile curving his lips. "I'm beyond saving." His face and voice were both as cold and remote as the arctic.

He was out of the car before I could even think of what to say. Numbly, I got out and followed him to the front door. We didn't speak as he pressed his finger against the doorbell.

After a moment, he pressed it again, but still no answer.

"I guess he's not home," I said with a shrug.

"I'll check out the back," Kade said. "You stay here."

Before I could protest, he was gone and I was left standing on the front porch. I looked around with a sigh. It was a decent neighborhood but older—one where the residents were either retired or worked during the day. Large trees dotted the street and I watched as a red cardinal landed on a bare branch nearby.

Impatient, I reached out and tried the handle on the door. To my surprise, it turned easily. Warily, I pushed it open. No alarm sounded and nothing tried to stop me, so I stepped inside.

It was silent, the kind of silent that made the hairs stand up on the back of my neck.

"Hello?" I called out. No one answered.

I proceeded cautiously past the dimly lit foyer. The house was darker than I had expected, considering how bright it was outside. There were few windows and those were covered with heavy drapes. I wondered where Kade was and thought maybe I should go open the back door for him. He used to be an FBI agent; he'd know what to do.

I moved past the empty living room, searching through the unfamiliar house for the back door. As I stepped into the kitchen, I stopped short in horror.

A man lay prone on the floor. And judging by the amount of blood around his body, he was no longer alive.

My stomach heaved, the smell of blood and death assaulting my senses. I stumbled backward, right into an unyielding body.

A scream was wrenched from my throat and I threw myself forward, away from the unknown person, terror licking at my veins. In an instant, I was spun around and a hand pressed over my mouth. My panicked gaze met Kade's. My relief was profound and I sagged against him.

"Are you all right?" he asked quietly, and I nodded.

He released me, carefully setting me aside as he approached the body. I stayed back—I certainly didn't need a closer inspection—and a moment later Kade returned.

"Gunshot wound to the head," he said grimly, "possibly self-inflicted, but I doubt it."

"Why?" I stammered. "Why would someone kill him?"

"No idea," Kade said curtly. "But we have to call the cops, and get out of here before we contaminate the scene any further."

Wordlessly, I followed him out of the house and back to the car. He turned it on so the heat would blow before he called the cops.

The next couple of hours were spent waiting for the police, then giving my statement several times. No, I hadn't known the victim. No, I didn't know who could have done this. No, I hadn't been here before.

In the middle of the officer taking down notes on what I said, I was distracted by a car squealing into the driveway. It had barely jerked to a stop before I saw a woman jump out of the driver's side and race toward the house, not bothering to shut the door behind her. A cop grabbed hold of her before she could make it past the police tape.

"Let me go! That's my husband in there!" she shouted.

I couldn't hear what the officer was saying to her as he held her back, but when the EMTs carried a stretcher through the door, a white sheet covering the figure on it, she sagged in defeat, sobbing.

My heart went out to her as the cop awkwardly patted her shoulder before moving away. She fell down to her knees in the snow, her face buried in her hands.

"Are we done here?" I asked the officer who had been interrogating me. He gave me a curt nod and I hurried over to the woman.

I sank down into the snow beside her and put my arms around her. She didn't say anything, she was crying too hard, but she leaned into me and allowed me to comfort her. Her gut-wrenching sobs tore at me until I, too, had tears leaking from my eyes on her behalf.

After a few minutes, her sobs subsided and she pulled back to look at me. She was older than me, looking to be in her late twenties, with dark brown hair cut to her shoulders and brown eyes, now red rimmed and swollen.

I stood and helped her to her feet, ignoring the soaked denim of my jeans.

"Are you all right, Mrs. Freeman?" I asked. A stupid question—of course she wasn't all right, her husband was dead—but I didn't know what else to say. What else was there to say in a situation like this?

She nodded, brushing her face with her hands. "Call me Jean," she said, her voice hoarse from crying. "Who are you?"

"My name is Kathleen Turner," I replied. "I'm the one who . . . found your husband. Me and . . ." I glanced around and caught sight of Kade standing a short ways away, watching us keenly. At my look, he walked over. "My friend and I found him," I finished.

"How? Why were you here?"

I decided now might be the only time I'd get to ask her anything about her husband's part on the mission in Iraq. "I was coming to ask your husband about Kyle Waters. The defense attorney on this case has been threatened and I thought there might be something your husband knew that could help us."

My words provoked a noticeable reaction from her. Her pale face drained of what little color remained and her eyes widened.

"I can't talk about it," she said, stepping back from us.

"Please," I implored her, realizing she knew something. "Whoever killed your husband might be after me and someone I . . ." My words stumbled and shied away from what I'd been about to say. ". . . care about," I continued. "If there's anything you know that could help me, please, tell me."

Jean studied me for a moment, then Kade, who hadn't said a word as I'd spoken. I held my breath, hoping she'd tell us what she knew.

"I think Ron was being threatened," she said.

"What do you mean? Why would someone threaten him?" I asked.

"He started getting these phone calls," she replied. "He'd have to go out once he got them and he'd never tell me who they were from or where he went. But then he suddenly wanted to know where I was all the time. I couldn't even go to the grocery store without telling him."

"How long has this been going on?" Kade asked.

"A couple of months, more or less," Jean said, shrugging. "I kept trying to get him to tell me, but he wouldn't. He said to just trust him. That's when he changed his testimony."

"He did what?" I asked, surprised. It was the first I'd heard about this.

"Ron had said in his deposition that all four of the SEALs agreed the man was a threat. After the phone calls started, he changed his story and said that Kyle had taken it upon himself to kill the guy."

"Which version is the truth?" I asked.

"They all agreed," Jean said. "I couldn't understand why he was doing that, why he'd lie and hang Kyle out to dry, but he refused to talk to me about it and he made me swear not to tell anyone. He told me our lives depended on it."

"If I were you," Kade said, "I'd leave town for a while. Go visit family, go on a vacation, whatever."

Jean nodded, her eyes wide with fear.

"Thank you," she said, backing up before turning and walking toward the police who stepped forward to question her.

I shivered, the cold and my wet clothes getting to me. Kade glanced at me out of the side of his eye.

"Let's get out of here," he said, grasping my elbow and guiding me to the car. I didn't resist, more than willing to get warm and leave this nightmare behind. It was already late afternoon and I had to get back for work tonight.

A few minutes later, we were headed down the highway, back to my apartment. I mulled over what Jean had revealed. Although it was an interesting twist, I didn't see how it fit with what was happening to me and Blane.

"Who would have had the power to make him change his story like that?" I asked, more thinking aloud than actually asking Kade. "And threaten him and his wife?"

"He was a SEAL," Kade replied. "It had to have been someone he believed would make good on the threats. SEALs aren't exactly easy to scare."

I silently agreed. "If they called him, maybe we could get authorization to pull his phone records."

"I can do that," Kade said, "and I won't even have to ask."

I remembered that he used to be in Cyber Crimes for the FBI, and realized he could probably hack his way into whatever he needed.

"Blane needs to know this," I said.

Kade changed direction, heading north toward the firm. "Agreed."

My heart leapt. I'd get to see Blane today after all, so long as he wasn't still in court when we arrived. I looked at my watch. He might be at the firm. Then I thought of something.

"Wait," I said, "what about Diane? I can't just go walking into the firm when I called in sick today. She'll fire me."

"You worry too much," Kade said, dismissing my concerns. "I'll take care of it."

I didn't know how he thought he was going to care of it, and I didn't want to ask.

Half an hour later, we were pulling into the firm's parking lot. I got out and nervously followed Kade inside. He walked quickly and I tried to keep up, rounding a corner for the elevators after him—and literally running into the one person I'd wanted to avoid at all costs.

"Diane," I squeaked.

Her eyes narrowed at me. "I thought you were home sick today," she said suspiciously.

"I am," I stammered. "I mean, I was. Then I was feeling better, so—"

"She's with me."

I looked up to see Kade had reappeared, his expression dark and forbidding as he looked down at Diane. Her eyes widened noticeably and she took a step back.

"Mr. Dennon, I didn't realize you were in town."

"I wasn't aware I was to report my comings and goings to you," Kade said with just enough sarcasm to make Diane flush in embarrassment.

"Of course not," she stammered, her gaze sliding to me. "And you say Kathleen is with you?" Her mouth tightened in a thin line and I could practically feel the anger and frustration emanating from her.

"It's Miss Turner," Kade corrected, "and her position here has changed. I'm promoting her and will notify you of her change in salary. Her comings and goings are no longer your concern."

"What?" Diane's shock would have been humorous if I wasn't feeling exactly the same way. I stared at Kade, my mouth agape. "Promoting her to what?"

Kade's lips twisted slightly, breaking the ice on his face but not his gaze when he replied, "Investigator. She'll report to me from now on."

Diane's mouth opened and shut like that of a fish gasping for air. Kade's fingers closed around my elbow as he tugged me with him. After a few steps, I looked back to see that Diane hadn't moved so much as a millimeter, still staring after us in stupefied shock.

Kade dragged me into the elevator and punched the button for the seventh floor. When I could muster a sentence, I said, "What was that about? How can you do that? How does she know who you are?"

Kade gave me a look. "You're a little slow on the uptake."

Suddenly, things clicked in my head. My eyes widened. "You work for Blane?"

"I bought in, actually," he corrected me, "when Gage was indicted. Thought it would be a good investment. I'm what you'd call a silent partner."

My mind reeled. "And you just . . ."

"Promoted you," he said, finishing my sentence for me. I was in shock and just looked at him. In less than five minutes, Kade had given me a new career and salary, and taken me out from under Diane's thumb.

"Surprised Blane hasn't done it himself," Kade mused.

I swallowed. "Well, maybe it didn't occur to him," I replied, wondering why I felt the need to defend Blane.

The doors opened and Kade stepped out, me in his wake. We walked into the foyer and I caught a glimpse of Clarice sitting behind her desk.

"You," Kade said, grasping my arm, "wait here." With a gentle yet firm shove, he pushed me down onto the sofa.

Exasperated, I popped right back up. "I want to come with you."

"You're supposed to be broken up, remember?" he said in exasperation. "Now wait here."

I rolled my eyes but kept silent, my lips pressed together so I wouldn't say what I wanted to say to him, which would have been foolish, considering his proximity.

"Unless you want to reenact last night," he smirked. A flash of the feel of his lips against my skin went through my mind and I took a hasty step back, hit the edge of the couch, and sat down heavily.

The smile disappeared from Kade's face as he watched me. "That's what I thought," he said. For an instant, he almost looked hurt, which made no sense, but then he was striding away toward Blane's closed office door.

Clarice used the intercom on her phone to tell Blane that Kade was there and I watched as he went in, shutting the door behind him.

"Kathleen," Clarice said, coming out from behind her desk, "would you mind manning the phone for me? I need to run downstairs and mail something."

"Sure, no problem," I said, taking her place at her desk while she left in the elevators.

I sat for a second, wishing that I was in Blane's office. Not only did I want to see him, I wanted to hear what Kade told Blane about what we'd been up to today.

"Where's Kathleen?"

I started in surprise, looking around for Blane, for that had been his voice. It took me a moment to realize that Blane must have left the intercom on in his office. I could hear his and Kade's voices coming from Clarice's phone.

"Relax. She's fine."

"What are you doing here?"

"Trying to figure out who's behind all this," Kade answered. "Thought you should know Ron Freeman is dead. Murdered. Professional hit, by the looks of it."

"You're kidding," Blane said.

"Wish I were," Kade replied. "But that's not the worst. Looks like someone was threatening him and his wife."

"That would explain his sudden change of heart on what he remembered from Iraq," Blane said grimly. "Kyle's ex-wife is testifying tomorrow for the prosecution. I wonder if she's being threatened as well."

"I can check it out," Kade said. "Where is she?"

I heard the shuffle of paper, then Blane read an address to Kade. Grabbing a scrap of paper, I jotted it down as well and shoved it in my pocket.

"I got another package today," Blane said, his voice turning cold. More rustling of paper. "Want to tell me why you were practically fucking Kathleen outside the bar last night?"

My breath caught and my palms grew sweaty. Suddenly, I was very glad I wasn't inside Blane's office.

"Nice photos," Kade said, seemingly unperturbed by Blane's anger.

"Kade," Blane said warningly.

"It was just a decoy, a ruse," Kade dismissed. "Hopefully that'll help throw off whoever's watching."

There was silence for a minute and I held my breath, waiting to hear what Blane would say. But he didn't speak next, instead it was Kade again.

"You know, judging by these photos, it looks like she was rather enjoying it. You might want to think about that before you put your life and career on the line for her."

"I could say the same to you," Blane said, his voice like ice.

"Knock it off, Blane," Kade replied, anger finally in his tone. "I refuse to become some cliché, you and me fighting over some chick. It's not worth it and you know it."

I heard the slap of papers on the desk and imagined Kade tossing the photos there.

"Whoever said we're fighting over her?" Blane asked in a deceptively calm tone. "Last she told me, she hates you."

I winced. I didn't hate Kade. Not really. I wasn't sure what I felt about him, but I didn't want him to think I hated him—an absurd notion, my not wanting to hurt his feelings. Kade had as much as told me he had no feelings that could be hurt.

"Well, there you go then," Kade said briskly.

"Even if she does hate you," Blane said evenly, "do it again, and you and I are going to have a problem."

"What do you care anyway? It's not like you're going to marry her. Isn't that role reserved for Kandi?" He said her name with disdain.

My stomach felt like lead as Kade said words I knew were true but still cut like razors.

"What's with the sudden interest in my love life, Kade? I thought I made it clear it's none of your business."

"When your relationships start putting expiration dates on your life, then it becomes my business."

"None of this is Kathleen's fault. I'd appreciate it if you'd try to remember that. She's not the enemy here."

"I'm aware of that. Which reminds me, since you've been too wrapped up in yourself to realize how miserable she is working for Diane, I promoted her."

"What do you mean she's miserable working for Diane? She never said anything to me about it."

"Please," Kade scoffed. "Diane knows you're sleeping with her and treats her like shit. You obviously weren't going to do anything about it, so I did."

"And you promoted her to what?" Blane asked. "Is she qualified for anything else?"

Ouch. That stung, no matter how true it was.

"I made her an investigator, reporting to me," Kade said flatly. "And your faith in her is staggering."

"It has nothing to do with faith," Blane shot back, "it's reality. She's smart, but she's young, inexperienced. What is she going to do as an investigator? And how much danger will that involve?"

"No more danger than you've already put her in. How long are you going to drag this out anyway? She's lasted longer than most of your relationships, I'll give you that, but it would no doubt be better for her if you ended it. Politics won't wait forever and neither will Kandi."

I barely breathed as I listened, nausea rolling in my stomach at the casual way Kade discussed Blane breaking up with me. I remembered what my mother had said about eavesdropping—you seldom heard what you wanted.

"Did I miss the part where we're telling each other how to run our lives?" Blane replied sarcastically. "Because if so, I certainly have some things I'd like to say to you."

"Speaking of changing the subject," Kade shot back, "did you check out junior? It wouldn't surprise me in the least if that little prick was behind this."

I remembered "junior" was Kade's pet name for James.

"He's got an alibi for where he was the other night," Blane replied. "So if it is him, he's working with someone."

"Thanks so much for watching the phones for me, Kathleen."

I started in surprise, spinning in my chair to see Clarice setting a pile of mail down onto the desk.

I looked at the phone with dismay. The voices had gone silent, though the light for Intercom was still lit. I was smart enough to realize it went both ways—if I could hear them, then they most certainly had just heard Clarice talking to me.

I heard a muttered curse—I couldn't tell if it was Blane or Kade—then I heard Blane say tightly, "Kathleen, please come in here."

The light on the phone went out.

CHAPTER NINE

I shot out of my seat, intending to make a quick getaway, but I wasn't fast enough. The door to Blane's office opened and Kade beckoned to me, the look in his eyes promising he knew what I was thinking, and that I wouldn't get far.

With a sigh of resignation, I reversed direction and headed for Blane's door. Kade smirked at me.

"You should learn what a mute button is if you're going to eavesdrop," he said quietly in my ear as I slipped past him.

"Thanks for the advice," I hissed back.

The door shut behind him, leaving me alone with Blane. I noticed he'd closed the blinds on the windows, shutting out any possible onlookers.

My stomach twisted. As much as my heart leapt in my chest to see Blane, the lead weight in my gut only grew. Kade had spoken as if it were a foregone conclusion that Kandi and Blane were meant to be together. I wondered how much longer Blane would toy with me before it was over. None of it came as a surprise, though it was a bit more than I'd bargained for to hear it spelled out in such plain, matter-of-fact words. I straightened my spine, determined to maintain my dignity.

"You summoned me?" I said flatly. I didn't know what to do with my hands, so I pushed them into the back pockets of my jeans. I kept my distance, though my eyes drank Blane in as he stood behind his desk. He'd discarded his suit jacket and tie, loosened his collar, and turned back the cuffs of his white dress shirt.

He frowned at my tone before rounding the desk to approach me. I took a wary step backward. Blane stopped in his tracks.

"You haven't done that in a while," he said grimly.

"Done what?" I asked, pretending ignorance.

In answer, Blane took another step and I couldn't resist the compulsion to inch back away from him. His face darkened even as mine grew hot.

"Why are you afraid of me again?" he asked.

"Don't be ridiculous," I snapped. "I'm not afraid of you." I wasn't sure how to feel at the moment, I just knew I was hurting. If he touched me, I might break down in tears, which was the absolute last thing I wanted. I needed to get away and pull myself back together.

He crossed his arms over his chest, regarding me silently.

"You heard what I said to Kade," he said quietly.

I shrugged, glancing away from him to study the wall over his shoulder.

"Kade is misinformed," Blane said. "I have no intention of going back to Kandi."

"It's none of my business." I pushed the words out past lips that felt numb.

"Of course it's your business," he shot back. "Do you think I'm just using you until I get bored?"

I didn't speak and didn't look at him. He'd just voiced the fear I wouldn't even admit to myself.

He cursed, then moved toward me so quickly I started in surprise. I stumbled backward, only to have his hands close firmly on my waist, holding me in place.

"After all we've been through, you'd still believe that of me?" His eyes searched mine, their depths the stormy gray I'd come to expect when he was angry.

"I don't know what to believe," I said, my voice hardly above a whisper.

He studied me, his lips set in a grim line.

"Believe this."

I barely had time to process the words before his lips touched mine. The familiar touch and taste of him was like a drug.

No. I couldn't let him do this. I knew I didn't stand a chance of guarding against him if he used my own body against me—my body that was even now straining toward his.

I wrenched my lips from his, turning my face away.

"No," I gasped, trying to squirm out of his grasp, but he was too strong.

Blane ignored my protest, his hands moving into my hair as he gripped my head, forcibly holding me in place as he kissed me again. My hands pushed against his chest, but it was like trying to move a wall of granite.

His lips moved against mine, their harshness gentled now, coaxing. I could smell his cologne and his own unique scent, spicy with an undercurrent of something darker, muskier. His skin was warm under my fingers, the heat of his body soaking through the linen of his shirt.

The rough pads of his thumbs brushed my cheekbones as he changed the angle of his kiss, his mouth slanting across mine. I tried to hold myself stiff, unaffected by his efforts. The warm heat of his tongue touched the seam of my lips, a gentle request. I gasped, sucking in breath, and his tongue surged inside my parted lips, taking advantage of my moment of weakness.

Blane took his time, stroking and exploring and beguiling me. My thoughts were fuzzy, incoherent. My bones melted as his arm curved around my waist, pulling my now submissive body fully against him. One hand threaded through my hair, his large palm cupping the back of my head.

Something seemed to crack open inside my chest as he held me, so tightly did his arm wrap around me to hold me close. If I allowed myself, I could almost believe I was something precious to him. But that path was dangerous; the near certainty of heartbreak loomed.

Blane lifted his head, his eyes now a brilliant green, his lips glistening and as swollen as mine felt. The air was thick with expectation and unsaid things.

"You're more to me than just a diversion," he said, his voice low and rough. "Do you believe me?"

I couldn't speak, afraid I'd give voice to all my fears and insecurities if I so much as released a single syllable. Did I believe him? I wanted to—too much so. Maybe that was enough. Hesitantly, I nodded.

Something close to relief flashed across his face, then was gone. His lips pressed against my forehead and my eyes slipped closed. It would be easy, too easy, to fall in love with Blane, and I was afraid I'd already passed the point of no return. He gathered me close, resting his chin on top of my head, and I savored how I felt secure and cared for in his arms.

"I have to go," I finally said, reluctantly pulling away.

"I think it would be a good idea for you to leave town for a while," Blane said, releasing me.

I gaped at him in surprise.

"It would be safer," he continued. "Kade can take you, go somewhere for a week or two, just until the trial is over."

"But that would leave you here alone," I protested. "They've been threatening you, too, Blane."

"I'll be fine," he said grimly. "It's you I'm worried about."

"Then we'll handle it together. I'm not running away."

"It may not be your choice," he said slowly, his jaw hardening.

"You'd force me to leave?" The very thought raised my hackles.

"If it gets any worse, then yes."

I shook my head, choosing to ignore his comment. I didn't want to fight. "I've got to get to work," I said, moving out of his arms.

"Remember the party tomorrow night," Blane reminded me. "Here's the address. You can meet me there." He grabbed a slip of paper off his desk and handed it to me.

My heart sank again. "I can't come," I confessed. "Romeo changed the schedule and I have to work."

"Damn it," Blane said in disgust, shoving a hand through his hair. "Why won't you quit that job?"

That hit my last nerve. "Because I need the money, Blane!" I exploded. "And it's great and it's nice that you want to help me, but that won't do me any good when this is over!"

He froze, anger emanating from him as he stared at me. His face was an unreadable mask, and I wished I could take back the words I'd spoken.

"I'm trying to tell you that I'm not going anywhere," he bit out, "and you already have me halfway out the door."

His words stung, the truth in them making me wince, so I lashed out. "Isn't that how you roll, Blane?" I snapped. "You think I don't know I'm just the latest in a very long line of women?"

"You're throwing my past up in my face?" In two strides, he was in front of me, his hand gripping my arm in a painfully tight grasp. I swallowed heavily as he loomed over me, his eyes flashing with fury. "I didn't know you then, Kathleen. What do you want from me?"

I tried to back up but couldn't. My heart pounded in fear, which only made me angrier. I knew he wouldn't hurt me, cowering was just instinctual. His anger was an intimidating thing.

"Nothing," I hissed furiously. "I don't want anything from you."

The door suddenly flew open. Both Blane and I looked to see Kade standing in the entry.

"Lovers' spat?" he smirked, but I noticed his eyes were serious as he took in the situation.

"I was just leaving," I said, more to Blane than Kade. I jerked my arm out of Blane's grasp. He let me go, his eyes locked on mine. I walked away quickly, casting one last glance back at Blane, who stood unmoving in the middle of the office, watching me walk out the door.

Kade said nothing as we walked to his car. Without a word, he tossed me my car keys. I looked questioningly at him.

"I think it's best if you have your own mode of transportation, just in case."

I nodded, grateful to get my car back. I drove to my apartment, Kade following me in his Mercedes.

He didn't speak until we were halfway up the stairs.

"Trouble in paradise?"

"Like you care," I muttered. Kade would probably turn a cartwheel if Blane and I broke up.

He took me at my word and didn't say anything further.

I found a note from Alisha taped to my door and was glad to read that she was home and waiting for me to bring Bits over. I walked him first before knocking on her door.

"How's your grandma?" I asked once I was inside.

It took a minute for her to answer since she was crouched on the floor saying hello to Bits as he jumped and licked her face. Eww. I knew where that dog's tongue had been and I certainly wouldn't want him licking my face, or any part of me for that matter.

"She's fine," Alisha finally replied, standing and taking the load of doggie toys from me. "I really appreciate you helping me out."

"No problem. Bits and Tigger got along really well actually."

"So," Alisha said, drawing out the syllable, "who's mister tall, dark, and handsome I saw you take into your apartment?"

I blushed and Alisha smiled knowingly.

"Yum," she said with a grin.

"It's not like that," I stammered. "He's . . . just a friend."

Alisha's grin faded as she looked at me. "You all right, Kathleen?" she asked, concern creasing her brow.

"I—" The words *I'm fine* stuck in my throat. It would be so nice to have someone to talk to. "Blane and I had a fight," I said.

She regarded me seriously. "Are you okay? He didn't hurt you, did he?"

"Of course not," I said, shaking my head. "Not that kind of fight. It's just . . . I don't know." I swiped a hand over my tired eyes.

"What did you fight about?" she asked.

"His ex, I guess." I shrugged. "He expects me to act like this is going to work out, when we both know it won't. I'd be kidding myself to believe that." Wouldn't I?

"He's been with a lot of women," Alisha agreed, "but you never know, Kathleen. It could happen."

Allowing myself to believe that terrified me. If I let that idea get a foothold, if I believed Blane when he said he wasn't going anywhere—that would make me vulnerable. And if I was wrong? If Blane was wrong? I couldn't stand the thought of what that might do to me. I shook my head.

"I've got to get ready for work," I said. "Thanks for listening, Alisha."

"Listen, Kathleen," she said, grabbing my hand. "I know it's hard, you want to try and protect yourself, but give him a chance. You might be surprised." She gave me a hug that was tighter and longer than usual. It felt good to have a girlfriend.

Twenty minutes later, I'd dressed in my work uniform and run a brush through my hair.

"Don't you want to eat first?" Kade asked.

"I'll grab something at the bar," I said with a shrug. I suppose I should have been hungry, but I wasn't. My stomach roiled at even the thought of food. I tried to hold on to my anger, but really I was just mad at myself, not Blane.

"So what's the story with Kandi?" I asked Kade, proud that my voice was strong and firm.

He glanced at me but I wouldn't meet his eyes, instead making a great show of finding my boots and putting them on.

"Her dad and Blane's dad were buddies," he answered. "Two strong political families, wealthy, connected. They raised Blane and Kandi side by side. She's a few years younger, but they always planned for them to get married. They've been on again and off again for years." I looked up to see him staring at me, assessing. "But then I guess he met you."

"Blane and Kandi broke up before he met me," I denied, somehow not surprised by the history between them. "I had nothing to do with it."

He didn't reply, his eyes gazing into mine before I looked uncomfortably away.

"She's quite intent on getting him back," I said with forced lightness. I remembered with a sinking feeling how beautiful and sophisticated she'd looked at the fund-raiser and in Blane's office. I couldn't compete with that, especially given her shared history with Blane.

"Kandi usually gets what she wants, yes," Kade confirmed. "Whether or not that's Blane remains to be seen." His voice clued me in on something.

"You don't like her," I said, studying him.

"She's a selfish, narcissistic bitch," he replied. "What's not to like?"

I laughed in spite of myself.

When we got to the bar, Kade pulled over to the curb but made no move to park in the spot next to me. I got out and went to his window, which he'd rolled down so he could speak to me.

"I need to check something out," he said. "I'll be back later. You good from here?"

"I'll be fine," I said. "Where are you going?"

"Thought I'd check on those phone records and swing by where Bowers was staying."

"Be careful," I told him.

His only response was a smirk. I rolled my eyes and watched Kade drive away, the taillights fading in the distance. I was nearly to the bar door when I reconsidered, going back to my car and getting Blane's gun from the glove box. I shoved it into my purse and headed inside.

I was not greeted with good news.

"We have to wear *what?*" I eyed the red velvet Tish was holding. "You've got to be kidding me."

"I wish I was," Tish said with a snort. "Romeo left them for us. Said we're supposed to wear them until Christmas is over."

The outfit I contemplated was a little red-velvet minidress with white fur trim around the hem and neckline. Except there wasn't really much of a neckline. It was strapless and sleeveless. Not only was I going to look like a tramp in it, I was also going to freeze my ass off. Tish was already wearing hers—of course it looked good on her. Unfortunately, my chest and ass were larger than hers.

I wanted to say a very foul word. With a shared look of long-suffering with Tish, I took the outfit and stomped to the bathroom to change. Tish gave me an extra pair of her nylons to wear—they would at least help keep me warm.

Tish had to help me zip the darn thing—I couldn't reach the zipper. I then studied my reflection in the mirror. Good lord, I looked like I was going to fall out of the top of the dress. I tried unsuccessfully to tug it higher on my chest. There was no way I was going to wear this all the way until Christmas. Romeo could just stuff it.

Now in an even fouler mood than before, I tied my apron around my waist and headed out into the bar. It helped to see the other girls were dressed as I was, though I determined that I wouldn't be shaking any martinis tonight—they'd just have to make do with stirred. Any shaking and I'd be giving more of a show than I already was.

We weren't terribly busy, just steady, and I suppose you could say the outfits helped with holiday cheer—for the male patrons anyway. I caught more than a few wives and girlfriends scowling at me. I wanted to tell them that it certainly hadn't been my idea to dress this way. The only thing keeping me from freezing was working and staying on the move.

I saw someone new sit down at the bar and turned to take his order. To my surprise, I knew him.

"Ryan," I said, recognizing him from my visit yesterday. "What are you doing here?"

He looked as surprised as I felt.

"I could ask you the same," he said. "I thought you worked for the law firm."

"I work two jobs," I said. "A girl's gotta pay the rent, you know?" I smiled at him. He was wearing a button-down charcoal-gray shirt and looking even better than I remembered, his chocolate eyes smiling back at me.

"Yeah, I know," he replied.

"What can I get you?"

He ordered a beer and I grabbed a bottle, pouring it into a frosted glass, which I set in front of him.

"That's some outfit," he said with a nod to my attire. He took a swallow of his beer.

"Yeah, not what I'd wear in subzero weather, if given the choice," I said wryly. "The owner has a different point of view." I pointed out the other waitresses in our identical red velvet.

"Well, I'm not going to argue with the owner," Ryan said with an appreciative grin.

"What are you doing downtown?" I asked, changing the subject.

"Had some business down here," he replied. "Thought I'd stop in for a drink before heading home. I would've come here sooner if I'd known a girl like you worked here."

I smiled at the compliment.

It had slowed down, so I chatted with Ryan for a while. He was a funny guy and had me laughing at some of the stories he told. It felt good to just relax and enjoy his company. The stress I'd been feeling with Blane and Kade had taken more of a toll than I had realized. I was surprised when I glanced at the clock and saw it was almost closing time.

"I'd better start clearing up," I said, "but thanks for keeping me company."

"Anytime, beautiful," he said, finishing his beer. "I'm hoping to change your mind about that dinner."

My smile grew forced, as I was abruptly reminded about my fight with Blane.

"Still involved?" Ryan asked, referring to the reason I'd given for not going out with him.

"I'm . . . not sure," I said honestly. After my outburst with Blane, I had no idea what the status of our relationship was. We'd both been so angry.

"That sounds promising," Ryan said. "Not to wish ill will on your significant other, but his loss is my gain. Are you working tomorrow night?"

"I am."

"Then I'll see you tomorrow," Ryan said with a wink. He tossed some money on the bar to cover his tab plus a tip and left.

I was a little behind, so I hurried to finish my work in time for closing. The bar was deserted now and I wondered if Kade was going to be back in time to follow me home. A hint of worry niggled at me, but I tried not to focus on it.

Tish came up to me after she'd locked the front door. She'd put on her coat and had her purse in hand.

"I'm going to head out," she said. Linda, the other waitress tonight, had already left at ten. "You good to finish up?"

"Yeah, I'm fine," I replied. "I just need to stock." I hoped Kade would be back soon. I wondered if I'd have to call Blane if Kade didn't show up.

Tish left and I made several trips to the storeroom to retrieve supplies for the bar. The place was still and quiet, as were the streets outside. This late on a weekday night, everyone was bundled up warm at home. I'd turned off nearly all the lights except the small lamps that hung directly over the bar. The amber glow from the streetlights filtered in through the blinds on the windows.

A noise made me go still. I listened intently, the hair on the back of my neck standing up. I heard it again—coming from outside.

I ran to my purse stashed under the bar, yanked it open, and pulled out the gun. I made sure it was loaded and knocked off the safety. The feel of the cold steel in my hands comforted me and I took a deep, steadying breath.

Going to the front door, I peeked outside. It took me a minute to make sense of what I was seeing. Four guys were in a scuffle across the narrow street. I looked closer. Wait, it looked like three guys were ganging up on one who was putting up a hell of a fight.

When they stepped into the light, my jaw dropped in shock. It was Kade. And those three guys—they were from the other night, when that one had hassled me and Kade had stepped in. It looked like they were taking the opportunity for a little payback.

Anger flashed through me and I jerked open the door, heedless of the cold and snow. Bracing my feet and grasping the gun with both hands, I fired a shot up in the air.

That got their attention.

"Let him go, assholes!" I called out, aiming my gun at the biggest of them. Bob was his name, if I remembered correctly.

"Well, look who's come to join us," he sneered. "If it isn't Miss High-and-Mighty herself. How you doing, bitch?"

"I said, let him go," I repeated. Two of his cronies each had Kade by an arm, and I couldn't tell if Kade was standing under his own power or if they were holding him up. Worry and panic flooded through me.

"How about we trade him for you," Bob said with a leer. He turned and before I could do or say anything, he punched Kade in the face. Kade sagged even lower in the grip of the other two.

Rage erupted inside me, white hot and dangerous. I welcomed it, the fury focusing my senses. Taking careful aim, I squeezed the trigger, smiling in satisfaction as Bob yelped.

"You fucking bitch!" he screamed. "You nearly shot my dick off!"

"You've got until three to let him go and get out of here!" I called out. "One . . ."

The two guys holding Kade dropped him, turned, and ran.

"Two . . ."

Bob cursed, aimed a last vicious kick at Kade, then took off after his friends. I ran across the street, my fury evaporating into worry as I took in Kade's crumpled form on the ground. Flicking the safety back on, I set the gun down and fell to my knees next to him. The cold, wet concrete bit into my nylon-clad knees, tearing the fragile fabric.

"Kade, are you all right?" I asked, grasping his shoulder and wondering if I should try to turn him over or just call 911. He groaned in response and panic fluttered in my chest. What should I do? I looked anxiously back at the bar, which seemed very far away. Should I leave him here and go call for help? I wavered in indecision, not wanting to leave Kade alone.

"I've had better nights, princess," Kade groaned, pushing himself painfully into a sitting position. Tears of relief stung my eyes and I quickly blinked them back. My hands fluttered uselessly, unsure how best to help him.

Kade's eyes focused blearily on me, and I winced at the blood and bruises already forming on his face.

"What the fuck are you wearing?"

"What?" I was so surprised, his words didn't immediately register.

"What are you doing in that getup? You do know it's about fifteen fucking degrees out here, don't you? You trying to freeze to death?"

"Last I looked, I was saving your ass," I snapped. "I wasn't aware that you required a dress code."

A grin flashed across his face but quickly faded into a grimace of pain. My irritation passed as quickly as it had come. I jumped to my feet, reaching down to help Kade stand. He grabbed the gun, shoving it into the back of his jeans. Moving slowly, we made our way to the bar, Kade leaning heavily on me.

I helped him onto a barstool and watched as he painfully shrugged off his jacket, which I took from him. I noticed then that his shirt was dark and wet in a spot on his chest, underneath his arm. "Kade, you're hurt," I said stupidly.

"No shit," Kade replied, grimacing again as he tugged off his shirt. I gasped when I saw the angry slice through his skin.

"We need to get you to the hospital," I said firmly, swallowing down my panic. There was a lot of blood on him.

Kade gave a huff of laughter. "For this? Please. Just get me some water and something to cover it. You have Band-Aids here?"

"You can't be serious," I protested. "That cut needs stitches."

He was already shaking his head. "You going to get me some water or should I do it myself? And I wouldn't mind a shot or two of bourbon."

"Fine," I groused, grabbing a clean towel from behind the bar and filling a bowl with hot water. Pouring a hefty portion of bourbon into a highball glass, I set it in front of him, then came out from behind the bar so I was close enough to clean him up. Kade moved to take the towel from me.

"I'll do it," I said, stubbornly gripping the towel tightly in my fist. "You can't even see what you're doing."

He relented and I dipped the towel into the water, carefully cleaning the blood off his face. Kade watched me as I worked, his blue eyes unfathomable. I worried my bottom lip between my teeth, his attention making me nervous yet I was determined to help him.

His lip was cut but had stopped bleeding and there was a deep abrasion on his cheek. I touched the skin gently, wincing even though he did not. It looked like it hurt.

"What happened?" I asked, breaking the silence and trying not to reopen the cut on his lower lip. "How did they get the drop on you?"

"I was . . . distracted," Kade replied. "My own fault."

"Distracted by what?" I asked, wondering what he could have been thinking about that would have allowed three guys to sneak up on him.

He didn't answer and I paused in my dabbing at the scrape above his eye. "What was it?" I repeated, my brow furrowing as he studied me. I watched as he turned away, grabbing the glass and downing the amber fluid in two swallows.

"Bowers's place was cleaned out," he finally said, replacing the glass and ignoring my question. "I watched and waited for a while, thinking he might show, but nothing."

"What about the phone records?" I resumed my task, frowning in concentration as I cleaned specks of blood from his jaw.

"Tracing numbers even as we speak," he replied. "I was headed back in when they jumped me. Then this Playboy Bunny showed up with a gun and scared the bad guys away."

I gave a tight-lipped smile at his teasing even as guilt assailed me. "I'm so sorry, Kade," I said, stopping again. "If it weren't for you helping me the other night, this wouldn't have happened."

"Don't mention it," he briskly cut me off. "Want me to get the rest? You're squeamish, aren't you?"

"Of course not," I replied automatically, wringing the towel out in the now slightly pinkish water. I turned back to Kade.

"Can you lift your arm?" I asked. He hesitated before obliging, bending his elbow and putting his hand behind his head so I could better see the cut. I was distracted for a moment, the muscles in his chest rippled with his movement, and I was suddenly aware of our proximity. Swallowing, I turned my attention back to his wound. It was angry and blood still seeped sluggishly from it.

"You should really get stitches for this," I said quietly, cleaning the cut as gently as I could. The water quickly turned a garish red as I worked. Kade didn't so much as twitch, even though I knew it had to hurt.

"Forget it," he said.

"What's the deal, Kade?" I asked in exasperation, feeling that my ministrations were woefully inadequate. "It only hurts for a second when they numb you and then—"

"And we're done here," he said briskly, lowering his arm. I stepped back in surprise, and then it hit me.

"You are kidding me," I said, stunned.

Kade looked at me strangely. "What?"

"You're afraid of needles, aren't you?" I asked.

"Right," Kade snorted, but I watched in disbelief as his ears turned pink. I couldn't help it—I laughed.

"It's okay," I said, grinning. "I swear I won't tell anyone." I held up three fingers. "Girl Scout's honor."

"I am not afraid of needles," Kade insisted.

I nodded as if I believed every word, though I couldn't wipe the grin from my face that said otherwise.

"Fine," he said with ill humor. "But I'm not afraid of needles. I just . . . don't like them. That's all."

I grabbed his glass, rounded the bar, and refilled it. "And yet," I said, pulling out the first-aid kit—which I'd insisted Romeo buy—from underneath the bar, "you have a tattoo."

I'd missed it before, but now I saw that on his upper arm was tattooed an intricate red and black dragon about the size of my palm. I moved closer to inspect it, running my fingernail along the myriad links and circles that made up the dragon's body and wings etched into Kade's skin.

"What does it mean?" I asked quietly, our eyes meeting. He glanced down, then away from my gaze.

"Tattoos are different," he said, swallowing the bourbon and turning the stool from me so he faced the bar. "Not like the needles they use in hospitals."

I sighed. He obviously wouldn't answer some of my questions, and there was no point in trying to pursue something he didn't want to talk about, though my curiosity about the tattoo was overwhelming.

Grabbing the antibiotic ointment, I squeezed some into my hand. "Lift your arm again," I ordered. Kade did as I said and I quickly smeared the gel into the cut. Kade stiffened. I worked as fast as I could, knowing the ointment probably burned like the devil. Peeling some Band-Aids, I pulled his skin taut and crisscrossed them over the cut, careful to keep the adhesive away from the wound.

"There," I said in satisfaction once I was finished, "that should work for now. Though you need a real bandage. We should stop at the drugstore on the way home."

Kade grunted and I smiled behind his back. That may be the closest he'd come to thanking me. I put the cap back on the ointment and was turning away when something caught my eye. I carefully set the first-aid kit back down and stepped closer to Kade, who ignored me.

The light above the bar shone directly down on Kade's back as he leaned against the counter, nursing his drink. I stared in shock at the dozen or so round pockmarks, each about the size of a dime, scattered all over his back.

"Kade," I choked out, then stopped, unable to say anything more.

He glanced at me over his shoulder. "What?"

"Your back . . ."

I reached out one shaking finger to gently touch one of the marks, the scarred skin slightly puckered.

"It's nothing," he dismissed, "just chicken pox scars. No big deal. Not everyone has perfect skin like you, princess."

He smirked at me, his smile fading when I said nothing. I could only stare.

"I know those aren't from chicken pox," I said, my voice hardly above a whisper. The only reason I even knew what they were was because of a horrible child abuse case my dad had once worked. A case where the stepmother had thought it amusing to put her cigarettes out on the child. "Who did that to you, Kade?"

My stomach lurched at the mere thought of Kade, an orphan at the age of six, enduring something like that. Blane had said that Kade would never tell him what had happened in the foster homes he ran away from, and I thought I might be sick just imagining what he'd gone through. I reached for him again—I wasn't sure why—but found my wrist suddenly caught in his viselike grip. Kade jerked me toward him, pulling me between his spread knees. My hand instinctively came up to his chest to brace myself.

"I don't want your pity," Kade snarled, his face inches from mine. Gone was the softening of his eyes, the genuine smile curving his lips. In their place, his eyes were empty pools of blue, his mouth set in a firm line. A nerve pulsed in his clenched jaw.

"I'm not . . . I don't—" I stammered, unsure what I was trying to say. Kade interrupted me.

"What are you doing anyway? This playing nursemaid crap?"

"I'm just trying to help you—"

"Well, I don't need your help," he bit out.

"Everybody needs somebody." He was starting to scare me. My wrist hurt from where he still tightly gripped it.

"I don't."

"Okay, fine. You don't need anybody." I wanted to cry. Whatever had happened to Kade, whoever had abused him so awfully, had taught him to not trust people—even those who cared about him. To my surprise, I realized I now fell into that group. I cared about Kade and I hated to see him hurting.

Kade abruptly released me, turning back to the bar to grab his shirt. I watched him uncertainly, thinking I should probably retreat while I had the chance but not wanting to. The scars on his back seemed to stand out in stark relief until Kade dragged his shirt down to cover them.

"Maybe," I began hesitantly, "you could talk to someone. There are people that specialize in that sort of thing."

"Why the fuck would I want to do that?"

I was at a loss for words, the hostility in his voice making me reconsider putting some space between us.

Shrugging on his jacket and grabbing his glass, he slid off the stool and approached me. I gulped but stood my ground. He watched me for a moment, then swallowed the last of the bourbon.

"I'm going to pretend this conversation never happened," he finally said, "and I suggest you do the same."

"But Kade—"

I gasped when he threw the empty glass on the floor at our feet, shattering it into pieces. I stared in shock at the mess. I could see shards of glass caught in the nylon covering my legs. Kade's boots crunched on the glass and suddenly his hands were on my shoulders. I winced when his fingers dug into my bare skin.

"Do you think I want to relive it?" he snarled.

I shook my head.

"Do you think I want Blane to feel guilty for what hap-pened?"

"No, Kade—"

"I don't want Blane to know anything—"

"I won't—"

"—and I don't need you feeling sorry for me—"

"I never said—"

"—and I don't want you inside my head!"

I was shaking now, the force of his rage both scaring me and making my heart break inside my chest. Tears spilled unchecked down my cheeks, but I didn't dare blink.

In the next moment, he was out the door and gone.

I stood alone in the silence for a long time.

CHAPTER TEN

I was woken up by my alarm clock the next morning and my hand slammed down on the snooze button, silencing the insistent beeping.

I groaned. I was exhausted. I'd been at the bar later than I'd planned, cleaning up the mess Kade had left on the floor, then I hadn't been able to sleep after I finally climbed into bed shortly after 2:00 a.m. Worry for Kade ate at me, and my argument with Blane made me feel sick to my stomach. I hadn't heard from either of them, which probably wasn't surprising.

I showered and got ready for work on autopilot. When I walked into the kitchen, I was startled to see that Kade's suitcase had moved. Glancing at the couch, I realized that the quilt from the Christmas tree farm had been neatly folded and left on the cushions. Kade must have come by last night after I'd gone to bed, and he was already up and gone.

I saw he'd made a pot of coffee that was still warm. As I poured myself a cup, I noticed a note on the counter: *Have business to take care of. Stay put. I'll be back to take you in tonight.*

Well, at least last night hadn't pissed Kade off so completely that he'd decided to forgo the whole security detail, which made me feel a little better. Though if he thought

I was just going to sit around my apartment all day watching Oprah and eating chips, he'd thought wrong. Kade had given me a new job and I was going to do it.

Digging in my purse, I pulled out a scrap of paper on which I'd scrawled the address of Adriana Waters, ex-wife of Kyle Waters. It seemed she was staying at the Crowne Plaza Hotel downtown for the duration of the trial, and since she was a witness for the prosecution, it was probably on the taxpayers' dime.

I grabbed my purse and coat and headed out the door. A half hour later, I walked into the lobby of the Crowne Plaza. Knowing they wouldn't just tell me her room number, I paused at one of the tables and pulled an empty envelope from my purse. Folding a hotel brochure, I stuffed it in the envelope and sealed it, then scrawled *Adriana Waters* on the outside. I walked to the front desk.

"Excuse me," I said, giving a friendly smile to the man behind the counter. "Would you please deliver this to Adriana Waters?"

He eyed me suspiciously, but I maintained my smile. Taking the envelope from me, he said, "Of course."

"Thank you." I turned and walked a few steps before pausing to glance back, watching as he slid the envelope into one of the myriad mailboxes on the wall behind the counter. The one he chose was marked 1282.

I took the elevator to the twelfth floor. The hallway was empty and quiet when I got out. The thick beige carpet muffled my footsteps as I walked. I passed a maid cleaning one of the rooms, the noise of the vacuum obscuring my passage. When I reached room 1282, I knocked and waited. No one answered. I knocked again, harder this time. I heard the scrape of a lock and the door eased open. A woman stood there, and I was taken aback by how young she appeared.

"Yes?" Her tone was cold as she surveyed me.

"Adriana Waters?" I asked.

"Who wants to know?"

"My name is Kathleen," I said. "I'm with the Kirk and Trent law firm, and I'm investigating your ex-husband's case. May I speak with you?"

She grudgingly nodded, standing aside so I could enter the hotel room.

The room was large, the space encompassing a large sitting room and dining area complete with a table and chairs for six. I walked to a sofa situated next to a chair and sat. Adriana sat across from me, crossing her trousers-encased legs primly at the ankles. She was dressed simply in a sweater, pants, and heels, all black. She was very fair, her hair nearly white it was so blonde.

"How may I help you?" she asked once we were both situated.

"I was hoping you could tell me of anyone who might hold a personal grudge against your husband," I said as I reached into my purse for a notepad and pen.

"You mean other than the family of that poor dead man?" she asked belligerently.

"Yes," I said simply.

She sighed. "I'm not surprised it's come to this. Those guys think just because they're SEALs and have guns, they can do whatever they want."

"Why do you say that?" I asked, startled at her accusation.

"Do you even watch the news, Miss Turner?" she asked condescendingly. "We shouldn't even be over there, but that's where Kyle is, killing unarmed civilians. That damn lawyer you work for turned it all around, made it seem like they did the right thing." She glared at me. "Lawyers are nothing but lying bastards."

"Blane Kirk is trying to get your ex-husband acquitted," I defended Blane. "Do you really want to see Kyle go to prison?" I couldn't imagine that. Even if they were no longer married, did she not care anything about what happened to him? What would happen to a US soldier put in a prison with thieves, rapists, and murderers?

"He deserves what's happening to him," she said angrily.

Now my temper was starting to rise as well. "Ms. Waters, do you know of anyone who would want Mr. Kirk to lose this case so badly they would threaten him?"

"Losing this case would move the country a big step forward," she said.

"Why do you say that?" I asked, surprised at her vehemence.

"You are so ignorant," she said with disdain. "If Kyle is convicted, that sets a precedent. The soldiers won't be allowed to just kill people anymore; they'll know they have to answer to the courts for their actions and the family members left behind."

Her gaze was unflinching and she spoke as though she were absolutely sure of the outcome of this case. The passion in her voice sent a chill through me. I wasn't at all sure her vision of what the military should be and do was the ideal solution.

"Do you have any idea where Brian Bowers is?" I asked. "He disappeared a few days ago and the police can't seem to find him."

She shrugged, unconcerned. "Brian is Kyle's buddy. You should ask him, though I wouldn't blame him for leaving town, the coward, rather than face the press and the public."

Something occurred to me as I studied her implacable features.

"You know," I said, "if it were me, I'd think it would have been really hard to handle my husband having such a dangerous job, and then to have him reenlist. That must have been difficult for you."

Adriana winced ever so slightly but didn't reply. Convinced I was on to something, I continued.

"You and he were married for two years. Did you and Kyle ever plan to have a family?" I asked.

Adriana's lips were pressed together in a thin line and I thought she wasn't going to answer me. I waited and after a moment, she spoke. "I was pregnant," she said.

"Excuse me?" I asked, sure I'd misheard.

"I was pregnant," she repeated, her voice very quiet. "When Kyle decided to reenlist. I told him that I couldn't do it, couldn't have a baby alone, constantly worrying that the next phone call was going to make me a widow and our child an orphan.

"Can you imagine what it's like?" she continued. "To love someone so much, only to realize that they don't love you in return? Kyle wouldn't put us first. He said he had to go back—that he was needed over there. It didn't matter how much *I* needed him—they came first."

I could hear the pain and heartbreak in her voice. I realized that all her bluster and anger was really a defense, protection against what had never healed.

"What happened to the baby?" I asked, afraid I knew the answer. The file hadn't mentioned any children.

"I miscarried four months into Kyle's deployment," Adriana answered. "I filed for divorce a month after that."

"I'm so sorry," I said.

Adriana's eyes were very bright, but no tears fell. "Be sure to fall in love with someone who loves you more than you love them," she said bitterly.

"So all of this is to just get back at Kyle for not loving you enough," I said baldly.

She flushed and abruptly stood. "I don't think there's anything else I can tell you," she said angrily, and I could see that the wall had come down again. The trace of vulnerability she'd shown me was nowhere to be seen.

"Okay, well thank you for speaking with me," I said, rising to my feet. She walked me to the door.

A few minutes later, I was back in the hotel lobby. I was glad to be out of there. Adriana's heartbreak and disillusionment had turned to anger and bitterness. It was sad to see.

It suddenly occurred to me that I had never given Adriana my last name, but she had called me "Miss Turner." It seemed Adriana knew more about this case than she was letting on. I decided to stick around and see if she left anytime soon. Taking a seat in the hotel's lounge, I ordered a Pepsi and waited. I could see people coming and going through the lobby from my vantage point.

Time passed and I had more Pepsi refills than I wanted to count, conceding to hunger at around one o'clock and ordering a sandwich from the annoyed bartender. I took my time, slowly munching on my cold french fries.

My patience paid off a short while later when I saw Adriana walk through the lobby toward the doors. I tossed some money on the table to cover my lunch and hurried to the elevators.

As I walked down the hall, an idea came to me, and I searched to find a room where a maid was cleaning. Following the sound of a vacuum, I came upon one.

"Excuse me," I called over the noise. Startled, she turned to see me standing in the doorway before hurriedly switching off the machine.

"I'm sorry to bother you," I said, "but I've locked myself out of my room. Can you help me?"

"Señorita?" she asked, confusion written on her face, and I realized she probably didn't speak English.

I mimed a key in a lock as I said, "Locked out. Help me?" Understanding dawned and she smiled. *"Sí, sí."*

I motioned for her to follow me and walked back to room 1282. I stood aside while she slid her key into the lock and opened the door.

"Gracias," I said, handing her a five-dollar bill. She nodded and smiled, pocketing the money. I slipped inside the room. I paused just inside the doorway, listening, but heard nothing to make me think I wasn't alone.

Even though I was the only one there, I still tiptoed into the bedroom. There was a desk in one corner. Thinking that looked promising, I went over and looked through the papers on it. There were some notes from the trial.

A few newspapers were piled up, all of them opened to articles about the trial. Blane's photo was prominent on the top one. As I moved the papers, I saw a cell phone lying underneath. I picked it up, wondering if it was Adriana's. Strange that she would leave without her cell phone. I slipped it into my pocket.

The sound of a door opening made my head jerk up. Alarm shot through me as voices filtered through the suite. I frantically looked around, searching for someplace to hide. With little else from which to choose, I scrambled into the closet.

The voices grew closer and my heart pounded. I struggled to breathe slowly and not gasp for air in case even that small sound might betray my presence.

I could hear now that the voices were those of a man and woman. I thought I recognized Adriana's voice, but the man spoke too low for me to distinguish what he was saying.

"You shouldn't be here," Adriana said. "What if someone saw you?" She paused while the man answered her. "That girl was here, Kirk's girlfriend. Nosing around and asking questions. I thought you were going to take care of her."

This last was said accusingly and a chill went through me. "Take care of." Well, that certainly sounded ominous. Finally, I could distinguish his words when he answered her.

"I told you I have a plan."

"If you don't get Kirk to lose this case—"

"Stop worrying," he interrupted her. "I'm taking care of it."

Their voices lowered as they moved farther from the bedroom. I hardly dared to breathe.

"Have you seen my phone?" the man asked. "I thought maybe I left it here."

"Just call it," Adriana said. "If it's here, I'm sure we'll hear it."

Panic surged in me and I fumbled with the phone in the dark, blindly feeling for the silence switch. I found it and flicked it, turning off the ringer—and not a moment too soon, as it began to vibrate in my hand.

I stared at the phone for a moment, then cautiously slid the bar on the screen to answer, pressing the mute button once it connected.

"Hello?" The man's voice was much clearer now and I realized it sounded familiar to me. "Anyone there?" I racked my brain, but I just couldn't place where I'd heard him before. The phone disconnected without him saying anything else.

"It's not here, but someone has it," the man told Adriana.

"Well, get a new one then," she said. "It's probably some teenager playing a prank."

I heard the door to the suite open and close. I listened carefully, wondering if both had left again. It seemed they had, for I heard nothing. I waited a little while longer for the coast to be clear. Deciding I had to chance it, I crawled out of the closet and eased through the bedroom door. A quick glance assured me I'd been correct—no one was there.

A few minutes later, I was out of the hotel and walking down the block to where I'd parked my car. I was nervous, afraid I'd been mistaken and they'd known I was there. Maybe they were following me. The cell phone seemed to burn a hole in my pocket.

I glanced behind me again, then let out a small shriek as I ran point-blank into someone. I would have fallen backward, but two hands grabbed my arms, holding me upright. I looked up to apologize, but the words froze in my throat.

"You should really pay more attention to where you're going, sweetheart," James sneered at me.

"What . . . what are you doing here?" I stammered, taken aback by his sudden appearance.

"None of your business," he replied, his eyes narrowing.

"Why aren't you in court?" I demanded, trying to step away from him, but his hands remained firmly locked on my arms, holding me in place.

"Recessed early today," he said with a smug smile. "It is Friday, you know. The judge likes to take it easy on jurors for this kind of trial."

Taking a quick look around at the crowded sidewalk, James released me, but before I could get away he grabbed my wrist in a tight grip, tugging me with him.

"What are you doing?" I spat at him, trying to pull free. He ignored me, dragging me behind him into the small alley between buildings. It was empty of people, the shadows thicker, and alarm shot through me. What if James had been the one with Adriana? What if he knew I'd heard their conversation?

"Let me go!"

My protest was abruptly cut off when James threw me against the wall, now grabbing both of my wrists and pinning them to my sides. His body pressed against mine, holding me in place so tightly I couldn't draw a full breath. His smirk made a shiver run through me.

"I'm looking forward to tomorrow night," he hissed in my ear.

My blood ran cold. "Tomorrow night?" I played dumb, hoping he didn't mean what I thought he meant.

"I told Simone I'd forget about the money she owes me if she got me you. For one night."

I couldn't speak. My eyes must have betrayed my horror, for he laughed.

"I'd tell you to not be so scared, but I rather like your spunk. Makes it more of a challenge."

"You're crazy if you think I'm going to sleep with you," I sputtered.

His eyes narrowed and his smile disappeared. "You'll be there tomorrow night, or I'll make sure you regret it," he threatened. "Jimmy may be dead, but there are others who took his place. You'll be begging to die once I let them get their hands on you."

I had no warning before his mouth was on mine, his tongue pushing inside my mouth. Nausea roiled in my stomach. I hated that he could use his size and body to bully me and I was helpless to stop him. Infuriated, I bit down hard on his lower lip.

James pulled back with a yelp and I was gratified to see blood on his mouth. Before I could brace myself, he backhanded me.

Pain exploded in my cheek and my head hit the brick wall behind me. For a moment, I saw stars, then I tasted blood. The class ring James always wore on his right hand had cut me.

"You'd better rethink any moves like that tomorrow," James growled at me, "or you may walk away with worse than bruises."

He abruptly released me and, in the next second, he was gone. I stood on legs that seemed too unsteady to hold me and leaned against the cold brick. I closed my eyes and tried to get a grip, silently calling James every vile name I could think of. Wiping the blood and the taste of James from my mouth with my sleeve, I hurried to my car to drive home.

I choked down some food while I watched television, trying to regain some control over my shattered nerves. *MacGyver* reruns left me feeling woefully inadequate. What that man couldn't do with a paperclip, matches, and a magnet.

When it was time to get ready for work, I grumbled as I pulled on the ridiculous red outfit Romeo had decreed we should wear, and brushed out my hair until it lay in shiny waves down my back. I didn't have a bruise on my cheek yet, though my mouth was swollen and split from where the ring had cut me. I covered it with some lip gloss and studied the effect in the mirror. It helped, sort of.

"Nice night, princess."

I spun around to see Kade leaning against the doorjamb of the bathroom, crooked smile firmly in place. I hadn't even heard him enter the apartment.

The knot that had been in my stomach all day finally eased. I hurriedly looked down, hoping Kade hadn't seen the relief in my eyes. I couldn't decide if I was glad he was back because I felt safer with him around, or if I was glad he wasn't still angry with me. Though that anger might reappear if and when he realized I'd been gone all day.

I cleared my throat.

"Hey," I said. It seemed we were going to ignore what had occurred last night, which was fine with me. I took a good look at him, glad to see the cuts on his face had begun to heal, and noticed he was wearing a tuxedo underneath a black overcoat.

"Going somewhere?" I asked.

"Kandi's Christmas party is tonight," he replied, his light tone belying the sharp look in his eyes as he watched me absorb this information.

The knot in my stomach was back, heavier than before. I'd forgotten. Tonight was the night I was supposed to meet Blane at the party but had to work instead.

"Is Blane going?" I asked, keeping my tone as light and uninterested as his. I moved past him into the living room to get my coat.

"It would seem so," Kade said, following me. Taking the coat from my hands, he held it while I slid my arms into the sleeves.

"What happened today?" he asked.

"What do you mean?" I said automatically, my mind busy turning over the information that Blane was going to Kandi's party, supposedly an intimate gathering of family and friends. No doubt everyone there would assume they were together since Blane would be going alone.

Kade's hand flashed out to grip my chin, forcing my eyes to his. When he was sure he had my attention, his gaze dropped to my mouth. His grip eased as his thumb brushed over my swollen and cut lip. I winced.

"This is what I mean," he said flatly. "I told you to stay put today. I see you did your usual bang-up job of not listening."

There was no way I was going to tell him what had happened, though the temptation was great. If I told Kade that James was the culprit, he'd either tell Blane himself or make me tell him, which would only cause a load of trouble for

Blane. Kade's solution of asking Blane for the five thousand dollars had evaporated when Blane and I had fought yesterday. Neither my pride nor my common sense would allow me to ask that of Blane. It would be foolish to think he'd just give me that kind of money. I'd find my own way out of the mess I'd made.

"It's nothing," I said, jerking my chin out of his hand and stepping beyond his reach. His blue eyes pierced mine and I had to look away. "And you gave me a promotion, remember? I had a job to do." I decided to change the subject. "Aren't you going to be late for the party?" I asked.

"Wanted to take you to work first," he replied. "Make sure you arrive alive." The teasing note in his voice belied the seriousness of the words. His eyes narrowed as he studied me.

"Great," I said quickly. "Let's go." I didn't want to think about Blane or the party or Kandi.

Thirty minutes later, I was clocking in.

Kade slid onto a barstool and I set a cup of coffee in front of him.

"You don't have to stay, you know," I said. "I can take care of myself."

Kade didn't reply, his eyes conveying his skepticism quite adequately as he peered at me over the rim of the coffee cup.

"I ran into some trouble today," I reluctantly acknowledged, "but I'm fine. So go. Have a good time tonight." My smile was brittle.

He hesitated for a moment, taking another swallow of the bitter liquid. "I'll be back by closing," he finally said, getting to his feet.

I nodded, watching him as he turned to go. The striking elegance of his formal attire was not the only thing that made Kade stand out in the crowd. Kade had a confidence about him, an assurance in his walk and a grace to his movements that drew the eye. The nearly palpable aura of danger surrounding him only added to his appeal. I couldn't tear my eyes away from him as he walked out the door.

The bar was busy already and Scott was my partner tonight. I noticed with disgust that he didn't have to wear a skin-baring uniform for the holidays, just a red silk shirt to go with his black pants. I grudgingly admitted he looked good in it, but then again, Scott looked good in just about anything.

"Damn, Kathleen," he said with a crooked grin, "you look amazing in that." His gaze drifted appreciatively down my body, lingering longer than usual on the ample cleavage on display.

"Trade you," I said, forcing a smile and nodding at his red shirt.

He laughed. "I don't think I'd look nearly as good in that as you do."

We were so busy that I didn't have much of a chance to even think for a while, which was a good thing. I felt very alone. I didn't see how I was going to get out of meeting James tomorrow night, and the prospect was terrifying. Ideas and plans formed in my head, each one more desperate and improbable than the last.

I tried not to think about what Blane was doing as I worked. The hands of the clock moved so slowly, I wanted to scream. If things would just slow down, maybe I could get Scott to cover for me so I could go. Blane had invited me to the party—I wouldn't be crashing it. But those hopes were dashed as the minutes and hours crawled by with business showing no sign of letting up.

It was after eleven when Tish called out to me. Finishing the garnish on the drink I'd just made, I handed it to a waiting patron, then hurried over to her.

"Someone's on the phone for you," she said, balancing a tray of drinks.

"Okay, thanks," I said, coming out from behind the bar and going to the phone in the back. There was no way I was going to be able to hear out front. I wondered who could be calling me.

"Hello?" I waited but heard nothing. "Hello?" I said more loudly.

"I bet you're wondering what your boyfriend's up to tonight." The voice was male and raspy and made the hair stand up on the back of my neck.

"Who is this?" I demanded.

"He's having a good time, by the looks of it," the man continued, ignoring my question.

His words penetrated and I realized that wherever he was, he was watching Blane. Helpless fury filled me.

"Leave Blane alone." My tone was as low and threatening as I could make it.

He laughed with a soft, derisive sound that made my knuckles turn white as I clutched the phone to my ear. When he spoke again, his words turned my blood to ice.

"I wouldn't worry. Kirk's only going to get what he deserves."

The line went dead. I stood, frozen in shock. The man knew where Blane was and was planning on giving him "what he deserves." Panic threatened and my hands shook as I grabbed my purse and yanked out my cell phone. I dialed Blane's number.

"Please pick up, Blane," I prayed aloud, listening in growing dismay as the cell phone went to voice mail. I tried Kade's, with the same result.

"Damn it!" I yelled, wanting to fling my cell phone against the wall. What's the point of having a damn cell phone if no one ever answers it?

I scrambled back out to the bar, flinging off my apron as I went.

"I've got to go," I said to Scott, digging my keys out of my purse.

"What? Why? We're swamped!"

"I know and I'm sorry," I said hastily. "It's an emergency. I swear."

I didn't wait to hear his response. Finding my keys, I clutched them tightly, the sharp metal cutting into my hand. I hurried out the door, running for my car. In my haste to leave, I'd not even grabbed my coat and the cold wind bit into my exposed skin. The inside of my car was frigid and I could see my breath.

Fear and panic made me fumble my keys and it took precious seconds to start the car. Finally shoving it into gear, I shot out of the parking lot.

I still had the address to Kandi's house, which Blane had given me, and I sped in that direction, praying I wouldn't pass a cop. I tried calling Blane again on the way, and again the call went to voice mail. I tossed the phone onto the passenger seat in disgust.

It took fifteen minutes for me to cross town and find Kandi's house. I pulled into the exclusive neighborhood, barely noticing the tastefully decorated homes that boasted two and three stories, their expanses looming on large plots of land. Cars dotted the street leading up to one house in particular. The lights inside made the numerous windows sparkle in the night, their warmth in stark contrast to the imposing mansion in which they were housed. That had to be Kandi's house.

Another car was pulling away and I quickly took the vacant spot. I jumped out, slamming the door behind me, and ran toward the house. My knee-high black boots weren't the best for this, but I didn't fall.

The driveway was mercifully short, ending in front of a wide set of stairs that led to a large porch—though that name seemed inadequate for the massive pillars and doorway that led inside.

I rapped on the door, my breath coming in gasps. The sweat from my exertion and panic was freezing on my skin and I began to shiver.

The door swung open to reveal a tuxedo-clad butler. An older gentleman, he took in my bedraggled appearance, his mouth turning down in distaste.

"May I help you?" he asked, his tone decidedly unfriendly.

"I'm looking for Blane Kirk," I blurted. "It's an emergency. Is he here?"

I peered past him, trying to see, but he moved, blocking my view.

"I'm sorry, but this is a private party," he said. "I'm sure Mr. Kirk will be happy to speak with you on Monday at his office."

"You don't understand," I said, frustrated. "It's an emergency—a matter of life and death. I have to see him."

The butler seemed to hesitate, so I pressed my advantage.

"Please. I'm begging you."

He sighed, stepping backward into the foyer. "Wait here, miss."

I nodded, eagerly following him inside, the door easing shut behind me. I watched as he disappeared down the corridor. I could now hear the noise of revelry—people talking, glass and silverware clinking, and the strains of holiday music.

I chewed on a ragged nail as I waited, wondering if the man who'd called me was inside the house as well. No doubt people like this hired a catering staff for their parties. Maybe he was masquerading as a waiter.

I drifted down the corridor, unable to quell the compulsion to find Blane, make sure he was all right. Make sure he knew someone was here—watching him, possibly waiting to kill him.

My hands clenched into fists as I struggled to keep my composure. My pace quickened, the tapping of my boots on the marble floor echoing down the hallway.

I burst through a doorway into a large ballroom. No one noticed my presence, engaged as they all were in conversation or dancing. A live band played in one corner. I searched the well-dressed crowd for Blane's familiar form but came up empty.

"Miss Turner?"

I jumped, startled to hear my name. Whirling, I saw Senator Keaston standing a couple of feet away. He looked as surprised to see me as I was to see him. Embarrassment shot through me at showing up dressed as I was, but concern for Blane overrode those thoughts.

"Senator," I said, "have you seen Blane? I must find him. It's very important."

"Of course," he replied genially. "I believe he stepped into the library not too long ago."

"Thank you." I turned to leave, then abruptly stopped. "Wait—where's that?"

"Across the ballroom, down the hall, last door on your left."

I shot him a quick smile then hurried across the room. If anyone noticed me rushing by, I didn't stop to look. The doors were a blur as I passed, the last one on the left my target. It was shut. My knuckles rapped twice before my hand wrapped around the brass knob and I pushed the door open.

My heart froze in my chest and I was left staggering in shock.

Blane was in the library, that much was true. What the senator hadn't mentioned—what perhaps he hadn't known—was that Blane was not alone.

A woman was astride Blane's lap as he sat in a leather chair in the far corner. They hadn't yet noticed me, as engrossed as they were in their kiss. Blane's hands were on the woman's waist, the skirt of the red-taffeta dress she wore pushed up her thighs. I was horrified to realize that they might be doing more than kissing—had I interrupted them actually having sex? Bile rose in my throat at the thought.

I must have made a noise of distress, for Blane abruptly pushed the woman off him and leapt to his feet, his gaze landing on me. The woman stood, seemingly unfazed by her sudden banishment from Blane's lap, serenely shaking out her skirts. Finally, she turned toward me, allowing me to glimpse her face.

Kandi.

I don't know if it would have been better if it had been just another of Blane's myriad nameless, faceless women— all I knew was that a shaft of pain cut through me so deeply, it felt as though I could no longer draw breath. Time seemed to stop for a moment, my aghast expression meeting Kandi's smug and self-satisfied one. I swung my gaze to Blane, who stood unmoving in the middle of the room.

The room was so silent, I was afraid he could hear my heart thudding in my chest, each beat painfully reminding me that this wasn't a nightmare from which I could awaken.

For a moment, we just studied each other. His expression was as unreadable as ever, though I thought maybe I saw a trace of regret in his eyes. I closed my gaping mouth with a snap, refusing to play the idiot girlfriend who had no idea this might happen.

"I'll just leave you two alone, shall I?" Kandi said with a smirk. As she passed, the stiff taffeta of her fabric rustled, concealing the words she hissed at me. "Nice outfit."

My fists clenched, as it took every ounce of self-control I possessed not to rip her hair out. Instead, I ignored her, my eyes still on Blane as the door shut soundlessly behind her.

Silence reigned.

"You have lipstick on you," I said quietly, my voice sounding foreign to my ears.

Blane took the handkerchief out of his tuxedo pocket and wiped his mouth. I felt frozen inside, stiff and breakable, as I watched him.

"What are you doing here?" Blane finally rasped.

I forced a tight smile. "You invited me, remember? Perhaps it slipped your mind." Venom filled each word as I struggled with both anger and despair. "I thought this was supposed to be a private family affair, Blane."

"I thought it was to be as well," he replied. "I was as surprised as you."

"I sincerely doubt that."

Silence again—so thick I thought it would smother me.

"Kat, it wasn't—" he began.

"Shut up!" I screamed at him, my control snapping. "Don't call me that!" The sound of the familiar nickname had sent rage rushing through me. I took a shuddering breath, pushing both of my hands through my hair and trying to regain control. When I spoke again, it was in a much calmer, though no less furious, tone. "I don't want to hear anything you have to say."

Blane said nothing, his lips pressed tightly closed. A nerve twitched in his jaw.

I was suddenly struck by the disparity of our appearances: Blane, dressed impeccably in a tuxedo that I could tell had been hand tailored. Myself, looking like a sleazy tart in my barely-there outfit, my hair disheveled and my boots old enough to show their age. I wasn't in Blane's league and never had been.

I broke our staring contest, dropping my gaze to the floor. Exhaustion hit me hard, overcome as I had been by the panic and rush of getting here, of finding Blane, and now this. I swayed on my feet.

"No." I held my hand, palm out, to stop Blane. He'd seen my moment of weakness and had moved closer—to catch me if I passed out, I thought grimly. As if I would give him that satisfaction.

A huff of laughter, devoid of humor, escaped my throat. I looked up at Blane, directing my icy words to his chest, refusing to look in his eyes.

"I actually came here to warn you," I said flatly. "A man called me, said he was watching you. Implied he was going to hurt you."

"I know," came Blane's soft reply. I laughed again.

"Of course you do." I couldn't disguise the bitterness in my voice. It had been for nothing then—the rush over here, the panic, the fear. My only reward had been to find him with another woman. The awful irony was not lost on me.

"Thank you," he said. "For worrying. For coming here."

"Yeah, well . . ." My voice trailed off. I still refused to look at him. My heart felt like it was breaking in two. I'd always known this fate awaited me if I fell in love with Blane—I'd been kidding myself to believe any other ending was possible. I swayed again.

"You need to sit down, Kathleen," Blane said, reaching for me.

"Don't touch me," I snarled, retreating a few steps. Blane stopped in his tracks. I swallowed, took a deep breath, and tried to regain some remnant of my fragile composure.

"I'm not quitting my job," I said flatly. "You'll have to fire me if you want me to leave."

"I'm not going to fire you," he said, watching me carefully.

Well, that was a small comfort.

"I've got to go." I had to get out of there, had to get away from Blane before I broke completely. I absolutely could not let him see how much he'd hurt me.

Without waiting for him to say anything more, I turned on my heel, rushing out of the room.

"Kathleen, wait!" Blane called.

I ignored him, nearly running in my haste to get away from him.

This time when I entered the ballroom, I was most definitely noticed. Dressed as I was, with tears running unchecked down my cheeks, pursued by Blane—I was hard to miss. Thankfully, most people were too stunned to do more than get out of my way.

I hit the hallway and tore through it toward the front door and freedom. It was hard to see, my vision blurry from tears. I was nearly to the door when I felt his hand close around my arm.

I swung around, acting more from the instinct of self-preservation than anything else. My fist came up and connected with Blane's jaw.

We stood in a frozen tableau, me in horror at what I'd done, and Blane . . . his expression was stricken as he took in my tear-stained face. I thought my hand probably hurt more than I'd hurt him, but the look of pain on Blane's face was unmistakable.

A crowd had gathered now and the silence in the foyer seemed condemning as dozens of eyes rested on Blane and me. With a jerk, I freed myself from Blane's grasp and walked out with as much of my tattered dignity intact as possible.

A few minutes later, I was in my car again. The tears were still falling freely and I let them. I'd done what I'd told myself I wouldn't do—I'd fallen in love with Blane Kirk. I rested my arms against the steering wheel and my forehead on my hands as I cried. What a fool I'd been.

I cried longer than I should have, wearily lifting my head to dig for my keys. No thought was in my head except the desire to get away, go home, and lick my wounds in private. I glanced up as I fumbled with the keys, and I froze.

The heat from my body and breath had fogged up the windshield and now I could see that someone had written on the glass directly in front of me, only one word: *BOOM.*

CHAPTER ELEVEN

I didn't move.

I didn't breathe.

My mind was having difficulty processing the very real possibility of a bomb in my car. My fingers were numb as they rested on the cold steering wheel. Time stopped for a moment, then rushed forward as panic set in.

"Kathleen."

I jerked in surprise, my head whipping around to look out the window at Kade standing next to the car, peering inside at me.

"Kade—" I gasped.

"Open the door," he said, his voice muffled from the glass. He reached for the door handle. "You're in no condition to drive."

"No! Wait!" I shouted. The panic in my voice must have gotten through to him, because he froze. "Look." I pointed at the windshield. Kade looked and I could tell when he'd made out the word because his expression turned cold and hard.

"Fuck."

My thoughts exactly.

"Don't move," he ordered before dropping out of sight.

"Wasn't planning on it," I replied weakly to empty air.

A few seconds later, he was back on his feet.

"Okay," he said, "now don't panic."

Those words weren't exactly comforting.

"There is a bomb underneath your car."

I suddenly felt so light-headed that I sagged in my seat.

"Don't you pass out on me, Kathleen!" Kade yelled, and I jerked upward, obeying the urgency in his voice.

"Listen to me," he said, intent but calm. "The bomb is rigged to something inside, but I can't tell what it is. It could be the door, ignition, radio, anything."

"That's not helpful," I said.

"It's also on a timer, Kathleen," he added reluctantly.

Oh God. My eyes clamped shut in terror.

"How much time?" I asked.

"Three minutes."

Three minutes to live. It didn't seem possible. I was only twenty-four. I had my whole life ahead of me. Granted, today hadn't gone well, but surely tomorrow would be better. And who would take care of Tigger if I died?

"You should go," I choked out. "Back off. I can try to open the door." There was no sense in Kade getting killed, too. I thought I had a pretty good shot that maybe it wasn't rigged to the door. Kade himself had said it could be attached to a myriad of things inside the car.

"I'm not leaving you, Kathleen."

I looked up to find him staring resolutely down at me through the glass, the tuxedo clinging to his body like it had been molded to him, though I noticed he'd loosened the tie and undone the top button on his shirt. I took a moment I didn't have to appreciate how good he looked. After all, this might be the last time I'd get the chance.

"Don't be ridiculous, Kade," I snapped, forcing my gaze away from him. "You don't even like me. Now go."

"I don't have to like you to save your life," he shot back. "Now roll down the window."

"Can't," I said. "Not without turning on the car." I never thought I'd miss the days of manual windows, but then again, I'd never pictured myself in this particular situation.

"Turn away then," he said.

Obediently, I turned away from the window only to hear a loud thud against the glass. Kade was trying to break the window. There was a second thud, the window splintering but rigidly holding together despite Kade's assault. When I cautiously glanced around, I saw Kade's elbow wasn't doing the trick and he was scanning the street for something to use as a ram instead. That's when I remembered.

"Wait!" I cried excitedly. Kade turned expectantly toward me. "I forgot about something."

Digging around under my seat, I unearthed an ice scraper and a lone glove. Frantic, I searched blindly until my fingers closed around what I sought.

"This!" I said, triumphantly brandishing my prize. It was a device about six inches long, with a sharp metal point on one end. My dad had given it to me when I'd first started driving at fifteen, mere months before his death. "In case you ever need to get out of a car in a hurry," he'd explained, showing me how one side of the tool could cut through a seat belt. I wasn't interested in that now, though, as I pressed the metal point into the window.

In seconds, the glass shattered, falling away in pieces. I had barely taken a breath before Kade was reaching through the window for me, pulling me out. Because of the Christmas getup, I had a lot of exposed skin on my arms and legs, and the sharp bite of the glass let me know I wasn't escaping unscathed. Once I was out, I reached back in and grabbed my purse off the seat. Kade grabbed my hand, jerking me backward.

"Run!"

No need to tell me twice.

We weren't far enough away to escape getting knocked off our feet when the explosion hit. Kade pulled me into him and twisted as we flew through the air, taking the brunt of the force when we landed.

For a moment, I just lay on top of him, stunned. Kade recovered more quickly than me, sitting up and dragging me onto his lap.

"Are you all right?" he asked.

My vocal cords wouldn't cooperate, so I gave a jerky nod. I was shaking uncontrollably, whether from the cold or the explosion or the still vivid shock of seeing Blane and Kandi. Probably all of the above.

But I couldn't think about that right now. I'd think about that later. Maybe.

Kade stood, helping me to my feet as well, then shrugged out of his tuxedo jacket and swung it over my shoulders. I was grateful for the coat, still warm from his body. Just then, a whole group of people swarmed outside from the party to see what the commotion was. My eyes fell on Blane, who was running flat-out toward us.

"Kathleen!"

He skidded to a halt a few yards away when he caught sight of Kade and me, then bent at the waist, his hands braced on his knees. After a moment in this position, he drew himself up again and moved toward us.

"Keep him away from me," I said to Kade, my voice only a whisper. "Please."

"She's fine," Kade said to Blane as he neared. Kade's arms tightened protectively around me, drawing me closer into his body. Blane stopped in his tracks, his expression shuttered.

Kade's arm was wrapped around my waist, and I thought I should be embarrassed by how much I needed that support to stay on my feet. Events had moved too fast before; now it was as though everything was in slow motion. I couldn't tear my eyes away from my car burning, the bright flames mesmerizing me.

That was almost me in there. I would have burned to death.

I couldn't get enough air. My lungs were inflating, but I couldn't breathe. My hands clutched at Kade and yet—I couldn't look away from the fire and I still couldn't breathe.

"Breathe, princess. Just breathe."

I heard Kade's voice, insistent in my ear, and I tried to obey. But the fire was growing dim now and I heard Blane as if from a long way off.

"She's going into shock, Kade. We need to get her to the hospital."

"Haven't you done enough?" The icy, accusing words came from Kade.

The last thought I had was that I didn't want them to fight.

~

The thing about passing out, it's really not as bad as it sounds. Rather, it's more like your body says, "You go on ahead—I'm just going to take a moment."

I stirred and opened my eyes, aware that I felt better. For one thing, I could breathe again, which is always a plus.

Where was I?

I was lying in a bed, but it wasn't mine. A small lamp was lit on a nearby table, allowing me to see the comfortable though nondescript room. Confused, I sat up, noticing as I did so that I no longer wore the hated Christmas slut outfit but a man's button-down shirt that swallowed me up and came nearly to my knees.

"Take it easy now."

My gaze swung to the doorway, where Kade was entering the room, holding two steaming mugs. He handed me one before sitting next to me on the edge of the bed. He'd changed out of his tuxedo, which was a real shame, and now wore his customary jeans and long-sleeved black henley. I noticed his feet were bare.

"Where am I?" I asked, taking a sip of the sweetened coffee. Somehow he'd known how I liked it.

"My place." Kade's simple reply threw me.

"Your place?" I asked, confused. "I thought you lived with Blane?"

He snorted. "Not likely. As if I could stand living with him for more than a few days."

I processed this as I took another sip. I had another question, but I wasn't sure I wanted to know the answer.

"Um, how did I get into this?" I asked, indicating the shirt I wore. It had to be Kade's.

"Yeah, that little red outfit's a goner. Sorry."

I certainly had no qualms about that. However, that also meant Kade had been the one to strip me and put the shirt on me. My cheeks heated and I looked down, letting my hair swing forward to conceal my face from Kade. To my chagrin, he reached forward, pushing my hair back and tucking the strands behind my ear. I glanced up.

"Would it help if I said I didn't look?"

The mischief in his eyes made me smile, though it was tremulous and quickly faded. I took another sip of the coffee. We sat in companionable silence for a few moments before Kade spoke again.

"Are you going to tell me what happened?" he asked quietly.

My eyes flew to his in surprise. "You don't know?"

He shook his head, his gaze sober.

I pushed my fingers through my hair and swallowed hard. I wanted to answer him, wanted to tell him what a dick his brother was, but that also meant I had to again relive the shock, the humiliation, and the pain.

I set the coffee on the bedside table with a hand that trembled.

"I'm going to need something stronger."

Kade watched in silence as I climbed out of the bed, following me as I left the bedroom and walked the short hallway to the kitchen. The kitchen was in the corner of a large open room. It had a small bar separating it from the living room area, where there was a flat-screen television hung on the wall, a couch, and a couple of chairs. The wall behind the sofa was all glass, the city lights sparkling in the night. I realized Kade must live in one of those expensive downtown loft apartments that overlooked the city.

Figuring I'd find what I needed in the cabinets, I began searching, starting down low and working my way to the higher ones.

"Can I help you find something?" Kade asked dryly, leaning a hip against the counter.

I stretched, trying to reach a high cabinet, frustrated that I hadn't yet found what I was seeking. Belatedly, I noticed the shirt I wore was riding high up my bare thighs. I abruptly tugged it back down. I glanced up at Kade, his eyes lingering on my legs before they traveled upward to my face.

"Where's your liquor?" I blurted, my cheeks burning again at the frank appreciation in his eyes.

He didn't answer, his gaze holding mine as he stepped into my personal space. My breath caught in my chest and I had to tip my head back to look at him.

"It's where it should be," he said, pulling open the door of the freezer behind me.

Startled, I turned to see several bottles of Belvedere in the freezer. Of course. I'd been looking for scotch—but that was Blane's drink, not Kade's.

Kade grabbed one of the bottles, pulled out the stopper, and set it on the counter.

"Straight?" he asked.

"Please."

Getting a couple of shot glasses off a shelf, Kade filled each with the chilled vodka. Handing me one, he clinked his to mine before adding, "Cheers."

I tossed back the cold liquid, almost instantly feeling the warm fire hit my belly. Sucking in a breath, I set the glass back on the counter, tapping it to signal a refill. Kade obliged, eyeing me as I rounded the counter and climbed onto one of the two barstools. As usual, my feet didn't reach the ground, but I didn't care.

I drank down the second shot and it was like balm to my shattered nerves. Kade was watching me, not speaking, and I appreciated his patience. Finally, I was able to say, "I walked in on Blane and . . . Kandi." I looked up at him, hoping he'd get the point without me having to spell it out.

His jaw tightened. "Doing what?" he asked. I cringed at the harnessed fury in his voice.

I just looked at him, then tapped my glass for another round. After a moment, he refilled both glasses and we drank in silence.

Inside me, tears threatened, yet I determinedly held them back. I don't know why I was so surprised by this outcome—I'd been telling myself it was going to happen for weeks. I guess expecting it and actually experiencing it were just two different things. One was all about my head, the other, my heart.

"You all right?" Kade asked, and I realized I'd been lost in my thoughts.

"I'm fine," I said automatically, and for the moment, it was sort of true. Alcohol was a great numbing agent. Screw the chocolate and ice cream—I'll take vodka to heal a broken heart.

Kade poured us both some more, emptying the bottle. It tasted really good now, going down smooth as could be.

Kade got another bottle out of the freezer and slid onto the stool next to me.

"People leave, you know?" I said out of the blue. It was a fact I'd always known but rarely stopped to dwell on. "They desert you, forget about you. People hurt you, betray you, don't love you anymore. They get hurt. They die." I studied my glass as I absently toyed with it. "I don't know why I thought it might be different with . . ." I couldn't finish that thought. Reaching for the bottle, I gave us refills, spilling only a little on the counter.

"Well, aren't you the cynic," Kade said, his mouth twisting into his telltale smirk, but his eyes were serious.

"When has anyone you've been close to not left?" I asked bluntly.

He eyed me for a long moment before replying, "I don't stick around long enough to give them the chance."

I frowned. "Why is that?"

He shrugged and threw back his vodka. "I'd rather be the one leaving than the one who's left behind."

I could certainly relate to that. Blane's betrayal burned like acid in my stomach. I wondered if he'd been sleeping with Kandi and me at the same time. The idea nearly made me ill. I pushed the thought away and drank my vodka.

"Why am I here?" I asked him. It was a strange choice to bring me to his apartment. "Why not just take me home?"

"You've nearly gotten yourself killed several times in the last few days," Kade said matter-of-factly. "It's easier to keep you safe here."

I snorted. "What do you care? Blane and I are through, so no one's making you play bodyguard anymore. You can't stand me as it is—you should be glad to be rid of me. I'm just the white-trash gold digger, remember?"

"I never said that."

"Which part?" I asked derisively.

Kade's face was inscrutable as he looked at me, his eyes the most beautiful blue. With the combination of those eyes and the wickedly arched brows that matched his nearly black hair curling slightly over the collar of the shirt, he could have been a fallen angel, he was so lovely.

"You need some food in you," Kade announced. "When was the last time you ate?"

I shrugged. I didn't remember or care. Now that I thought about it, I didn't care about much of anything at the moment. That was nice. I sighed and reached for the bottle of Belvedere.

"Nope," Kade said, snatching it easily from my hand. "Not until you eat."

"But I'm not hungry," I protested. Actually, it came out more like a whine.

Kade ignored me, sliding off his stool and rounding to the cabinets. He pulled out a box and dumped some little packages onto the counter. I picked one up.

"Moon Pie?" I'd heard of these but never tried one. I don't think I remembered even encountering them before in a store in Indiana. "Where did you get these?"

"I have my sources," Kade said, ripping open one of the packages. I watched as he broke the chocolate-covered circle in half, what looked like marshmallow fluff oozing out of the middle. Kade took a bite from one half, his eyes sliding shut in appreciation. It seemed incongruous but was apparently true—Kade had a sweet tooth. His eyes opened, catching me staring at his mouth. I flushed.

"Try it," Kade insisted. "You can't have that much booze on an empty stomach or you're going to be puking, and I'm not holding your hair for you."

I grimaced. It didn't look very good, chocolate notwithstanding, though he had a good point about the puking. Kade made an impatient noise at my hesitation.

"Here, just try." Instead of offering me the hunk of pie, he took his finger and scooped out some of the marshmallow, holding it out to me. Surprised, I looked up at him, only to see a hint of a challenge in his gaze. He no doubt thought I wouldn't do it.

I leaned forward and wrapped my lips around the creamy fluff, Kade's finger sliding into my mouth. I heard Kade's sharp intake of breath and smiled to myself. It wasn't often I was able to best Kade at his own game.

The rough pad of Kade's finger felt very nice on my tongue. But soon the fluff was gone and I let his finger slide from my mouth. Taking a half of a Moon Pie, I took a bite, waiting to see what Kade would say. He didn't disappoint.

"If I'd known you'd do that to anything covered in marshmallow, I would have put it in a different location."

I chuckled, the vodka helping me appreciate his sense of humor.

I finished the Moon Pie, licking the melted chocolate from my fingers. Kade watched me in such a way that I thought it might be a good idea to renew my interest in going home.

"Are you going to take me home now?" I asked.

"Wasn't planning on it."

His curt answer irritated me. It wasn't like I could just stay here with him. "I need to go home," I insisted.

"And then what?" Kade retorted. "In case you haven't noticed, you have no car. No car means no transportation."

I stared blankly at him, realizing he was right. My car was a smoldering pile of ruins. The thought of having to buy another one made me sick to my stomach. The meager amount in my savings would be entirely depleted. And what was I going to do without a car until then? I had no boyfriend to loan me a car and didn't want to be a burden to my few friends by having them cart me around.

My aloneness hit me with the force of a sucker punch. I'd gotten accustomed not only to Blane's company but also to his solid presence in my life. Now it was gone and I was once again on my own. The tears I'd been holding back welled in my eyes, spilling over and down my cheeks.

Kade cursed, hurriedly rounding the counter to me. He took me in his arms and I didn't resist; the temptation to lean on him was too great. He held me as I wept, one hand wrapped around my back, the other running soothingly through my hair, over and over. With my head tucked under his chin, I could hear the slight rumbling in his chest as he spoke to me.

"Shh. I'm sorry, princess. Don't cry. Please."

My chest hurt with a physical pain, my heart breaking inside. I didn't want to think about why Blane would cheat on me, why he would choose to hurt and betray me in this fashion. Now I had nothing and no one. I sobbed harder.

"Please, Kathleen," Kade pleaded. "Please don't cry."

With an effort, I stopped. My eyes were swollen and my head was pounding. I tried to calm down, but my breath kept hitching in my chest.

"There, that's better," Kade said softly. His hands cradled my face, his thumbs brushing away my tears. "I'm sorry Blane's such a bastard. And I'm not any better. But you're not alone, okay?"

I forced a weak smile. "But I am," I whispered sadly.

"You have me."

The fierceness of his declaration surprised me and I stared at him. His face was inches from mine as he gazed into my eyes before gently pressing his lips to my forehead.

Leaning back to look at me, he smiled a real smile, not his usual mocking smirk. It wiped the cynicism from his features and was worth the effort to smile back. He placed a comforting kiss on each cheek while I sniffled. His hands cupped my jaw, his long fingers reaching back into the hair at the nape of my neck. Kade's hands were large and strong, and I had the passing thought that he could snap my neck in an instant if he wanted to.

His lips on mine took me by surprise before I realized this was a kiss of comfort, not sexual, but that didn't stop me from sucking in my breath or my pulse from leaping under his fingers.

When he drew back to look at me, his eyes held a question. I couldn't help my gaze drifting down to his mouth. The tension between us grew thick as we stood there, my tears forgotten. I could smell the scent of cologne on his skin, the cotton of his shirt soft under my fingers, the warmth of his skin seeping through the thin fabric.

I felt as though we were hanging on a precipice—only a millimeter from falling over the edge—and I couldn't say whether I wanted that to happen or not. He was so beautiful, and for once his eyes held no mockery, no derision, as he gazed at me. With a brilliant clarity, I remembered being in the motel in Chicago with Kade and how he had touched me, laid his head on my lap, placed a kiss on my knee. It seemed Kade trusted no one, was close to no one, and I was humbled that he'd let me in even this much.

Unbidden, my hand reached to push back a lock of his silky dark hair that had fallen over his brow. As my fingers slipped through the strands, Kade groaned softly, a sound somewhere between pleasure and pain, and then the choice was no longer mine to make.

His mouth met mine with an intensity that left me reeling. Kade's hands cradled my head as he kissed me, his lips tender yet demanding a response.

"Kiss me back, princess," he murmured against my mouth.

I couldn't deny him, this man who put his own soul at risk to save others from a terrible fate. He wanted me and I needed him.

Kade's kiss was different from the one and only other time we'd kissed. That had been purely sexual. This time, it was as though he were worshipping me with his lips and tongue. The room seemed to spin and I held on tightly to him, the only thing sure and grounded and real. His tongue slid against mine, a whisper of heat and satin, not claiming so much as exploring and entrancing me.

When he finally raised his head, the look in his eyes was one I couldn't decipher. My breath was coming in pants and I wanted him to kiss me and never let go.

"Why'd you stop?" I whispered.

"You're drunk," he answered roughly, his fingers softly threading through my hair. I closed my eyes, leaning into his hand. "And I have no interest in being your rebound guy."

I heard him speaking, but his words didn't really penetrate, too enraptured was I by his touch, gentle and sweet. I swayed on my feet. He steadied me, his arms sliding around my waist.

"Come on," he said. "You need to get some rest."

"No," I protested, trying ineffectually to pull away. "I don't want to sleep." I was terrified that if I slept, I would dream. Would I escape the exploding car in my nightmares?

Kade studied me and I felt as though he could see right through to my innermost thoughts, his blue eyes piercing my few remaining defenses.

"All right," he said, turning and leading me by the hand into his living room.

The furniture and walls were all in a palette of ivories, beiges, and coffee; the floor a beautiful hardwood that was chilly on my bare feet. The space was masculine without being overbearing, classy and yet comfortable. I looked around, then sank onto the couch that faced the wall where the television hung. I tucked my legs Indian-style, tugging Kade's shirt down over my exposed thighs. The room was a little cold.

"Where's your Christmas tree?" I asked as Kade sat down next to me on the couch.

He just looked at me.

"What?" I asked. "Everyone should have a Christmas tree, even if it's only a little one."

"I'll keep that in mind," he said dryly, pulling my unresisting body into his arms and laying us side by side on the couch spoon-style, my bottom tucked up against his hips.

Seeing a remote control on the nearby ottoman, I grabbed it, finding and pressing the power button. I flipped channels until I stumbled across *A Charlie Brown Christmas* playing.

We didn't speak, merely watched the story of Charlie Brown and his search for the true meaning of Christmas and the scraggly little Christmas tree that just needed a little love. As the closing credits rolled, I spoke.

"Thank you," I said quietly.

Kade glanced down at me. "For what?"

"Saving me. Again."

The corner of his mouth twisted upward. "I have told you you're a shitload of trouble, right?"

I smiled. The words he'd once uttered in loathing now seemed like a teasing endearment. "I believe you may have mentioned that."

The brilliant blue of his eyes held me captive until I forced myself to look away.

"Did you use to watch this as a kid?" I asked, searching for something to say. I indicated the television.

Kade's expression grew cold and distant. "I might have," he said. "I don't really remember."

I frowned. "You don't remember?"

"I spent the days and nights just trying to survive when I was a kid," he said flatly. "Holiday specials weren't a big part of that."

With a pang, I remembered the burn scars on his back. I wriggled until I was turned toward him. He'd rested his head on his palm, his elbow braced on the couch as he looked down at me.

"Tell me?" I softly asked. My hand stretched upward to push through his hair, my fingers pale against the midnight locks.

His brow furrowed and he opened his mouth to speak but hesitated. I waited patiently, warm from his body pressed against mine on the couch, his hand resting lightly on my hip.

"Not everyone was bad," he finally said, the words seeming to come difficult to him. "But a few were the stuff of nightmares. Those, I ran away from. But there was one . . . I couldn't run away."

"Why not?" My question was almost a whisper, caught as I was by the haunted look in his eyes.

"There was a little girl there, too, younger than me. She didn't know, didn't understand, and he'd go after her."

I barely breathed as I listened. Kade's eyes were on mine, seeming to beg my forgiveness even as he told this horror to me.

"I figured out I could distract him, make him stop, if I pissed him off. Kind of like a diversion. He was a mean son of a bitch. Liked to do the cigarettes and the belt. His fists when he was too drunk to find something else. A few times, a broken bottle, a knife."

Tears started leaking from my eyes, but I couldn't look away from the pain in his.

"Eventually, the girl left. The state took her away. Blane found me shortly after that."

"What happened to the girl?" I asked.

Kade's mouth twisted. "You've met her," he said. "It was Branna."

I could only look at him, surprise etched on my face. Branna had been the gorgeous brunette who had helped us in Chicago, along with Terrance and Rusty. I'd known then that she was in love with Kade, though I'd had no idea of their history together, of how much Kade had sacrificed to protect the weak and innocent, even back then.

More tears spilled from my eyes and Kade frowned, brushing them lightly away.

"I didn't tell you that so you'd feel sorry for me," he said.

I shook my head. "I don't feel sorry for you, or pity you. I feel . . ." I struggled to put my thoughts into words. "Rage and helplessness. Sorrow and despair. I hate that you had to endure such things and I hate the people who did them to you."

Kade studied me, but I couldn't tell what he was thinking. My hand still moved through his hair and I didn't dare look away, wanting him to read the sincerity in my eyes. Somehow I doubted he'd told this story to very many people—maybe to no one—and I didn't want him to regret telling me.

"I lied, you know," he said casually.

My hand froze and my entire body went still beneath his.

"I did look."

It took my fogged brain a moment to puzzle through what he meant, then I let out a relieved huff of laughter. Of course. He was talking about when he'd changed my clothes earlier and then implied that he hadn't looked. The twinkle of mischief was back in his eyes, his lips twisted again in a teasing grin.

I marveled at how a week ago, if I'd been told I'd be in this situation with Kade, I'd never have believed it. Of course, if I'd also been told a week ago that Blane would cheat on me with Kandi . . . Well, that I might actually have believed.

∽

When I awoke the next morning, it was to hear raised voices coming from Kade's living room. I rubbed my bleary eyes, looking for a clock. It was after ten. The voices quieted, so I got out of bed, groaning. The vodka was making its aftereffects known—my head was pounding. Easing my way to the bathroom, I found a brush to run through my tousled hair. An extra toothbrush lay on the counter, still in the packaging, and I mentally thanked Kade. My mouth felt like it had been filled with cotton overnight.

When I came out of the bathroom, I listened but heard nothing. Figuring the voices had just been the television, I stepped out of the bedroom, only to freeze in my tracks at the sight of Blane and Kade standing in the living room.

Both turned to look at me. Blane's gaze swept me from head to foot, taking in that I wore only Kade's shirt. Seeing as how I'd just stepped out of Kade's bedroom, I watched as he made connections in his mind, his expression turning to icy granite that I knew boded ill. I shrank backward, momentarily afraid of him. But then my fear turned to horror when he turned and launched himself at Kade.

The solid crack of Blane's fist hitting Kade's jaw made me shriek. Kade must have been as shocked as I was, because it took him a few precious seconds to defend himself. They grappled, Kade landing a return hit in Blane's gut. Blane was bigger than Kade, but Kade was slightly faster, making it an even match.

I watched with dismay, uncertain what to do or how to stop them. This was not what I wanted. Together, they were all the other had. I couldn't let them rip each other apart.

"Stop!" I cried. "Stop it! Both of you!"

They ignored me. I winced at the sound of knuckles hitting bone again. Tossing aside caution and all good sense, I ran forward.

There was a space between them and I threw myself into it just as Blane's fist came flying toward Kade—only I now stood in front of Kade. I cringed and squeezed my eyes shut, flinching away from the blow. I expected to feel pain exploding through me at any second, but when nothing happened, I carefully opened my eyes.

Blane's fist was a hair's breadth from my cheek. I'd seen the force with which he'd thrown that punch, and it would surely have shattered my cheekbone had he not pulled it back at the last possible second.

No one moved or spoke, the only sound that of their breathing, which I could barely hear over the pounding of my heart. My eyes slowly lifted from Blane's fist to his face. For an instant, there was naked fear written there, before it faded into a mask of anger.

"What the fuck are you doing?" he snapped, jerking backward. "Do you know how close I came to hitting you?"

"Well, if you hadn't been fighting, you wouldn't have almost hit me!" I yelled back. My hands were shaking, so I clenched them into fists. "Why would you do that anyway? Why would you hit your brother?" Anger filled me, burning away the sorrow and heartbreak.

Blane's expression didn't change and he didn't answer me.

"I didn't sleep with her," Kade said flatly, crossing to the freezer and taking out an ice pack, which he laid alongside his jaw.

"Is that what you think?" I said to Blane, my voice dangerously quiet. "That I'd screw your brother to get back at you? That's the sort of person you think I am?" An insistent little voice in the back of my head reminded me about kissing Kade last night. I ignored it.

"Like you have any room to talk, brother," Kade said mockingly. "Or are you the only one allowed to fuck around?"

"Kathleen, I—" Blane started.

"Save it," I snapped. Turning on my heel, I went back into the bedroom, slamming the door behind me. Only when I was alone in the bathroom, safe from prying eyes and ears, did I allow the tears to fall.

Seeing Blane, without any warning at all, had been as though someone had shoved a hot knife into my chest. Then for him to automatically assume the very worst . . . I'd thought he knew me better than that. Of course, he could just have assumed I'd cheat the same as he had. What's good for the goose and all . . .

300

As I stood in front of the mirror, with nowhere to hide and no one to see, I thought about whether I would have stopped Kade last night if he'd wanted more from me than just a kiss. I hoped I would have, but the reality was that I didn't know. I'd been reeling from Blane's betrayal, terrified that I'd nearly been killed, and loneliness had sapped whatever remaining willpower I'd possessed. If Kade had pushed the issue . . . Well, I should probably not fault Blane for thinking the worst. I'm no hypocrite, though perhaps I'd skirted the edges a little this morning.

I sighed. What was done was done. I'd just have to be more careful around Kade from now on. The memory of last night came back to me and I shivered. There had been an energy between Kade and me, an attraction and chemistry that was both compelling and dangerous. If this morning had shown me anything, it was that I had the power to come between Blane and Kade, and I had no desire to do so. Some women might get off on that, but not me. I had no family left—I wasn't about to be responsible for separating two brothers.

I took a shower, wrapping myself up in a towel before exiting the bathroom. Kade had left a pair of sweatpants and a long-sleeved T-shirt on the bed, which I gratefully pulled on. Both were way too big, and I had to roll the waist of the pants down and the legs up just so I could walk.

I cautiously entered the kitchen. To my relief, Blane had left.

"How's your jaw?" I asked Kade as I poured myself a cup of coffee and climbed onto the barstool next to him.

"I'll live," he said shortly, turning toward me. His eyes narrowed. "You have a bruise," he said, his fingers brushing my cheek. "Are you going to tell me who hit you?"

"And what will you do if I tell you?" I asked.

"Kill him."

I smiled at his matter-of-fact answer, though I wasn't one hundred percent sure he was joking. "Well, I'm not going to say, so just forget about it. It doesn't matter anyway."

"You need to take a self-defense course or something," Kade replied. "You're too little to take chances."

I snorted. "Little? Please." He obviously had not seen me from the back.

Kade's eyes narrowed. "You're five foot nothing, have bones I could break with my bare hands, and no doubt weigh about a buck ten. You couldn't stop an overgrown fifth-grader from pushing you around."

"I'll have you know, I'm five foot one and three-quarters," I said archly. No way was I commenting on his weight guess.

"Exactly."

"Like a self-defense course would have stopped Blane this morning?" My tone was sarcastic, but I didn't think it was a bad idea. On the contrary, it would be nice to be able to defend myself in some way.

"I didn't say it would make you smarter," Kade said. "Interfering was a bad idea."

"I had to do something," I said. "I couldn't just watch you two kill each other."

"Next time, leave it alone."

I really hoped there wouldn't be a next time.

"I'll set up the class," Kade said. "The firm will pick up the cost." He smirked at me, adding, "It's cheaper than a hospital bill."

"How pragmatic of you," I said, then changed the subject. "I went to visit Adriana Waters yesterday."

His eyes sharpened, focusing on me. "And?"

"And she's working with whoever is doing this," I said. "I broke into her hotel room and—"

"You what?" Kade said, interrupting my story. "You broke into her room? How?"

"Well, I got a maid to let me in, so I guess that's not really breaking in. Anyway," I continued, "she came back with a man. I didn't get to see who he was, but they talked about getting Blane to lose this case. I think they're behind the threats that made Ron Freeman change his testimony."

"Did they say anything else?"

I shook my head.

"Blane wants me to find Bowers," Kade said. "He thinks Bowers might have been threatened as well, into changing his story, but decided to go into hiding rather than betray Kyle."

I agreed. "Do we know anything about him? What his hobbies are? His friends? Maybe he's hiding out with a girlfriend."

"I'm going to do some digging today," Kade said.

"What about me?"

"You are going to chill here, relax, and stay safe."

"I can't just sit around all day and do nothing," I protested.

"Of course you can," Kade said lightly, getting up and tucking his gun into its holster at his belt. "You've had a rough couple of days. Take it easy today." He shrugged into his leather jacket and turned away.

"Kade," I said urgently, sliding off the stool.

He paused and turned. I stopped awkwardly in front of him.

"Want a kiss good-bye?" he smirked.

I forced a smile. "I just wanted . . . just . . . be careful today, okay?"

His brow furrowed for a moment at my tone, which was tinged with desperation.

"No worries," he reassured me, leaning down to brush his lips against my forehead. Then he was gone.

I swayed on my feet, overwhelmed with what I had just remembered, right before Kade walked out the door: Tonight was the night I had to meet James. With Kade gone and Blane now with Kandi, I had no one to save me except myself.

My stomach heaved and I barely made it to the bathroom in time.

CHAPTER TWELVE

I needed to go home. I understood Kade's wanting to keep me here, keep me safe, but I just couldn't stay. What if Blane came back? I didn't think I could face him again so soon. Not to mention that I had to get home and take care of Tigger.

Lack of transportation was a problem. I'd have to call a cab. With that thought, I remembered Frankie giving me his number, in case I ever needed another ride. Considering how I was dressed, it would be better to have someone I knew pick me up rather than a complete stranger.

Digging Frankie's number out of my purse, I called it, relieved when he answered.

"Frankie?" I asked. "This is Kathleen."

"Hi, K-K-Kathleen," he said, sounding surprised to hear from me.

"I hope you don't mind, but I've run into some car . . . trouble," I hedged, not sure how to explain that my car had been blown to bits. "Could I possibly ask you for a ride home?"

"Sure. Where are y-you?"

Good question. I had no idea. "Um, just a sec." Going back to the bedrooms, I opened the second bedroom door, hoping it was an office. I was in luck—the room held a massive cherrywood desk, with a computer and four flat-screen monitors. Although I hated to go through Kade's things, I saw a small stack of envelopes and picked them up. As I'd hoped, they had an address printed on them, which I read off to Frankie. With his apartment located on Meridian, Kade lived only a few blocks from Monument Circle. I didn't want to think about how much this place cost a month.

Frankie said he'd be there in a few minutes and I hung up. Glancing around, I remembered how Kade used to work for the FBI, in Cyber Crimes. There was a lot of computer equipment in here, and his computer itself looked state of the art.

Some file folders lay to one side of his desk, and I looked at them for a long moment, trying to decide if I should snoop. I'd already conceded that it would be extremely tacky and rude of me to go through Kade's things, but the temptation to know more about him was strong. I sidled a little closer, looking over my shoulder as if Kade would appear at any moment.

Casually, I reached out and flicked open the cover of the file on top. My jaw dropped in shock.

My own face stared up at me from the folder—a candid shot of me walking downtown that I knew had been taken without my permission. I snatched up the folder and flipped through it, my stomach churning with each turn of the page.

Everything there was to know about me was right there in black and white. My high school and college transcripts, my bank account records and current balance, credit report, obituaries of both my mom and dad, the deed of sale for my parents' house, overdue medical bills I still owed for my mom's care—everything.

Not only had Kade lied to me when he'd said he knew nothing about me, apparently he'd done his own background check, though this was more thorough than that. He'd dug into my personal history—photos of me in high school and college were documented as well as a short list of my friends from home and an even shorter list of past boyfriends. Good God, did he have video of when I'd lost my virginity as well?

Furious, I hurled the folder across the room, watching as the papers flew everywhere. Rage and betrayal coursed through my veins. Apparently, Blane and Kade weren't as different as they seemed. I'd fallen for their lies, believing both of them could be trusted. Kade had never gotten over his distrust of me and the proof lay scattered all over the floor.

Grabbing my purse, I jabbed at the button for the loft elevator in the corner of the living room, then entering when the doors slid open. Once inside, I realized Kade lived in the penthouse. Of course he did. Bitterly, I punched the button for street level.

A doorman whose nametag read *Paul* opened the door for me and I returned his smile with a forced one of my own. To my relief, Frankie's taxi was already waiting and I quickly climbed inside.

"Thank you so much for coming to get me, Frankie," I said, trying to quell my anger. After all, it wasn't Frankie's problem Blane and Kade were such jerks.

"It's n-not a p-p-problem," he replied, giving me a shy smile.

"How are you doing?" I asked.

"Aw, fine. J-just wor-working, you know?"

"Yeah, I know." Speaking of which, I didn't know how I was going to get to the hotel tonight. Well, one obstacle at a time.

We pulled up in front of my apartment building and I dug out some money to pay Frankie, who again protested.

"Not this t-time," he said firmly. "Th-this one's on m-m-me."

Before I could say anything, he had driven away. I was grateful for his kindness, though he could ill afford it, and I shoved the money back in my purse.

I was nearly to the top of the stairs when I saw a man step out from the shadows by my door. I froze in my tracks, staring stupidly at him.

He was huge—his massive shoulders encased in a black jacket—and seemed to fill the entire landing. In three strides, he stood in front of me as I hesitated on the stairs.

"Kathleen Turner?" he asked, his voice a deep rumble in his chest.

I nodded uncertainly. "Who are you?"

His smile sent chills down my spine.

"Simone sent me," he said. "She thought you might need a little reminder about tonight."

Alarmed, I tried to retreat backward down the stairs but was abruptly stopped when he grabbed my shirt, fisting the cloth around my neck. He yanked me forward and I stumbled, abruptly realizing I'd lost my grip on the banister and now stood with only the tips of my toes touching the stairs. I clutched at his arm, terrified he was going to let go and send me tumbling down the concrete steps.

"It'd be too bad if you had an accident," he sneered at me. "So just remember—if you don't show up tonight, I'll be payin' you another visit tomorrow."

I glanced over my shoulder, the stairs looming behind me. I'd surely break something, or worse, if he pushed me.

"You understand?" he growled, shaking me.

"Yeah," I said. "I get it."

He shoved me backward and I screamed, clutching wildly at him before he pulled me back. My feet connected solidly with the stairs as I gasped for air, my heart racing.

The man laughed, shoving me aside as he went down the stairs. I watched as he climbed into a gray Camaro and peeled out of the parking lot.

"Are you all right?"

I started, looking up into Alisha's concerned face.

"I heard you scream. Who was that guy?" she asked, her eyes wide.

Shaking, I climbed the few remaining steps up to her before bursting into tears.

A couple of hours later, I was back in my own clothes, curled up on my couch with Tigger in my lap, Alisha sitting next to me. I'd broken down and told her everything—about seeing Blane cheating on me with Kandi, about my car blowing up, staying the night with Kade and then finding his file on me, to my dilemma of what I was going to do about James tonight. To her credit, Alisha had listened very well, offering sympathetic noises when appropriate but mainly just letting me pour my troubles out to her.

"So how much money do you owe Simone?" she asked, getting up from the couch.

"Five thousand dollars," I replied glumly, stroking Tigger's fur and watching as Alisha straightened a slightly crooked picture on one wall. I wondered how long she'd been staring at it, itching to fix it.

"How much do you have in savings?"

"Only about three hundred." I glanced at the clock. It was nearing the time I'd have to get ready and go. I didn't want to call a taxi again. "Do you think I could borrow your car?"

"Of course you can," Alisha said, "but what are you going to do? Sleeping with this guy to pay off a debt just seems like such a third-world, women-as-property kind of thing."

I had an idea—just forming at the back of my mind—and even as I thought it, I wondered if I could pull it off. Unless I resigned myself to sleeping with James, I didn't have a choice. The price of failure, though, would likely be worse than sex. I made a decision. It didn't matter if I failed—I had to try. I was sick to death of being pushed around, not only by James but by Kade and Blane as well. I'd get myself out of this mess or face the consequences.

"I have a plan . . ." I said slowly. "Sort of. But I need help. Could you help me?"

Alisha eyed me, then nodded. "So long as your plan doesn't include a threesome, I'm in."

~

A few hours later, I was entering the Crowne Plaza Hotel, trying to maintain a semblance of calm over my anxiety. I tightened the belt of my long coat as I made my way through the luxurious lobby to the front desk. Although a few people milled about, the sound of conversation was muffled by the thick carpet. In one corner of the lobby, a man played the baby grand piano, the rich tones warm and inviting.

"May I help you?" The man behind the desk cast a practiced eye over my clothing, no doubt judging its quality and price tag. His nametag read *Bernard*. He was the man Gracie had told me to ask for.

"I was told you'd have something for me," I replied. "Something for Lorelei."

A glimmer of understanding lit his eyes, but he carefully kept his expression blank as he opened a drawer beneath the counter.

"I believe this is for you," he said, handing me a white envelope with a room number written on the back.

"Thank you," I replied absently, already turning away. Inside the envelope was a room-key card. Taking a deep breath and steeling my resolve, I headed for the elevator.

A few moments later, I was walking down a long hallway on one of the hotel's top floors. I passed a mirror, then paused and returned to it. I shed my coat and studied my reflection.

Part of the plan had been to dress the part, cooperation from James being necessary for this to work. To that end, I had borrowed a top from Alisha that I'd been surprised she'd even owned. It was a halter, made of a silky silver material, that tied behind my neck and at my waist, leaving my arms and entire back bare. I didn't have the type of bra you'd wear with a shirt like this, so I'd gone without—a fact that was obvious as the thin material clung to me. I'd paired the shirt with a black skirt that was too short and too tight for me to wear anymore, a scrap that had been buried in the back of my closet. The hem stopped several inches above my knees, and I gave it a sharp tug to pull it down a bit. Alisha had lent me a pair of black stockings that came to midthigh and had a seam running down the back of each leg.

Last of all, I had dug out the peacock-blue heels I'd bought at Nordstrom with the money Kade had given me. It seemed fitting they'd be used for this purpose. They gave me height and a bit of courage, the little blue, green, and silver jewels affixed to them glinting in the light. I'd left my hair down and had tousled it, the long locks curling over my shoulders and down my back. The sapphires Blane had given me sparkled at my ears.

The thought flittered through my head that though I had declared my independence from both Kade and Blane, it seemed I was taking both of them inside the hotel room with me tonight—perhaps as a reminder, perhaps for courage. I shook off the uncomfortable thought. I didn't need Blane or Kade to take care of me. I could take care of myself just fine, thank you very much.

Grabbing my coat and purse, I faced the door, unsure whether to knock or just walk in. Considering that I'd been given a key, I supposed that knocking was out. I slid the card into the key slot and watched the light turn green, the lock clicking free. Turning the knob, I entered the room.

I was taken aback by what I saw. Candles were lit throughout the room, giving it an ethereal glow. Beyond the entry was a bank of windows, the curtains open to display the twinkling lights of the city below. A bottle of champagne rested in a silver wine bucket filled with ice, two empty flutes standing nearby.

I swallowed uncomfortably, frowning. What was this—some kind of seduction scene? That didn't really coincide with what I'd been expecting. James hadn't bothered to be anything but cruel to me since our one and only date. I walked farther into the room.

"I must admit, I'm a little surprised you showed up."

Turning, I saw James standing a few feet behind me. He wore gray slacks and a white button-down shirt, no tie. His eyes flicked over me and it was all I could do not to cross my arms over my chest. I felt dirty, even with nothing more than his gaze touching me.

"I wasn't aware I had a choice," I said, smiling tightly. "You made that quite clear yesterday." I turned my head slightly, displaying the bruise that darkened my cheek.

"I wouldn't have had to do that if you'd just cooperated," he said, moving closer to me. I forced myself to stand still and not retreat.

"Oh, so it's the woman's fault if the man beats her up?" I asked sarcastically.

"Precisely."

His hand lifted to brush the skin of my arm and a shudder of revulsion went through me. His eyes were glued to my chest. Taking a step back, I said, "Aren't you going to offer me something to drink?"

James smiled and the sight of it produced another shudder in me.

"Where are my manners? Would you like a glass of champagne?"

At my jerky nod, he uncorked the bottle and poured the sparkling, golden fluid into the two flutes. After I took one from his outstretched hand, he guided me to the sofa, pulling me down to sit next to him. I was squeezed into the small space between his body and the arm of the sofa. I took a sip of the cold champagne.

"I must say, I like the outfit," James said, his voice low, near my ear. His hand rested on my nylon-covered knee.

"I assumed this is how you like your prostitutes to dress," I said coldly.

"*Prostitute* is such a harsh word. I prefer *female companion*."

I pressed my knees tightly together when his palm slid up my thigh. "It doesn't change the fact that you're blackmailing me into having sex with you," I said baldly, taking another sip of champagne.

"Taking advantage of your . . . circumstances . . . isn't a crime," James said lightly. He took the champagne from me and set it on the table.

"Your involvement with the prostitution ring will get out sooner or later," I said quickly. "You won't be able to play this game forever."

"I'll keep that in mind," he replied, curling an arm around my shoulder. I felt his fingers work at the ties to my blouse.

"Why does Simone owe you money anyway?" I asked, my hands clenching into fists.

He shrugged. "Like it's any of your concern, but she owed me for the take from the party. A party which you attended, I might add."

314

"You mean the one where you didn't lift a finger to help me when your dad told Jimmy to kill me?" I said angrily.

"Now, now," he said condescendingly, "don't hold a grudge. It all turned out all right. You're not dead."

"Only because Blane saved me."

At the mention of Blane's name, James's fingers tightened painfully on the back of my neck. I struggled not to wince.

"Ah yes. Kirk. He does seem to fuck up the best-laid plans." James's voice hissed in my ear. "But he's not here to save you tonight, is he?"

I twisted away from his grip on my neck just as my hand shot out to grasp between his legs, my hold firm and tight on his balls. James froze.

"I don't need him here to save me," I spat at him, digging in my nails through the thin fabric of his slacks. James sucked in a breath through his teeth. "I can do that all on my own."

"What the fuck are you doing?" he snarled.

"Reminding you of who you're screwing with," I said. "I'm glad you were so talkative tonight, especially since it's all been recorded." With my free hand, I plucked the small Bluetooth earpiece, hidden by my hair, from my ear. I'd phoned Alisha from it when I'd gotten off the elevator. "Perhaps what you did isn't a crime, but somehow I doubt the public would view it that way."

"I'll kill you for this," James threatened, his eyes narrowing in anger. I squeezed tighter and he grunted in pain. I smiled coldly.

"Good to have that on record, too," I said sweetly. "Keep going, Mister District Attorney. I'm sure you're really helping your reelection chances. Tell me—should I send the tape to the cops? The press? Or just put it on YouTube?" My heart pounded in my chest, anxiety twisting in my gut, but I kept my expression serene.

In a move that startled me, James swung his elbow, catching me on the side of the head with a sharp crack. I gasped in pain and my grip on his body faltered. With a roar of anger, he swung again, catching me in the jaw and sending me careening to the floor. My teeth clanked shut and I tasted blood from where I'd bitten my tongue.

Ignoring the pain and jerking upright, I had just enough time to see James coming for me. Fear and adrenaline shot through me and I lashed out with my foot, the wickedly sharp stiletto heel on it catching him directly on his shin.

James howled in pain, dropping to his knees. I didn't wait to see what he did next but turned back over, scrambling to where my purse had fallen to the floor a few feet away. I could hear James spitting curses, the table overturning as he lunged for me.

I gasped in shock as the ice from the bucket hit my back. James's hand closed around my ankle. I kicked out blindly, earning another reprieve when I met solid flesh and heard him grunt with pain.

"You are so dead, you fucking bitch!" he yelled at me. I didn't waste time replying; my grasping hand finally clutched my purse and I dug inside it. I turned back toward him.

"Don't ever threaten me again, you bastard," I growled through clenched teeth. I jabbed the stun gun I'd borrowed from Alisha against his arm and pushed the trigger.

James's body jerked, then was still, his eyes rolling up into his head.

Relief flooded through me and I gasped for breath. Adrenaline was still coursing through my body, making my hands shake. I stumbled to my feet, wanting desperately to get out of there, and shoved the stun gun and Bluetooth back into my purse. A vindictive thought had me reaching for James, relieving him of his wallet and car keys. Taking what cash he had, I found the bathroom and tossed the wallet into the toilet. Spying his cell phone on a nearby table, I dropped it on the floor and ground the heel of my shoe into the screen, shattering it, then I was out the door and walking quickly down the hall toward the elevators.

I punched the down button and hauled out my phone, calling Alisha.

"Are you all right?" were the first words out of her mouth.

"Yeah, I'm fine," I said, hoping it was true. I turned toward the mirror in the hallway and grimaced. Blood trickled from the corner of my mouth and my hair was a wreck. I shoved a hand through it for a quick finger-comb, wincing when I touched the spot where James's elbow had connected. "Did you get it all on tape?"

She answered in the affirmative as I surveyed my shirt, now wet from the ice and plastered to my skin. My nylons were ripped where James had grabbed me.

"Gotta go," I said. "I'll be back soon."

"Kathleen, wait, I need to tell—"

The rest of her sentence was lost as I disconnected. I shoved the stockings down and off my legs before putting my bare feet back into my shoes. Looking around, I spotted a nearby potted plant and hurriedly shoved my wadded-up stockings into the pot just as the elevator dinged. Crap. I hoped the elevator was empty.

I shook out my coat as the doors slid open. I had one arm inside a sleeve when I spotted Blane standing inside the elevator.

I gaped in surprise, then froze.

"Get in," he growled at me.

His command jerked me out of my stupor and I stiffened my spine.

"I think I'll catch the next one," I said coldly.

In a flash, he reached out and snagged my arm, yanking me into the elevator with him. He jabbed a button behind me and the doors slid closed.

Furious, I stared daggers at him. He ignored my fuming glare, his eyes resting on the blood by my mouth, then dropping lower. Before I could stop him, he roughly pushed aside my coat, taking in my clothing. I shoved his arms away, clutching the coat closed around me.

"Do you mind?" I hissed.

Blane's eyes met mine and I instinctively stepped away from the rage I saw there, the wall of the elevator coming up against my back.

"Actually," he bit out, "I do."

The elevator dinged again, then Blane was dragging me out of it, his grip unyielding on my upper arm—not hard enough to bruise, but too tight to get away. I stumbled next to him, my heels not made for moving at this pace.

"Where are you taking me?" I asked, holding on to my anger.

"We need to talk."

"I don't want to talk." Like I wanted to hear his excuses, his explanations. As if anything he had to say would erase the image of him kissing Kandi from my mind. The thought made me angrier.

He was dragging me down a deserted corridor that looked like it was on the same level as the conference rooms, all empty at this time of night. He stopped in front of a door marked Conference Room 125. Opening the heavy wooden door, he pushed me inside, then closed the door behind him.

The room was large, the ceiling at least twenty feet high, and with only a few lights that were half lit. A scattering of big, round tables were arranged in the space, covered with black linen cloths. Chairs were stacked along one wall.

Eager to get some space between Blane and me, I moved away, turning so my back wasn't to him. I needn't have worried. He'd halted inside the doorway. Darkness shrouded him and I squinted to see him through the shadows, cursing the faint light I'd stepped into.

"What do you want, Blane?" I asked. "What are you doing here?"

"I came to stop you from making a stupid move," he answered flatly. "But I see I was too late."

My heart sank. I don't know how he'd found out why I was here, but he had—and he thought I'd gone through with it. I shouldn't have cared, but I did. My eyes stung, which only made me angry.

"It's none of your business, Blane," I choked out. "I don't need you. I can take care of myself."

"Can you?" His voice was both skeptical and sad. I squinted into the darkness, wishing I could see his face. As if he'd heard my thought, he moved toward me. Alarmed, I backed away.

"Kade told me what Simone wanted you to do tonight," he said, coming closer.

I bumped into something and stopped, glancing around to see I'd come up against one of the tables.

"I paid that money to her already," he continued. "You coming here tonight was completely unnecessary."

My eyes jerked to his in dismay. "But . . ." I stuttered. "But James said—"

"James?"

Blane's shocked outburst had me clamping my mouth shut, aghast at what I'd just stupidly revealed.

"James was the one who—" Blane stopped, seemingly unable to complete the sentence. Without another word, Blane turned on his heel, striding for the door.

"No! Blane! Wait!" I scrambled after him, cursing my stilettos for slowing me down. In the dark, I couldn't see where I was going. My heel caught on the carpet and with a cry, I fell, my ankle twisting sharply beneath me.

In seconds, Blane was crouching at my side. "Are you all right?" he asked.

I grimaced, nodding. "I just twisted my ankle."

Without another word, he lifted me in his arms and set me onto a nearby table. Dropping down, he lightly pressed my ankle, feeling the joint. I hissed at the pain. Damn it. This was all his fault, I thought crankily.

"What do you expect when you wear shoes like these?" he asked.

"Well, I hadn't planned on running in them," I retorted.

He didn't say anything to that, merely continued massaging my ankle, carefully bending my foot. It felt a little better and I turned the joint in a circle. No break, thank God.

Incongruously, I suddenly wanted to cry. The sight of him bending down, taking care of me, reminded me too much of what used to be. The anger over his betrayal was still there, but now I felt an overwhelming sadness, too. I was glad I'd never told him I loved him. That would have been humiliating.

That thought steeled my resolve, even as I fought the urge to reach out and run my fingers through his hair. He was wearing dark jeans and a deep-green sweater, which I knew would make his eyes appear like emeralds. The feel of his hands on my skin was bittersweet.

Blane swam in my vision and I cleared my throat, blinking rapidly. Best not to dwell on it.

"I'll, um, find a way to pay you back," I said roughly. When he looked up at me, my breath caught. I'd been right about his emerald eyes and their brilliant depths held me mesmerized.

"You say that as if I care about the damn money," he said flatly.

The fight was drained out of me—I was sick of arguing, so I just shrugged in response.

He stood, standing close to me, his chest at eye level. I sighed inwardly, knowing that a week ago, I could've leaned forward and rested on his broad chest, been comforted by his strength.

Blane's fingers under my chin forced my head up until I was looking at him. His thumb brushed the corner of my mouth.

"James did this, didn't he?" he growled, his jaw tight. "What else did he do that I can't see?"

Before I could stop him, he'd pushed my coat down and off my arms, examining my exposed skin as if searching for more marks and bruises.

"He didn't do anything that I didn't pay him back for," I said, folding my arms across my chest. I felt very exposed in this outfit, more vulnerable because it was Blane looking at me in it.

Blane frowned. "He didn't . . . force you to . . ."

He trailed off, but I got the gist. "No. I recorded him saying some rather incriminating things—things that would destroy his career if they were made public. So let's just say he came around to my point of view." I lifted my chin defiantly.

Blane's eyes glimmered, his lips twisting in a tiny smirk. I couldn't help the curl of pleasure his approval gave me in the pit of my stomach.

His eyes dropped to my arms covering my chest, then lower to where the hem of my skirt had climbed to the tops of my thighs. My skin burned as if he'd touched it and his hands, resting lightly on the bare skin of my knees, felt like a brand. The air seemed to thicken in my lungs as I remembered the last time I'd sat on a table, only it had been a desk and it had been in Blane's office . . .

I abruptly pushed myself off the table, gingerly testing my weight on my ankle. It hurt, but it would hold. Blane's arm slid around my waist and I flinched at the touch of his hand on my naked back. I tried to step away.

"Let go of me," I told him. "I'm fine."

He didn't listen—shocker, that—and instead pulled me closer to him, wrapping his arms around me and tucking my head against his chest. I could hear his heart beat through the fabric of his clothes. My fists clenched at my sides as I fought the overwhelming need to hug him back.

"God, Kat," he began, his voice tight, "when I saw your car blow up last night, I was sure you were dead. And tonight, when I thought you were here with some bastard . . . I wanted to kill him before I even knew who it was."

I didn't know how to respond. "I'm sorry," I mumbled, though it was a ludicrous thing to say.

"You're sorry?" He gave a short bark of humorless laughter. "That's the last thing you should be. All of this—you nearly getting killed too many times, you having to put up with Kade, James a constant threat to you . . . This is all my fault. Last night, I could have lost you forever."

I looked up at him. His eyes traveled over my face before he softly ran the back of his knuckles down my cheek. I could feel every inch of my body pressed against his—and a little voice in the back of my mind was urging me to forget about last night, forget about Kandi. Who cared about that? If Blane still wanted me, still felt something for me, I'd be a fool not to take what he offered for as long as he was offering it.

Just like all the other women he had dated.

That thought brought me up short and I stepped back out of his arms.

"But you did, Blane," I said simply.

His face was a blank mask as I gathered my coat and purse and walked away, each step harder to take than the one before. I could feel Blane's eyes burning a hole in my back and I didn't breathe properly until I reached the safety of the hallway.

I belted my coat tightly around my waist and left the hotel, dropping James's keys down a drainage pipe off the street. Bitchy and vindictive? Absolutely. But recovering from lost keys and a broken phone was a pain in the ass, and was the least James deserved for how he'd treated me, not to mention that I would have liked to watch him retrieve his wallet from the toilet.

I delivered Alisha's keys and her stun gun to her apartment, which was how I found out how Blane had known where I was. He had stopped by my place and Alisha, who was worried about me, had told him where I had gone. Well, that solved that little mystery. I couldn't be mad at her, though, she'd only tried to help me—and if things had worked out differently and I hadn't been able to get my hands on that stun gun, I would have been glad to see Blane show up.

It was late and I was exhausted when I let myself into my apartment and shucked my coat. I reached to turn on a lamp but paused. Perhaps it was a testament to how often he showed up when I least expected him, but seeing Kade sitting on my sofa in the ambient glow of my Christmas tree lights didn't surprise me all that much.

"What do you want, Kade?" I wasn't in the mood to see him.

"I saw you took a tour of my office. Then left. Something I remember quite clearly telling you not to do."

His tone was biting, making a shiver of unease creep down my spine. I squared my shoulders.

"Seeing as how you have a rather detailed file on me," I
retorted, "I'm surprised you'd expect any different."

"Yes, the file currently decorating my floor. The file
you're all pissed off about. The one I refuse to apologize for
making."

He'd gotten to his feet and taken three steps, stopping
only when he was directly in front of me. I swallowed, but
I wasn't going to back down. That was my new mantra—no
one was going to push me around anymore.

"And where the fuck have you been?" he continued. He
eyed me, his gaze skimming down to my shoes and back up.
"Dressed like that, I can only guess you thought you'd keep
your appointment for Simone."

"I took care of myself," I said defensively.

"I'll bet you did."

The derision in his tone set my teeth on edge.

"I didn't screw him, Kade," I snapped. "I blackmailed
him."

Kade frowned. "Blackmail? Who?"

"James."

"James Gage?"

At my nod, Kade's eyebrows lifted in surprise. "Junior?
James Gage—the DA? You blackmailed the district attorney?"

I nodded again.

His eyes narrowed as they flicked down to my chest. I
fought the urge to cross my arms.

"And how far did it get before you pulled off your Big
Plan?" The words were soaked in his usual sarcasm, igniting
my temper.

"That's none of your business," I spat.

"Dressed like that, I'd be surprised if he let you go before screwing you, no matter what you threatened."

I was furious. How dare he criticize me? "Oh, you like the outfit?" I preened, smiling tightly as I smoothed my hands provocatively over my hips. "You should—after all, you bought the shoes."

It seemed I'd once again taken Kade by surprise, but he recovered quickly, his eyes gleaming as though I'd just dangled a t-bone in front of a tiger.

"Then I should take a closer look."

Before I could react, he'd crouched down and slid a hand behind my knee, pulling my stiletto-clad foot off the floor to rest on his thigh. Off-balance, I clutched his shoulder so I wouldn't topple over.

"What the hell are you doing?" I sputtered, my nerves jangling with all kind of alarms at his touch.

"Taking a closer look at the merchandise," he said calmly.

I gritted my teeth.

"These are definitely Come-Fuck-Me shoes," he said, leisurely inspecting my foot. "They must have set you back some."

"Well, you were quite generous last time you were here," I sneered, trying not to think about the feel of his hand sliding along the back of my knee—or about how he was so near, I could feel his breath on the inside of my thigh.

"It was stupid of you to send all that money to the bill collectors," he said flatly, reminding me of how he'd come by that information.

"Why the file, Kade?" I asked. "Why would you put me under the microscope like that? Invade my privacy?"

"You were dating my brother," he said, his use of the past tense making me wince. "I told you once before that I won't take chances with Blane. I needed to find out who you were."

Kade looked up at me, the electric blue of his eyes like a shock to my system. A lock of his hair had fallen over his brow. Again I was reminded of a fallen angel, beautiful and dark. His self-appointed role as Blane's protector defused my anger, though I still felt violated.

"It seemed to be very . . . thorough," I protested, wishing he'd stop touching me.

"Yeah, well, that's what it became."

I looked at him, confused. What was he talking about? He'd stopped examining my shoe and now just studied me, slowly running his hand up behind my leg until his fingers curled around the back of my thigh.

I had heard of someone undressing you with their eyes but had never experienced it—until now.

Kade's gaze felt almost like a physical touch, caressing my hips, my stomach, my breasts. With James, I'd felt dirty when he had looked at me. With Kade looking at me as though he could see through to my skin, my body responded completely differently. My nipples tightened, straining at the thin fabric covering them. Desire pooled between my legs and my breath came faster. It was wrong and I knew I shouldn't think of him in that way, but he was heartbreakingly lovely and was gazing at me as though I was one of his Moon Pies about to be devoured. After being betrayed by Blane, being wanted by Kade was an unexpected, sinful pleasure.

He slowly stood, his hands trailing up my thighs, catching the hem of my skirt. I stiffened when his fingers brushed my bare skin.

"How about I spend tonight in your bed instead of on the couch?" he whispered in my ear.

"Kade, stop," I protested. "You shouldn't . . . touch me like that." I tried to step away but didn't get far. His hands gripped my flesh more tightly, pulling me against his body. I gasped, his aggression making my heart race even as I castigated myself. The last thing I should do was encourage him.

"Why not? We're two consenting adults." He leaned forward, his lips by my ear. "I know you want me, princess."

My eyes slid closed in dismay even as a tremor went through me at the lightest touch of his mouth. "Just because you have a file on me doesn't mean you know me or what I want," I managed, grasping his wrists and tugging them from underneath my skirt. He allowed me to move his hands, but they only retreated to my waist.

"I know you better than you think," he said, his eyes boring into mine. "I know that you wanted to be a lawyer, which is why you got a job at the firm. I know that piece of crap car you had was one of your sole possessions. I know that you avoid sad movies because you hate to cry."

"What are you doing, Kade? Why are you telling me this?" His intensity was scaring me, as was how much he really did know about me.

"I also know that the last thing you want to do is trust someone, because everyone you've ever loved has left you. And I know this because we're the same, you and me. Trust, love—those things are more dangerous than knives or bullets."

I was shaking now, feeling the weight of his words sink in. It was true, all of it. I'd been terrified of trusting Blane, afraid of how I might grow to care about him and then be hurt when he didn't feel the same. Of course, I'd been right.

"Trust is hard earned, princess, and I didn't mean to break the little trust you had in me."

I was startled. That almost sounded like an apology.

"The file on you started as a background check. Then I met you." His eyes flicked down to my mouth and his hands moved to frame my face. "Then I kissed you, touched you, worked side-by-side with you."

I waited, barely breathing, to see if he would say more. His gaze seemed fevered, so intently was he staring into my eyes.

"And suddenly, I care about more than just Blane and my own hide," he confessed. "And I didn't want to. I've fought it and I tried to hate you, tried to despise you—but I can't."

My emotions threatened to overwhelm me. It was too much. All this time, I'd thought Kade had hated me, barely tolerated me. Now he was telling me that I'd been very, very wrong. I was floored, stunned. I drank in the honesty in his eyes, my chest aching.

I wanted to tell him. Wanted to say that yes, I cared about him, too. That despite how he'd treated me—like a wounded animal lashing out at anyone who tried to care for it—I had grown to want him in my life, to want him with an intensity that frightened me.

Kade wanted me. The idea rocked me. He was a man who had cared for no one and nothing but himself and Blane for as long as he could remember. The sudden thought of

Blane caused the words to die on my tongue, unspoken. What would he do if he found out? Would he and Kade be estranged from each other because of me? After what had happened this morning, I couldn't be sure that wasn't exactly what would happen. I couldn't live with myself if that were true.

Making matters even worse were the feelings I had that were still very much caught up in Blane. Were Blane and I over? Absolutely. Was I ready to move on? After the scene in the hotel and my tumultuous emotions, that answer seemed to be a pretty definitive no.

"Kade," I whispered, "I can't. Blane—" I didn't know what else to say, my mind in a whirl of thoughts and feelings. I searched Kade's gaze, hoping he would know what I meant, but I could tell the moment the name left my lips that Kade assumed I was rejecting him, choosing Blane instead.

It was as if a door slammed shut, his eyes regaining their cold, calculating distance even as his face grew still and shuttered. I could have corrected his assumption, but what did doing so matter in the end? He wouldn't understand that my reason for keeping my distance was to ensure that he and Blane stayed close. It was only this morning that he'd told me to "leave it alone" when it came to him and Blane.

"Of course. I should've known you'd still want Blane," he said, his lips twisting in a humorless smirk. "Even if he is screwing someone else."

The icy anger in his eyes belied the lack of emotion in his voice. I didn't know what to say, how to make it better. I'd hurt him, though he would probably cut off his own arm before admitting it—and he wanted to hurt me back. I didn't want to lose him, couldn't bear to lose someone else I cared about.

"I don't want Blane," I said, ignoring the little voice in the back of my head that laughed in outright derision at that whopper. "But I can't have you. Don't you see that?"

His eyes searched mine before he finally replied, "You're the only one who sees that." He stepped away from me and toward the door.

I panicked. I couldn't just watch him walk out and leave me. Isn't that what he said he always did? Leave before anyone got too attached?

"Wait!" I called out.

He paused, his hand on the doorknob.

"You said I wasn't alone," I reminded him. "That I had you. Were you lying to me?" I was ruthlessly using his own words against him. I needed him and I wasn't about to let him go, no matter the many reasons why I should.

He turned, his face a mix of shadows cast by the light from the tree.

"No," he said, the word seeming to cost him something to utter. "I wasn't lying. I won't leave you alone. It's just better for me to not be in here tonight. I'll be close."

The knot inside my stomach eased and my eyes shut with relief. When I opened them, he was still watching me.

"Will I see you tomorrow?"

"We have a case to solve," he reminded me, "and it's not going away. Just put some fucking clothes on before I see you again," he said, twisting the doorknob to open the door.

I stiffened. "You know I don't normally dress like this!" My protest was directed to his back as he walked out the door, closing it behind him. I turned away with a frustrated sigh, shoving my fingers through my hair only to jerk back around when the door reopened.

"And the next time I see you wearing those shoes," Kade said, "they'll be the only thing you're wearing."

CHAPTER THIRTEEN

I didn't sleep well. Kade's last words echoed in my head and I wasn't sure if the churning in my stomach was dread or . . . something else. I couldn't concentrate. My feelings for Kade were too wrapped up in the anxiety and terror dogging my every move, augmented by what I'd learned about him and the horrors he'd endured when he was young. Were we similar creatures? I didn't know. What I did know was that I hadn't wanted him to walk out that door and leave me with no idea of when I'd see him again.

Yet, I could still feel Blane's arms around me, holding me tight as he told me how he'd been afraid he'd lost me forever. In the dark, I imagined what might have happened if I'd given in, hugged him back and let him hold me. Would he be here with me now? Was I sorry he wasn't?

Tears ran down my cheeks into the pillow as I stared sightlessly at the dark ceiling. I wanted to sleep for a week, a month, waking only when the aching inside my chest became bearable. I was consumed by worry and dread as I wondered if James would try to retaliate, and if whoever had blown up my car would try again to kill me. If women were akin to cats, then I'd used up several of my nine lives. How much longer could my luck hold?

I was up at the crack of dawn, sighing at the dark circles etched under my eyes as I surveyed my reflection in the bathroom mirror. Too tired to care, I gathered my hair back in a tight twist, pinning it securely. As I pulled on jeans, I noticed the waist was loose. Well, I guess that's one good thing to come out of all this worry and anxiety—looks like I'd lost a couple of pounds, though I didn't think I'd be recommending the Stalker Diet to my friends.

Abruptly, I remembered the phone I had stolen. Grabbing my purse, I rummaged until I'd found it. I pressed the buttons and the screen lit, asking for an unlock code. Crap. Okay, well, I could give it to Kade. Maybe the cybergenius could crack it.

My phone rang, interrupting my thoughts.

"Hello?"

"Um, hi," a female voice said hesitantly. "Is this Kathleen Turner?"

"It is," I replied. "May I ask who's calling?"

"This is Stacey Willows. You came by the other day to ask me about Kyle and the mission in Iraq?"

A hint of excitement bubbled inside my chest. This could be the break I'd been waiting for. "Yes, I remember," I said, careful to keep my voice calm. "How are you, Stacey?"

"I'm . . . not sure," she said. "I think I'm in trouble."

"How can I help you?" Images flashed through my mind of Ron Freeman's dead body on the floor of his kitchen.

"I think I'm being followed," Stacey said, speaking quickly, "and I don't know what to do." She paused. "I'm scared."

"I can help you," I assured her, hoping that was true. "Just tell me where I can meet you."

"I'm afraid to leave my house," she said. "Can you come here?"

"You bet," I said, shoving my feet into my boots. "I'll be there as soon as I can."

I hung up the phone and grabbed my purse and coat, then paused. I knew better than to go somewhere without telling Kade first. I dialed his number on my cell.

"Morning, princess," Kade answered.

"Good morning," I replied. "Hey, I need to run an errand," I said. "Stacey Willows called. I think she's being threatened as well. She wants to see me."

"I'll come get you," he said.

"I can get a ride. I think I need to get there asap. She sounded really freaked out."

"Not cool with that," Kade warned.

"I'll be fine," I said. "Isn't this what you're paying me to do?"

"I'm paying you to investigate, not throw yourself into obviously dangerous situations," he retorted.

"What do you think she's going to do to me?" I asked. "Her fiancé is Kyle's commanding officer. Nothing's going to happen. I'll call you as soon as I'm done."

"Fine," he capitulated. "But don't take chances. Get out if it looks bad."

"Got it," I said.

A few moments later, I was knocking on Alisha's door. When she answered, she was pulling on her coat.

"Hey," I said. "Are you going somewhere?"

"I was just headed to the store," she replied. "Bits is out of treats."

"Would you mind dropping me off?"

"Sure, no problem."

I gave her Stacey's address and she drove me there. I'd figure out a ride home later. It had sounded like I needed to get to Stacey's soon.

"You sure you just want me to drop you off?" Alisha asked, eyeing Stacey's house. "I can wait, you know. It's not a problem."

"No," I said. "I don't want to keep you. I'll be fine." The last thing I wanted was for Alisha to get hurt should something go wrong.

Alisha still looked uncertain but nodded.

"Thanks again," I said as I got out. I walked up the sidewalk to the front door and knocked, watching as Alisha drove away. Stacey answered quickly.

"I'm so glad you could come," she said, opening the door wide enough for me to step through. Her face was pinched and white, her eyes red rimmed as though she'd been crying.

"I want to help you in any way—" I began, turning back toward the entry just in time to see Stacey swinging something at my head. It was too late to duck, and I watched in stunned horror as whatever it was hit me with a sickening crack.

∼

Consciousness came slowly, and with it, pain. I'd had headaches before, but never before had my head hurt like this. I slowly opened my eyes, then blinked to be sure they were open. I was in total darkness.

Gingerly, I put my hands out, feeling. I was on something hard, the floor. My hands came up against a wall. Getting painfully up on my knees, I followed the wall, realizing I was in a small room, probably a closet, by the dimensions. I reached upward, my fingers skimming until I found a door handle. Scooting closer, I felt something wet seep into the fabric of my jeans. I reached down, feeling a puddle of water that seemed to be coming from underneath the door.

I paused and took a deep breath before trying the knob. I wasn't surprised to find it locked. Reaching into my pocket, I silently cursed when I discovered my cell phone was no longer there.

I put my ear to the door and listened for several minutes. I heard nothing, no sound to indicate someone might be inside the house, if indeed that's where I was.

Turning so my back was braced against the back wall, I lashed out at the door with my legs, gritting my teeth at the sudden pain radiating in my knees and my head. I paused, waiting to see if the loud noise would alert anyone that I was no longer unconscious. When nothing happened, I kicked again, gratified to feel the door shudder slightly. It took several more kicks before the doorjamb finally gave, the splintering enough for me to push the latch open.

I hurriedly stood and stepped out of the closet, only to stumble over something on the floor and then fall, landing in more water. Looking over my shoulder, I saw a dark heap on the floor.

Alarmed, I scrambled up, searching for a light in the dark room. Finally, I found the switch and flicked it on, barely stifling a scream.

Stacey's body lay on the floor, her eyes staring sightlessly at the ceiling. The water I'd fallen in was actually blood, a large pool of it stemming from the gash across her throat.

I looked down at myself, horrified to see I had her blood all over me—on my hands, clothes, everywhere.

For a moment, I couldn't do anything—couldn't move, couldn't breathe, couldn't think. I was paralyzed. All I could hear was my heart pounding in my chest.

I closed my eyes, blocking out the scene for a minute. I had to get a grip. I had no idea how much time I'd been unconscious, but Stacey looked like she'd been dead for hours. Whoever had done this was probably long gone. What to do now? The police. I had to call them.

Stepping carefully over Stacey's body, I left the empty room, realizing it must be a bedroom in her house, and walked to the kitchen, where I picked up the phone and robotically dialed 911.

I sat perched on the edge of Stacey's sofa while I waited, unable to get her image out of my head. Why had she knocked me out? Who had killed her? Why hadn't they killed me, too?

The police were there within minutes. I haltingly told my story while a paramedic checked the huge bump on the back of my head. The cop took notes, asking me questions about why I'd been there and why Stacey would hit me over the head.

"I have no idea," I answered honestly. Looking down, I again saw the blood on my hands. I wanted it off. "Please, can I wash my hands?" I asked.

"Not yet," the cop answered.

When I looked up at him, it was to see that he was regarding me with suspicion in his eyes. My stomach dropped. Oh God. What if they thought I had killed Stacey?

"Who's in charge here?"

Both the cop and I looked up at the sound of a new voice coming from the other room. I knew immediately that it was Blane. I heard the other cop talking to him.

"Where's the victim? I want to see the body," Blane demanded, stepping into the living room. His gaze landed on me and I had to physically dig my nails into the couch to stop from jumping up and running to him. His stark expression relaxed infinitesimally, the fists at his side loosening.

"Let's go, Kathleen," he said, moving toward me.

"Not so fast," the cop next to me said, standing and blocking Blane.

Blane's eyes narrowed. "Why would you detain her?" he asked. Dressed casually in jeans and a long-sleeved pullover, his demeanor was no less authoritative as he addressed the cop.

"She's a witness," the cop said, "as well as a possible suspect. She's been present at two murders in as many days, though she maintains that she only found the victims."

"She's my employee," Blane dismissed. "She had nothing to do with it."

"Oh, really? Why is your employee here?" The cop crossed his arms over his chest, regarding Blane through narrowed eyes.

Blane turned to me and I told him the same thing I'd told the police, that Stacey had called and asked me to come see her. When I arrived, she'd hit me over the head. Blane's hands clenched into fists at that part, his jaw tightening into steel bands as I explained how I'd woken up, escaped from the closet, and found Stacey's body.

"Have the paramedics examined her injury?" Blane asked the cop, his voice no-nonsense.

When the cop answered in the affirmative, Blane then asked, "And have you found the closet from which she escaped?"

Again, the cop gave a grudging affirmative.

"Do you have the murder weapon?"

I could tell the answer to that one was a no by the way the cop's lips pressed firmly together before he gave a quick shake of his head.

"Then you have nothing to hold my employee on," Blane said, reaching for my arm and pulling me to my feet. "If you need to speak to her, call me." He handed the cop his card and walked me out the door into the night. We didn't stop walking until we'd reached his car, parked on the street.

I stood in silence, watching from afar as police drifted in and out of the house, most of them leaving as the ambulance drove away with Stacey's body.

Blane opened the passenger door of his car and leaned inside. I was startled when something cold and wet touched my hand. Looking down, I saw that Blane had taken one of my hands in his and was gently and methodically wiping the blood off with a wet cloth. I couldn't look away from the white cloth that was slowly turning red. When Blane had finished one hand, he got a new cloth and started on the other.

"I'd ask if you're all right, but I already know what you'll say," he said roughly.

I didn't reply.

"You should probably go to the hospital," he continued, "but I know what you'll say to that as well."

I swallowed. "How did you know I was here?" I asked.

"Kade," Blane answered. "When he didn't hear from you, he called me."

"Why didn't he come?" I asked, wishing for the first time ever that it had been Kade to show up instead of Blane.

"Because I said I would," Blane said stiffly.

"Well, thanks," I said, trying to sound grateful. After all, I was certainly glad I wasn't still in there with the suspicious police. Spending a day or two in jail was not on my schedule.

"What were you doing here?" he asked, gently swiping at my jaw and cheek. I looked up at him, both wishing he wasn't standing so close and wanting him to come closer.

"Working," I answered simply.

The cloth was fisted in his hand.

"Then you're fired," he ground out.

My mouth fell open in outrage. "What? You can't fire me! I was just doing my job!"

"A job you have no business doing," he retorted, his eyes flashing in anger. "That could have been you in there with your blood all over the floor."

"Well, it's not," I shot back. "And it doesn't matter if you fire me, because I'm not stopping. Whoever is behind this has tried to kill me three times. It's personal."

The anger seemed to drain out of him at my words, and he bowed his head with a sigh. He looked down at my clothes and frowned. Stepping back slightly, he surprised me by pulling off his shirt. Underneath, he wore a white T-shirt. It fit him like a second skin, stretching tightly over his chest and shoulders.

"Here," he said, eyeing my blouse and offering me his shirt. "Take that off and put this on."

"I can't just strip out here," I protested. It was dark, but a streetlight nearby still cast too much light for me to be comfortable about taking off my clothes.

"I'll shield you," Blane said. He opened his arms and pressed his hands against the car, trapping me between him and the door. He was close enough for me to smell his cologne and feel the warmth from his body, but he was right—no one could see me.

"Close your eyes," I demanded. I didn't wait to see if he complied. I quickly unbuttoned my shirt and slipped it down my arms, letting it drop to the ground. I pulled Blane's shirt over my head and tugged it down over my skin. The smell of Blane enveloped me and I flinched at the sharp pain that produced.

My hair was in complete disarray, half the pins gone, so I took the rest out, letting the heavy mass fall past my shoulders. When I was once again presentable, I looked up to see Blane's eyes on me, his jaw like granite. Of course he hadn't closed his eyes and they burned with a familiar intensity, but something else was written on his face, an emotion I couldn't name.

"Kathleen, I—" he began.

"How's Kandi?" I asked, interrupting whatever he'd been about to say. I couldn't withstand an explanation—something that might offer me an excuse to forget about her.

Blane's expression shuttered.

"You're not going to listen to me, are you?" he replied flatly.

"Listen about what?" I knew I was being a stubborn pain in the ass, but I didn't care. Call it self-defense, call it keeping my sanity, call it whatever you want—I just knew I had to keep my emotions at bay.

"Kandi is serving her purpose," he said carefully.

I frowned at his odd choice of words.

"Kirk! What the hell is this?"

Blane spun around, one arm behind him to keep me in place and out of sight. I peeked over his shoulder and wanted to faint on the spot when I saw James striding across the lawn toward us. He hadn't seen me yet, his furious gaze on Blane.

"Another witness turns up murdered? How convenient for you." James stopped a foot or two from Blane, his lips curled in a sneer of contempt.

This was so not a good time for James to pick a fight with Blane. I curled my fingers around Blane's biceps in what would no doubt be a futile attempt to hold him back if he decided to tackle James. I could feel the coiled tension in his body. He couldn't go after James, not here with cops around. I knew without a doubt that James would press charges, and tomorrow it would be all over the papers.

"Get the fuck away from me, Gage," Blane growled.

James suddenly spotted me. In an instant, he was enraged.

"You fucking whore!" he yelled, lunging for me.

Before I could even react, Blane had grabbed James by the neck and slammed him up against the car.

"I should rip you to shreds," Blane threatened him, his voice dripping with menace.

James was clawing at Blane's hand, trying to free himself. Unable to do so, he swung his fist, connecting with Blane's jaw.

The blow seemed hardly to faze Blane, though he released James, only to sink his fist into James's gut. James doubled over, coughing and retching. Blane stepped back.

"Give it your best shot, Gage," Blane taunted James, and I realized he wanted James to attack him, just so he'd have an excuse to beat him up.

James exploded outward, swinging wildly at Blane, who easily sidestepped him and landed a punch to James's ribs. He stumbled, then swung again. This time Blane landed a solid hit to James's face and I heard the crack of bone.

Bent at the waist, James took a moment to recover before he stood upright. Blood dripped from his nose and I thought it might be broken. He glared at Blane with hatred in his eyes.

"You know I fucked your girl there, Kirk," he said, smirking in spite of his injuries. "Not a bad lay. But she could use a few more pointers on how to give a decent blow job."

I gasped, aghast at his lies, then realized too late what he was doing.

"Blane, no!" I cried, but it was too late. Blane attacked James with a furious energy that sent a jolt of fear through me. I ran forward, throwing my arms around Blane's waist and tugging.

"Blane, stop!"

I pulled with all my strength, calling his name and trying to reach him through his haze of rage. To my relief, Blane finally released James. He was breathing heavily, sweat dampened his T-shirt, and his skin was hot beneath my hands. James stumbled, barely keeping on his feet.

By now two cops had approached the street. I watched in alarm as they came near.

"Arrest him," James ordered, gasping for breath as he wiped the blood off his mouth with his sleeve. "He assaulted me."

The cops watched Blane warily, neither of them moving to do what James said. For his part, Blane just stared daggers at James before turning toward his car, pulling me along with him.

"What the hell is wrong with you two?" James blustered to the cops. "Arrest him!" He came after us, stopping short when Blane spun around to confront him.

"Shut up, Gage," Blane hissed. "Arrest me and my girl may have something she'd like to show the good officers as well."

James went still, his gaze flying to mine. I winked and blew him a kiss. Jackass.

"Let's go," Blane said, grabbing my hand.

I didn't protest when he put me in the passenger side of his car. Despite my bravado in front of James, I felt shaken to the core.

Blane drove hard and fast, and we flew through the streets of Indianapolis. I'd never seen him drive this fast before, and I clung to my seat. Finally, I couldn't take the silence anymore.

"Why would you do that?" I exploded. "Why would you jeopardize your entire case because of James?"

At my words, Blane jerked the wheel and the car whipped onto a deserted side street, screeching to a halt in front of a darkened streetlamp. He threw the car into park and turned to me. His face was as blank as slate, only the burning in his eyes betrayed his emotions.

"James had it coming," he said coldly, "and I'd do it again in a second."

I shook my head. "I don't understand why you'd act that way, Blane." I'd watched him for months with other women and in all kinds of situations. Blane was always in control. "It's beneath you, to beat up an ass like James. Especially when he was lying, just trying to get a rise out of you."

"Then he succeeded."

I combed my fingers through my hair, frustrated. From my peripheral vision, I could see Blane watching me. I looked at the clock on the dash, then cast him a quick glance. "I need to get to work." It was after five already. I had to be at work by six. "Please take me there."

"No."

Startled, I looked up at him.

"Not until you listen to me," Blane demanded.

My eyes narrowed in anger. There he was, pushing me around again.

"Fine," I retorted. "I'll walk."

In a flash, I was out the door and running down the sidewalk. I couldn't think straight. My head hurt like the devil and I was freezing, the icy wind biting into my skin. I knew I was acting unreasonably, my anger at Blane feeling out of control, but I couldn't stop it. So I ran.

I didn't look behind to see if Blane was following me, so I wasn't prepared to suddenly be snatched off my feet. I shrieked in surprise.

"Let me go!" I yelled, kicking and squirming, but his arms were like bands wrapped around my torso and waist.

"Not until you listen to me!"

He hauled me back to the car, bracing my back against the cold metal door and imprisoning my arms at my sides. I couldn't move—his body pressed against mine—and I had to tip my head back to see his eyes.

"What do you want me to hear, Blane?" I fumed. "That you didn't mean for me to see you and Kandi together? That you're real sorry it ended like that between us, but hey, it was fun while it lasted? I get it, okay? Let's just move on."

His expression was cold, like marble, but he winced at my words. If I had any sense, I'd have been afraid at the anger burning in his eyes. His nearness was accentuated by the cold of the night, only the heat from his body warming me.

"I didn't sleep with her."

His voice was low and tense.

"Does it matter?" I retorted. "You had your tongue down her throat. What were you doing, Blane? Giving her mouth-to-mouth?"

"She instigated it, Kathleen, not me," he insisted.

"Oh. Well, that makes it all okay then," I said, my sarcasm thick.

"I didn't say it was okay, or right," Blane said calmly. "But I thought you should know my reasons."

"What reason could you possibly have that would make me not care, Blane?" I asked in disbelief.

"Her father is on the House Budget Committee," Blane said. "I think the person behind these attacks has an agenda, more than just a twisted sense of justice. The Defense Department is slated to get their budget cut by billions next year. They've been fighting it. If I lose this case, public opinion will turn against the military and the cuts will go through. I suspect that Kandi is the one leaking information. That's the only way someone could have known all about you and she's the only one with the motivations and connections to do it."

His grip on me loosened. I felt like I'd just been knocked upside the head. Oh wait, I had. A bubble of hysterical laughter crawled up my chest and I swallowed it down.

"If she's behind it," Blane continued, "then being with her would shift the focus away from you. And if she wasn't, whoever was would still see that you and I were no longer together, that hurting you wouldn't affect me. Kandi is simply a means to an end—a way to keep you safe. That is her only value to me, especially if she's the one who helped them target you."

I didn't know what to say. My stomach roiled, and I thought I might be sick again. I'd gotten it wrong, Blane hadn't betrayed me. But was he telling me the truth? Could I believe him? The doubt must have shown in my eyes, because Blane cradled my face in his hands.

"Believe me, Kat. Trust me," he implored earnestly. "I never wanted to hurt you. My only motivation has been to do everything in my power to protect you." His eyes were intent on mine, willing me to believe him.

"Why didn't you tell me?" My voice came out a whisper.

"I wanted to," he said, his brow creasing. "I was going to, the night of the Christmas party. But then you had to work, and you said you weren't coming. I knew someone was there, watching. They had this delivered to me."

Blane reached into his jeans pocket and produced a creased piece of paper. I took it, opening and reading the scrawled phrases:

Roses are red,

Violets are blue.

Bet you don't see me,

But I can see you.

A chill ran down my spine. At least I'd gotten that right. He had been there that night, stalking Blane. My fingers were numb as Blane gently took the paper back from me, pushing it back into his pocket.

"When you showed up, I couldn't have scripted a more public breakup, especially knowing he was there, watching. I hated myself for hurting you like that, but I thought it was better than the alternative."

"Which was?"

"You being dead."

That made me pause for a moment. "You let me believe the worst," I protested.

His jaw hardened. "If you hated me because I betrayed you, it was more believable. I'd have done anything to keep you out of danger. Just look at what happened tonight— what nearly could have happened."

I stiffened. He thought he knew what was best for my life. He had made that decision without ever consulting me.

"Then why are you telling me this now?"

"Because I nearly lost you again, Kat," he said roughly, cradling my cheek in his palm. "If I'd kept you close, I could have protected you. Let me."

Blane's hands moved behind my neck, his fingers threading through my hair. The way he was looking at me sent a shiver down my spine and made the center of my chest ache. I knew that feeling, and it terrified me.

With a gentleness that contradicted the strength with which he held me, Blane pressed his lips to my brow, my cheek, a feather-light touch near my eye, speaking softly to me between each kiss.

"I'm so sorry," he whispered. "Say you forgive me, Kat. Trust me."

His lips settled over mine with heartbreaking tenderness.

The moment his mouth touched mine, something broke inside me and I wrenched away from him. Unprepared, he let me go.

"Blane, I can't—I don't know—" My tongue stumbled over the words. I wasn't sure what I was trying to say. My mind was warring with my heart, and I didn't know what to think or feel. I wanted to fling myself into Blane's arms and tell him all was forgiven, that of course I trusted him. He'd proven himself worthy of my trust in so many ways.

Yet something prevented me. As much as I wanted to, alarms were screaming inside my head that I'd be a fool to go back to him. Seeing him with Kandi and believing he'd betrayed me had hurt me deeply. I didn't know if I could withstand it again, and wouldn't it eventually come to that? Why go back to Blane when another breakup would just loom on the horizon to break my heart all over again?

I had to get out of there. I backed up a few steps, glancing around for any way out. To my amazement and relief, I saw a car turn down the street toward us and recognized it as a taxi.

Turning back to Blane, I shook my head. "I'm sorry," I said, tears clogging my throat. "I just . . . I can't."

"Kathleen, wait—"

He reached for me, but I was already in the street, flagging down the slow-moving taxi. To my relief, it abruptly stopped and I climbed in.

"Go! Drive!" I ordered before collapsing back against the cold vinyl. The driver obeyed, stepping on the gas. I stared out the window, refusing to look back at Blane.

"K-K-Kathleen?"

My head jerked up. "Frankie?"

"Yeah."

What a stroke of luck! Something of which I'd had precious little lately. He seemed to turn up when I needed him most.

"I'm glad you were around, Frankie," I said, giving him the address for The Drop.

"M-me, t-t-too," he stuttered. "Wasn't th-th-that your b-boyfriend?"

"Not anymore," I said, roughly scrubbing my wet cheek with the back of my hand.

"I'm s-s-sorry."

Yeah, me, too.

When I got to work, I borrowed some clothes from Tish. We were still on slutty Santa duty, so even though Kade had managed to destroy my costume, I was ever so fortunate Romeo had another to replace it. I made myself as presentable as I could before clocking in, tossing my blood-encrusted jeans in the trash.

Tish eyed me as I stocked the bar.

"You all right?" she asked.

I smiled tightly. "Massive headache," I explained. "That's all."

"Want some medicine?"

"Thanks," I said gratefully, accepting two painkillers she dug out of her purse.

I worked on autopilot, unable to shake the feeling that I'd made a mistake, that I'd made the wrong decision with Blane. The instinct for self-preservation was strong, but maybe the heartache was worth the time we'd have together. God knows, the time I'd been with Blane had been some of the best in my life. I missed him.

"Hi there, beautiful."

I looked up, shaken out of my inner musings to see Ryan sliding onto a stool at the bar. I smiled back.

"Hi," I replied. He looked good, wearing jeans and a cream-colored cable-knit sweater that fit snugly over his broad shoulders. The color contrasted nicely with his tan skin and dark hair.

"You look surprised to see me," Ryan said. I popped the top off a bottle of beer and placed it in front of him. His hand curled around it. "I came by Friday, but the guy bartending said you'd left early, but that you would be here tonight."

"Yeah, I had a . . . family emergency," I explained.

"Everything all right?"

I nodded, wondering if he knew about Stacey being murdered. The words were on the tip of my tongue, but something held me back and I didn't say anything.

"How was your day?" he asked.

There was nothing about my day I could tell him, so I was deliberately vague. "The usual. Cleaning, laundry, grocery shopping," I hedged. "You?"

"I took care of some business," he replied. "Boring stuff."

"Working on the weekend?"

"Not all of us can be the idle wealthy," he teased.

I laughed. "Yeah, that's me," I said wryly. "Money to burn."

We chatted for a little while, me taking breaks to fill orders, but overall we weren't very busy for a Sunday night.

"Have you reconsidered my offer?" Ryan asked after he'd finished his second beer.

"Which would be . . . ?"

"Dinner," Ryan said. "Tomorrow night. Are you free?"

I thought about it. There was really no reason to say no. Blane and I were through. I didn't dare think of Kade. Going out with Ryan suddenly sounded appealing. He seemed nice, had a steady job, was good-looking, funny, and carried none of the drama with which my life had lately been overwhelmed.

"Sure," I said. "That sounds nice."

"No more boyfriend?"

My smile was forced. "Not anymore."

"Great! Pick you up at eight?"

I agreed, jotting my address down on a napkin and giving it to him.

"I don't suppose I could convince you to wear that tomorrow night, could I?" he asked, motioning to my outfit with a mischievous grin. "I've been picturing you wearing that all day," he continued.

I blushed. "Maybe if you're lucky," I flirted.

"Luck has nothing to do with it," Ryan said, his lips curving in a slow smile. "See you tomorrow." He tossed some money down on the bar, pulled on his coat, and left.

I sagged against the bar once Ryan had gone. I was exhausted and my head still ached. Glancing at the clock, I saw there was only an hour left before we could close. Thank God. It was taking everything I had just to stay on my feet.

"No offense, Kathleen," Tish said, dropping off a couple of trays on the bar. "But you look like hell. What's going on?"

I sighed. "Having trouble sleeping, that's all."

"Did Blane try to explain away his date with that chick?" she asked. I recalled how Tish had been privy to the "fake" breakup with Blane here in the bar.

"Yeah," I said, Blane's explanation of why he'd been with Kandi echoing in my ears.

"Did you believe him?"

I slowly nodded. "Yes, but I still told him it was over." Even to my own ears, I sounded miserable.

Tish squeezed my hand sympathetically. "Breakups are hard. If you love him, you could always give him another shot."

"But . . ." I began, "but what if he does it again? What if I trust him, and he breaks my heart again?"

Tish studied me. "He might. But he might not. It's a risk only you can decide to take."

I had no answer. Confusion, fear, and self-doubt held me back. My feelings must have shown on my face, for Tish leaned forward and gave me a quick hug.

"It'll be all right," she said, tucking my hair behind my ear. "Just call him."

I forced a smile. I doubted Blane would want to hear from me after I'd rejected his apology and rejected him.

I was just finishing prep work for the next day when Kade walked in the door.

"I see you didn't listen to me," he said derisively, looking me up and down. "You're going to catch pneumonia wearing hardly any clothes in the middle of winter."

"If only I could be so lucky," I shot back. Compared to being shot or blown up, pneumonia sounded like a vacation.

"Brought you an early Christmas present," he said, tossing something at me. Reflexively, I caught it. Bewildered, I stared at the set of keys in my hand, then up at him.

"Well, I'm certainly not going to chauffeur you all over town," he snorted, reaching across the bar to grab a bottle of beer. He twisted the cap off and took a swig.

"You . . . got me a car?" I could hardly form the words, certain I was wrong but not knowing what else to think.

"Thought you could use a little Christmas cheer," he said dismissively, taking another drink. "Consider it an advance on your salary and a tax deduction for the firm."

I was stunned, my jaw hanging open. The keys bit into my palm as I clutched them in my fist. Kade watched my reaction, even as he pretended nonchalance, his fingers casually holding the neck of the beer bottle.

"Kade," I began, "I don't know what to say—"

"Thank you is customary," he said dryly, his lips twisting in an almost smile.

"Thank you," I said. "But I can't accept this. It's too much." I regretfully held the keys back out to him.

"Please," he scoffed, not taking the keys. "It's not like I bought it for you." He took a swig of his beer.

My brows lifted in an unspoken question.

"The firm bought it," he said with a shrug. "An investigator has to have wheels. It's a company car."

I hesitated. If it was a company car, then that wouldn't be so bad. That would be nice, actually, having someone else take care of the insurance payments and taxes.

"Are you sure?" I wavered in indecision, the offer tempting me.

"You really think I'd just go buy you a car?" he asked derisively.

Well, when he put it like that . . .

I stepped out from behind the bar and put my arms around him for a hug. I must have surprised him, because he was stiff for a moment before awkwardly hugging me back. "Thank you, Kade. This is a huge load off my mind."

Kade pulled back so he could look at me. "No problem," he said. "And if you'd like to thank me further, I could give you a few ideas, several of which prominently feature those shoes you wore last night."

My face heated and stepped away, giving him a smack on the arm as I did so. "Drink your beer," I told him, crossing back behind the bar.

I dug inside my purse, pulling out the cell phone I hadn't been able to get into because of the pass code. I handed it to Kade.

"I took this cell phone from Adriana's hotel room," I explained. "But it has a code on it. I thought you might be able to break it."

"No problem," he said, pocketing the phone. "I was able to trace the phone calls made to Freeman."

"Who called him?" I asked.

"Someone with a lot of resources," he said. "Government resources."

My eyebrows shot up. "Blane said he thought that might be the case, that the Defense Department budget is supposed to be cut by billions next year."

"Yep," Kade confirmed. "Always follow the money, princess. Nine times out of ten, it's all about the cash."

"And the tenth time?" I teased.

"The tenth time is personal," he shot back. "Everyone knows that."

"Ryan Sheffield came by tonight," I told him. "I'm going on a date with him tomorrow night."

"You realize he works for the government," Kade said. "He could be our mysterious caller. Or our shooter. Why the date?"

I shook my head. "No, I don't believe that. He doesn't strike me as the type. And why not a date?" Last I checked, I was excruciatingly available. "Maybe he knows more than he's telling, though. If he does, I'll get it out of him."

"And how do you plan on doing that?"

"Men the world over all have the same weakness."

"Really?" Kade said mockingly. "Do enlighten me, princess."

I crossed my arms on the bar and leaned over. Sure enough, Kade's eyes flicked downward to my cleavage. I laughed. "Breasts, of course."

"Point taken," Kade conceded, clearing his throat.

"What about Stacey Willows?" I asked, grabbing a towel and drying the glasses I'd just taken out of the washer. "You know she was murdered today."

"So Blane said," he replied. "What happened?"

I explained how my day had gone and how I'd found Stacey's body. "She said she was being threatened, too, that she was supposed to testify against Kyle."

"And you were so sure she wouldn't hurt you," he mocked. I chose to ignore that comment. "I'll check her phone records, too," Kade said. "But why would she knock you out? Were there signs of a struggle?"

"You mean other than her slit throat?" I asked sarcastically.

"Smartass," he replied without heat. "If she knew her killer, she would have trusted him, let him into the house. Otherwise, there would have been signs of forced entry, a struggle, something to signify she'd fought."

I frowned, remembering the spotless condition of the house and door. "I don't think there was any kind of struggle," I said finally. "Her body was right outside the door of the closet she'd stowed me in. Maybe she was going to show him she had me when she turned her back and he took advantage of the moment, killing her before she could tell him about me."

"So it seems you're lucky to be alive this evening," Kade said, his gaze shrewd.

I shrugged, not wanting to talk about it. If I didn't talk about it, I wouldn't have to think about my conversation with Blane that had followed. "Any luck on finding Bowers?"

Kade shook his head. "These guys are good. If he doesn't want to be found, I don't know if I'll be able to find him."

Kade finished his beer and tossed a bill onto the bar, but I snatched it up and handed it back to him.

"The drink's on me," I said. "It's the least I can do."

"The sooner I can track down who's making these calls, the sooner we can catch whoever's doing this," Kade said.

"Then go do it," I said, waving him away. "I don't need you dogging my every move anyway."

"Since when?"

His sarcasm only masked his concern, so it didn't bother me.

"Go home, Kade," I insisted. In the back of my mind, I knew it would be a bad idea to have him sleeping in my apartment again.

I walked him to the door so I could lock it, but before he stepped through, he surprised me, pressing his lips to my cheek.

"Car's parked out front," he said, lightly brushing my bare shoulder with his fingers and sending a shiver through me. "I'll see you tomorrow."

I hurried through the rest of my work, excitement giving me new energy. I still couldn't quite believe he'd gotten me a car. I braced myself for a hulking monstrosity built in 1982, but when I finally walked outside there was only one car parked nearby—a shiny black Lexus SUV.

Unable to believe my eyes, I tentatively hit the unlock button on the key fob Kade had given me and saw the car's lights blink on.

I climbed inside—the leather interior smelled rich and decadent. The engine turned over with a gentle purr. My hands slid over the beautiful wood-grain dash and steering wheel. I had never in my life had a brand-new car, not even close.

I was almost afraid to drive it, it was so gorgeous, but it handled beautifully. It was big and I felt safe behind the wheel. When I parked in my lot, I locked it, noticing that it also had a car alarm. That was a good thing, considering the neighborhood.

Once inside, I checked out my answering machine, which sadly proclaimed no messages. Well, what did I expect? Why would Blane call?

I showered and fell into bed, asleep almost before my head hit the pillow.

～

I was awakened by the ringing of the telephone. I groaned, blearily looking at the clock, which indicated 3:43 a.m. Grabbing for the phone, I mumbled something resembling hello into the receiver.

"Kathleen?" A girl's voice, vaguely familiar.

"Yeah?" I sat up, rubbing my tired eyes.

"Kathleen, it's CJ."

Now I was awake. "CJ," I said, "are you all right? What's the matter?" Phone calls in the middle of the night were never good.

"Um," she hesitated, "I'm sorry to bother you, but I didn't know who else to call."

"It's not a problem. What's wrong?"

"I-I've been arrested," she said, her voice wavering.

"Arrested! For what?" I gripped the phone tightly, imagining her stuck in a jail cell downtown.

There was a pause before she answered. "Treason."

I was so surprised I was speechless.

"Kathleen?" Her voice was anxious. "Are you still there?"

"Yeah, yeah," I said quickly. "I'm still here."

"Kathleen, can you help me?"

"Yes, absolutely. Of course I'll help you," I assured her. Actually, I had no idea what I was going to do. "Just sit tight, all right? I'll be right there."

"Okay." Her voice, so small and trusting, steeled my resolve.

I hung up, then hurriedly climbed out of bed to throw on some clothes. I knew what I had to do—knew the only way I could help CJ—but was dreading doing it. I dressed and pulled my hair back in a ponytail. Picking up the phone, I stared at it, taking a deep breath.

I had to call Blane.

CHAPTER FOURTEEN

Blane answered on the third ring.

"Kirk."

His voice was deep and sleep roughened. When I heard it, I had a brief flash of lying next to him in bed and waking up to his voice in my ear, then I remembered that he may not be alone.

"Blane," I said hesitantly, praying Kandi wasn't there, or if she was, that I wouldn't hear her voice. "It's me. It's Kathleen."

A pause, then he said, "Kat? Are you all right?"

"I'm fine," I said quickly. Nerves were making my voice shake and I clutched the phone tightly.

I heard a sigh and the rustle of sheets. "I'm glad you called," he said quietly. "God, I really fucked up, Kat." He paused. "I miss you."

My gut twisted at his words. "I . . . I miss you, too." I abruptly remembered CJ. This wasn't a personal call—it was supposed to be business. Panic made me blurt, "Blane, I need you."

"I need you, too, Kat," he said in a tone so deep and full of sensual promise it sent a shiver down my spine. "Just say the word and I'm on my way."

Oh God. He thought this was a . . . a booty call. My cheeks burned.

"I didn't mean—that's not why—" My tongue stumbled over the words. "I need your help. It's CJ. She just called me. She's been arrested."

Silence on the line.

"Blane?" I asked, worried he'd hung up on me. "Are you there?"

"You're calling me because you need a lawyer?" His voice was completely different. Gone was the soft, sexy growl. Now his words were cold and hard, and I cringed at the underlying anger in them.

My palms were sweating now. "Yes. I mean, no." I hesitated. This had been a bad decision. "I'm sorry. Never mind. I shouldn't have called." I'd just have to figure out some other way to help CJ.

"Wait."

I heard him just as I was about to hang up the phone.

"Kat? Are you still there?"

"Yes," I answered. I felt like the worst kind of heel. He'd thought I was calling because I wanted to be with him again, which I did, but I'd messed everything up and now it was all topsy-turvy. But I couldn't suppress the surge of pleasure that Blane wanted me, would have come at my beck and call to be with me.

I heard him take a deep breath. "Tell me what's going on."

It didn't take long to relate my conversation with CJ. When I was through, Blane said, "All right. I'll pick you up in fifteen minutes." He hung up before I could tell him that I didn't need a ride.

I brushed my teeth and splashed water on my face while I waited. If anything, I looked worse now after a few hours' sleep than I had before. My skin was stark white and my eyes had what looked like bruises beneath them, I was so tired. I tucked my black turtleneck inside my jeans and cinched my belt, pushing my feet into a pair of sneakers.

I thought I was prepared for Blane's arrival, but the knock on my door startled me so badly, I dropped the brush I was holding and it clattered loudly to the floor.

Taking a deep, steadying breath, I opened the door.

Just as it always did, Blane's presence enveloped me. I'd never developed an immunity to the charisma and personality that was a force of nature. He stood head and shoulders above me, his hair ruffled by the wind. His expression was impenetrable and I stepped back to allow him inside.

He wore a leather coat similar to Kade's, with jeans and a dark sweater. The only light in my apartment was coming from the Christmas tree he'd gotten for me and the glow drifting from my partially closed bedroom door. Belatedly, I wished I'd turned on a light.

As if he had read my mind, Blane reached behind me and flipped on a lamp. I blinked in the sudden brightness, disconcerted to find him studying me, his gaze shrewd. Blane's eyes never missed anything, and I was embarrassed by how I looked at this hour. Kandi probably woke in full makeup and heels. Turning away, I grabbed my coat. I began to shrug it on, but Blane had taken hold of it and held it open for me.

"Thank you," I said quietly, pushing my arms into the sleeves. His fingers brushed the nape of my neck as he lifted my ponytail out from under the collar. Unnerved, I stepped away and cleared my throat. "You didn't have to come get me," I said, turning to face him. "I can follow you there."

"You don't have a car, remember?" he said.

"I do now."

He shook his head, his eyes searching my face. "You look like you can barely stand, much less drive a car. You'll ride with me."

I wanted to argue but knew that CJ was waiting for me. It wasn't worth the time it would take, not to mention that knowing Blane, I'd still end up riding with him no matter what I said to the contrary.

I knew I looked like hell, whereas you would never know I'd just dragged him out of a dead sleep in the middle of the night. Grossly unfair.

We rode in silence, the tension thick between us. I stared out the window as we flew through the cold, empty streets.

"Are you ill?" Blane asked out of the blue.

"What?" I turned toward him, wondering where that had come from.

"You're white as a sheet," Blane said frankly. "And I'm guessing you can't remember the last time you ate."

"It's been a rough week," I replied. Blane didn't respond, though his hands gripped the steering wheel more tightly. I turned back to the window.

I chewed my lip in indecision, twisting my hands in my lap. Should I say something? Should I tell him that I believed him about Kandi? I glanced sideways at him as he drove. His expression was as cold and forbidding as I'd ever seen it. I swallowed heavily, wishing I had the courage and energy to say what I wanted to say, but I sensed this wasn't the time or place. It would have to wait.

When we reached the police station, Blane led us inside, his hand guiding me at the small of my back. The clerk at the desk recognized him, though his eyebrows flew upward when Blane told him who he was there to see.

"The treason case?" he asked. "The feds brought her in. We're just holding her until they can arrange transport to Washington."

"To my knowledge, everyone is given the right to an attorney," Blane reminded him.

The cop sighed. "All right. But she'll have to wait here." He pointed at me.

"But—" I began, only to have Blane squeeze my arm, silencing me.

"That'll be fine," he said to the cop.

Blane led me to a small bank of blue plastic chairs. "Sit here and wait for me," he said. "I'm the one she needs to see."

I wasn't stupid enough to question the truth in that, though I was disappointed I couldn't verify for myself that she was okay.

"All right," I sighed, sinking tiredly into a chair. "Just tell her I came, okay?" I didn't want her to think I was cozy at home in bed while she was sitting in jail.

"I will," Blane assured me.

I closed my eyes and leaned my head back to rest against the wall. For a brief moment, I thought I felt the brush of Blane's hand against my cheek, then he was gone.

I tried not to fall asleep, jerking awake whenever my head bobbed, but I must have succumbed, because the next thing I knew Blane was gently nudging me awake. I sat up with a start, realizing I'd stretched out onto the chair next to me.

"CJ," I said, rubbing the sleep from my eyes. "Is she all right?"

"She's fine," he said, his brow creased in concern as he crouched in front of me. "Better than you, actually."

"What happened? Why is she here?" I asked, ignoring his comment.

"We'll talk about it in the car," he said quietly, with a meaningful glance at the cop behind the desk.

I nodded, understanding that he didn't want to say anything that could be overheard.

"Are you awake enough to leave?" Blane said.

"Of course," I replied.

Blane stood and I rose to my feet as well. The room tilted in a slow spin and I abruptly sat back down.

"What's wrong?" Blane asked, crouching in front of me again. He took my hands in his. "Your skin is clammy." He felt my forehead.

"I'm fine," I insisted. "I just stood up too fast."

Blane pinched the back of my hand.

"Ouch! Cut it out!" I tried to pull my hand away, but he held firm, looking at my skin.

"You're dehydrated," he announced. "Which is why you're so tired."

"I'm so tired because it's nearly five in the morning and I worked until one," I retorted.

"Come on," he said, standing and pulling me to my feet. He wrapped his arm firmly around my waist so I wouldn't fall.

The room didn't tilt this time, though it still did a slow turn. I stumbled and Blane's arm tightened, keeping me upright and glued to his side.

"How would you know if I'm dehydrated?" I asked as we walked. The cold air outside hit me and I started shivering. Blane tucked me more closely to his body, shielding me from the wind.

"I'm a SEAL, remember? I know the signs."

Oh yeah. Duh.

Blane bundled me into his car, then drove to a nearby all-night convenience store. Leaving me to wait, he jumped out and was back within a few minutes, carrying a small paper bag.

"Drink this," he said, opening a plastic bottle and holding it out to me.

I looked at the label—something fruity with electrolytes.

"Eat this, too."

Blane handed me a banana. I noticed as I took it that he'd already broken the peel for me. For some reason, it struck me as sweet that he would do that.

We drove toward my apartment while I slowly chewed on the banana.

"So what did CJ say?" I asked.

"It's complicated," he replied. "Apparently, her parents are missionaries who went to China several years ago, leaving her to stay with an uncle when she was sixteen.

"Things were fine for a few months, then she and her uncle stopped hearing from them. Eventually, she found out her parents had been detained and sent to a labor camp for inciting separatism."

"That's horrible," I breathed. I'd heard enough news stories about Chinese labor camps to know what fate awaited her parents. "Are they still there?"

"That's part of the problem," Blane said, glancing at me. "When the US Embassy produced no results in getting her parents released, CJ decided to take matters in her own hands. She approached the Chinese looking for a deal, offering to work for them in exchange for getting her parents released."

"That's why she sent the election results there," I said, "from TecSol's server."

"Yes," Blane confirmed. "They were supposed to release her parents upon completion of that project."

"But they didn't?" I guessed.

He shook his head. "Since the hack was discovered and the project shut down, they said she didn't complete her mission and their agreement is void."

I rubbed my forehead, feeling the throb of the headache I'd fought all day since Stacey had clonked me over the head. I knew I had done the right thing with TecSol, yet I felt awful that CJ's parents were still prisoners.

"So why is she in jail?" I asked.

"She threatened them, told them she was going to go to the US government with what she knew if they didn't release her parents. They retaliated, leaking information on her first. She said she's been on the run for a while but was arrested tonight after trying to use her ATM card."

"Why would she use her ATM card? She's smarter than that." Even I had seen enough movies to know you weren't supposed to do that.

"I think she was desperate."

My heart went out to her and I wished she'd stayed with me longer than just a night. "What can we do to help?"

We reached my apartment and Blane got out of the car, coming around to my side to help me out. I felt better after the banana and drink, but was still weak and didn't resist when Blane's arm slid supportively around my waist.

"I'll make some calls tomorrow," Blane said, using his key to unlock my door and lead me inside.

"What can I do?" I asked. There had to be some way I could help.

"Nothing," Blane said firmly. "These aren't some two-bit criminals, Kathleen. CJ is involved with some extremely dangerous people. Let me see what I can do to help her. You stay out of it."

I chewed my lip as I discarded my coat. I understood Blane's concern but hated to be put in the position of just sitting around and waiting.

A knock at the door startled me, but Blane moved forward to answer it as though he was expecting someone.

"Thanks for coming," he said when he'd opened the door.

A man stepped past Blane into the apartment. He was shorter than Blane by several inches but solidly built. The whiteness of his teeth contrasted starkly with his dark skin. Dark hair and eyes completed the picture. I guessed from his features that he had a Latin background. If not for his friendly smile, he would have appeared very formidable indeed. He wore a pair of glasses with thin wire frames. As Blane closed the door behind him, the stranger moved forward, holding his hand out to me.

"Hello," he said. "I'm Eric Sanchez, a friend of Blane's."

I automatically shook his hand, casting a questioning glance at Blane.

"Eric," Blane said, "this is Kathleen, an . . . employee of mine." He seemed to hesitate before identifying me as an employee. "Eric is a doctor," Blane explained to me.

"And why is there a doctor here?" I asked, my eyebrows climbing.

"You hate hospitals," Blane said with a shrug, as if that explained Eric's presence.

"Let's sit down," Eric said, still holding my hand. He drew me toward the couch and sat next to me. I watched as he opened the leather case he carried, removing typical doctor paraphernalia—a stethoscope, blood-pressure checker thing, and thermometer. "I understand you've not been feeling well?" he asked.

"I'm fine," I replied, trying to decide how I felt about Blane actually arranging for a doctor to make a house call for me in the middle of the night. On one hand, it was incredibly presumptuous, big surprise there. On the other, it was very thoughtful of him to be concerned and to remember how much I despised hospitals.

"You had a rather significant injury today, is that correct?" Eric asked.

"A bump on the head," I reluctantly answered.

"And tonight you had a dizzy spell?"

I looked accusingly at Blane, the blabbermouth. "Just a small one. I'm a bit tired, that's all."

"She was dehydrated," Blane said, crossing his arms over his chest and leaning against the wall behind me. "I gave her a banana and sports drink."

"Did that help you to feel better?" Eric asked, picking up an instrument and peering into my eyes with it.

"Yes." My grudging answer seemed to amuse Eric. I saw his lips twitch before he controlled his expression.

"Do you often have dizzy spells?"

"No."

"Any loss of appetite recently? Nausea?"

I remembered throwing up at Kade's yesterday morning. "Yes."

Eric wrapped the blood pressure cuff around my arm. "Any chance you could be pregnant?"

His nonchalance was a stark contrast to the shock those words produced in me. It took everything I had not to look behind me to Blane. I felt the blood drain from my face.

We had always used protection, but nothing was a hundred percent, everyone knew that. What if . . . ? I couldn't finish the thought.

I suddenly realized my silence had produced a tension so thick I could nearly feel it emanating from Blane standing behind me. Eric seemed oblivious, though, scrutinizing the blood pressure gauge before glancing up.

"Is there?" he asked again.

I did math in my head, my eyes squeezing tightly shut as I realized that yes, there was a chance. According to my calculations, I was a couple of days late. Unable to speak the words, I gave a quick nod.

"Well, that might be the culprit then," he said mildly. He put his tools back in his bag and produced a small packet. "This is a very mild sedative," he said. "If you are pregnant, it won't hurt the baby but will help you sleep. You need rest and proper nutrition." He smiled kindly, pressing the packet into my numb fingers. "I prescribe a good night's sleep, followed by three square meals tomorrow and plenty of liquids. You also might want to grab a pregnancy test from the drugstore in a few days."

Blane let him out the door and I caught Eric saying in an undertone to him, "Employee, huh? Right, Blane. Tell me another one."

"Thanks for coming," Blane replied.

"Anytime," Eric said. "You know that."

The room was silent after Blane shut the door. I stared in front of me, seeing nothing. The idea that I might be pregnant . . . the thought was too incomprehensible for me to process.

I was startled from my thoughts by Blane crouching in front of me, taking my ice-cold hands in his.

"Kat," he said softly, "it'll be all right. Don't worry. Okay?"

I stared at him. "How can it possibly be all right?" I choked out in a whisper.

His mouth curved into a smile, a real one that lit up his eyes, and he leaned forward, kissing me lightly on the lips. "Trust me."

I let myself do what I'd been aching to do for days and leaned forward, tentatively resting my head against his shoulder. His arms slid carefully around me, as though any sudden movement on his part would startle me away. His hand cupped the back of my head, and I closed my eyes with a sigh. The tension and worry I hadn't even been aware of eased inside me. Blane was here.

Blane gathered me in his arms and I didn't protest as he helped me to my bedroom. Laying me on the bed, he methodically removed my shoes and jeans before covering me with the blankets. I watched him take off his shoes and shirt before sliding under the covers next to me. Wrapping an arm around my waist, he pulled me back to spoon against his body.

My whole body relaxed at the feel of him holding me. "I believe you," I said after a while, my voice quiet in the dark. "About Kandi."

Blane went still behind me and I waited to hear him speak. After a few moments, he said simply, "Good." I felt him press his lips to my temple as he fit me more snugly against him. His hand found mine resting against my abdomen and entwined our fingers together. Within moments, I was asleep.

~

I woke up slowly, stretching and feeling rested for the first time in days. Opening my eyes, I checked the clock, startled to see that it was past noon. Turning over, I saw the bed was empty beside me. Disappointment made me frown, but considering the time, Blane would have had to get to work hours ago. I sat up and my hand landed on something that crinkled. I picked up the piece of paper, recognizing Blane's handwriting:

Would have stayed with you, but had to be in court today.
Rest and eat something. I'll call you later.
— B

PS—Don't go anywhere.

Checking my cell phone, I saw I had a couple of missed calls from Blane. I was glad he'd left the note rather than just leaving without a word. I'd slept better last night in his arms than I had in several days.

I showered, my hand skimming over my stomach, and I wondered if it could possibly be true—if I could be carrying Blane's child. It was both terrifying and at the same time incredibly fantastic. The impact it would have on my life was so mind-boggling, I resolved to try not to think about it anymore until I got a pregnancy test.

I nearly jumped out of my skin when I walked into the kitchen and found Blane's housekeeper, Mona, peering into my refrigerator.

"I'm sorry, dear," she said. "I didn't mean to startle you."

"It's all right," I said, a bit breathless. "I just wasn't expecting someone to be here."

"Blane mentioned you were feeling under the weather, so I thought I'd bring something by that might help." She closed the fridge and motioned to a large pot on the stove. "Just some chicken noodle soup, nothing fancy. And I took the liberty of stocking a few other items in your cupboards. I hope you don't mind." She smiled kindly.

I was completely taken aback. "Not at all," I blurted. "I appreciate that. You didn't have to go to the trouble, though."

"It's no trouble at all," she said, gathering up her coat and purse. "If you need anything else, just let me know."

"Thank you so much." I followed her to the door.

"You're welcome, dear." She gave me a brief hug before she left and I was too startled by the gesture to return it before she released me. I watched her leave before shutting the door, wondering about what had just happened. Then I smelled the mouthwatering aroma of chicken noodle soup. Filling a huge bowl full, I promptly devoured every bite. I couldn't help envying Blane someone who could cook like Mona.

I had a few hours until Ryan came, so I did some laundry and cleaned. My apartment was sadly lacking in terms of my attention lately. When that was finally done, I collapsed on the couch and flipped on the television.

In the middle of *Judge Judy*, my cell phone rang—Blane was calling. I glanced at the clock. It was after five. He must be out of court by now.

"Hello?"

"Kat. It's me," Blane said.

"Hey," I replied.

"How are you feeling?"

"Better."

I heard him blow out a sigh. "Good. Did Mona come by?"

"Yeah, she brought soup. It was great. Thanks." My fingers twisted the corner of the quilt I'd thrown over the couch, the one Martha had given me. It felt like ages ago. "And thanks for last night," I quietly added.

"It was my pleasure." His voice had dropped into a deeper register and I cradled the phone more closely to my ear. "Can I come by later?" he asked.

"Yes" was on the tip of my tongue before I remembered. I had a date tonight. "Um," I hedged, unsure what to say, "tonight isn't good."

A pause. "Why not?"

"I, um, have plans," I said, twisting the quilt fabric again.

"What kind of plans?" His tone was guarded now, and I recognized his courtroom interrogator coming out.

I squeezed my eyes shut and blurted, "I have a date."

Silence. I squirmed uncomfortably, pressing my lips tightly together. I would not be the first to speak. What was there to say? Even if he hadn't slept with Kandi, he'd kissed her and God knows what else. I refused to feel guilty for going on a date.

"I see," he finally said. Then, "Will you go on a date with me?"

"I—" my words faltered. He'd taken me by surprise. "Why?"

"I want you back, Kat," he said bluntly. "I'll do whatever it takes. I don't care who else you date, so long as you give me a chance to win you back."

I took a moment to absorb this, surprised at his declaration. Surprised and gratified. I still found it hard to believe he felt something more for me, more than the typical impulse to attain someone who had rejected him. Even suspecting this, I couldn't deny him—Blane Kirk, my own personal weak link.

"All right," I said carefully. "I'll go on a date with you."

"Good," he said, satisfaction in his voice. When he spoke again, it was in the low timbre that sent a shiver through me. "I could smell you on my skin this morning," he said. "It took every ounce of self-control I had to not touch you the way I wanted to."

My heart skipped a beat, then sped up. I closed my eyes, absorbing the sound of his voice in my ear.

"Do you know what you do to me, Kat?" he asked.

"No." My response was barely audible, my mind conjuring images of Blane in my bed and the things we had done there.

"You must know," he said. "You make me lose control, forget about everything and everyone. Until all I know is that I have to be inside you, feel your legs wrapped around my waist, your cries of pleasure echoing in my ears."

Oh God. I could barely breathe. His voice was like a potent wine, filling my mind and making my blood heat in my veins.

"I miss you, Kat," he said. "I miss your smiles. I miss your crankiness in the morning before you've had your coffee. I miss how excited you get when it snows. I miss how you won't eat popcorn unless you have a Pepsi with it. I miss listening to you sing in the shower when you think I can't hear you. But mostly, I miss how I feel when I'm with you."

I sucked in a breath, his declarations overwhelming me. I missed him so badly, it was a physical pain. His words frightened me as much as they thrilled me.

"I—I have to go, Blane," I stammered.

"All right." His voice was calm and even. "But I hope you think of me while you're with him."

The line went dead, Blane's words lingering in my ear as I hung up.

I stared at nothing for a while, my apartment growing dark around me, Blane's words echoing in my head. When had life gotten so complicated?

I glanced at the clock. Ryan would be here in less than an hour and I hadn't done anything other than shower. I shifted into high gear. Thinking pants were better for this weather than a dress or skirt, I pulled on a pair of dark jeans that fit me like a second skin. I added a black silk blouse with a scooped neck and flowing sleeves. It was pretty and feminine and went nicely with the jeans and my black boots. I left my hair down, blowing it the rest of the way dry before putting on my makeup.

My phone rang a few minutes before Ryan was supposed to arrive. It was Kade.

"Nice of you to tell me the big news," he said, his voice flat.

I sucked in a breath. I hadn't counted on him finding out that I might be pregnant. "I don't know what you mean," I said, playing for time to think.

"I talked to Blane. He told me."

I winced at the underlying anger in Kade's voice. Was yet another truce between Kade and me about to be broken? How would he feel if I was carrying Blane's child? Would he think I'd planned it to try and trap Blane?

"I'm sorry, Kade," I stammered nervously. "I didn't mean for this to happen. I'm not trying to get Blane to marry me, if that's what you're upset about."

"Damn it, Kathleen," Kade bit out. "That's not why I'm pissed. Blane knows better than to be so careless."

I took a moment to process this before replying. "It's not for sure," I said quietly. "Probably just a false alarm. I've been under a lot of stress, you know."

"Yeah, I know." His tone was grim.

A knock at my door proclaimed Ryan's arrival.

"Ryan's here," I said. "Gotta go." I disconnected before he had a chance to reply.

Taking a deep breath to steady nerves now shot after the conversation with Kade, I opened the door to see Ryan standing there, looking gorgeous in jeans, a heavy brown coat over a button-down shirt, and cowboy boots. His dark hair curved over his forehead in delicious waves.

"Hey, beautiful," he said with a grin, looking me up and down. "You look good enough to eat."

"Thanks," I said with a smile. "Want to come in?"

He stepped inside and I was uncomfortably reminded of my lack of height. He was as tall as Blane and just as broad. I swallowed heavily. Kade's comment last night about Ryan ran through my mind, but I pushed it away. Just because he believed the worst of everyone didn't mean it was true.

"I'll just get my coat." I grabbed the coat Blane had given me, but Ryan took it out of my hands, holding it open for me just as Blane had.

"Any particular preference for dinner?" he asked as we stepped outside.

"Not really," I said as we walked down the stairs. "I'm not terribly picky. Just no sushi."

"No sushi," he said, grinning as he opened the passenger door on a big pickup truck for me. "Got it."

He drove me to a restaurant downtown known for its steaks. The place was dark and quiet on a Monday night, and we settled into a leather-covered booth.

Ryan ordered a bottle of wine as we looked at the menus. I'd had the soup not long ago, so I wasn't terribly hungry. Still, a free meal was a free meal and I could always take home the leftovers. I ordered the petite filet. Ryan ordered a bone-in rib eye, rare.

We chitchatted for a few minutes while the waiter uncorked and poured our wine. I just took tiny sips, the uncomfortable reminder that I might be pregnant lingering in my mind.

"So you and Kirk aren't together anymore?" Ryan asked out of the blue.

I choked on my wine. "I didn't realize you knew it was him," I sputtered, once I could breathe again.

"I know you used to be his girlfriend," Ryan said casually, pouring more wine into our glasses. He turned toward me and I realized he was much closer than I was comfortable with.

Just then, my cell phone rang. I looked at the caller ID. It was Kade again.

"I'd better take this," I said.

"Sure," Ryan said affably.

I scooted out of the booth and headed toward the restrooms, stopping in the hallway where it was quiet.

"Hello?"

"Get out of there, Kathleen," Kade said without preamble.

"What? Why?"

"I cracked that phone you lifted," Kade replied. "It belongs to Ryan Sheffield. From the photos I found, he's been sleeping with Adriana Waters."

"They're having an affair?" I said, incredulous.

"It would seem so," Kade replied.

I was floored. Adriana was having an affair with Ryan? I had thought she hated everything about the military. Why would she get involved with another Navy man? Then another thought hit me. "That must have been him that I heard in the hotel room." Talking about "taking care of" me.

"Right, which is why you have to leave. Now. I found an account in Grand Cayman that belongs to Ryan. It's recently received over five million dollars in deposits. In case you're not aware, they don't pay enlisted men that kind of money."

My heart sank and I blew out a sigh. I didn't know how I could still be surprised at what wrongdoings people committed. Naiveté, I supposed, wanting to believe the best rather than the worst. Maybe I should be more like Kade.

"But why would he kill Ron and Stacey, Kade?" I asked. "Or come after me? He's JAG, not a SEAL. They would've laughed in his face if he'd been the one threatening them."

"Because before he was JAG, he was CIA."

"What?" I was aghast. "But . . . that's not possible," I stammered.

"I'm on my way," Kade said. "Ryan's neck deep in this shit. Get out of there. Tell him anything."

"Okay. I'm downtown, at—" I was cut off when my phone was suddenly snatched out of my hand. Startled, I spun around to see Ryan standing right behind me. He raised the phone to his ear.

"I'm sorry but Kathleen can't come to the phone right now," he said. "She'll have to call you back later."

Kade must have said something then because Ryan's eyes narrowed. "Tell Kirk that if he wants to see her alive again, he should make sure he loses this case." Ryan hung up the phone and shoved it into his pocket.

"Shall we continue our dinner?" he asked, taking my arm in a tight grip and ushering me back to the table.

"Why are you doing this?" I asked. "I heard you on the stand. You thought Kyle did the right thing. You said so yourself."

"Who do you think leaked the story to the press?" he asked. "Once that shit hit the fan, it didn't matter what anyone said. Kyle was going to be crucified. And he would have been, too, if Kirk hadn't defended him. Too bad for you he's too good at his job."

Just then our food arrived, the waiter carefully setting down our plates. Ryan politely thanked him.

It seemed Ryan had been behind the threats to me and Blane the whole time. But for what? Just money? And where had that kind of money come from? I watched him as he calmly began cutting into his steak, the rare meat oozing red juices.

My gaze fell on the large steak knife the waiter had brought me. Just as my hand lifted to grab it, Ryan snatched it away.

"How rude of me," he said. "Let me cut your steak for you."

We didn't speak as he cut decisively through the meat, taking the knife and laying it far beyond my reach when he was through.

"It's your last supper, so to speak," Ryan said, picking up his fork again and stabbing a hunk of steak. "Eat up."

My eyes darted wildly around the room, seeking any kind of help. There were few patrons tonight and the waitstaff was nowhere to be seen.

"No one's going to save you tonight," Ryan said between bites. "So whatever you're planning, forget it." He barely glanced at me, trapped as I was inside the booth. "Now eat."

"Why do you want Kyle to go to prison so badly?" I asked.

"I don't care one way or the other," he replied indifferently. "But I work for people who care a great deal and have paid me very good money to make sure of this trial's outcome."

"Who are these people?" I asked. "Do you still work for the CIA?"

"You know," he said, his tone turning irritated in the blink of an eye, "it really pisses me off when I spend good money buying a woman dinner and she won't eat it because she's on some diet or doesn't want to appear as though she actually eats." He grabbed my arm in a painful grip and jerked me toward him, pushing his face close to mine. "Eat your fucking dinner."

It was like Dr. Jekyll and Mr. Hyde, so quickly did he turn from genial and calm to coldly lethal. I hurriedly picked up my fork, fumbling with it since my hands were shaking so badly, and put a bite of meat in my mouth. Ryan watched, easing up once he was satisfied I was chewing.

"That's better," he said, resuming his own meal.

The meat was like sawdust in my mouth, the lump of matter getting harder to swallow the more I chewed. I choked it down, taking a drink of water before eating another bite under Ryan's watchful eyes.

"I quit the CIA, by the way," he said conversationally. "But that doesn't mean the training I have doesn't come in handy."

"Why would you join the Navy if you left the CIA?" I asked, confused.

"Who said I joined? It helps to have friends in high places."

"I know you're sleeping with Adriana," I accused.

"Was," he replied shortly, his knife slicing through his steak. "Past tense."

"What do you mean?"

"I guess you haven't heard," he said. I waited while he chewed another mouthful of meat. "Adriana was so traumatized by what Kyle did to her, causing the miscarriage of their child, that she took her own life earlier tonight."

I gasped in horror. Ryan didn't even bother to look my way. "You killed her," I breathed. Poor Adriana. First she'd lost faith in her marriage, then her child. Now she was dead.

"Public opinion is a fickle thing," Ryan said. "The suicide of Kyle's ex-wife should take care of any sympathy people might have toward him."

I was aghast. "And now you're going to kill me?" I asked.

"I have to do whatever it takes to make Blane throw the case. If he hadn't been so quick that night in his office, I'd have got you."

My blood ran cold at the casual way Ryan spoke of killing me.

"What about the bomb in my car?" I asked.

"Did you like that?" Ryan laughed. "Creative, right? Didn't get you, though. You must have nine lives, sweetie, but your time's up." He wiped his mouth, glancing at my plate with a sigh. "I guess that's all you're going to eat. You can't say I didn't try to give you a decent last meal, beautiful."

"Why kill me?" I asked. "I haven't done anything to you."

"Collateral damage, sweetness. You can thank Kirk for getting you involved at all. We got all our info from his ex. Turns out, she's an old sorority sister of Adriana's and does she ever hate you. She was full of useful information. Using you as leverage on Kirk was a no-brainer once we realized he was in love with you."

"Who is 'we'?" I asked. "Who are you working for?"

"Can't answer that."

"Blane's not going to lose this case," I said, anger at the terror Ryan had put me through giving me a shot of courage. "He sees Kyle as his brother in arms, and he won't abandon him. That should prove to you that I don't mean a thing to him. Everything you did to me was for nothing."

"Save it," Ryan said coldly. "You think I'm an idiot? That I didn't see through the big breakup scene? Kirk will go to any lengths to protect you."

Terror made my heart race. "You won't get away with this," I bluffed. "You're despicable and a disgrace to this country."

"Like I give a shit," Ryan snorted. "I'm just doing my time until I can get out and get a real job. Completing this mission ensures I have a very plum job waiting for me. Always wanted to work in politics."

Seizing my chance, I took the fork I still had in my hand and brought it down with as much force as I could on his thigh. Ryan jerked, grunting in pain. I scrambled away, climbing across the booth, panic pushing me. To my dismay, I was brought up short by Ryan's fist closing over the belt in my jeans. In a flash, he'd hauled me back next to him.

"Nice try, you fucking bitch," he seethed, yanking the fork out of his leg. It hadn't penetrated very deeply, the thick denim and my lack of leverage stopping it from doing any real damage. I struggled to get out of his grip.

The cold press of metal pushed against my skin and I froze.

"You see that happy little family over there?" Ryan hissed in my ear.

I looked over to see a man and woman eating dinner with two kids, a boy and a girl. The boy was older, maybe ten, and the girl was perhaps five. She had the curliest blonde hair I'd ever seen.

"Make any more scenes and those kids will be orphans."

I watched, unable to take my eyes off the family, as the little boy hid his peas under his potatoes and the man re-filled the woman's wine glass. The little girl swung her feet, encased in hot-pink sparkly tennis shoes. I obeyed Ryan, stilling my efforts to get free.

Ryan threw a couple of hundred-dollar bills on the table and stood, pulling me up with him. He walked us toward the door where the maitre d' stood. This was my last chance to get help. Ryan nudged his gun against my ribs.

"Try it and I'll kill him," Ryan hissed at me, making the words I'd been about to say die on my lips. We passed the man as he held the door for us, smiling affably and wishing us a good evening.

Once we were outside, I looked around, scanning the area for anyone or anything that could help me. Ryan jerk-ed me along to his truck, pushing me up against the side and stepping back slightly.

"You're a pain in the ass," he said calmly, reaching into his pocket. I froze in horror, wondering if he was going to kill me right then, but he removed a small packet. I watched as he shook out a cigarette and lighter. "You don't mind if I smoke, do you?" he asked sardonically. I recognized the same brand as that of the butts that had been left on the ground outside my apartment.

He lit up and took a deep drag. I didn't move, watching him as I would a snake, waiting for him to glance away and give me a split second. I knew I wouldn't get far if I ran, but being shot in the back was preferable to just standing here waiting to die.

Ryan took another deep drag of his cigarette, knocking the ashes to the ground. Looking at me, he opened his mouth to say something. I never knew what it was because just then his head exploded.

CHAPTER FIFTEEN

For an endless moment, I couldn't move. I watched as Ryan's headless body collapsed as if in slow motion to the ground, the cigarette he'd lit still burning in his lifeless grip. Blood and gore were streaked on my clothes, in my hair. I dropped to my knees next to Ryan's body, reaching a hand toward him, to do what, I didn't know. He was beyond my help.

Another gunshot hit the truck above my head. I collapsed onto my stomach. A scream clawed its way up from my chest. I couldn't think what to do, then I remembered my cell phone.

My fingers scrabbled at Ryan's pockets, the horror of touching his dead body overcome by my panic and fear. Another shot hit the truck just as my hand touched the smooth metal of my phone. I yanked it out, then crawled underneath the big truck, pulling myself forward on the rough asphalt until I reached the other side. Stumbling to my feet, I ran.

I didn't know where I was going—my mind was in a turmoil of shock and terror. Fumbling with my phone, I dialed.

"Help me," I gasped when the line picked up.

"What's happening?" Kade shot back.

"I don't know," I replied, pausing to duck into an alley. I gasped for air, my hands shaking violently. "They shot Ryan."

"Who?" Kade asked. "Who shot Ryan?"

"I don't know!" I sobbed. "His head just exploded. And now they're after me." I was fighting hysteria as I looked down at the bloodstains on my shirt and arms.

"Take it easy," Kade said soothingly. "Breathe, Kathleen. Keep it together. I'm coming for you."

"K-K-Kathleen? Are you all r-r-right?"

I spun around at the sound of the voice, my heart in my throat, then nearly collapsed in relief.

"God, Frankie, you scared me."

Frankie stood near me, the light from the street behind him casting his face in shadows. He didn't say anything as he moved closer toward me.

"Frankie?"

"What's going on?" Kade asked, his voice urgent in my ear. "Who the fuck is Frankie?"

"I'm s-sorry, K-Kathleen," Frankie stammered.

"What? What do you mean?" It was then I noticed him carrying a rifle. I had a split-second warning, gasping "No!" before everything went black.

∾

This was the second time in as many days that I'd gotten knocked upside the head with something, and waking up this time was no better than before.

I groaned. My head was splitting with pain, making me seriously reconsider opening my eyes. It was freezing, wherever I was. My hands were nearly numb and the cold bit into my skin.

The smell hit me next and nearly made me gag. It smelled like rotten meat, wherever I was. I forced my eyes open, realizing I was lying on a cold concrete floor. There was very little light, just enough for me to make out my surroundings.

I was in a small room, the walls dark and dank. The meager light seemed to be coming from a glassless transom window over the one and only door. I painfully rose to my feet, making my way to it. It was made of a heavy, sturdy wood and had no inside knob.

Turning, I jumped when I saw another person in the room with me, hidden in the shadows.

"Frankie?" I asked tentatively. The person didn't answer. "Who are you?" Still no answer.

Tentatively, I moved toward the figure, realizing as I did so that the smell was becoming stronger and more potent the closer I got. An ominous awareness shuddered through me, but I made myself keep going.

Sinking down next to the person, I tentatively reached out. At my touch, they slumped over on the floor and I shrieked in surprise, stumbling backward and falling. Light now shone on a man's dead face and I could see an empty eye socket, the other eye wide and staring at me. As I watched, maggots crawled from his open mouth.

My stomach heaved and I turned over, retching and vomiting until there was nothing left in my stomach. I wiped my mouth, my hands shaking violently. Without the strength to stand, I crawled on my hands and knees as far away from the dead man as I could get.

"I s-s-ee you've m-m-met my other g-guest."

I looked up to see Frankie had opened the door and now stood in the opening.

"Why are you doing this?" I asked. None of it made any sense. Why had Frankie kidnapped me? Why was he keeping a dead body in his cellar?

"For my f-father," he said.

"Your father?" I was utterly confused.

"My f-father and I c-c-con-converted to Islam. He w-went to Iraq to f-fight. I'm g-g-going, too, as s-s-soon as I k-k-kill his m-m-murderers."

Frankie stammered, but the hand holding the gun trained on me was steady.

"Frankie," I said, trying to reason with him, "you're not a murderer."

He laughed and the sound sent a chill down my spine. "Wh-who do you think k-k-killed Ron Freeman? Or the m-man n-next to you?"

I was horrified at his confession. Frankie had seemed so sweet, offering me free rides, always being there when I needed him . . .

"Oh my God," I breathed. "You've been following me." I knew it had to be true. It was too coincidental, now that I looked back on it, how Frankie and his cab had always been nearby. He'd been there when my car had the flat tire, and when I'd fought with Blane right after finding Stacey dead. My eyes widened in shock and realization. "Did you kill Stacey?"

"You led me t-t-to her," he admitted. "I p-p-put a t-t-tracker in your p-purse the night I t-took you home."

I felt light-headed with realization. I'd led Stacey's killer right to her door. I couldn't think or process all that he was telling me.

"You followed me and Blane to the Christmas tree farm," I said numbly. "And took the photos you sent to Blane. And all that time, I thought it was luck that you were around when I needed you."

"S-s-stupid whore," he said contemptuously.

"Why?" I asked, my voice a thin thread in the room. "Why me?"

He didn't answer for a moment as he studied me. "You l-l-look like my s-s-sister."

I remembered Frankie telling me that, the first night we'd met. I frowned in confusion. "Then why are you doing this to me?"

"Because you're just like her!" he suddenly shouted, making me jump. His face was blotchy and red and he used the gun for emphasis, pointing it jerkily at me. I instinctively recoiled, cringing against the wall. "She used to be s-so g-g-good. P-pure. Then she s-spread her legs and l-l-let him f-fuck her!"

Spittle flew from his mouth and his eyes were bright, almost feverish. His eyes were wet as well, but I didn't think he noticed.

"And she wanted to m-marry him, turn her back on our beliefs, our family," Frankie sneered. "Father was right t-to do what he did."

I almost didn't dare ask the question, afraid as I was of the answer, but the words came despite myself.

"What did he do, Frankie?"

"He upheld our family's honor." He seemed calmer now, which was even more terrifying.

"How?"

"We beat her. Then we k-killed her."

My stomach heaved and I thought I was going to be sick again. Frankie had helped murder his own sister.

"I'm not Muslim, Frankie." I tried to reason with him, though I knew Frankie was far beyond logic.

"Even more reason you should die," he said. "One less American whore." He moved closer to me and I instinctively shrank away. "B-b-but f-first, let's m-make you useful."

He pulled a phone out of his pocket and I recognized it as mine. After turning it on, he punched a few buttons, and held the phone up so I could hear it ringing. He'd put it on speaker.

"Kat, where the hell are you?" Blane answered, his voice anxious.

"I have her," Frankie said. "I thought you m-m-might want to s-s-say good-bye."

A pause. "Who is this?" Blane's voice was like ice.

"The man who's going to k-kill K-K-Kathleen. Then I'm going to k-kill you and K-Kyle," he said. "Do you want to listen?"

My terror spiked when Frankie carefully set the phone on the ground before moving closer to me. I couldn't look away from the gun still steady in his grip, and was taken aback when he grabbed my hand.

"No! Stop!" I cried, trying to jerk away. In the next instant, I heard a sickening crack as fierce pain shot through my hand. I screamed. He'd broken my finger. I cradled it to my chest and bit my lip to keep from making any further noise. Tears ran down my cheeks.

"Kathleen! What the fuck are you doing to her?"

"She will pay for what she is," Frankie said, speaking with utter conviction.

"I am going to hunt you down and kill you," Blane rasped. His voice reeked of menace and sent a chill down my spine. I'd never heard him sound that way before.

"I'm going to shoot her and let her bleed like my father bled. Then I'm going to burn the hair she's so proud of. Then if she's still screaming, I'll cut her throat."

Terror shot through me. "No, please," I managed, my voice strangled. Frankie's stammer was strangely gone, his demeanor preternaturally calm as he described how he would torture and kill me.

"Any last words, Kat?" Frankie mimicked Blane's nickname for me. I looked at the gun in his hand, the look on his face, and realized that this was it. I was going to die. I would never see Blane again.

"Can you hear me, Blane?" I called out.

"Yeah, babe, I can hear you." His voice was gentle now, the sound of it breaking my heart.

"Blane," I choked out. I took a deep breath before quickly blurting out, "His name's Frankie. He's driving a city cab, about five seven, twenty years old, hundred fifty pounds, clean shaven—"

Frankie slammed the gun against the side of my head, abruptly cutting off my words as pain exploded in my face. I cried out as I fell to the floor.

"Kat!" I could hear Blane through the tinny speaker-phone, but I was fighting to stay conscious and couldn't reply.

"Time's up," Frankie interjected.

Before I could even shut my eyes, he fired the gun. I screamed again as the bullet tore into the flesh of my thigh.

Frankie walked toward me, then stood over me. His eyes were completely empty of all emotion. They were the cold, remorseless eyes of a killer.

"I'll see you soon, Kirk," Frankie said. He brought his heel down hard on the phone still lying on the floor, shattering the glass.

I clutched the wound in my leg, trying to stop the hot flow of blood—my flesh felt like it was on fire. I'd never felt anything that hurt so badly in my entire life.

Frankie crouched down next to me. I glared at him, hatred in my eyes.

"B-Because of your big mouth, I'm going to have to f-f-find him b-b-before he finds us," he told me, stammer again intact. "And once I do, I'll b-be back to f-finish you."

"He'll kill you first, you sick fuck," I hissed. Pursing my lips, I spat at him.

The spittle hit his face and he flinched in surprise, wiping it off before backhanding me again.

"Just for that, I'll m-m-make him s-s-suffer," he hissed.

He was gone before I could do more than make a feeble grab for him, the wooden door slamming shut with a finality that made me want to scream.

Sweat rolled down my face, even though the room was freezing. I could see the puffs of air as I panted for breath. I knew I had to do something to stop the bleeding. Reaching up, I ripped at my sleeve, jerking until I heard the shoulder seam tear. Taking the fabric, I wrapped it around the wound in my leg, cinching it tightly. I gritted my teeth at the pain. I had to keep going, had to get out of here. If I didn't, I knew I would die here in this cement hole. I fought to keep from passing out, but knew I wasn't succeeding. I slumped over several times, only to jerk awake. I had no idea of how much time had passed since Frankie had left, but it felt like hours.

I looked up at the window. It seemed very far away, at least two feet or more above my head. My eyes fell on the dead man and I had an idea, an awful idea, but I was desperate.

I crawled toward him, turning him over on his back. Dog tags peeked from his shirt and I picked them up. Brian Bowers. It looked like he hadn't disappeared of his own accord.

"I'm so sorry, Brian," I said to him, tears choking me. "But I need your help."

I dragged his stiffened body toward the window, stopping every few feet to retch. The smell was overpowering. Feeling something on my hand, I looked to see that maggots were crawling up my arm.

I shrieked, flinging them off. I collapsed on the floor, the pain in my leg agonizing. Hopelessness and despair rose in me. I couldn't do it. I was going to die here while Blane might be dying out there.

The thought of Blane had me back up on all fours, grabbing Bowers and resuming my ordeal. After what seemed an eternity, I reached the wall. I rose, barely able to put any weight on my injured leg. The tourniquet seemed to be helping—the bleeding wasn't as bad. Or maybe it was the cold that kept the blood moving only sluggishly.

It took all my strength to prop his body against the door. I took a deep breath, steeling myself for what I had to do. It felt wrong, but I prayed that Brian would have understood.

Using his body as a human ladder, I grappled my way up until I was able to stand on his shoulders. The transom was now at my chest. I grabbed on, struggling to pull myself into the small opening. Making one last monumental effort to heave my body upward even as Brian shifted and slid out from beneath me, I lay with half my body through the window, my legs still dangling inside the room.

Spots danced in front of my eyes and I panted for breath, waiting for them to go away. When they did, I looked down at the floor, several feet below me. I knew it was going to hurt like hell, but I pulled myself the rest of the way through and dropped to the floor. The ground met my feet and pain shot through my wounded leg. I collapsed, stifling a scream at the pain, biting my lip hard enough to draw blood. When I finally caught my breath, I struggled to my feet to look around.

It was some kind of basement, the wood floor dusty. To my right, a flight of stairs led upward. Groaning, I limped toward them, both hands scrabbling against the rough wall for support, every moment causing pain to shoot through my leg. The stairs were excruciatingly slow going as I dragged my wounded leg up each step. I prayed this would be the way out because I didn't have it in me to go much farther. Sweat poured from me and blood ran freely down my leg, soaking my jeans. Chills wracked my body.

The stairs opened into a kitchen. It wasn't kept well, with dirty dishes piled in the sink. My eyes locked on the doorway and I limped toward it. My single-minded focus was getting to the front door.

In the doorway, I had to stop for a moment. My breathing was fast and shallow, and I was afraid I was going to hyperventilate, pass out, or both. Clutching the doorframe to stay on my feet, I tried to regain my breathing. A slight noise made me raise my head.

Blane stood not twenty feet away, a gun in his hand. I started in surprise to see him and opened my mouth to speak but stopped when he laid his finger against his lips in the universal signal to stay silent.

I realized that Frankie must still be in the house. Spots danced in front of my eyes again and my heart rate spiked in fear. My grip tightened on the doorframe.

Suddenly, someone grabbed me from behind, arm locked around my neck, and jerked me backward. My feet skittered on the floor and the pain shooting through my leg made me cry out.

The cold metal of a gun pressed against my temple made my breath freeze in my chest.

"Kirk," Frankie snarled. "Did you c-come looking for your whore?"

Blane didn't say a word, his gun trained steadily on us. His face was a cold, hard mask.

"I'll k-k-kill her first," Frankie said, "then I'll kill you."

"You can't get both of us," Blane said, his voice deadly calm. "You shoot her, I kill you."

Frankie laughed. "S-s-stalemate."

"I'll put down my gun—" Blane began.

"No—" I said before Frankie yanked his arm back hard against my windpipe, choking off my words.

Blane's steely eyes followed the movement of Frankie's arm before he continued, as though I hadn't spoken. "I'll put down my gun, and you let her go. I'm the one who's going to get Kyle off. Remember, he's the man who shot your dad. I'm the one you want."

I pulled at Frankie's arm, my nails digging into his skin, and he yanked again on my neck. My eyes were frantically trying to meet Blane's, but he carefully avoided my gaze.

"Do we have a deal?" Blane asked.

Frankie nodded. "P-put down your gun, K-K-Kirk."

I watched in dismay as Blane slowly complied, his eyes locked on Frankie and the gun held to my head. I could hardly breathe, unable to believe that Blane was about to be shot right in front of me and I was powerless to stop it.

The instant Blane stood after laying his gun on the floor, Frankie whipped his hand around to point it at Blane. He fired.

"No!" I screamed, watching in horror as the shot hit Blane in the chest, knocking him backward to the floor. My knees collapsed and I fell to the ground, Frankie releasing me as I dropped.

A second gunshot sounded, then another in quick succession. My head swung up to look at Frankie behind me. He still had an expression of surprise on his face, even as red blossomed on his chest. His knees gave out and he collapsed on the floor in a heap.

Behind him I could now see what had been hidden.

Kade.

He must have come in a back entrance while Blane had come in the front. Kade hurried to me, quickly holstering his gun.

I was trying to get back up on all fours to crawl to where Blane lay motionless, but my body wouldn't cooperate. I gave up and started pulling myself forward on my arms.

"Hey, take it easy," Kade said, falling to his knees. He pulled me back and gently cradled my head and shoulders in his arms.

"Blane—" I choked.

"Shh. Don't try to talk," he said. His hand cupped my cheek.

"But Blane—" I couldn't understand why he was just letting Blane lie on the floor.

"I'm fine, Kat. I'm right here."

I jerked my head and was stunned to see Blane crouching next to me.

Speechless, I sluggishly tried to comprehend seeing Blane, alive and unhurt, next to me.

Blane turned to Kade. "Call 911," he ordered.

"I'm on it," Kade replied, handing me carefully to Blane before moving down the hall.

"Blane, how did . . ."

"I had a vest on, Kat," he explained. He probed my arms and legs, looking for other injuries.

I started to cry. I couldn't help it. I'd thought for sure he was dead.

"You're going to be okay, Kat," Blane said softly, his fingers combing through my tangled hair. "You're strong, Kat. Stronger than you realize."

"Why would you do that?" I rasped. "He could have killed you."

Blane regarded me seriously, his finger brushing the skin of my cheek as he replied, "That was a chance I was willing to take."

I wanted to say something, tell him how much I loved him. The close call we'd both had made my fears and insecurities seem so trivial, but the words died on my lips as dark oblivion overtook me.

∼

When next I opened my eyes, it was dark. Afraid it had all been a dream, that I was still trapped in the cold cellar with Brian Bowers's dead body, I struggled to sit up.

"Take it easy. You're okay. You're safe."

A hand rested on my shoulder and I realized Kade was standing next to me. I collapsed in relief back onto the bed.

"Where am I?" My throat was dry and hurt, my voice barely a whisper.

"Indiana University Hospital," he replied.

I processed this. "Hate hospitals," I rasped.

"That's what Blane said. But you needed to come here. They had to remove the bullet from your leg and you'd lost a lot of blood."

"Thirsty."

Kade grabbed a cup from a nearby table. Placing an arm behind my shoulders, he helped me sit up, holding the cup to my lips so I could take a drink. The water was the best thing I had ever tasted and I drank deeply.

"Thank you," I said once I'd had my fill.

"No problem," Kade said, easing my head back down into the pillow.

"How'd you find me?" I could still remember how stunned I'd been to see Blane.

"I put a tracking device inside your cell phone after the first time you disappeared on me," Kade answered. "I wasn't about to lose you again." He paused. "Though it seems I nearly did."

I recalled how he'd been sitting at my kitchen table that morning and had gone through my purse, finding the names and addresses I'd written down. That must have been when he'd planted the tracker. Not that I was complaining. If he hadn't done that, I might still be in that house—only dead.

"What time is it?"

"Around five a.m.," Kade answered. "You were missing for over six hours. We would have gotten there sooner, but the asshole must have turned the phone off. It stopped sending a signal. All we had to go on was about a square-block radius."

Something Blane had said to Frankie came back to me. "How'd Blane know about Frankie's dad?"

"He was with me when Frankie called. I heard what you said, the description you gave. That was enough for me to track him down. Frankie was Franklin Randall Wyster. Son of James Walter Wyster, aka Ahmed el Mustaqueem."

It seemed like it had been ages since Clarice had told me the name of the man killed in Iraq—Ahmed el Mustaqueem.

"Frankie and his dad allegedly committed an honor killing a couple years ago," Kade continued. "The victim was his daughter, Christine Wyster. She was fifteen at the time. They were never prosecuted."

I shuddered, horrified at the thought of what the poor girl must have endured at the hands of people who were supposed to love and protect her. "I thought Ryan was the one who killed those people," I said, "but really it was Frankie."

"Frankie may have killed them," Kade said, "but Ryan was the one threatening them into changing their testimony. I don't know who he was working for, but I'm going to find out."

I took internal stock of my body. I didn't have a lot of pain, but felt . . . strange. My brain felt sluggish and slow and it was difficult to concentrate.

"Why do I feel funny?" I asked.

"Painkillers" was his curt reply.

That explained why my leg didn't hurt. Thank God for modern medicine, but it was making my mind sluggish, almost like I was drunk. My eyes wanted to stay shut when I blinked, but I struggled to stay awake. "Knew you'd find me," I slurred.

"Six hours was a long fucking time, princess," he muttered. Kade's hand closed around mine, the gentleness of his grasp belying the harshness of his tone.

The familiar nickname brought a smile to my lips, although I couldn't pry my eyes open.

It was a moment before Kade spoke again. "Go to sleep, Kathleen," he said, his other hand smoothing over my head. "You need your rest."

His hand slipping out of mine made my eyes fly open.

"Don't leave," I protested, reaching for him.

"I'm not going anywhere," he assured me, and the feel of his hand in mine made my body relax back into the mattress.

Then sweet oblivion took me again.

∽

"Are you sure you don't want a wheelchair?" The nurse was quite persistent.

"No," I said, adamant. "I can use the crutches just fine." The last thing I wanted was to be wheeled out like some invalid.

"I'll help her," Blane said reassuringly to the nurse, who gave him a nod before leaving. I harrumphed in exasperation.

"Can we go now?" I pleaded, desperate to leave the hated confines of the hospital. This was the second day I'd had to endure it and I'd reached my limit.

"Absolutely," he said, grabbing my purse and handing me my crutches. I eased them under my armpits and took a tentative step. I could handle it all okay. We started making our way cautiously down the hallway.

"Thanks for being here," I said, swinging the crutches forward. It was slow going.

Blane had been by my side nearly the entire time at the hospital, leaving only to meet with the police, Judge Reynolds, and the prosecution. I'd been relieved when he'd told me that, given what had happened with Ryan and Frankie, Judge Reynolds had dismissed the case. Blane had seen Kyle off at the airport mere hours ago.

"Of course," Blane said evenly. "Happy to help."

It was awkward between us. He'd put his life on the line for me—would have died if Frankie had aimed for his head instead of his chest—and I wanted to know why. Was it just

Blane being Blane, the military man? Or did he do it because he felt something deeper for me?

Blane helped me into his car and I leaned back into the leather seat with a sigh. Crutches were hard work and my broken finger didn't make things any easier.

The doctor had told me they'd done a blood test when Blane had brought me in to see if I was pregnant. The test had turned up negative. I hadn't yet told Blane. The words stuck in my throat as he got in the driver's seat and started the car. I made myself speak.

"I'm not pregnant," I blurted.

Blane glanced at me as he shifted the car into gear. "Okay."

"I . . . I just thought you should know," I said, my voice faltering. "Sorry for the scare."

Blane looked at me again, the intensity of his gaze making my breath catch. "I was never scared," he said.

I didn't know what to say, so I remained silent.

He took my hand, holding on to it as he drove. I noticed we were heading in the opposite direction of my apartment.

"Where are we going?" I asked.

"I thought you should stay with me for a while," Blane said easily. "Mona can help you until you're back on your feet."

I frowned. His high-handedness rubbed me the wrong way. "I'll be fine, Blane," I said crisply. "You can take me home."

He turned to look at me. "Please, Kat," he said quietly. "Come stay with me."

My heart skipped a beat, his sincere request soothing my irritation. I nodded, acquiescing. I wondered where I would sleep, in "my room" . . . or Blane's? Which did I want?

We drove the rest of the way in silence. The elephant in the car remained in what was left unsaid. I didn't know how to bring up, "So, why were you willing to die for me?" without sounding incredibly narcissistic. And what if he just looked at me and replied, "I'm a SEAL. It's what I do." I would feel idiotic and foolish.

Blane parked in his driveway, helping me out of the car and handing me the crutches. We made our way slowly up the sidewalk to the front door. Mona greeted us, holding the door wide open so I could get inside.

"I'm so glad you could come stay!" Mona exclaimed, her smile warm and welcoming.

"Thanks for having me," I said. "I hope I'm not too much of an imposition."

"Not at all," Mona assured me. "Tigger has settled in nicely." She motioned to the bay window, through which the sun was shining. I could see the marmalade lump of fur curled on the sun-dappled carpet, proclaiming Tigger's presence.

"Let's get you upstairs," Blane said. Stepping forward, he swiftly swept me up in his arms, handing the crutches to Mona.

"What are you doing?" I asked, alarmed. "I need those crutches."

"No, you don't," he said, heading toward the stairs. "You just need me."

I was completely at a loss for words, watching his face wordlessly as he climbed the stairs and took me to the bedroom I'd stayed in before, setting me gently on the bed.

"What's going on, Blane?" I asked.

He crouched in front of me so we were at eye level. "You do know what day it is, don't you?"

I looked questioningly at him. I had absolutely no idea what day it was. The past few days had been a blur.

He smiled widely and it took my breath away. "It's Christmas Eve, Kat," he said gently.

Christmas Eve. It didn't seem possible.

"I know I messed up, making you think I'd betrayed your trust," Blane continued, "and I'm sorry." His hand moved to cup my cheek. "When I heard that gunshot, Kat—" He shook his head, as if he couldn't go on. His gaze lifted to mine. "Is it too late?" he asked, his voice pained even as his thumb brushed my cheek. "Am I too late to put us back together?"

I swallowed heavily. "I . . . I don't know, Blane," I managed. "You left me out of your plans. You didn't tell me what you suspected about Kandi. You knew I'd think the worst and you let it happen anyway." I looked at him. "I don't think I'm the only one with trust issues."

My emotions were balanced on a knife-edge as it was, the stress—physical and emotional—of all that had happened weighing on me. I loved him, I knew that much, but couldn't make myself say the words that would bring us back together. The image of Kade drifted unbidden through my mind.

Blane nodded, his eyes keenly watching me.

410

"Maybe you're right, Kat." Leaning forward, he pressed his lips gently to mine. "I'll earn your trust again," he whispered lightly.

He stood and I had to clench my hands into fists to not reach for him.

"Do you want to shower?"

Washing the hospital smell off sounded immensely appealing, so I nodded. "That sounds wonderful."

Blane disappeared and I heard the sound of the water turn on in the shower. When he returned, he helped me hobble into the bathroom.

"Turn around," he said, and I complied.

Blane's fingers hooked underneath my shirt, dragging it up and over my head. My breath caught in my throat as he unhooked my bra, the fragile straps sliding down my arms.

"I can do it," I protested weakly when his fingers moved to the waistband of my pants.

"I know," came the rough reply before he pushed the cotton down over my hips and legs, taking my panties with it.

My pulse jumped at the feel of his warm breath against my skin, his hands tracing up the backs of my thighs. The heat of his mouth against the small of my back made the flesh between my thighs ache.

Blane stood behind me, his hands drifting lightly up my sides. "You'd better get in now," he growled.

I swallowed hard before stepping into the steaming shower, the hot water sluicing over my skin. I was glad the hospital had put a waterproof bandage on my thigh. A shower was much better than a sponge bath. I didn't turn around, but I could feel Blane's eyes on me. After a moment, I heard the bathroom door close.

I washed as quickly as I could, shampooing and conditioning my hair proving difficult with a broken finger. I scrubbed until I finally felt clean again. When I turned the water off, the bathroom door opened again and Blane stepped back inside.

"Feel better?" he asked, sliding the shower open and holding out a fluffy white towel for me.

I nodded even as I tried to ignore the way his eyes drifted over my body. I stepped forward and he wrapped the towel around me. Our eyes met, and for a moment, I couldn't breathe. His gaze dropped to my mouth and I nervously wet my lips. Blane's hands tightened on my hips, tugging me toward him until I could feel his arousal pressing against my abdomen.

"You're not playing fair," I breathed.

"I never said I would," he rasped in my ear, sending a shiver through me.

Tearing myself away, I hobbled into the bedroom and dried off while Blane got in the shower. Searching through the bureau, I found some panties and put them on. In another drawer, I found a white nightgown and slipped it over my head. I was exhausted and climbed into bed. I struggled to keep my eyes open, but it was a losing battle and I was asleep before Blane came out of the bathroom.

∽

Something woke me. I lay still, trying to figure out what it was. Then I realized someone was in the room with me.

Turning, I saw the outline of a man against the curtains. For a moment, I panicked, then realized that the outline was a familiar one.

"Kade."

He moved forward until he stood next to my bed. I instinctively reached out to grasp his hand. I hadn't seen him since the first time I'd awoken in the hospital.

"Didn't mean to wake you, princess," he said quietly.

"It's fine," I replied with a yawn, pushing myself to a sitting position. I rubbed my eyes and pushed my hair back from my face, struggling to wake up. "Are you all right?" Kade seemed to come to me at the oddest moments, and most often at night. I wondered when he slept.

"You're the one with a gunshot wound and you're asking me if I'm all right?" His voice was bitter.

I was glad he was here. I hadn't been in the proper frame of mind to thank him when I'd awoken in the hospital two nights ago. If he hadn't planted that tracking device, I might be dead now. Scooting over on the bed, I tugged on his hand. He briefly resisted before perching hesitantly next to me.

The light filtering in between the blinds covering the window was enough for me to see his face. His brow was creased, his lips tilted downward as he studied me.

"Thank you," I said, "for coming after me."

"We were nearly too late."

"I'm fine, Kade," I said, giving him a small smile. I felt stronger, even after the horrifying experience. "I'll heal. I survived."

His expression didn't ease. If anything, it became more forbidding. "He died too quick after what he did to you."

I tried to speak, but he pressed a finger against my lips and I remained silent.

His eyes drifted over me and a wry smile twisted his lips. His finger brushed over my lower lip, dropping until his hand curled around the back of my neck underneath my hair. "You even look like a princess," he mused. "White gown, blonde hair tumbling over your shoulders, blue eyes so wide and innocent. All you need is a knight in shining armor to come to your rescue."

"You came to my rescue, Kade."

A grimace of pain passed over his features. "Blane's the white knight. Not me."

My heart went out to him. He couldn't see himself the way I saw him—strong, brave, loyal, trustworthy. As noble as Blane, though I was sure Kade would disagree. "Sometimes knights wear black," I said quietly. Our eyes caught and held, then my leg twinged and I winced.

"What? What's wrong?"

I shook my head. "It's nothing. Probably just time for another pain pill."

In a moment, Kade was gone and then back with a glass of water. I took it as he opened a nearby bottle and gave me a pill. I swallowed it and handed him the glass, which he set on the bedside table. He rose to go.

"Wait," I said, catching his sleeve. "Where are you going? Are you going to your place?"

He nodded and I breathed in relief. He wouldn't be far, then. I didn't examine why that was important to me.

"Do you mind," I began tentatively. "I mean, if it's not too much trouble—"

"What do you need?" he asked. "Are you still in pain?"

"No." I hesitated. "I just . . . don't want to be alone." I could feel my face heat and was glad for the darkness. "It's . . . dark." He didn't say anything, so I blundered on. "Just until I fall asleep. Then you can leave." The thought of being alone in the dark made me fearful in a way I hadn't felt since I was young and the dark held the boogeyman and monsters under my bed. A real-life monster had tried to kill me, had planned to do so in a torturous, gruesome fashion. During the day, I could shove that fact to the back of my mind and not think about it, but the night was difficult for me.

Without a word, Kade rounded the bed and lay down next to me, on top of the covers. Relieved, I snuggled under the quilt, turning on my side and scooting as close to him as I dared. He made me feel safe, protected. Nothing would get by Kade, not even my nightmares. My whole body relaxed.

After a few minutes of silence, he spoke, his voice quiet. "Kathleen."

"Yes?" I replied, my voice as soft as his.

"How did you get out of that cellar?"

I stiffened, the memory of Bowers's dead body engulfing me. The smell, the sound it made as it scraped across the floor, his sightless eye and empty socket staring at me as I climbed to his shoulders.

"I used Brian's body as a ladder," I whispered, the horror of it making tears fall from my eyes.

Kade must have heard the regret in my voice, for I felt his arms encircle me and pull me close. "Shh," he said, smoothing my hair in a comforting gesture. "You did what you had to do. He wouldn't have wanted you to die there, too."

His acceptance of what I'd done felt like forgiveness. I wasn't a monster to have done that to Brian.

"Those men didn't deserve any of this," I said quietly.

"Nope," Kade replied with a tired sigh. "They were just pawns. Bowers and Freeman were threatened into changing their testimony, then killed by a fanatic looking for revenge."

"And Stacey," I added sadly, "caught up in it just because of who she loved."

It was only after that sentence left my mouth that I realized the irony of my saying those words. After all, if it hadn't been for Blane, I wouldn't have gotten caught up in any of this either.

We lay like that for a long while, Kade absently stroking my hair. I could hear his heart beat, and feel the rise and fall of his chest as he breathed.

The grandfather clock downstairs tolled the hour. I counted twelve. Midnight. It was Christmas Day.

"Merry Christmas, Kade," I said softly.

"Merry Christmas, Kathleen."

CHAPTER SIXTEEN

I awoke to a room only dimly lit by weak sunlight. It was early. I rubbed my eyes, sensing another person in the room with me.

"Kade?" I blinked, then jerked in surprise when Blane stepped into view.

"It's me," he said quietly, and I had to look away from his penetrating gaze, my cheeks flushing.

My first thought was that Kade must no longer be in bed with me, because there was no way Blane would be just standing there like that if he was. I surreptitiously felt behind me with my hand, and indeed, the space in the bed was empty.

"Come with me," Blane said. "I have a surprise for you."

I sat up, glancing at the bedside clock to see it wasn't yet six o'clock. "Okay," I replied. "Just give me a minute."

I hobbled into the bathroom to put myself together as quickly as I could. I dragged on a pair of black yoga pants and a long deep-cranberry sweater that was soft to the touch.

"Let me help you," Blane said as I sat on the bed, struggling to pull on a pair of boots. My stitches pulled when I bent my leg too sharply and I watched in relief as Blane knelt at my feet to help me. A few minutes later, he was bundling me into a coat and leading me by the hand to his SUV, which was idling outside.

It had snowed overnight, and our feet crunched through the thick blanket of snow and ice. I wondered where in the world he was taking me at this hour of the day, and on Christmas.

As we settled into his car, Blane handed me a steaming travel mug. I smelled coffee, the rich aroma teasing my nostrils.

"Thank you," I said, sipping the brew.

"It was completely self-serving," he said dryly.

I laughed lightly, his quip reminding me that I was rather cranky without that first cup of joe in the morning. "Regardless, I appreciate it."

That seemed to break the ice between us. Blane drove faster than most people would in this weather, but his reflexes and skills were much better. We slid and Blane caught the wheel, easily turning into the skid and regaining a grip on the pavement.

"Where are we going?" I asked, curiosity getting the best of me.

"It's a surprise," Blane said. "If I told you, it wouldn't be a surprise."

I harrumphed. "Fine. Whatever. Don't tell me."

"Wasn't planning on it."

Our eyes met and his lips twitched in an almost-grin.

I flipped on the radio, switching stations until I found one playing Christmas carols. I hummed along as Blane drove. Before long, I realized we were nearing the airport.

"Going somewhere?" I asked, my eyebrows climbing. My grip tightened on my coffee mug when I thought of Blane leaving.

"No," he shook his head, glancing at me. I knew the tightness in my voice hadn't escaped his attention. "We're just the welcoming committee today."

I frowned, trying to puzzle out his words.

A few minutes later, Blane parked and helped me out, his grip firm around my waist as we made our way across the slick pavement.

The warmth of the terminal hit me as we entered and I took a deep breath. The whole airport was nearly deserted at this hour and on this day. Blane led me past check-in and through security, flashing something in his wallet and speaking with the guard on duty. Finally, we reached an empty gate and Blane carefully helped me settle into one of the chairs.

"It shouldn't be long now," he said, glancing at his watch.

I was dying from curiosity and suspense, and could not even begin to imagine what could be going on. Blane moved to the window and watched the tarmac outside. Getting to my feet, I hobbled over to him.

"What are we waiting for?" I asked, my breath fogging the icy window.

"That," Blane said, pointing.

I looked and saw that a small plane had just landed. As I watched, it rolled slowly to the gate where we stood.

Hearing noise, I turned around and saw people heading our way. To my surprise, I recognized one of the figures.

"CJ?" I asked in disbelief.

She smiled broadly when she saw me and hurried over.

"Kathleen!" she exclaimed, pulling me into a tight hug. "I can't believe it! Can you? And it's all thanks to Blane."

She pulled away, her eyes bright, while my jaw hung open in surprise.

"CJ," I stammered, "I thought you were in jail."

CJ shook her head. "Blane got me out," she said. "Didn't he tell you?"

I turned accusing eyes to Blane, who ignored me, directing his words to CJ. "Things have been busy the past few days."

But CJ didn't really hear him, her attention caught by others coming up the jetway. I saw two people, a man and a woman, accompanied by two men in uniform.

CJ rushed toward the couple.

I gripped Blane's arm tightly, looking up at him. "Are they . . . Is that . . ."

He just smiled at me. "Watch," he said quietly.

I turned back in time to see CJ hurtle into her father's arms. I could hear her sobs and saw the tracks of tears down her mother's face as she hugged CJ. My eyes stung and I quickly passed my hand over my face, wiping away the wetness on my cheeks.

The reunion was beautiful to watch. I threaded my fingers through Blane's, silently wanting to share the moment with him. He seemed to understand, his hand closing around mine.

The men with CJ's parents waited patiently for them to finish greeting their daughter before ushering all three away, leaving Blane and me alone again.

"Where are they going?" I asked.

"They'll need to be debriefed," he answered. "Then they'll relocate them somewhere, help them get their lives back in order."

I looked up at him in stunned amazement at what he had done. "How? Why?" I asked.

Blane's hand cupped my cheek, his thumb brushing over my skin. "The how isn't important," he said. "As to the why—for you, of course. Merry Christmas, Kat."

Something softened inside me and I reached up, pulling his head down to mine. Our lips met and it felt like coming home. I savored the familiar scent and feel of him.

His hands slid underneath my hair to cradle my jaw, the rough pads of his thumbs brushing my cheeks. He deepened the kiss and I eagerly kissed him back. When we finally broke apart, my pulse was racing and his eyes had darkened.

I cleared my throat awkwardly, combing a nervous hand through my hair as I stepped back. "Thank you," I said. "That's an amazing thing you did."

He shook his head. "Thanks aren't necessary," he said lightly, taking my hand. Blane led me back outside to his car and drove us back to his home.

The sun was high in the sky now, about midmorning, and we were greeted with the smell of bacon and coffee as we walked in through the door.

"Merry Christmas!" Mona said, stepping out of the kitchen. She wore an apron over black slacks and a dove-gray sweater. "I hope you're hungry."

"Starving," I replied. "It smells wonderful, Mona."

A familiar *meow* drew my attention and I looked down to see Tigger winding himself around my legs.

"Merry Christmas, Tigger," I said, leaning down to give him a pat.

Blane helped me into the kitchen, where we filled our plates and ate. Mona was a fabulous cook and I was glad I wasn't living here permanently or I could easily gain ten pounds. She sat down with us, as did her husband, Gerard. They were in high spirits and chatted easily, telling me stories of when Blane was a child and of his refusal through those years to go to bed on Christmas Eve because he was determined to catch Santa.

I laughed, looking at Blane, who smiled good-naturedly with the teasing while he sipped his coffee. His arm was resting possessively on the back of my chair, his hand now and again touching my neck through my hair. One ankle rested on his other knee and his whole body was turned fractionally toward me.

It was nice and I really enjoyed it. It had been several years since I'd had people with whom I could share Christmas, and before that, Mom had been sick. The kitchen was warm and cozy and smelled like a home. Gerard and Mona made me laugh and I could see the brilliant white snow outside glistening in the morning sunshine. I didn't want the time to end, but eventually my yawns could no longer be hidden.

"You need to take a nap, dear," Mona gently chastised me. "You haven't got your strength back yet."

"No," I protested, rising from my chair. "I want to help you clean up."

"Nonsense!" She waved me aside. "Blane, take her upstairs, please. She needs to rest. We'll have dinner at six this evening. Bob and Vivian are joining us."

Blane led me from the room, his hand on the small of my back, gently guiding me.

"The senator?" I asked.

Blane nodded. "He and Vivian often come for Christmas dinner, if they're in town."

"Is Kade coming, too?" I asked, trying to sound casual, as if I weren't holding my breath while waiting for his answer.

"He'll be here" was Blane's curt response.

I didn't say anything more until we'd reached my room. I sat down on the bed with a tired sigh. My leg ached and I was glad to be off it. I watched as Blane moved to the window, bracing an arm against the frame as he peered outside.

"Why would you think I was Kade?" Blane abruptly asked.

"What?" I was taken aback by the question.

Blane turned toward me, his eyes meeting mine. "Earlier this morning," he clarified. "Why would Kade be here?"

I scrambled for an explanation, knowing I couldn't give the real one—that Kade had been here last night with me. It had been innocent, yes, but I knew Blane's possessive streak might make it impossible for him to see it that way. "I was half-asleep, Blane. I don't know what I said." The fib felt sour on my tongue, but I wasn't about to instigate something between Blane and Kade.

"He cares about you."

I shook my head in denial. "Kade cares about Kade, Blane. He was just doing what you wanted him to—keeping me safe."

His lips twisted into a slightly bitter smile. "Yes, ironic, isn't it? I pushed him on you, and now I may pay the price."

I tried to puzzle out what he meant. "I don't know what you mean," I finally said quietly. Weary, I passed a hand over my eyes.

"It doesn't matter," Blane said, coming to my side. "I shouldn't have said anything. Get some rest. Do you need another pain pill?"

I shook my head as I climbed under the covers. "No, I'm done with those," I replied. I didn't like how they made me feel. Bending down, Blane placed a light kiss on my lips.

"Don't let me sleep through dinner, please," I said as he turned to leave.

"I won't," he replied before exiting the room, the door closing gently behind him.

Blane's words turned over in my head as I lay there. It almost sounded as though he were jealous, but there was nothing to be jealous of. Kade and I had grown closer over the past week—that much was true—but I knew nothing could happen between us. I refused to become a wedge between Blane and Kade.

The sexual attraction between Kade and me couldn't be denied—I wasn't stupid—but if my relationship with Blane had taught me anything, it was how very vulnerable making love with a man had made me. I'd been devastated when I'd seen Blane with Kandi, no matter that I believed the reasons he'd had for allowing it to happen. I wasn't anxious to put myself and my heart at someone's mercy again—not until I knew I could trust him. Blane had vowed that he'd earn my trust back, that he wanted us to be back together. I wondered if he could—and if I would let him.

Eventually I drifted to sleep, thoughts of Blane and Kade twisting through my mind.

~

The Kirk household dressed for Christmas dinner. *Really* dressed. I looked at the black-velvet dress Blane had left for me and wondered if I'd be able to fit into its confines. Blane may have underestimated the exact size of my ass, I thought, as I regarded the dress skeptically.

I'd showered again and washed my hair, blowing it dry and curling it. It now lay in soft ringlets down my back. I'd applied a smoky-gray shadow to my eyes and a red gloss to my lips. The makeup helped accentuate my blue eyes, which stood out sharply against my fair skin.

I stepped into the dress, pulling it up over the black bra and matching panties I'd put on. I had to wriggle a bit when it hit my hips, but then it fell into place. I pushed my arms through the short cap sleeves, smoothing the soft velvet over my abdomen. The dress clung to me, falling to midcalf and covering my bandage. A slit in the back made it easy for me to move in it. Reaching behind me, I pulled the zipper but couldn't get it up all the way.

A knock at the door made me turn and I called out, "Come in."

Blane entered and the sight of him momentarily robbed me of breath. He'd dressed in a black suit, the shirt beneath a blinding white, his tie a deep burgundy. The jacket stretched across his broad shoulders, making him appear even larger than he was.

His eyes moved appreciatively down my body and back up, lingering at the low neckline, which with the help of the bra displayed an impressive amount of cleavage, right on the line between tasteful and tacky.

"Can you help me?" I asked, turning my back to him and lifting my hair so he could reach the zipper.

I could see his reflection in the glass of the window as he approached me. His fingers brushed the skin of my back and I caught my breath.

Blane took his time zipping my dress, easing it up millimeter by millimeter. He was so close, I could feel the warmth from his body at my back. I could barely breathe, my response to his nearness something I couldn't control—as though I belonged to him and he could command my body.

I released my hair, only to have Blane softly sweep it aside, placing his lips on the skin between my neck and shoulder. His arms slid around my waist, enveloping me. I felt small and protected in his arms, my eyes slowly closing at the touch of his tongue against my skin. The slight abrasion of his jaw made me shiver.

"You look gorgeous," he rasped, lifting his eyes to meet my gaze in the window.

"Likewise," I said breathlessly, my pulse racing.

The corners of his mouth lifted in an almost-smile and I could see the glimmer of satisfaction in his eyes that he knew he was affecting me.

"Shall we?" he asked.

I nodded, slipping on a pair of black flats. Heels, with my leg still tender, seemed like a bad idea. Lightly placing his hand on my back, he guided me out the door and assisted me down the stairs. I was glad that I no longer needed the crutches.

The long dining room table I'd seen the first time I'd come to Blane's house was now laden with china, silver, and crystal. The candelabra in the center glowed with lit candles.

I expected to be seated at the table, but Blane kept us moving past the dining room.

"I thought it was time for dinner," I whispered.

"Cocktails in the library first," he replied.

I nodded, my hands twisting together in a sudden fit of nerves. Christmas dinner with my family had meant jeans and sweatshirts and filling our plates in the kitchen to carry to the table.

We entered the library and I was surprised to see not only Senator Keaston and Vivian but also George and Sarah Bradshaw, Keaston's campaign manager and his wife.

"Good evening," Blane said with a smile, guiding us to where the foursome stood talking, drinks in hand. "Merry Christmas."

"Merry Christmas to you, Blane," the senator said jovially.

Vivian stepped forward and clasped Blane's hands. "Merry Christmas," she said as Blane brushed a kiss on her cheek. She turned to me then.

"You remember Kathleen?" Blane asked.

"Indeed I do," Vivian said with a gentle smile. "Merry Christmas, Kathleen. How are you feeling?"

"Better, thank you," I said quietly.

Blane had been drawn into the circle of men talking when Mona approached me, holding a martini glass.

"Cocktail, dear?"

I gratefully accepted, hoping it would calm my nerves. I sipped the cold liquid, the glass rimmed with festive red sanding sugar and garnished with three fresh cranberries on a skewer. I could tell the vodka was premium, slightly tinted with cranberry juice and a splash of vermouth. It was divine.

"I'm quite glad to see you again," Vivian said to me. "You and Blane make a beautiful pair."

"Thank you," I said for lack of knowing what else to say.

"So many of Blane's female friends come and go," she continued. "I'm encouraged that you're here this evening."

I smiled tightly and nodded, my cheeks flushing. I didn't care to be compared to the rest of Blane's numerous flings.

"Yes, I agree," Sarah said, joining our little group. "If he's going to run for governor, Blane needs to find a woman he can settle down with."

"Absolutely," Vivian said. "Kathleen—"

"Tell me, Vivian," Mona interjected, "are you still considering chairing the fund-raiser this spring?"

They began talking about some charity thing and I gratefully eased away. I glanced at Blane, who was conversing with George and the senator. Sensing my gaze on him, he looked my way, tipping his head slightly in approval, a smile curving his lips.

Walking to the window, I peered outside. I watched as snow fell softly from the sky, giving the scene a storybook feel. Lights from other houses nearby twinkled in the night.

"Penny for your thoughts."

I turned, a wide smile breaking across my face at the sight of Kade standing a mere foot away. Like Blane, he wore a black suit, but the shirt underneath was also black and no tie adorned his neck. The top two buttons on his shirt remained undone, revealing the smooth skin of his throat.

The suit was expertly tailored, encasing his shoulders and cutting inward to his lean waist and hips. His black hair and brows were a stark contrast to the piercing blue of his eyes, which targeted me from beneath thick, dark lashes.

"You're here," I said, belatedly realizing how stupid that sounded.

Kade's lips twisted in an amused smirk. "Stating the obvious. Let's hope that bullet to your leg didn't affect your brain." His eyes dropped to my cleavage and lingered for a moment.

I blushed but was too glad to see him to be bothered by his teasing.

"Looks like you could use another drink," he said, taking my empty glass. "I know I do," he muttered conspiratorially, glancing at the separate clusters of men and women talking.

His fingers threaded through mine, drawing me to him as he approached the bar on the sideboard. He set aside my sugarcoated glass with a snort of disgust, taking two highball glasses and filling each with ice, vodka, and tonic before handing me one.

"To your continued good health," he toasted, clinking his glass against mine. The twinkle in his eyes made me smile and I took a sip of the cold liquid.

"Glad you could make it, Kade," Blane said, suddenly appearing next to me. His arm slid proprietarily around my waist.

Kade's eyes didn't miss the gesture. "Wouldn't have missed it, brother," he said easily, his eyes on mine as he took another swallow of his drink.

Vivian joined us then, giving Kade a hug before sliding her arm through his and leading him away, talking animatedly.

"Holding up okay?" Blane asked quietly.

I tipped my head back to see him properly. "Yes," I said with a smile. "It's nice." I still felt a bit like an outsider, but it was good to be with people and celebrating one of my favorite holidays. I also knew that I was happy because I was sharing it with Blane and Kade. They had quickly become two people I cared deeply about, and aren't those the people you want to be with on Christmas?

Soon after that, we all went into dinner. Each course was served with a different wine, and by the time dinner was over, I was feeling very mellow indeed. Blane helped me from my seat, leading me to the family room, where everyone gathered in seats by the fireplace. The ten-foot tree in the corner twinkled brightly with its many lights and countless ornaments.

It seemed I wasn't the only one whom the wine had affected. Both Vivian and Sarah laughed more easily and slightly louder than before as they chatted. Their gaiety made me smile.

Blane sat me next to him on a leather loveseat, his hand clasping mine as it rested on his thigh. I listened to the conversation with half an ear, gazing at the tree and the fire dancing merrily in the fireplace behind its grate.

"It's so nice to see you so happy, Blane," Vivian suddenly said. She smiled indulgently at the two of us seated together.

"Indeed," the senator added. "Though I have to say, it's not often—ever, actually—that I've seen you take the kind of risks you've taken lately, Blane."

Blane's hand tightened almost painfully on mine.

"What do you mean?" I asked.

"Robert—" Blane began in a warning tone. That was the first time I'd heard Blane refer to Senator Keaston by his first name.

"I suppose he hasn't told you," the senator interrupted him, "but it took considerable effort on Blane's part to free your friend and her parents."

My stomach clenched. Deep down, I'd known it hadn't been easy for Blane to do so, but I had accepted at face value the brush-off he'd given when I'd asked.

"You may very well have placed yourself in an extremely vulnerable position," Senator Keaston continued, speaking directly to Blane. "You now owe some very powerful people, Blane."

"That's enough." The tightly controlled anger in Blane's voice made me flinch, though it seemed to have no effect on the senator. He merely took another swallow of his drink.

The sudden tension in the room was palpable. Blane's grip on my hand hadn't eased. It seemed no one knew what to say. Except Kade.

"Now it's Christmas," Kade deadpanned, handing Blane a glass with a shot of scotch glowing amber in its depths.

I grimaced, even as Mona chuckled and Vivian gave a small smile. Blane's body relaxed somewhat, as did his grip on me, and feeling began to return to my hand. Conversation resumed around the room.

"I didn't know," I said quietly, so only Blane could hear.

"You weren't supposed to," he replied stiffly. "It's nothing." He downed the scotch in one swallow.

My mind processed what I'd just learned. Blane had put himself at risk for me, not only physically—willing to take a bullet to save me—but also risking his career. I hadn't thought of the kind of influence necessary to free CJ's parents from China, but it had to be considerable. The thought of Blane being indebted to an unknown person who wielded that kind of power made me cringe. What had I done? What had I asked of him?

"Play something for us, Blane," Mona cajoled, her request abruptly breaking through my scattered thoughts.

"Oh yes, please do," Vivian seconded.

Blane smiled easily. "Only if Kathleen sings," he said.

My eyebrows flew upward and I immediately started shaking my head. "No, I can't possibly," I stammered.

"Of course you can," Blane said, brushing aside my protest. "You have a beautiful voice."

"Yes, she does." This from Kade. My gaze flew to his and I realized both of us were remembering my rather risqué Britney Spears performance at The Drop on Halloween. His lips twitched.

"Come on," Blane said, tugging me to my feet.

Going to the piano in the corner, he guided me to the side of the shining ebony instrument while he slid onto the leather bench. I was nervous about being the center of attention, everyone looking expectantly at us.

Blane played a few notes, glancing up at me. I recognized the tune and gave a tiny nod. He played the introduction more fully and I took a deep breath before launching into a slow, melodic rendition of "The Christmas Song." My voice was still a little rough from my ordeal with Frankie, but the hoarseness lent more of a throaty quality to the pitch that went well with the tune.

I kept my eyes on Blane as I sang, until I felt more comfortable, the familiar words and melody helping me relax.

And every mother's child is going to spy, to see if reindeer really know how to fly . . .

I raised my chin and looked out over the assembled guests, the rich sound of the piano filling the room. Anyone looking in on this scene would liken it to a perfect storybook Christmas. And it very nearly was. Almost.

Although it's been said many times, many ways . . .

Kade watched me avidly, the look in his eyes making me unable to look away from him. I couldn't decipher it.

Merry Christmas . . . to you . . .

I drew out the last few words as the notes from the piano lingered in the air.

When the song ended, I was taken aback by the enthusiastic applause. I smiled shyly, adding my own applause and turning to Blane. He'd played beautifully, his fingers moving easily over the ivory keys.

Shortly thereafter, the guests departed while Mona and Gerard left for their home, which adjoined Blane's property. I retrieved my gifts for Blane and Kade which Gerard had been kind enough to fetch from my apartment for me, reappearing to find them sitting in opposite wingback chairs by the fire.

"Merry Christmas," I said brightly, handing each of them a brightly wrapped package. The size and shape of the gifts were identical.

Toeing off my shoes, I carefully settled on the sofa. I looked up to see them both just sitting there, watching me.

"Well, open them!" I said in exasperation.

Blane and Kade glanced at each other before opening the gifts. My hands twisted in my lap and I nervously bit my lip.

They uncovered the presents at nearly the same time, both looking at the small paintings I'd had commissioned. Neither of them spoke, which alarmed me.

"It's Lake Winnipesaukee," I explained hurriedly. "Blane said you two used to go there together when you were young. I thought you might like it, hoped that it would remind you of good memories you share."

Blane held the small painting I'd chosen for him, a view of the lake in the shining sunlight, the sun glistening off the gentle waves. Kade held its mirror image, the lake at night, moonlight reflected in the still waters.

Still, neither spoke. My heart sank.

"You hate it," I said to them both.

"No, absolutely not," Blane said quickly. He glanced up at me and I was startled to see the brightness in his eyes. "It's beautiful, Kat. I hadn't realized you'd remembered that story."

"Of course I did," I replied, somewhat offended that he assumed I'd forgotten.

"What story?" Kade asked.

"The time we were diving and I couldn't find you," Blane replied.

Kade gave a small laugh. "Ah yes," he said. "You were supremely pissed off."

"More at myself than you," Blane corrected.

"Thank you, Kathleen," Kade said sincerely.

I smiled, relieved. The paintings weren't large—I couldn't afford anything bigger—but I thought they suited them.

"I guess it's time for my gift then," Blane said, setting aside the painting and reaching inside his jacket. Pulling out an envelope, he stood and brought it to me, perching on the arm of the sofa.

"But you already gave me something," I said, bemused. A gift that, in retrospect, had cost more than I would have been willing for Blane to pay.

"I couldn't pass this up," Blane said, grinning.

I opened the envelope, pulling out the pieces of paper and studying them. When I realized what they said, I gasped.

"You got me front-row tickets and backstage passes to the Britney Spears concert?" I asked, incredulous.

"What else would I give her biggest fan?" Blane teased.

I squealed in delight, reaching up to give him a tight hug. He laughed at my exuberance.

"Just don't expect me to go with you," he admonished.

"That's fine." I sank back down into the sofa, avidly studying the tickets. "I'm sure I can find someone else to go with me," I said distractedly. I couldn't imagine how he'd gotten his hands on these.

"I'll go," Kade offered.

"Really?" I said, still studying my tickets. "It's in July." The backstage passes were like gold to me, Britney's face emblazoned on them.

"Absolutely," he replied.

"Why would you want to do that?" Blane scoffed. "You suddenly a Spears fan?"

"I don't mind taking Kathleen to see her favorite pop star," Kade said, almost too casually. "In the middle of summer, I'm sure it'll be steaming hot, right, Blane? We'll have a few drinks, enjoy the show. Maybe Kathleen will even wear her Britney outfit again."

I laughed at that, still admiring the passes. "Do you suppose she'd think it's funny?"

When neither man responded, I glanced up to see them locked in a staring contest. I was confused—what had I missed? Blane's jaw was clenched tight and Kade's smirk was chilling.

"What? What's wrong?" I asked anxiously.

"Nothing, Kat," Blane said, breaking his glare at Kade and smiling tightly at me. "I think I'm going to call it a night. May I help you upstairs?"

I was tired and going to bed sounded lovely, but I was loath for the night to end. Still, I agreed and rose from my seat.

Going to Kade, who had risen as well, I stood on my toes and gave him a hug. I knew Blane was watching, but I was determined not to let his scrutiny keep me from showing Kade some affection. It was Christmas, after all.

"Merry Christmas," I said, wrapping my arms around his neck. I leaned against his chest and gave him a squeeze.

His arm curved around my waist and I felt his lips brush my hair.

"Merry Christmas, princess," he said softly.

I released him, turning to get my tickets, which were resting on the sofa. Blane had my shoes dangling from his fingers on one hand and held his other hand out to me. I took it and followed him upstairs.

My room was dark and Blane didn't turn on the light. I stood in the middle of the room while he put my shoes down and took the tickets from my hand.

"Do I get a hug as well?" he asked roughly.

"Of course," I said, my cheeks heating at his implication. I reached for him.

Then his hands were on my waist and his mouth was on mine. I gasped in surprise and his tongue slipped inside.

The kiss was hungry and I became lost in it. My arms reached upward to twine around his neck. Blane's hands skimmed from my waist over my hips and around to cup my rear. Pulling me closer, I felt the hard press of his erection against my stomach. An answering rush of heat between my thighs made me whimper.

His mouth released mine to trail down my jaw to my neck, nipping and sucking lightly at my skin. I clutched Blane's shoulders as my knees weakened, tilting my head to give greater access to Blane's questing mouth.

The sound of a zipper being lowered made me realize Blane was unzipping my dress. He pushed it off my shoulders and down my body, the soft velvet barely making a sound as it slid down my legs to puddle on the floor at my feet.

My hormones had kicked into high gear and I reached for Blane's tie. His hands caught my wrists easily, holding them away from him.

I looked questioningly at him. "Isn't this what you want?" I asked, confused. My resolve to not sleep with him lay somewhere in the puddle of velvet at my feet.

His eyes glittered in the shadows, sending a new rush of arousal through my body as he stared intently at me—he still fully clothed while I stood in only my bra and panties.

"I do want you, Kat," he said, "but not just for the night."

Blane released me, stepping away. I missed the warmth of his body immediately. Taking my hand, he lifted it to his lips, pressing a soft kiss to my knuckles before turning my hand and pressing another to my palm. My breath caught.

"You let me know when you want that, too," he said quietly.

Then he was gone and I was left standing alone in the bedroom, my body achingly aroused.

Utterly confused as to what I did want, I shucked my bra, then picked up my nightgown and dragged it over my head.

As exhausted as I was, I couldn't sleep. I tossed and turned, the words Senator Keaston had said about the "risks" Blane had taken on behalf of CJ's parents reverberating in my mind. There was no way to undo what Blane had done for me. The weight of guilt lay heavy on my heart. I heard the clock chime downstairs and strike the hour. Two o'clock, with sleep nowhere in sight. With a sigh, I rose from the bed.

When I entered the hallway, I looked to my right, where Blane's bedroom was silent and dark. I stood for a long moment, staring at that door. My nails bit into my clenched fists. I wanted so much to climb into bed with Blane, feel his arms around me, but the guilt of what he'd done on my behalf—what he may have sacrificed—weighed heavily on me. What if he resented me for it? I regretted ever involving him with CJ.

Unable to riddle my way through my confusion—the scales tipping first in favor of one decision, then in favor of another—I turned away and eased down the stairs. I was drawn to the living room and the Christmas tree. It would be nice to just sit and enjoy looking at it a little while longer, even though Christmas was now officially over.

The tree was still lit and a fire still danced in the fireplace. It was beautiful and I sighed.

"I thought no creature was supposed to be stirring."

I started, turning to see Kade sitting in the far corner of the sofa. It was lost in the shadows of the room and I had to squint to see him.

"I didn't realize anyone was still up," I said.

Kade rose from his chair and I watched as he set an empty glass on the table and approached me. He'd discarded his jacket and folded back the cuffs of his crisp black shirt, exposing his wrists.

"It's so not a good idea for you to be down here," he said when he was inches from me.

"Why?" I asked. My eyes narrowed. "Are you drunk?"

"I wish I were," he said softly. "It would be easier."

"What would be easier?" My voice had lowered to match his. His blue eyes were intent on mine and I couldn't look away.

"Leaving," he said.

My hands clenched into fists. "You're leaving again?"

His smile was without humor. "Duty calls," he said lightly.

"What duty?" I asked.

"Something I found on Ryan's phone," he replied. "I need to look into it."

"Did you find out who he was working for?"

"Maybe," he said. "If I'm right—and I really hope I'm not—then it affects Blane in a major way. I have to find out the truth."

"Protecting Blane," I said softly, a rueful smile on my lips. "You're a good brother, Kade."

He studied me for a moment before murmuring, "I don't know if that's true anymore."

Before I could ask what he meant, he changed the subject. "I didn't have a chance to give you my present."

I watched as he reached into a pocket and pulled something out. Taking my hand, he turned it palm up and deposited a small token. It was metal, warm from being next to his body.

I looked down at my hand. The metal sparkled in the firelight.

"Kade," I managed to say, "you didn't have to—"

"I wanted to," he said, cutting me off. Taking the gold locket from my hand, he opened it. Tears immediately sprang to my eyes.

"How . . . how did you . . . ?" I couldn't speak anymore, emotion clogging my throat. Inside the locket was a picture of my parents, identical to the one from the ornament on my Christmas tree.

"Turn around," he said, and I complied.

He placed the chain around my neck and I lifted my hair so he could fasten the clasp. The locket rested between my breasts, close to my heart. I pressed my hand over it, touched more than I could say. His hands came to rest on my shoulders as we both stared into the dancing flames of the fireplace.

"I wish you would stay," I dared to whisper, turning back to face him.

"I can't," he said. "Do you think I'm blind? Blane wants you back. If I stay, I'll have to watch you and him together. Don't ask me to do that."

Tears sprang to my eyes, spilling over and down my cheeks before I could stop them. I couldn't say why I was crying, only that it felt like part of my family was leaving me, the same way my dad had left and then my mom. I was one step closer to being alone again.

Kade cursed, his hands moving to cup my jaw while his thumbs brushed my tears away.

"Don't cry, princess," he pleaded. "Please."

"When will you be back?" I forced out.

"In time for Britney," he teased, and I smiled feebly.

"Please," I said, my voice barely above a whisper. "Please be careful. Don't get hurt. Don't die."

"I didn't know you cared," he said dryly.

"You know I do," I retorted without heat.

Kade wrapped an arm around my shoulders, pulling me close in a one-armed embrace, his other hand resting lightly on my hip. I hugged him back, my arms tight around his waist—I was terrified it might be for the last time. He released me and it took every ounce of pride and self-control I had to not clutch at him.

I opened my mouth to say good-bye, but he pressed a finger to my lips.

"Shh," he commanded. "Don't say it." Leaning down, his lips lightly brushed my forehead.

I watched him shrug into his suit jacket and grab his coat, his eyes on me, before he turned and walked out of the room without another word.

Going to the window, I watched and waited. Several minutes later, I saw Kade outside, walking to his car. The snow continued to fall, the white flakes disappearing when they touched his dark form. He got in his car and I stayed at the window, watching, long after the red taillights of his car had disappeared into the night.

EPILOGUE

Blane watched the embracing couple before disappearing silently back into the darkness of the hallway. Easing open the front door, he stood on the porch and waited, arms crossed against the cold.

He'd heard Kathleen get up tonight. For a moment, his heart had leapt, hoping his door would open and she'd be there. To his disappointment, no knock had come and the door had remained firmly closed.

Blane had risen from his bed, thrown on a pair of jeans and T-shirt, and followed her. When he heard her voice with Kade's, he'd paused in the hallway.

As he listened, Blane realized he'd severely underestimated Kade. He was shocked, in a way. He'd grown so used to Kade not caring about anyone, he hadn't thought to be wary, to keep a distance between Kade and Kathleen. It hadn't occurred to Blane that Kathleen would form an attachment to his prickly, sarcastic, emotionally unavailable brother—or that he would form one in return.

Scarred from the years of abuse before Blane had gotten to him, Kade never let anyone get too close. He had thought Blane didn't know what the "chicken pox" scars on his back were, and Blane had never let on otherwise. He knew Kade didn't want pity. It had taken years before Kade had slept soundly through the night without being plagued by nightmares. Guilt had ridden Blane hard for his failure to persuade their father to take Kade in when his mother had died. He should have tried harder, not given up so easily.

For all that the guilt of the past haunted Blane, it was the jealousy of the present that ate at his peace of mind. Earlier, he'd thought he'd perhaps mistaken the double meaning in Kade's speech about taking Kathleen to the concert. Now he knew he'd interpreted the challenge correctly. Despite what Kade had said to the contrary, Blane knew that Kade felt something for Kathleen.

Blane had wanted to tell Kathleen how he felt today—spell it out so she'd know without a doubt how much he cared about her. As skittish as she was, though, Blane wasn't sure if his doing so would draw her closer or scare her away, so he'd kept silent, hoping his actions would speak for themselves. Despite everything that had happened between them, Blane was convinced now more than ever that Kathleen wasn't yet ready to hear what he had to say.

The front door opened, a shaft of light hitting the porch as Kade stepped outside. He stopped abruptly when he saw Blane before closing the door behind him, leaving them enveloped in darkness.

"Eavesdropping's not your style, brother," Kade chided quietly, his tone light.

"Where are you going?" Blane asked. "And what is going to affect me? What did you find?"

"I'll let you know," Kade said evasively. "You've got a job to do, remember? Shouldn't you be declaring your candidacy for governor any day now? Isn't that what you want?"

"I haven't decided," Blane replied.

Kade's eyes narrowed. "And have you decided whether or not what you want includes Kathleen?"

"Why do you ask, Kade? I thought you didn't care about her," Blane reminded him. "Told me you couldn't care less if she lived or died."

Kade's jaw tightened and his eyes narrowed. "What more does she mean to you than another conquest, Blane? When has any woman ever said no to you?"

"You think that's what this is about? Me wanting the unobtainable?"

Kade's silence spoke volumes.

"Fuck you, Kade," Blane said coldly.

"I've seen the way you play with women," Kade said in disgust. "You use them, then toss them aside." He paused. "Kathleen could have been pregnant. Would you have married her, Blane? Or sent her a monthly check? It seems you have more in common with dear old Dad than you thought."

Blane fought the urge to hit him, Kade's arrow hitting its mark with deadly accuracy. Only Blane's self-control stopped him from retaliating for that remark.

"And you think you're any better?" Blane's voice was like ice. "Correct me if I'm wrong, Kade, but when was the last time you spent more than a single night with a woman? I'm sure that would be a nice dose of reality for Kathleen."

"I never said I was better," Kade shot back. "I'm just trying to show you that it's not a game, not this time. She's gone through too much for you to treat her like another one of your easy lays."

"You don't trust me," Blane said abruptly, surprised by the sudden revelation. The realization cut deep. Earning Kade's trust had been a difficult thing—to think that it was now in jeopardy was devastating.

Kade's gaze didn't waver. "You've made some bad decisions lately, Blane. How can you expect me—or Kathleen—to trust you?"

For the first time in a long time, self-doubt assailed Blane. Was he hurting Kathleen more by being with her? Pursuing her? Should he just let her move on?

Kade moved closer, clasping Blane on the shoulder. "She loves you, Blane," he said quietly. "Don't fuck it up."

He turned and walked away. A moment later, Blane heard his car start.

Going back into the house, Blane saw Kathleen still standing at the window, looking out. Oblivious to the confrontation between him and Kade, she stood quietly, her fingers playing with something around her neck. She was lit softly by the firelight, and her white nightgown seemed to almost glow with an ethereal quality. Her hair tumbled in a disarray of waves down her back. Blane watched her for a long while, debating whether to go to her. Finally, he entered the room, not stopping until he was directly behind her. Their eyes met in the window's reflection.

"Kade left," she said quietly.

"I know."

"He looks out for you, you know," she said. "For anything that could hurt you."

Blane had known this, but the words coming from Kathleen only increased the sense of guilt he carried inside. He slid his arms around her waist, pulling her back toward his chest until they touched. Her hands rested lightly on his arms, which crisscrossed her abdomen.

They stood in silence, looking out at the darkness, both lost in their own thoughts.

"Let's go upstairs," Blane said finally, breaking the quiet. He was unsettled, not knowing what she was thinking—about him, about them, or about Kade.

To his relief, she nodded. Blane took her hand, which felt small and fragile inside his own, and led her back to bed.

ABOUT THE AUTHOR

Tiffany Snow has been reading romance novels since she was too young to read romance novels. After fifteen years working in the Information Technology field, Tiffany now works her dream job of writing full-time.

Tiffany makes her home in the Midwest with her husband and two daughters. She can be reached at tiffany@tiffanyasnow.com. Visit her on her website, www.TiffanyASnow.com, to keep up with the latest in *The Kathleen Turner Series*.

Turn the page for a sneak peek at the third book in *The Kathleen Turner Series, Turning Point*.

Turning Point

CHAPTER ONE

S omeone was following me.

The streets of downtown Indianapolis were busy this Friday night. Even though it was the second week of February, after two months of nothing but cold, snow, and ice, a spell of unseasonably warm weather had brought the residents of Indy and the surrounding suburbs out in droves.

Laughter and gaiety surrounded me as I hurried through the crowds oozing down Capitol Avenue. My pulse beat quicker and the hair on the back of my neck stood up. I chanced a quick glance behind me, but saw no one paying the least bit of attention to me.

I knew he was back there. Just because I couldn't see him didn't mean he couldn't see me.

He'd been following me for several blocks, always staying just out of sight when I turned around, and I'd caught only glimpses of an arm, a shoulder. But he was getting closer. I could feel it.

A group of men were strolling in front of me. An idea struck and I eased my way in front of them. My height—or lack thereof—had its advantages, I thought, as I slipped past them into an alley. Hopefully, they'd concealed my movements long enough to lose the man following me.

Unable to withstand the temptation, I stopped and peered behind me. When no figure stepped into the alley, I slumped against the brick wall at my back, releasing a pent-up breath.

"Nice move, princess. You almost lost me."

I gasped, jerking around.

"Damn it, Kade! You scared me to death!"

Kade Dennon, former FBI agent and current gun-for-hire, was completely unfazed by my outburst, the smirk I knew all too well curving his lips.

"It was a good thought." He crossed his arms and leisurely leaned one shoulder against the wall. "Use your weaknesses to your advantage. Being short doesn't have to be a detriment."

"I'm not short," I groused. "I'm"—I searched for a more palatable word—"petite."

"Whatever," he said with a snort. "Let's try again. I'll give you a sixty-second head start. Go." He looked down at his watch, timing me.

"Wait." I held up my hand. "It's getting late and I have a date with Blane tonight. Can we call it good for now?"

Blue eyes framed in lush, dark lashes and topped by wickedly arched brows peered at me. It didn't matter how often I saw him, Kade's dark beauty never failed to take my breath away. His square jaw, roughened with a day or two's growth of stubble, tightened. Black hair—which I knew from experience was soft to the touch—fell over his brow. I likened him to a fallen angel, and the description had never been more apt, clad as he was in his customary dark jeans, black shirt, and black leather jacket. I also knew a gun was holstered at his hip, and somewhere on his person was concealed another, as well as a wickedly sharp knife.

"Fine," he finally said, the word clipped. "But your wake-up call tomorrow is six a.m."

"On a Saturday?" I protested.

"And no coffee beforehand," he ordered. "I don't want you puking on me."

I didn't have a chance to reply before he was gone. With an ease I envied, he'd slipped into the crowd and disappeared.

I sighed in defeat as I trudged to my car parked a few blocks away, wondering if this was ever going to work.

Kade had shown up at my door a couple of weeks ago, declaring that if I was going to be of any worth as an investigator, I needed to be trained.

Well, that's putting it more delicately. His exact words had been, "You need to be trained before you really fuck something up, end up dead, or both."

How could I say no?

In truth, I'd been excited and nervous about my new job as investigator for the law firm of Kirk and Trent. I'd worked there as a runner, delivering documents, until Kade had given me an abrupt promotion right before Christmas. I guess you could call him a silent partner in the firm.

So far, the training had included time at the firing range with my new gun (courtesy of Kade), daily early morning runs (also courtesy of Kade), self-defense classes with a Marine, and these impromptu lessons that had no name. I ached all over from hitting the mat too many times in the self-defense lessons, dreaded the morning runs like a condemned man awaiting execution, and had only done so-so on what I privately thought of as the "cloak-and-dagger" training. The only place I'd held my own was the firing range.

Not for the first time I wondered if this was a job I could actually do.

I unlocked the door and climbed inside my black Lexus SUV, a company car paid for by the firm. Twenty minutes later, I was back at my apartment.

I lived on the top floor of a two-story apartment building near downtown, in a neighborhood where people didn't walk their dogs after dark, at least not alone. When I'd first moved to Indianapolis almost a year ago, this had been the best I could afford. Even then I'd had to work two jobs just to make rent and pay the bills—I was a runner for the law firm during the day and bartender at night at The Drop. Luckily, my new promotion meant an increase in salary and I'd been able to quit the bartending gig.

I hurriedly showered, pinning my long strawberry blonde hair up so it wouldn't get wet. There wasn't enough time for me to blow it dry before Blane arrived.

My heart beat a little faster as I thought of Blane, anticipation making my stomach flutter. Blane Kirk: high-powered lawyer, former Navy SEAL, rich playboy, my ex-boyfriend. One of those labels didn't seem to fit with the others. Our introduction had been less than what romance novels were made of, consisting as it had of my tripping and falling face-first into his lap during a client meeting. I still cringed when I thought about it.

We'd broken up before Christmas, after I'd found him in a clutch with his former girlfriend, Kandi-with-an-i. What I hadn't known then—what Blane didn't tell me until later—was that he'd suspected her of being the leak behind repeated attempts on my life. He'd thought that by breaking up with me and dating her, he'd be able to keep me safe. That hadn't worked out so well.

Since then, Blane had been "courting" me, for lack of a better word, in an attempt to win me back. I'd been leery of jumping back into a relationship, even though I knew I was in love with him. His list of ex-girlfriends was as long as my arm—both my arms, actually—and I had no interest in having my heart broken a second time.

Yet those reservations hadn't stopped me from going out with him, spending time with him, kissing him. It seemed no matter my resolve, I was helpless when it came to Blane.

My phone rang just as I was checking the clock; Blane was a few minutes late, which was unlike him.

"Hello?"

"Kat, it's me," Blane said.

Kat. That's me. At least, that's what Blane calls me. My full name is Kathleen Turner and, yes, I was named that on purpose. My father, Ted Turner, and my grandmother, Tina Turner, were only too happy to pass on the family tradition of naming a kid after a famous Turner. Since I had no brothers, it was up to my only cousin to carry on the dubious honor. Not that I knew if he would, since I hadn't heard from him in years.

"Hey," I said, sinking down onto my leather couch. If he was calling rather than knocking at my door, it couldn't be good news.

"I'm sorry, Kat, but I'm going to have to cancel our date."

I held in a sigh. "That's okay," I replied, keeping my tone light. No need for him to know how disappointed I was.

"I have to leave town for a few days. Something's come up."

A slight stiffness to his words made me frown, a hint of worry creeping in.

"Is everything all right?"

"Absolutely," he said easily. "I'll call you, okay?"

"Yeah, sure," I said, wondering if I had imagined something that wasn't there.

A few moments later, we'd disconnected, and I was left thinking about what would make Blane leave town on a Friday night. I'd been too taken aback to ask where he was going, and now I mentally kicked myself.

I changed into an old T-shirt, baked a frozen cheese pizza, and ate it while watching the latest episode I'd recorded of *Dancing with the Stars*. Not exactly the evening I'd planned.

Finding some rocky road ice cream buried in the back of my freezer, I scraped the carton clean, absentmindedly licking the spoon as I thought about Blane. I'd moved out of his house and back into my apartment two weeks after Christmas. My excuse for temporarily living with him—the fact that I'd been shot in the leg by a psychopath—was no longer viable. The physical and emotional wounds had healed well enough by then.

But I hadn't wanted to leave.

It was nice, living with Blane. I loved that he was the first and last person I saw every day. He was true to his word, giving me space and not pressuring me, though he had no compunction against using the explosive chemistry between us to tease and torture me. Each night he would kiss me before leaving me alone in my bedroom, and his kisses weren't chaste and sweet. They were hot, skilled, and demanding—always leaving me wanting more—which, of course, was his intention.

It was during one of these heated encounters that I had abruptly decided I needed to go back home. I couldn't think around Blane. Everything I wanted and felt was confused when his arms were around me, when he was touching me, kissing me. What did it mean, this pseudo-relationship and my living with him?

"Wait . . . stop," I'd said breathlessly, wrenching my lips from his.

That didn't deter him. His mouth trailed a scorching path across my jaw and down my neck.

"Blane—"

Blane kissed his name from my lips. I became lost in his touch again for who knows how long.

"I should go back home," I blurted.

Blane's entire body went still. I could feel his heartbeat racing as he pressed against me. Or maybe that was mine. He raised his head, his green eyes glittering in the semidarkness of the bedroom.

"You want to go back to your apartment." It didn't come out as a question, but rather a statement.

Nervous butterflies danced in my stomach. "It's not that I want to," I stammered. "But maybe it would be for the best."

Blane didn't say anything for a moment, and the silence seemed oppressive. I couldn't hold his penetrating gaze, so I stared at the white linen of his shirt.

"I'll take you home in the morning," he finally said.

When I looked back up, I couldn't read anything from his face. Before I'd even realized what was happening, he'd placed a kiss on my forehead and disappeared out the door.

I lay in bed, staring at the ceiling for a long time. I didn't know what had happened, what Blane wanted from me. Had he expected that I'd just continue living with him?

That just wasn't me.

Then I heard the sound of the piano downstairs.

Glancing at the clock, I pulled on a matching white robe to cover my nightgown. It was after one. Padding downstairs on bare feet, I followed the sound to the library. Inside, there wasn't a single lamp burning. The only light was filtering through the windows from the streetlamps outside.

Blane sat at the piano with his back to me, his hands moving furiously over the keys. Music filled the room as though it were a living thing. I watched in silent awe. I'd never seen him play like this before. His careful control was gone; only passion remained.

I don't know how much time passed before he suddenly stopped and turned around, startling me. I'd moved closer without even realizing, so engrossed in the music had I been. Now I stood mere feet from him.

He was disheveled, his dark-blond hair tousled, the neck of his shirt open, and his sleeves carelessly pushed up. Blane was almost always impeccably dressed, every inch of him screaming "powerful attorney." Seeing him with his armor off and guard down was a rare thing.

The overwhelming silence in the library and Blane's seemingly accusing look made me feel as though I'd rudely intruded on a private moment.

"I'm so sorry," I said softly, taking a step back. "I heard music . . ."

"That's all right," he replied, his voice a soft rasp. "I didn't mean to keep you up."

Since he didn't seem angry, I halted my retreat. Cautiously, I asked, "What were you playing?"

"Rachmaninoff."

I nodded as if that meant something to me, though I would have been hard-pressed to even repeat the name he'd just said.

"It was beautiful," I said sincerely. "But why are you playing at this time of night, Blane? What's wrong?"

He didn't answer for several moments and I held my breath. Finally, he glanced away. "Nothing's wrong, Kat. Let me help you back upstairs."

My breath came out in a huff as frustration reared inside me. I pressed my lips firmly together to keep from saying the words on the tip of my tongue. It seemed a recurring theme: Just when I thought Blane might open up to me, really open up, he pushed me away.

The next morning, he took me home.

For all that we'd been through together, Blane kept an emotional distance from me. He'd done so much—even put himself in mortal danger for me—but I didn't know if it was because of me, or simply because that's who he was. And he'd never said.

Since I'd moved out, we'd been dating. It was a combination of nice, sweet, and frustrating all at the same time. We were getting to know each other better, but it still seemed like Blane kept me at arm's length. Except when he was kissing me.

I fell asleep thinking about him and wondering where he'd gone, what he hadn't told me, and when he'd call.

∾

The covers were ripped from my body and I jerked upright, barely stifling a shriek. Kade was standing in my bedroom, the corner of my blanket in his hand.

"You're late," he said.

I flopped back onto the mattress with a groan, turning so my back was to him, and buried my head in the pillow. "Go away," I mumbled. "It's still dark outside."

He didn't respond, and for a blessed moment, I thought perhaps he'd heeded me.

"Black's my favorite color. How'd you know?"

It took a moment for my sleep-fogged brain to process what he had just said. The cold air brushing my backside brought things abruptly into focus.

"Kade!"

I shot up and yanked down the T-shirt that had ridden up to my waist overnight, exposing the black lace of my underwear.

His eyes drifted slowly over me, from my sleep-tousled hair, down my chest to my bare thighs.

"Five minutes," he said, abruptly turning and leaving the room. The door shut behind him.

I blew out a breath and pushed a hand through my hair, calming my suddenly pounding heart. Kade and I hadn't spoken of what lay between us, not since he'd told me that he cared about me. I'd hurt him that night. Not that I'd wanted to, but there'd been nothing I could say that wouldn't drive a wedge between him and Blane—his half brother.

I just knew I liked seeing him turn up on my doorstep, even if that meant getting up at the crack of dawn to go running through the streets of downtown Indianapolis.

Dragging myself from the warm confines of the bed, I hurried into the bathroom. Ten minutes later I was dressed in layers, with my hair pulled back in a ponytail.

"Ready," I said as I laced up my shoes. Kade was waiting impatiently with arms crossed in my living room.

"It's about time," he grumbled, heading for the door. I stuck my tongue out at his back.

"I saw that," he said warningly, his back still turned. He held the door open for me.

"You did not," I said with a laugh, smacking him on the arm as I passed by.

"Ah, so you did mock me," he said, following me down the stairs. "You should practice lying, princess. You don't have a deceitful bone in your body."

Kade started running as soon as we hit the pavement. He went at a pace I could keep up with, at least for a little while.

"I can lie," I protested, my breath coming out in puffs of cold as we ran.

"Please." Kade rolled his eyes. He wasn't even breathing hard. "I don't think I'll be taking you to Vegas anytime soon."

"Why do I have to lie anyway?"

"It comes in handy," he said. "Being able to make someone believe a lie can save your life."

I was turning this over in my mind when he added with a wicked grin, "And get you laid."

I went to smack him on the arm again, but he moved out of my reach.

"I'm the bad guy, princess. Catch me."

And just like that, he took off.

"Shit," I muttered miserably before putting on a burst of speed myself.

I ran as fast as I could through the streets, now starting to glow with the light of dawn. I knew I was never going to catch him, his legs were too long and he was just too fast. He rounded a corner up ahead and I abruptly changed direction, heading off to my right.

I ran harder, cutting through empty yards and a parking lot. Tearing around the edge of a building, I raced down an alleyway, only to find a chain-link fence blocking the end.

I quickly spotted a Dumpster shoved into the corner. Wrinkling my nose in distaste, I climbed up on top of it, hunched down, and waited.

Sure enough, about five seconds later, Kade came running down the street. He had slowed down quite a bit and was looking over his shoulder, no doubt wondering where I'd gone. I waited . . .

Now!

I jumped, hurtling through the air. He looked up, but not in time to get out of the way. The breath rushed out of his lungs when I tackled him, and we both went crashing to the ground.

Pressing my advantage of surprise, I climbed on top of him, grinning in glee at my victory.

"Caught you!" I said. "Betcha thought I couldn't do it, right?"

In a flash, Kade had flipped me over onto my back, straddling me and holding my wrists prisoner above my head.

"And what exactly were you planning to do with me once you'd caught me?" he asked, his voice a sibilant whisper in my ear.

I heard the words but couldn't concentrate enough to reply. I could smell the musky aroma of his sweat and feel the press of his thighs against my hips. His face was inches away, his blue eyes locked on mine. My breath was coming in pants, my chest heaving, and time seemed to stand still. His gaze drifted down to my mouth.

"What the hell? What's going on here? Get off her!"

The shouting broke my trance and I jerked my head around to see a heavyset middle-aged man hurrying toward us. He was carrying a bat. I squirmed frantically and Kade leisurely got to his feet.

"I'm okay." I forestalled the would-be rescuer, jumping up. "I'm fine."

The man halted. "Are you sure?"

I nodded. "Absolutely. I just . . . fell . . . and he was helping me."

The man snorted in disbelief, but turned and walked back in the direction he'd come from.

I could feel Kade's eyes on me, but I avoided looking at him. I nervously readjusted my ponytail, which had come loose in our tussle.

"Let's go," Kade said, and he broke into an easy jog.

I hurried to catch up to him and we ran back to my apartment in silence.

"Meet me at the gym at six o'clock tonight," Kade said, glancing at his watch. His breathing was deep and controlled, whereas the sound of my sucking air into my lungs would have embarrassed me if I hadn't felt like I was going to throw up any minute. I clutched at a stitch in my side.

Kade lifted an eyebrow, his mouth twisting in amusement. My eyes narrowed, daring him to say a word.

"Six o'clock," he said again.

I nodded to show I'd gotten the message and watched as he slid into his black Mercedes. In a few moments, he was gone.

Lugging my aching body back into my apartment, I collapsed flat out on the floor and groaned. Tigger seemed to think that was an invitation to cuddle. He was stretched out next to me in short order, his loud purr vibrating against my side. I halfheartedly patted his marmalade fur, too exhausted to raise my arm for a proper petting.

The only thing that got me off the floor was the thought of a hot shower and coffee.

I whiled away the afternoon doing laundry, making lunch, and trying to pick a practice lock Kade had given me. It was a difficult task and I grew frustrated quickly. When the lock finally tumbled and opened, I crowed with delight.

"Only took"—I glanced at the clock above my television—"an hour and a half."

I sighed. Well, Kade had never said this would be an easy job.

Speaking of which, it was time to go to the gym. When I'd imagined a gym before, it was with vague thoughts of a place filled with exercise machines, maybe a pool, weights, stuff like that. That wasn't the kind of gym Kade sent me to.

This dingy place wasn't in a great part of town, and considering where I lived, that was saying something. The fading sign over the door outside read Danny's Gym. Inside, the usual smell of sweat and linoleum hit me, though it wasn't entirely unpleasant; the gym was kept immaculately clean. There were free weights and weight sets over in one corner, and heavy punching bags along the wall. The center of the room was dominated by a large boxing ring.

Today, the gym was nearly empty save for the owner, Danny, the Marine who had been training me. A head taller than me and sporting a crew cut, he stood with his arms crossed over his massive T-shirt-clad chest, watching two people in the ring.

I frowned as I got closer, studying the figures. Then my eyes flew open wide in surprise.

Kade and Branna were sparring.

They circled each other, Kade barefoot and dressed only in gray sweatpants that clung to his hips and thighs. His hands were taped as though he'd been boxing.

Branna was wearing formfitting black yoga pants and a black tank top. Her long, nearly black hair was tied back in a French braid. I felt dowdy in my shorts and T-shirt, my hair in a ponytail.

I hadn't seen Branna since Chicago, when Kade and I had infiltrated a data center and she had hacked into the security cameras. Kade had told me that he and Branna had shared a foster home, that she had been abused as a child and he had done what he could to stop it.

I didn't want to feel anything for her—she barely tolerated me. I'd known the moment she first looked at Kade in Chicago that she was in love with him. But the knowledge of her past raised a reluctant sympathy in me, though she would hate me even more if she knew those thoughts were going through my head.

Kade made his move. He was fast and I held my breath. Branna was a small, delicate-looking woman, but she dodged him, pivoting on her toes. He snagged her arm, but she easily twisted away, doing something to his hand that made him wince. They moved again, grappling, and I was sure he was going to hurt her. Then suddenly Branna grasped his arm, used his momentum to twist him . . . and a moment later, Kade was flat on his back. My jaw dropped in astonishment.

Beside me, Danny clapped. "Nice one," he said.

Kade groaned, accepting Branna's outstretched hand as he got to his feet. "I'm getting too old for this," he groused.

She laughed lightly. "Don't be ridiculous." I could hear the slight trace of her Irish accent. "I'm just better than you are."

He rolled his eyes at this, then spotted me. "Perfect timing," he called out.

Branna turned to see who Kade was talking to, and I could almost feel the temperature drop ten degrees when she saw me.

"What's she doing here?" Her voice held none of the warmth from when she'd teased Kade. It seemed she was no fonder of me now than she had been in Chicago.

Kade gave her a sharp glance. "She's here to train."

He climbed out of the ring and made his way over to Danny and me. Branna remained where she was.

"Make sure you lock up when you're done," Danny said, glancing at his watch. "I'm meeting a buddy, so I'm outta here."

"Will do," Kade replied. He turned to me as Danny left.

I tried and failed to not ogle his bare chest, carved in planes of muscle and glistening with sweat. Kade wasn't a huge guy, but the lean sinew of his body was honed to perfection.

"So how'd your date go last night?" The question seemed innocuous on the surface, but the sarcasm in his voice gave it a whole other meaning.

I shifted uneasily. Blane's and my relationship was a touchy subject with Kade, ever since he'd seen me fall apart after witnessing Blane and Kandi together.

"Blane had to cancel," I said.

Kade lifted a single eyebrow in silent question.

I shrugged. "He said he had to leave town for a few days," I explained, frowning. "Didn't he tell you?" Blane and Kade kept rough tabs on each other, from what I knew of their relationship.

"I'm not his keeper," Kade said, then abruptly changed the subject. "Today I want you to train with Branna."

"What? You must be joking," I stammered in surprise. "I've been training with Danny. Why Branna?"

"She's closer to your size and a woman. She has a better understanding of how to train you than Danny does, though he's been great at showing you the basics."

Before I could protest further, he took me by the arm, leading me over to the ring, where Branna still stood, glaring at us.

"You didn't tell me I'd be having to train the bartender," Branna said, her voice rife with condescension, ignoring me completely as she glared at Kade.

"You get paid no matter what," Kade said indifferently, handing me into the ring.

I reluctantly took off my shoes, eyeing Branna's malicious gaze.

"You don't have to turn her into a ninja, just show her some moves, defense techniques. Danny's been working with her, but you're going to be able to show her things he can't."

The ringing of a cell phone preempted anything Branna might have said, and Kade dug into a duffel bag stowed alongside the wall. "I have to take this," he said as he glanced at the number. "Be right back."

He walked to the back, where Danny's office was. When he was out of sight, I returned my attention to Branna.

For a moment, neither of us spoke. I could again appreciate how beautiful she was, even with her lip curled in distaste. Black hair, green eyes, and near-porcelain skin had a dramatic effect. She was small but curvaceous, and I envied the narrowness of her waist. Kade was correct, she and I were about the same height. But that's where the similarities ended.

"Danny's been training you," she stated rather than asked.

I nodded. "A bit." Which was a nice way of saying I ended up on the mat a fraction less often than I would have a month ago.

"Well, then," she replied with a smile I wasn't sure I liked. "Let's see what you've got, shall we?" Her accent made the words sound innocent, but the gleam in her eyes said otherwise.

All kinds of alarm bells were going off inside my head as I watched her assume a fighting stance. I desperately wanted to get out of the ring, but I didn't know how to do so without looking like a coward. Her disdain and contempt made me angry, and I wished I had the skills to put her in her place. Unfortunately, I could see how this was going to go. I grimly hoped none of my bones would be broken before Kade reappeared.

Branna moved and I watched her warily, caution making me keep my distance. We circled slowly, each observing the other for a sign, whether of weakness or opportunity I couldn't say. When she did come at me, I was unprepared, taking a blow to my stomach. My legs were swept out from under me and I hit the mat hard.

Branna's tinkling laugh made my hands curl into fists as I coughed, trying to get my breath back. My stomach burned from her hit, but I gamely got back to my feet. Branna looked simply delighted now. Gone was the irritation at having this chore handed to her by Kade. I guessed the prospect of kicking my ass was an agreeable one to her.

The next few minutes were a blur of pain and sweat. Branna toyed with me like a cat with a mouse, and I knew I was going to be sporting black-and-blue marks all over later. I kept a tight grip on my temper, though I was furious. Branna was a bully.

I was on all fours, sweat dripping down my nose onto the vinyl, wondering how much more my body could take, when I decided I'd had enough.

"I don't think Kade's going to appreciate your training methods," I wheezed, painfully sitting back on my haunches.

"Then he should have thought of that before," Branna replied haughtily. Not even her hair was mussed from the tight braid. I hadn't been able to lay a finger on her.

"Does he know you're in love with him?" I asked. "Because you don't strike me as his type."

Branna's eyes narrowed.

"I hear he likes blondes." I smiled.

At that, she came at me as I'd known she would, but this time I was prepared. Still on my knees, my hands shot out to catch her calf as she kicked out at me. I gave it a hard twist and yank. She grunted in pain as she hit the mat. I launched myself to my feet, sure I was going to pay for that, and I wasn't wrong. Her rage at being bested, even if only fleetingly, was scary. In seconds, I was facedown on the mat with blood dripping from my nose, and this time, Branna was giving me no time to recover, yanking me by my hair until I was on my knees.

"Branna! What the fuck is going on?"

The pressure on my hair suddenly eased and I collapsed back down on the mat, groaning. Kade had finally returned, and if I hadn't been so relieved to hear his voice, I would have gladly killed him for leaving me alone with the Terminator.

"I told you to train her, not kill her!"

"It's not my fault your little protégé can't hold her own in a fight," Branna defended herself.

The vinyl felt blessedly cool against my cheek, and I wouldn't have moved for quite a while if Kade hadn't gently turned me onto my back. As I blinked blearily up at him, the look of dismay on his face as he surveyed me was replaced by cold anger.

"Jesus Christ!" he exploded, the anger in his voice making me jump. "Why do you always have to make it personal, Branna?" Kade asked in disgust. "I needed you to do a job, not release your inner bitch."

I thought that Branna's "bitch" wasn't so much "inner."

"If you don't like the way I do things, then you shouldn't have called me," Branna shot back, though I noticed that her fair skin had turned a shade of crimson at Kade's words.

"Get out," Kade said.

He returned his attention to me and helped me sit up. The pain in my stomach made me catch my breath. I gritted my teeth, not wanting to give Branna the satisfaction of hearing me make a sound.

"Fine," Branna bit out, grabbing her bag from along the wall. "But do your own damn training from now on."

"No shit," Kade replied, barely glancing her way as she slammed out the door.

"I don't like her very much," I managed to say while using the hem of my T-shirt to swipe at the blood accumulating beneath my nose.

"At the moment, neither do I," he said. "Can you stand?"

I nodded and tried to rise, but Kade had to help me. I maintained a tight grip on his shoulder as his arm curved around my waist. The strength in his muscles and the feel of his skin beneath my fingers distracted me from my aches and pains.

He helped me to a bench and I gratefully sat, resting my head against the wall and releasing a sigh. Kade got up, returning a few moments later with a wet cloth.

"I'm sorry, princess," he said quietly as he gently wiped the blood from my face. "I wouldn't have left you alone with her if I'd known she would do that to you."

I didn't mind the nickname Kade had coined for me. Though it had begun as something disparaging, it had turned into a type of endearment. He'd begun using it after watching me do a karaoke performance of my beloved pop princess Britney Spears. I wasn't good at a lot of things, but I could do a dead-on Britney impression.

"It's all right," I dismissed his apology. "It wasn't your fault." I left unsaid, "That Branna's such a bitch."

"Come on," he said, getting to his feet. "I know what'll help."

I stood slowly, wincing, and followed him to the back. I glanced around curiously at lockers and shower stalls lining the walls. Kade pushed his way through another door, which he held open for me.

As I stepped inside a small wood-paneled room, I was immediately assailed by humidity and the smell of chlorine. A bubbling hot tub sat in the middle of the room.

"Get in," Kade said, nodding toward the tub. "It'll help with the ache."

I glanced down at my attire uncertainly. I hadn't brought an extra change of clothing.

"I won't look," Kade snorted, then smirked. "I've seen it before anyway."

I blushed at the reminder. Kade had seen me naked before, that was true. He'd helped save me from being turned into a cinder when my car had been blown up. The damage to my clothes had been irreparable, and he'd taken care of that, though I'd been unconscious at the time.

I still hesitated and Kade heaved a long-suffering sigh. "I'll be back in fifteen."

He left the room and I could no longer resist the allure of steaming water. Stripping down to my plain white cotton underwear and bra, I eased into the water. It was blissful, and I could feel the coiled tension in my muscles loosening up. Sinking down to my neck, I rested my head against the side and closed my eyes. It felt heavenly.

I had nearly fallen asleep, so I was surprised when the door opened and Kade stepped back inside. I groggily lifted my head. He'd changed into jeans and pulled on a T-shirt. I briefly mourned the loss of the view of his naked chest.

"Time's up, princess," he said, holding out a towel for me. He turned away to shut off the hot tub, then left the room again.

I stripped off my wet bra and underwear, pulling my T-shirt and shorts on over my bare skin. It felt weird, but I was only going home. Holding my dripping clothes, I emerged from the room to find Kade by the doors, staring out at the darkening streets. When he heard me approach, he turned, taking in my appearance, including the small bundle I held.

"You going to be all right?" he asked.

I shrugged. "A few bruises. Nothing I can't handle."

He gave a short nod.

When he said nothing further, I smiled nervously. "Well, I guess I'll see you tomorrow."

"Let's grab some dinner," he suggested. "I'm starving."

I blanched. "I can't go somewhere like this," I protested. "I'm not wearing any—" I abruptly cut off, my face heating.

Kade looked briefly pained. "Wear this," he said, digging inside his duffel bag and tossing me a hoodie. "And don't remind me about what you're not wearing."

I shrugged into the hoodie and zipped it up. It smelled of Kade. Whereas Blane always wore cologne, Kade rarely used the stuff. The aroma drifting from the cotton was a mix of leather, spice, and warm musk—nothing that could be captured in a bottle, and all uniquely Kade.

"I'll drive," he said, and I didn't argue as I followed him out the door.

The Mercedes was an expensive car, and I enjoyed riding in it. I surreptitiously watched Kade's hand deftly handle the gearshift. If I allowed myself to think about it, I could almost imagine I was Kade's girlfriend rather than his employee. Sitting in his car, wearing his clothes—it was not an altogether unwelcome notion. I knew that few, if any, women had been allowed this close to Kade.

The image of Blane abruptly intruded, and guilt hit me hard. I shouldn't be thinking about these things. It was classless and tacky to entertain thoughts of Kade like that when I was dating Blane. The sexual tension between Kade and me was thick enough to cut with a knife, but that didn't mean I had to act on it.

I deliberately looked away, turning to stare unseeing out the window.

A few minutes later, Kade stopped the car. We were parked on the street near a building marked simply Tavern. I raised my eyebrows in silent question at Kade.

"What?" he asked innocently. "They've got great burgers."

I followed him inside. It was a busy Saturday night, and the tables, booths, and barstools were full of people. Kade slipped into the crowd and I grabbed a fistful of his shirt hem so I wouldn't lose him. Reaching behind his back, he unfastened my hand from the cloth and laced my fingers through his. A warm sensation flowed through my veins at the gesture and the feel of his thumb brushing across the top of my hand.

A moment later, we slid into an empty booth in a far corner. I sat with my back to the room while Kade's was to the wall.

A waitress whose nametag proclaimed her to be Cindy handed us menus. Kade ordered a beer and so did I.

I began perusing the menu, waiting. I didn't have to wait long.

"What did you see?"

It was the standard question Kade had begun asking. This was my observation lesson, and I'd been practicing. I put down my menu and looked at him as I answered.

"There are two exits, the front and the one at the rear past the bathrooms. Five waitresses and two bartenders, plus two cooks. They must have trouble relatively often, because the phone number for the cops was taped to the wall near the phone. A possible problem tonight will be the five men at the bar arguing over the basketball game—IU versus Purdue. IU is winning in the second half, but the Purdue fans appear drunker."

The corner of Kade's mouth twitched in approval, and the warm feeling from earlier spread.

"Oh, and there's a hooker reeling in a john at the other end of the bar," I added.

"Nice job. Though I think you forgot the two guys who checked out your ass on the way in," Kade said with a smirk.

"Likewise I didn't mention the three women who watched you walk across the room like you were sex on a stick," I retorted.

I'd wanted to scratch their eyes out.

Kade's grin widened. "Sex on a stick?"

I didn't give him the satisfaction of replying.

"Any helpers?" he asked, getting back to business.

I nodded. "Two guys at the table in the southeast corner. One of them's wearing an IFD T-shirt." Kade had taught me to look for anyone who might be in the police, military, or fire department, as they'd be most likely to help a complete stranger in trouble, especially a woman.

The waitress came back with our beers and took our order.

"Address?" he asked once she was gone.

I told him where we were.

"Nearest cross street?"

I told him that, too.

"Why'd you move out?" he asked out of the blue.

I stared at him in confusion. "Move out of where?"

"Blane's."

Oh. I took a nervous sip of my beer. "I was just staying there until I healed."

"And he let you go?"

I bristled. "Let me? I wasn't aware I had to wait for him to 'let' me do anything."

"Don't get your panties in a twist," Kade said. "Oh wait, I forgot." He leaned across the table. "You're not wearing any."

He took another swallow of his beer, his eyes glittering with mischief as he watched me.

"Thought I wasn't supposed to remind you about that," I said archly.

Kade shrugged. "Doesn't matter. It's all I can think about anyway."

I swallowed. "Kade, I'm dating Blane. You know that."

Kade's jaw tightened and he finished off his beer without replying. The waitress appeared with another, as well as our food, which she set before us on the weathered wooden table surface.

"Are you sleeping with him?"

I choked on my beer. "I can't believe you just asked me that," I spluttered, my cheeks burning.

"That means you're not," he said, and there was no mistaking the satisfaction in his voice. "It's been six weeks. If Blane hasn't sealed the deal by now, it's open season."

I was almost afraid to ask. "Open season on what?"

The look in his eyes made my breath catch. "On you."

Here ends the first chapter of
Turning Point.

Check Tiffany's website—www.TiffanyASnow.com—for
more information on *The Kathleen Turner Series.*

ACKNOWLEDGMENTS

Thank you to my cheerleaders—Paige, Emily, Stephanie, Kristi, Nicki, and Lisa—for your encouragement and enthusiasm. What a blessing all of you have been to me!

Thanks especially to my head cheerleader extraordinaire—Nicole. Without you and your unwavering enthusiasm and persistent heckling for more chapters, this book might still be unfinished. I love you!

Thank you to Nikki. Every writer should have a person like you whom they can ask "Is this utter crap?" and know they're going to get an honest answer—whether they like it or not. Thank you to Zoi. Your willingness to share your expertise in editing this manuscript humbles me and I'm grateful for you.

Thank you to Tracy. Newfound friend and fellow book lover, thank you for letting me exploit your awesome kindness (and excruciating logic and attention to detail). This book is better because of you.

Lastly, thank you to my wonderful family. I appreciate your patience in enjoying fewer homemade dinners, instead enduring frozen pizzas and takeout as I spent evenings typing away on the computer. And yes, Erica, one day when you're older I'll let you read it.

Made in the USA
Lexington, KY
15 September 2019